A Picture of
Innocence

(Die Waisen von Posen)

by

David S T J Lane

A Picture of Innocence

(The Orphans of Posen)

(Die Waisen von Posen)

Book One

by

David S T J Lane

A CIP catalogue record for this title is available from the
British Library.

Published in 2012 by FeedARead Publishing
V.20V7

©2012 David Laurie St John Lane

ISBN 978178176976

First published in 2012 by FeedARead Publishing
Second Edition January 2013

email: orphansposen@yahoo.co.uk

Cover design by Linda Fowler – Glint Print

To my wife Penny,
my step-daughters Leonie and Brioney

…and to my daughter - Sophie

The Polish German Borders 1939

Poland, as attacked on 1 September 1939 - from a contemporary newspaper illustration.

The characters, circumstances and events described in this book are largely factual. Where I have quoted numbers, dates, or figures, these may be taken to be based on relevant sources. However, since this work explores the period of 1939 to 1966 from a German perspective, where sources conflict, I have consciously used the German interpretation of events and figures to reflect the views that characters would have held at the time. **A full list of characters, terms and expressions, and the author's notes appear at the back of this book.**

"In war, whichever side may call itself the victor, there are no winners, but all are losers."

- Neville Chamberlain, 1938

PART I

Chapter 1

28 August 1939: Warsaw Conservatoire

Zbigniew sat back in his chair with a wry smile and looked across his study at Julie Scholl, 'You know, I've taught piano here since 1916 and that is the first time I have ever really been convinced by that piece. Excellent performance young lady…excellent.' He sat up and closed the score on his lap, 'But tomorrow we go back to the *Ballades* – after all you didn't come to Warsaw to study Rubinstein did you?'

He walked over to the piano and they sat for a few minutes at the keyboard examining the music while he made some suggestions on pedalling and dynamics, tempi and phrasing. She listened intently, scribbling in the margins of the score and smiling where he accused her of excessive *sentimentality*.

At fifteen, Julie was Zbigniew's youngest student, and though he had initially doubted her ability to cope without her family and so far from her home in Berlin, she had proved to be something of a joy to teach: bright, sociable, perhaps a little mature beyond her years, but willing to study and quick to learn. And, after the misery she had described enduring in Berlin, the atmosphere in Warsaw had seemed to set her free.

Julie finished making a few faint pencil notes in the score and began to gather her things while her professor paced across his study to see her out, wrestling with his desire to say something more to her - to breach his general rule that he confined himself to an interest in his student's academic work - but he now found this impulse impossible to contain. Everywhere the talk was of war – imminent war, and the Germans who could leave Warsaw had already gone, their houses boarded up and abandoned, their possessions hurriedly sold off or sent north to East Prussia. Even the Embassy was preparing to evacuate, but Julie remained, inexplicably and without news. He was almost at the door when he turned with an expression of fierce anxiety, 'Julie, I simply *must* ask; have you heard from your father in Berlin? Has he said anything about your situation here?'

1

Julie nodded while she clumsily returned her music to a leather satchel.

'So you *are* leaving.'

She turned to face him, her head slightly bowed, 'My father called Madame Beck last night. He says things are very serious and I should leave as soon as possible.'

'They are, Julie, and to be perfectly honest I am surprised you are still here – you must be one of the last. So, tell me; when do you leave - and why didn't you speak to me before?'

Julie looked up, her cheeks flushed, 'He has arranged for Madame Beck to escort me home in three days. I'm sorry but he forbade me to say anything until you had received his telegram.'

'And now I have made you break your promise.'

'I would have said something sooner…I wanted to…'

He held up his hand in a gesture of reassurance, 'I quite understand that he should want to say something to me first. But now it is time for him to consider other issues, and your safety comes first. I am just astonished that he has waited so long…and to wait another three days as things are now! What can he be thinking of?'

'He's been ill – very ill. He wanted to do something three weeks ago but he was in hospital and had to have an operation and since my mother died he's lived alone. Madame Beck *has* been trying to call him every day.'

Zbigniew shook his head and walked back to his desk, picking up a notebook, 'Well, if we still have three days, we have time for one last lesson – a Chopin *Prelude* perhaps – a farewell to Warsaw.' He picked up a score and began to flick through it, looking for a suitable piece, while Julie walked over to the open window.

Outside the heat of the day was starting to ebb and she could already hear the familiar cry of pedlars and newspaper vendors and the chatter of office workers making their way home. In the distance the whine of tramcars rose and fell as they rattled though the tree-lined avenues, their monotone bells marking their passage. She suddenly caught the scent of flowers carried on a breeze from the blooms which hung in the quadrant below and became nostalgic for the lazy days she had spent with her guardian's daughter, Sophie, in the parks and cafes.

'The last *Prelude* – it seems to have the necessary drama for the times in which we live!' Zbigniew exclaimed, with sudden vigour. Julie jumped, lost in her thoughts, and took the score from him. She

2

studied the three pages of music with a look of trepidation. He smiled. 'Well, let's just see how far you get shall we?'

As Zbigniew took Julie's hand to bid her farewell there was a knock on the door and a tall man in a dark double breasted suit and crisply knotted bow tie entered the room. Her professor's face lit up and he greeted him with a warm embrace. 'My dear Sikorski, I always wanted to introduce you to my most talented pupil, Fräulein Scholl – I'm sorry to say our only remaining student from Berlin. Fräulein Scholl, may I have the honour to introduce you to our Professor of Composition, Kazimierz Sikorski.'

Sikorski took Julie's hand and bowed respectfully, appreciating as he did so her simple beauty and the captivating intensity of her dark brown eyes. He paused for a moment, still slightly stooped, 'Yes, I heard you play Chopin's Third Sonata last month – you have some very mature ideas.'

Zbigniew gestured Julie back to the piano and brought forward a chair for Sikorski, 'You must hear this - this is very special; please Julie, just the theme and first three variations.'

As Julie returned to the piano Sikorski gently pushed away the chair again, his voice sombre, 'I'm afraid this is not a chance encounter and time may be against us, so I will need to be brief.' Julie sat at the piano, looking over anxiously at Sikorski. 'I have just come from the Principal's office. We've learned that the Government is preparing to intern German nationals. I'm afraid, Fräulein Scholl, this means that you may be arrested.'

Julie looked at her professor and then at Sikorski, seemingly unable to take in what he had said. Zbigniew sat slowly, shaking his head, 'Are you sure…the city is full of rumours?'

'Yes...I'm quite sure. I have a private student who works as a clerk at the Interior Ministry. He tells me he's been preparing cards for the last week. He said there are three kinds: red, for arrest and house search; pink, for internment - applicable particularly to German nationals; and yellow, for evacuation to eastern Poland. The cards are now with the police, awaiting orders from the Government. My student tells me that when he was filling in the cards with the names of those to be arrested he copied them from a master list. He says Fräulein Scholl's name was on the list.'

Zbigniew leaned forward and put his head in his hands, 'But Julie is only fifteen!'

3

'My student tells me they are talking about a general mobilisation within days. That almost certainly means war with Germany. It also means that Fräulein Scholl may only have a few hours to leave Warsaw if she is to avoid being interned.' Sikorski placed his hand on Julie's shoulder and looked into her eyes, 'You must come with me to Poznan - tonight. I taught in Poznan a few years ago. I still have friends there. It's in the west. Ethnically it's still part German. I know of some German nuns there who run an orphanage for girls. I'm told you can stay there - at least until the crisis passes and you can cross back into Germany.'

'Who organized this?' Zbigniew asked.

'The Principal has felt for some time that we have a duty towards those foreign students remaining – in the event of an emergency. I volunteered to help. We think it's better for Fräulein Scholl to go immediately than risk internment.'

'And what if you are stopped?'

Sikorski shrugged, 'We have a moral duty, particularly to our younger students. It's simply too dangerous for any German to stay here now.' He reached into his jacket and pulled out an identity card. 'This belongs to one of our singing students – you know her, Julie Daase, she's from Poznan. She looks enough like you to get by at a casual glance. It is crude, but it's better than nothing. If you go on to the streets now, with German papers…anything can happen. Daase knows this plan of course. Tomorrow she will tell the authorities her papers are lost and take the consequences – a small fine, nothing much. I've thanked her for you, but there is no time to lose - will you come?'

Julie nervously secured the buckles of her satchel, then turned with tearful exasperation, 'Yes, but I wish I didn't have to. I've been happy here…and I don't want to go. I wish they would just leave us alone.'

She walked over to her professor and embraced him with an affection and warmth for which he was unprepared. 'Thank you so much.' she whispered. 'I shall come back to you, I promise…next term – and I'll practice the last Prelude until then.' She stood back, wiping her eyes.

Zbigniew kissed her gently on the hand, but knew at that moment this was goodbye. And, despite his own desire for her to return safely to Germany, to him Julie had also represented the illusion

4

of a continuing normality which had now been stolen from him. As she made to leave the room he took her hand again gently, 'You must take care and you must believe in yourself. This madness will pass...eventually. You have a rare gift...and I shall miss you.' Julie felt his hands slip from her arm and he turned away, momentarily overcome. 'Goodbye' she said, but his back remained turned, and then, urged on by Sikorski, she left, with a sense of bewilderment and apprehension, closing the door behind her.

Later that evening, after feverish packing and brief tearful farewells with Sophie Beck and her family, Julie found herself in the chaotic approaches to Warsaw's Główna station. She had hastily bundled her most prized possessions - her mother's letters, some photographs and scores - into a piece of borrowed hand luggage which she clutched tightly, while Sikorski struggled with the heavy suitcase containing her clothes and shoes.

The station was only half finished, though it had been started in 1932. It was supposed to have been *the* great symbol of the Second Polish Republic. Instead it had become a public symbol of the corruption and mismanagement of the military dictatorship which had seized power in 1926. Lately it had been damaged by fire, the rotting debris still lying about and filling the air with acrid odours; but the trains still ran and the people still came.

Julie drew up the collar of her raincoat and Sikorski clasped her arm tightly to his side as they crossed the street opposite the grand entrance. They began to merge with the crowds, and when Julie collided with an elderly lady she gestured apologetically but said nothing. She knew her Polish was passable but her accent was still clearly German and, for the first time, she saw a look of suspicion and apprehension in those around her.

When they turned the corner into the main concourse their hearts fell. A sea of military uniforms of every description surged in front of them, while would-be civilian escapees to the east filled what little space remained. They could see no hope of reaching the ticket hall, still less of buying a ticket in time for the Poznan departure, and so Sikorski decided they should go straight to the platform. Julie could see the strain in his face and for a moment she was gripped by a sense of panic - that she might lose him in the crowd, that someone might recognise her, that she might be rounded on as a German. Sikorski

5

gripped her hand tighter until she cried in pain, but she hung on, dragged and buffeted behind him though the confused jumble of kitbags, luggage, and people.

As they approached platform five the crowd thinned. At the barrier itself there were no ticket collectors, policemen, or even loitering passengers. Sikorski looked at Julie.'This doesn't seem right. This can't be it!'

While they stared anxiously down the gloomy platform and along the line of dirty, soot stained carriages, towards the plumes of steam rising from the locomotive in the distance, an engineer emerged from the coupling between two of the carriages and leaned on a large wrench. Sikorski called down to him and after wiping his face with a rag and raising a sceptical eyebrow he confirmed that the train would go to Poznan, 'If that's really where you want to go!' Sikorski needed no encouragement and soon they were hurrying along the platform looking for the first class coaches toward the front of the train.

Once they had settled into their compartment and assumed the trappings of permanent residence, a newspaper, book, some boiled sweets, and a coat laid on adjacent seats to discourage others, Julie began to recover her composure. Presently, after much shouting and slamming of carriage doors, there was a whistle and a lurch and the train slowly began to pull away. As the end of the platform slid past them they exchanged brief relieved smiles and reclined into their seats, glad to be out of the immediate clutches of the Warsaw authorities.

Beyond the city, beyond the few factories and outlying villages, they found themselves peering silently into the featureless night. Occasionally the lights of a remote station or signal box flashed by to mark their progress, but otherwise all in the window was reflection. 'So why Warsaw, why not Berlin, or Vienna?' Sikorski asked eventually, breaking into Julie's thoughts.

'I was in Berlin, but I didn't like it.'

'Because?'

'I wanted to study music. They wanted me to study in accordance with the principles of National Socialism – whatever that means. Everything in Germany *now* is politics – even music is politics.'

6

'Someone told me, I can't remember who, that you had a passion for Jewish music. A little provocative in Germany I would imagine...even a little provocative in Poland.'

'I like Rubinstein that's all. He was my mother's favourite composer and I wanted to learn the Theme and Variations. We were banned from playing Jewish music at the *Koservatorium* and Herr Gieseking wouldn't let me study it. They told me that as a German and a Catholic it was out of the question for me to even *keep* the music, but I wanted to learn it for my mother and *she* gave me the music...At least in Warsaw I still had that choice.'

Sikorski thought for a moment, removed his glasses and began polishing them, 'But how did you remain so free of it. You must have been through the Nazi education system?'

'No, I didn't grow up in Germany. My father *is* from Berlin, but he worked in Spain, where he met my mother, and then Argentina from '31. We lived in Buenos Aires mainly - he's an economist - I was very free...and happy there. You can't imagine how beautiful it was in the city and how different it is to Europe. Then in '36 my father felt that it was our duty to return to Germany. But from the moment we arrived I felt like a stranger. The people were just so different...not like Argentina at all. Then my father got a very good job at the Ministry of Economics, but I was never happy at the *Konservatorium*. They insisted I had to join Party organisations, go to political lectures, carry a book where my tutors could record my *ideological fitness*. Eventually my father sent me to study in Warsaw just to save us both a lot of trouble with the authorities. We didn't want to be parted but he knew I couldn't be happy...and Herr Geiseking was wrong for me anyway.'

'And when was that?'

'That was the beginning of '38 - March I think.'

'And your mother, what of her?'

Julie looked down at her hands, 'She died...in '35...in childbirth.' she said quietly. 'I think that may be partly why we came back. My father was different after that. He used to laugh and joke a lot, but now he buries himself in his work. She was the daughter of a Spanish politician – she played the piano too, and gave me my first lessons. They married and left Spain in the '20s – I think I have a lot more of *her* in me than my father. He says I have her temperament! He is always joking that I don't make a very good German...too much

Spanish blood he says!' Julie smiled. 'But before I play she always comes to me. She's still there - somewhere.'

Sikorsky put his glasses back on and looked at her for a moment, 'Yes, I rather sensed something of that other world when you played the Sonata last month.'

After a while he could see Julie begin to drift off to sleep and catch herself with a jolt, 'It's alright...' he said putting his coat over her, '...it will be gone eleven before we arrive in Poznan. Try to sleep for a few hours. Sister Schmidt from the orphanage will be waiting for us at the station.'

Moments later a Polish officer slid open the compartment door and, seeing Julie asleep, quietly asked if he could join them. As the officer brought in his suitcase and removed his greatcoat Sikorski wondered if he might be better informed about the general situation in the west than the newspapers he had brought for the journey. The officer held out his hand, whispering, 'Colonel Rybicki, my apologies for the intrusion but I was late catching the train – that station is a disgrace.'

Sikorski nodded, 'Kazimierz Sikorski and my pupil Julie Daase.'

'From the Conservotoire?'

Sikorski was taken aback, 'Yes, my apologies, but have we met?'

The Colonel smiled, 'I am a reservist - a lawyer by training but a musician by temperament. I used to come to the lunchtime recitals every week – now, of course, it's a matter of when I'm on leave. But I'm sure I recognise you from there.'

'Are you going to Poznan?'

He nodded, 'And then to Leszno to join my regiment. I've been doing this journey once a fortnight since March when they called up reservists - what a waste!'

'So do you think this will blow over?'

The Colonel shook his head, 'Marshal Smigly says Poland *wants* war with Germany. Hitler is only waiting for the opportunity to strike. No, I think we will fight this time. It's madness, but there we are – unfinished business.'

'Are we ready?'

'We're ready for the *last war* - not what's coming. We should have modernised like the Germans. But we do still have the fourth

8

largest army in Europe, so we should hold them until the British and French mobilize and attack from the west. Then perhaps we can settle these borders once and for all and go home to our beds.'

'And you think they will help us – after abandoning the Czechs to the Germans in March?' The Colonel smiled to himself, seemingly entertained by a passing thought. Sikorski looked at him askance. 'Why do you smile?'

'Because we stuck the knife into the Czechs too – we marched into Teschen last November. Or had you forgotten about our *arrangement* with the Germans?'

'But we never accepted the position after Versailles. Teschen was rightfully Polish, not Czech.'

'But under international law it *was* Czech…and the majority of the inhabitants *were* Czech, or doesn't that matter to anyone anymore?'

Sikorsky shifted uncomfortably, 'The Czechs *have* accepted the position.'

'Of course they have…with a gun at their head. But the *reality* is that we carved up the country along with the Germans and the Hungarians. And now we're expecting the British and French to save our skins – to uphold the *territorial integrity* of Poland, to honour their guarantees…like gentlemen.' The Colonel shook his head, 'Just don't become too indignant if the French and British have second thoughts about going to war for the generals back in Warsaw.'

As Sikorski digested the Colonel's comments he heard the door sliding open in the adjacent compartment and the ticket inspector rousing the occupants. He reached for his wallet and began to fumble through its contents in a way calculated to attract the Colonel's attention.

'A problem?'

'I think I've lost our tickets.'

The door slid open and a grey haired man in an immaculate inspector's uniform entered, while behind him a bored policeman maintained a distant watch. The Colonel showed his travel warrant and the inspector saluted him respectfully.

Sikorsky had rehearsed his explanation for their missing tickets a number of times in his head during the journey, but now the inspector fixed him with a steely gaze and his nerve failed him. 'I seem to have lost our tickets.' he said, lamely.

'Then show me your identity papers - and the girl - and I will issue you with replacements. But you will have to pay again, Sir.'

Sikorski leaned over to Julie who awoke startled by the presence of so many strangers. The inspector repeated his request and Julie nervously produced her papers while the policeman, alerted by the conversation, also entered the compartment. The inspector looked at her. 'Will you please stand?' he said with an edge to his voice.

Julie rose to her feet unsteadily, her heart racing, her eyes flitting between Sikorski and the Colonel. The inspector looked at her papers critically and passed them to the policeman, whispering to him and pointing at them purposefully. The policeman looked up at Julie and then at the papers again, before noticing that her hands were trembling. His expression hardened and he looked over at Sikorski, 'Outside...*now* Sir, if you please!' The three of them left the compartment, shutting the door behind them, leaving Julie and the Colonel alone.

She began to gather her things with an expression of hopelessness, but the Colonel leaned forward smiling, 'Don't worry, everyone's on edge these days. The west of Poland is full of German spies and saboteurs - according to the papers! They've even tried to blame the fire at Główna station on German agents. It's all nonsense, of course.'

She stopped gathering up her things and sat down again, 'What will they do?'

'Nothing; I'll sort this out if necessary – I know Sikorski.'

'You do?'

'I was a regular at the Conservatoire before I was called up. I recognised his face – as I think I do yours. What is your instrument?'

Julie leaned back into the corner of the seat where the shadows fell. 'I am a singer.'

The Colonel smiled. 'My wife says I have many faults, one of them is that I always remember a pretty face...but I will spare your blushes on this occasion. Let us be content to say that I admired your performance last month - am I right?'

Julie hesitated, unsure whether to betray herself and then decided it was futile to persist, 'Thank you.' she said quietly.

The compartment door slid open again and the policeman entered. 'You are to come with me. You will alight at Torun for further questioning.'

10

The Colonel stood. 'I will take these passengers to Poznan. Any questions that need to be answered can be answered there. I know this man and this girl. I take full responsibility for them.'

The policeman clicked his heels and saluted, while the ticket inspector huffed, 'But the tickets?' The Colonel gestured to Sikorski, who quickly found forty zloty and with that the inspector issued two new tickets and moved on.

When they had resumed their seats the Colonel looked at Sikorski, 'So, you are trying to get to the border?' Sikorski faltered for a moment, unsure how to respond, searching Julie's expression for some clue as to what might have been said in his absence, but the Colonel continued, 'It's quite alright, I understand, I approve - unofficially of course. Poland is no place for Germans - not now.'

Sikorski leaned toward the Colonel, 'We thought we would go to Poznan tonight and then, in a few days, if things have settled down, try to get to the border.'

The Colonel nodded thoughtfully and looked over to Julie, 'Then I think tonight you've had your first piece of luck…but we must all hope that it lasts - for a few more days at least.'

Chapter 2

Julie awoke in the orphanage the following morning chilled by harsh reality. Yesterday she had woken-up in Warsaw, surrounded by everything she could want or need, secure in the comforts of her life with the Beck family. Today everything that she owned was contained in a single suitcase and the piece of hand luggage next to her bed. She was homeless and destitute. Even her identity was now borrowed. As she lay, looking out over her fellow room-mates she felt frightened, adrift, with no idea of where she really was, what would happen to her, or how she would complete her journey. It suddenly seemed madness to have come this far into the unknown, to have left her friends and the security of familiar surroundings. But now she was here, and in the cold light of dawn she realised she would have to try to come to terms with the situation and trust in Sister Schmidt.

When she had arrived the previous evening it had been late and long after the other girls had been sent to bed. She had sensed them watching her then, as she nervously undressed and crept between the sheets. Now she wondered about them as they slept, unsure how they would react to her arrival, uncertain even how orphans lived and how they might feel about an outsider entering their enclosed, strictly ordered world.

As these thoughts nagged away at her, a dim light began to penetrate the dormitory. She turned restlessly and stared up at the ceiling, at the plasterwork reliefs of cherubs, Bacchus, and Pan; harps, lyres, and other dance themes. She remembered Sister Schmidt saying that the room had been a place for dance instruction and noticed, from the corner of her eye, a long set of mirrors along the end wall and a hand rail. She thought it strange to have found such an ornate room in an orphanage. And so her mind wandered, with nothing but these images and her anxieties about the future for company.

Later, her thoughts were disturbed by the sound of a column of vehicles some distance away, muffled shouts and orders of command in Polish. She drew the blanket around her, feeling a knot tightening in her stomach – the sounds an unwelcome reminder of the world outside and the reasons for her sudden escape from Warsaw.

Julie lay trapped in this state of nervous tension until Sister Olga entered the room at six o'clock with a small bell which she tinkled briefly before the lights were turned on. The girls rose from their beds sleepily, stretching, yawning, and glancing furtively at the new arrival, not confident enough to approach, but watching her with intense curiosity.

As Julie sat on the end of her bed, uncertain of what to do, a tall slender girl of perhaps sixteen approached her, securing the cord of her dressing gown. She smiled, extending her hand, 'Hello I'm Helene. Sister Schmidt told me you were coming. Welcome, you must feel very lost.'

Julie stood and shook her hand gently, 'Yes, I feel completely lost. My name's Julie.'

Helene gestured towards the door where the other girls were gathering and smiled reassuringly, 'Yes of course, but first we must get washed and dressed, say our prayers and have some breakfast. Then I will introduce you – but I'm sure Sister Olga will do that over breakfast anyway. Later there will be lots of time to talk.'

Julie went to the washroom with Helene and the other girls in silence, but once there, out of Sister Olga's sight, she realised that their jostling curiosity was beginning to get the better of them. Finally a thin delicate girl dropped her soap at Julie's feet and picked it up, meeting Julie's eyes as she did so. She had made her opportunity to engage the newcomer and was determined to be the first to find out about her. 'I'm so sorry...by the way my name's Jutta. You are from Warsaw? I hear you came on the train last night. Is that true?'

'Yes.' Julie said, studying the pale delicate face of the brunette, emerald eyed girl who stood next her.

'One day I shall go there. I so want to live in a big city and see all the pictures at the cinema. Have you ever been to a cinema?'

'Yes.' But before she could elaborate a girl who introduced herself as Ursula spoke from the other side of her, 'Sister Olga says the cinema is full of sinful things - and the theatre. She says Vienna is a better place to live than Warsaw - Warsaw is too Polish. I think I will go to live in Vienna one day.'

13

'Hello, I'm Dorle', a pretty blonde girl of fourteen said from behind her, 'Are you really from Warsaw? My mother came from there.'

Helene could see Julie being slowly surrounded. She clapped her hands and shook her head in despair, 'After breakfast!' She shrugged at Julie, 'I'm sorry, it's always like this when a new girl comes.'

Julie was struck by Helene's maturity and their respect for her, but it didn't seem 'forced' in any way and there was no apprehension in them, just a sense of the older sister trying to make the best of things and keep everything in some kind of order. But even with these small morsels of snatched conversation huddles soon started to form as Julie's every answer became the source for further feverish speculation.

'How many of us are there?' Julie asked as they walked back towards the dormitory.

'Sixteen now you are with us. The youngest is Viktoria, she's nearly fourteen, and I'm the oldest at sixteen. And how old are you?'

'Fifteen - sixteen next February.'

'That's strange – I thought you were older. Oh well, it'll be so nice having some new company to talk to. I'm afraid we don't see many new faces – not anymore. Waltraud was the last girl to join us and that was a year ago.'

'Why not?'

'Because this is a German orphanage and each year more Germans are forced to leave. In a few years I don't suppose there will be any need for places like this – there won't be any more German orphans; but for now we are happy enough. And now I'll take you to *breakfast*.' Helene nudged Julie, raising an eyebrow, and Julie immediately knew that she needed to lower her expectations of this meal, despite her gnawing hunger. But she also warmed to Helene, who seemed, by this simple gesture, to have accepted Julie as a friend and equal.

Sister Olga was rotund and barely taller than Viktoria, the youngest of her charges, but her presence was considerable and her manner decidedly 'no-nonsense'. Julie smiled at her briefly as they filed in to breakfast for a bowl of oats. Sister Olga nodded pleasantly enough in return, but maintained her station, inspecting their extended

14

hands for cleanliness before they ate. Even Julie dared not assume any special privileges, so now imitated the behaviour of those around her and answered the roll call in turn.

After breakfast Helene, as Head Girl, was assigned to go to the bakers with two large baskets and Sister Olga decided that Julie should go with her while the other girls were at their lessons in the school room. As they descended the steps to the street Julie took one of the baskets from Helene who smiled appreciatively, 'Have you been to Posen before?' Julie shook her head. 'Oh it's a lovely city. So are you an orphan?

'No, but I feel like one.'

'Where are your parents?'

'My mother died four years ago and my father works for the Economics Ministry in Berlin – I was studying in Warsaw.'

Helene thought for a moment, 'So you are *Halbwaise* - part orphan?'

'Yes - I don't suppose I'd thought of it that way. And you…have you been here long?'

'Since '26 - since I was three years old. My parents lost everything – their farm was taken from them by the Polish Government. We were German and my parents refused to take Polish citizenship so they were forced off their land. It was the Poles way of getting us out – and then they couldn't feed me so had to give me up. They killed themselves afterwards – which is a sin isn't it?'

Julie winced, 'But how do you know all this if you were only three?'

'Oh, Sister Schmidt is very honest with us about our past. She believes the past and the future are in God's hands while only the present is in ours – and that's a question of faith.'

'Do you like the orphanage? The other girls seem very happy. It's not what I imagined when Herr Sikorski told me I was coming here.'

'Yes, everyone has an image of what it must be like, but they are all different. We are all friends and don't be fooled by appearances; we are very pious when we have to be but we have a lot of fun when Sister Olga and Sister Schmidt are out of sight. There's just one of us you have to be careful with and that's Waltraud – the girl I told you about who joined us last year.' Julie caught an expression on Helene's face, 'She was brought to the orphanage by the

15

police. She'd been living on the streets, begging. She was attacked by some drunks. She's very highly strung – very nervous. Sometimes she has nightmares and wakes everyone up, but don't take any notice. I usually take her to the school room for a few minutes and bring her around. Don't come and help, it's become a bit of a routine. It's best to keep it that way.'

After leaving through the heavy stone archway entrance they had begun to walk up Thorner Strasse, biding their time and enjoying their freedom in the warm fresh air. Julie had been totally absorbed in their conversation, but now looked around her, taking in the unfamiliar surroundings. The street seemed pleasantly green, with mature leafy chestnut trees either side of the narrow cobbled roadway. The pavements were shady and cool, the sunlight penetrating the canopy in vivid shafts of light around them. The houses fronting the street were modest - one or two floors at the most, with irregular and slightly bowed roofs covered with mossy tiles and crowned with decaying chimneys. From all these buildings the orphanage stood out as a later addition of almost ecclesiastical design, perhaps the reason it had maintained its place as a Catholic orphanage when the dancing school had closed in the autumn of 1914.

By the time they reached Glogauer Strasse it was nearly eight o'clock and the road was clear of the columns of vehicles and troops that Julie had heard from her bed that morning. Everything seemed peaceful. They stood at the junction for a moment basking in the warm glow of the sun. In contrast to Thorner, the high tenement buildings that rose above the wide boulevard of Glogauer Strasse reminded Julie of Berlin and, for a moment, she dreamed that she was there and her father appeared from a doorway smiling and put his arm around her and took her home. Helene interrupted, pointing into the distance at the famous trade centre building rising high and imposing on the skyline and telling her about the crowds that came for the annual fair and how it transformed the city.

They turned right, towards the Central Station, and strolled for a while, chatting happily as they went. But as they approached the bakers they could see four or five men wearing armbands stopping customers as they entered. Helene clasped Julie's arm, 'I'll speak Polish – just smile and don't say anything…I'll speak for both of us.'

As they neared the shop door the men looked at Julie and Helene appreciatively, and stood aside with a show of courtesy, whilst halting an old man with a walking stick who tried to follow them. The elderly Polish baker took their baskets and filled them with small loaves of bread. As he passed them back to Helene he took her arm, looking warily toward the men in the shop doorway, 'Don't come tomorrow. I will come to you after I close.' He leaned forward, 'Today those men are unsure of themselves, they hesitate, but tomorrow…who knows. Better to stay off the streets.'

As they left, the group remained absorbed in questioning and jostling the old man whose stick had now been grabbed and was being used to prod at him. As they walked away they heard a shout and turned to see the old man on the ground, kicks raining in from all directions on his back, head and stomach, 'Walk on…,' Helene said quickening their pace, '…walk on!'

When they had made distance Helene looked back anxiously, 'They were from the *Straż Obywatelska*. He was an ethnic-German; I've seen him in there before. He's a harmless old man – I just can't believe they could attack him like that.' Helene seemed close to tears.

Julie reached out and took her hand, 'Who are the *Straż Obywatelska*?' She felt Helene's clasp tighten.

'It's just a title.' she said with exasperation, 'They're Polish…patriots…*citizens guards*. If war comes we'll see more of them I'm sure.'

'Are you frightened?'

'Of course - I pray, I hope. But there aren't many of us Germans left. How can we protect ourselves?'

Julie tried to blank out the knowledge of what was happening behind her, but her heart was still pounding and when they reached the safety of the orphanage they stood in the entrance for a few minutes trying to catch their breath and settle their nerves, looking back up the street anxiously. Julie held her hand in front of her face and Helene could see that it was shaking, but when she reached out to hold it steady they smiled nervously as she found that her hand was also shaking and far more violently. And so they clasped their hands together tightly to steady themselves and began to ascend the orphanage steps with their baskets of bread.

Sister Schmidt had exchanged few words with Julie the previous evening when she met her at the station, but now sat her down for their formal introduction in her small but densely furnished wood panelled office, cluttered haphazardly with pictures, books, bric-a-brac, icons, and a scattering of religious pamphlets.

The Sister was in her late middle-age, with grey hair, an aristocratic poise, and with a pleasant down-to-earth manner. 'Helene has been looking after you?' she said still looking at the papers in front of her.

'I am very grateful…'

'Yes well, I must register you with the authorities and you must tell me how to contact your father without delay so that we can make arrangements. Are you a Catholic?'

'Yes, but I'm afraid I do not go to mass as often as I should.'

'Oh don't *fear* child - that's not the way. I hope you will find us a happy and supportive community during your stay. Herr Sikorsky told me that you are a pianist?' Julie nodded. 'Good, then you shall make use of that wonderful old piano in the school room while you are here. It's wasted on my meagre talents.' She paused, 'Do you know this was a dancing school in the old days?'

Julie nodded, realising that Sister Schmidt had forgotten their conversation of the previous evening, but deftly sidestepped, 'I saw the inscription over the entrance.'

'I do like the girls to dance – does that shock you? Do you have a rather dour picture in your mind of how we live in orphanages?'

Julie smiled, 'I'm not sure I ever really thought about it.'

'Ah, but then you see I was a young girl once and loved to dance, before the last war, before I became a nun. *That* sort of dancing was art and a high achievement if done well. You had to be strong in mind and body and that is what I want to give these girls, a sense of moral certainty through Christ and a sense of their own spirit and joy through activity and dance. Do you like the sound of that?' Sister Schmidt beamed at her with a radiant smile that Julie found irresistible.

'Would you like me to accompany the dances?'

Sister Schmidt rubbed her hands heartily, 'What a splendid idea.'

As Julie rose to leave, she remembered the baker's warning to Helene to stay off the streets. She repeated his words to Sister Schmidt who was clumsily folding Julie's registration papers into an envelope. The Sister looked up unperturbed. 'Julie, there were 87,000 Germans in the city of Posen when I first came in 1910 to see Kaiser Wilhelm II

18

accept the keys to the Imperial Castle. Then, after the war, in 1919, when Poland became master of *Poznan* as they call it, they wanted us out, so they made us take Polish citizenship and seized German homes and farms – I am sure you know Helene's story. Now, if you speak German in the street you can be harassed and if you read a German book in public you put a Polish dust cover on it so as not to attract attention. German newspapers are seized, the German Cultural Association is banned, and the leaders are in prison. Now there are just five thousand of us here. We have weathered the storm for this long and I am sure we will continue to do so.'

Thorner Strasse, Posen, August 30, 1939

It was twenty past three the following day when Wladislaus the baker came to the orphanage with their bread. He sat in Sister Schmidt's office looking shocked and distracted. 'Whatever is wrong?' the Sister said taking the baskets from the table.

'It was on the radio…,' he said in broken German, '…they've ordered a general mobilisation.'

'Who?'

'The Polish Government.'

'And the Germans?'

'No…there was nothing about that, but everyone knows the Germans are ready - it will be the end of Poland.'

'Why…' said Sister Schmidt with almost military zeal, '…you have an army! You haven't been forced to give ground like the Czechs. Surely you will fight?'

Wladislaus looked at her shaking his head. 'The army's been resting on its laurels since we beat the Russians – that was nineteen years ago and then we still had General Pilsudski. The new men - they're incompetent! Sister, the officials are leaving even before the fighting starts; they're handing the streets to the army and the mob - looking after themselves. There'll be no administration left in a few days…and then what?'

Sister Schmidt pushed an envelope towards Wladislaus, 'Can you take this to the police? It's the registration papers for a new orphan here. I'm afraid any irregularity now could cause us terrible problems with the authorities. Can you do it?'

He nodded, smiling briefly, 'Ah, even in the middle of a crisis, the German passion for paperwork - for German order! Yes, of course, I will do it now, before things get too difficult.'

As he was leaving he turned and looked at the bread, 'I can't guarantee when you will see me next. They're closing all the small bakeries for now to conserve stocks – in case war comes. If I can help you I will.'

Sister Schmidt stood and embraced him, 'You have been a good friend to us Wladislaus. God bless you.'

That evening the girls assembled for dinner either side of the long wooden table as usual, with Sister Olga at one end and Sister Schmidt at the other. The diet of the orphanage had never been generous, but now the girls looked forlornly at the thin soup and slice of bread and sensed a change for the worse. After grace and a brief flurry of utensils they sat disconsolate, spoons scraping their empty bowls in a manner designed to register the very slightest of reproach towards their all giving Lord.

Eventually Sister Schmidt put down her spoon and identified a suitable subject for rebuke. 'Gabriele!' A dark haired young girl of fifteen blushed slightly, lips pursed in anticipation of her admonishment. She stood facing the Sister. 'Why are you making such a lot of noise? Did you find no food in your bowl?'

Gabriele looked at the other girls briefly for support and then turned to face Sister Schmidt, 'I'm still hungry Sister…I'm always hungry.'

Julie saw an unexpected look of contrition cross the Sister's face and she gently gestured at Gabriele to sit down again. Sister Schmidt cleared her throat, 'It has never been easy for us Germans here, but this has rarely been because of the attitudes of our neighbours. Our kindest and most generous supporters over the years have been Polish, like the baker and farmers who donate their vegetables for a few złoty. But now we must prepare for the possibility of war between Poland and Germany and what makes things more difficult is that part of this war may be fought on the basis that we, the Germans of Poland, need to be saved from Polish persecution. This will make us the enemies of the Polish State and the Polish people. I think you must understand this if, as I expect, war actually comes and we are visited by the Polish authorities. In that situation we must

20

remain together and you must answer all questions truthfully and honestly and offer no comment on any actions taken in this orphanage – we must offer no provocation to these men. I shall speak if there is speaking to be done. But my children, until this situation is resolved, we *must* conserve what we have, and that means we must eat more modestly and, I'm afraid, this means we may go hungry – at least for a few days.'

As the Sister rose from the table she saw that Waltraud's hands had begun to tremble. She walked over to her, clasping her rosary beads around her waist with one hand while placing the other on Waltraud's head, and said a brief prayer which seemed to calm her. When she had finished she looked at Helene and Julie and discreetly gestured they should join her.

When they were outside the refectory the Sister turned to them, 'You are perhaps the girls here who have the greatest maturity and understanding – I'm sorry Julie but that is how it is – and you are so new here. I know war and what it does to men. I know too that we are defenceless here. Our strength ...' her words froze and they all suddenly became alert to the sound of distant shooting. They stood rigid and motionless, listening nervously and straining their ears, but after a few seconds of intense concentration Sister Schmidt seemed to interpret these sounds and smiled reassuringly. '...Our strength is in numbers - in staying as one body. You must both ensure that the girls are in either one place or another from now on, never scattered. Choose your group and if we are visited bring the two groups together as quickly as possible in the dormitory. And there is another thing; the city is being abandoned by the civil administration. You must gather every container and fill it with water. Our supply may fail and it will be too dangerous on the streets. We must prepare well. If we do that and we are ready, I'm sure everything will be alright.'

Julie and Helene looked at each other and then reached out to hold hands, relieved that even in these circumstances, Sister Schmidt seemed to offer security and strength of purpose, their grip on each other's hand tightening momentarily to acknowledge their own bond, and their own special determination to look after each other.

As Sister Schmidt reached the door Helene whispered to Julie, 'Her father was at Tannenburg you know, he was a cavalry officer – you can see it in her manner can't you.'

'Did he survive?'

Helene's brow furrowed, 'I don't know. Does it matter?'

'I hope not. I hope she really does believe everything will be alright.'

Helene suddenly grew nervous, 'So do I...' Then their eyes met and without a word they hugged, quietly drawing from each other a feeling of strength that, at this moment, they could find in nobody else. Then, arm in arm, they began walking slowly back to the refectory.

'Will you take Waltraud in your group?' Julie said, breaking the silence.

Helene nodded, 'I'll take her to the chapel to pray – she seems very fragile today – much worse than usual. But could you have Erika and Viktoria in your group? They drive me to distraction and they might get on Waltraud's nerves too.'

'Why?'

'Oh, they're always laughing – giggling to each other; and nobody ever knows why. It's some sort of chemistry between them.'

Julie smiled, 'I'm very fond of them. I think they are like sisters - and so do they. I don't mind.'

Thorner Strasse, Posen, 31 August 1939

'I have actually spoken to your father's secretary at the Economics Ministry in Berlin – to my astonishment...' Sister Schmidt announced as she entered the school room where Julie was practising the piano, '...she says your father is in Russia – the Soviet Union. She's going to contact him.'

Julie stopped playing and, for a moment, seemed stunned, 'But I don't understand. I thought...I thought at the very least he would be looking for me...waiting for news.'

Sister Schmidt hesitated, 'Your father has duties and obligations Julie...he must answer to the Minister as well as to his conscience. We cannot always be the masters of our own destiny. You must understand that.' Julie looked down at her hands, unwilling to meet Sister Schmidt's gaze. 'So what will you do child - if we can find a way for you to go safely to Germany?'

Julie shook her head, her voice tinged with bitterness, 'Go to my uncle in Remagen-Kripp I suppose. He has an inn there.'

'Good, well I'm sure your uncle will be very pleased to see you...and I'm sure your father *will* be waiting for news.' Sister Schmidt clasped her hands together, 'Now Julie, I want the girls to dance! They need to be taken out of themselves. There was more shooting this morning and it's set them on edge.'

Julie seemed to recover herself, 'Do you know what it was – the shooting? You seem to listen differently to us.'

'When you have lived through war you know the sounds that are to be taken seriously and those that are just frayed nerves. The Poles are very jumpy; it makes them want to shoot at something.'

She turned abruptly and went to fetch the girls, leaving Julie wondering if the shooting had really been at something, or *someone,* given Sister Schmidt's unusually fretful manner. And then she realised she didn't really want to know the answer - that the truth no longer mattered to her. She needed to believe in Sister Schmidt - they all did. She was all there was left to cling to, and the distant hope that the crisis would pass.

When Julie opened the windows of the school room to let in some air before the girls arrived she saw the street for the first time since the visit to the bakery. It was silent and empty, but for a few distant barricades. Groups of men in irregular clothing and armbands loitered, looking about them and up at the sky occasionally. The city seemed to be slumbering, airless and oppressive.

For the rest of the day the school was a hive of activity, Sister Olga and Sister Schmidt determined to provide no opportunity for the girls to dwell on their situation. They drilled them in their dance steps as they might a platoon of infantry - exacting, impatient and unyielding when they complained.

In the evening they all went to the small chapel and prayed. Julie prayed with them, finding herself reciting the ancient Latin verses with the same intensity as all the girls around her, willing God to help them, pleading for some sign of hope, while in her heart the voices of fear and apprehension grew louder.

When the girls were in bed that night and all was still, Sister Olga and Sister Schmidt returned to the office exhausted, unable to think or feel or stand. 'Why today?' Sister Olga said clutching her sore feet.

Sister Schmidt looked at the telephone. 'It's been dead since this morning. I was talking to a secretary at the Economics Ministry when it was cut – about Julie's father. I tried all day, on and off, but the line's still down.'

'Meaning?'

'When men run out of words they reach for their swords. It can only be hours now. I'm sure it's an omen.'

Sister Olga shook her head, 'What will you do?'

'Pray for a swift victory.'

Sister Olga hesitated, 'Whose?'

Sister Schmidt looked up, 'Does it matter?'

Helene went to the bathroom in the early hours of the following morning and found Julie sitting on the tiled floor, her knees drawn up under her chin, gazing into the distance. Their eyes met, 'What's wrong?'

Julie shook her head, 'I couldn't sleep.'

'Is there something on your mind...something you want to talk about?'

Julie half smiled, 'My father...Sister Schmidt called the Economics Ministry in Berlin yesterday.' Her voice was subdued, 'It seems I'm not his only concern. It seems he's gone to Russia.' Julie paused, 'I had always expected, after my mother died, that we would become closer. Now I feel as though I've lost him too.'

Helene sat down next to Julie and took her hand, 'But he must know how much he means to you?'

'He's all I have Helene...and I love him. But he's not there for me is he...even now, when I am stuck in Poland and a war could break out? I just don't understand how he could do it...just abandon me like that.'

'I can't think that could be true...of course he loves you. You are his daughter. There must be a reason.'

Julie shrugged, 'But how do you explain his going to Russia...unless he really doesn't care. I can't.' Julie thought for a moment. 'Perhaps it's easier when you're an orphan...when they can't hurt you like this.'

Helene shook her head, 'Never say that Julie...never. I would give anything to have my mother and father back.'

24

Julie nodded, 'I know…I'm sorry. But this isn't the first time he's not been there for me when I needed him…he walked away in Berlin too, when I had problems with the authorities. I tell people it was Gieseking, or the Nazis that made me leave, but the truth is he didn't want trouble for himself either…that's why I really left…so he could be free of the problems I was creating at the *Konservatorium*.'

'But I thought you wanted to go to Warsaw?'

'Yes, we had a discussion. It was very *practical,* but I think I expected him to fight for me to stay…I even asked if we could go back to Argentina. He said *no*. And then, when I left, he didn't even see me to the station. He had a meeting…or something. We embraced and he put me in a taxi at the house and that was it. He even gets his secretary to type his letters to me…I'm sure of it…at least that's how they read.'

Helene remained silent for a moment, 'Did you know your mother?'

Julie looked up and smiled, 'Yes. She taught me the piano at first. I loved her so much. We adored each other. She was always much more emotional than my father, always hugging me and kissing me…a very warm person. I was eleven when she died. I cried and cried when my father told me she wasn't coming back from the hospital and the baby was lost too. I don't think I stopped crying for a year – every time I thought of her, or saw something that reminded me of her. And then I had to stop crying when we came back. I had to try and live in Germany – to study. I learned to cope.'

'Do you know how much I would give, just for that one kiss from my mother, to have been hugged by my father just once?'

Julie ran her hands over her face, 'Helen, I'm sorry. I don't know how I can talk like this to *you* of all people. It's just that I'm frightened. I want him to be here. I need him. I thought I was coping, I thought I could pretend that everything is going to be alright, but now…I'm not so sure.' Julie looked up, 'But yes you're right. I am lucky. This must all sound so stupid to you. But these things, my father going to Russia, the way I left him in Berlin, my mother's death; they keep going around in my head. But thank you for listening.'

'It's part of surviving…we all need someone we can talk to. You know I will always listen. I've even seen Viktoria and Erika comforting each other!' Julie smiled at the thought. 'At least, *somewhere* out there you have your father. For us there are just the Sisters and they never comfort us like a mother would. For them our

25

needs can be met through prayer and the love of Christ, but it isn't the same is it?' Helene smiled. 'Did I ever show you my locket with a picture of my parents?'

'No. Why don't you wear it?'

'It's forbidden by Sister Schmidt.'

Julie shook her head, 'But why?'

'All jewellery is forbidden.'

'That's silly. But if you were only three when your parents gave you up how did you come to have it?'

'Most of us have something; some object that was left with us as babies when we were orphaned…something that belonged to our parents…it's a tradition. I have a silver locket from my mother with a picture of my parents inside. Erika has her mother's wedding ring. Dorle has her father's watch…most of us have something. It's strange but we all cling to them like icons…our only link…this one tiny object. But Julie, you have more than that. You have a real father. Don't give him up, please.'

Julie smiled and clasped Helene's hand, 'You know I had lots of friends in Warsaw. I was never still, always meeting people, always going places, always filling my time with books and study…the cinema. But now I have time to think, and it's difficult for me sometimes.'

'I am here.'

Julie nodded, 'I know you are. It's just that now I'm away from all those people I thought mattered, the people I filled my life with…I realise I didn't have any real friends at all. I could never have spoken to them like this…the way I'm speaking to you.' She smiled, 'It seems strange that I had to come to an orphanage to find true friendship.'

Helene stood up, drawing Julie to her feet, 'Everyone is important here…you are part of the family too.' Helen leaned forward and hugged Julie who clasped her tightly. She stood back with a look of panic, 'And that reminds me, I came here for a pee!'

Thorner Strasse, Posen, 1 September 1939

Gunfire woke the orphanage the next morning. Julie sat up and exchanged alarmed glances with Birgit who lay wide eyed but motionless in the next bed. Some of the girls got up, stood anxiously and then retreated back under their covers.

After a few minutes Helene got up and balanced precariously on her bedhead, looking toward the high windows, but could see nothing and sat again. The firing seemed more menacing and purposeful than before. When the first aircraft flew low over the city a little later drawing desultory fire from rooftops along Glogauer Strasse, Birgit joined Julie on her bed where they huddled for mutual reassurance. Now nobody dared move about, but sat in silence listening and waiting for something to happen, their hearts pounding and their nerves jangling with every slight sound.

Sister Schmidt entered the dormitory and restored some semblance of normality, shooing the girls to the washroom with an imperturbability that settled them slightly.

There followed a pattern of sporadic shooting across the city in the near and far distance and explosions which occasionally rattled the glass in the windows. Once or twice something hit the building roof and they would hear it rattle over the slates and drop into the cast iron gutters. Each time this happened their nerves became a little more frayed and their glances more strained.

After breakfast, in the school room, Julie discovered that her group of girls was greatly impressed with her stories of foreign lands and unfamiliar places – even those parts she made up - so she told them the story of her life, of Buenos Aires, the people and the places, of sailing over the oceans, of Hamburg, Berlin, and Warsaw. It seemed to transport them away from Poznan and provide a welcome escape.

'So…,' she said finally exhausting her imagination and looking at the still expectant faces, '…when I am older I want to be a concert pianist and travel the world. What do you want to do? Agnes, let's talk about our lives when we are grown up. Everyone has a turn…'

There was a ripple of excited agreement and they all looked intently at Agnes. She rolled her eyes and smiled broadly, 'I want to be a farmer's wife. I want to marry for love - not money - and have a large family. I want to have my husband's parents living nearby and lots of friends. And I will invite you all on my Name Day every year. Then we shall have a big party.'

'And you, Erika – you are always scheming, what do you want to do?'

Erika's eyes widened and she furrowed her brow. 'I want to travel the world first, before I meet the man of my dreams, I want to

27

see lions and tigers, India and South America – like you. And then I want to meet a rich American and live in New York.'

'And you Ottilie?'

Ottilie put her hands together. 'I think I want to give my life to orphans, like the Sisters here. I want to help in some way. I think I would like to give myself to children who have nothing.'

The other girls nodded their approval. 'Of course, if I were rich, I could have my own orphanage.' Erika added.

'And you Therese?'

Therese nervously plaited and un-plaited her long strawberry blonde hair, 'I think I would like to find someone special, someone I could be with for the rest of my life. I don't care where…I suppose it would be nice not to be poor…yes we would have to be comfortable. I don't think I want to live here. I think…Paris. I think I would like to be a doctor and live in Paris.'

They looked at Viktoria who grinned mischievously. 'I would like to travel with Erika – before she got married – and then marry her husband's really, really, really rich brother and have two orphanages named after me.' With this she thrust out her tongue at Erika and they descended into fits of giggles again, while Julie looked on shaking her head.

Suddenly Sister Olga came into the schoolroom and stood looking at Julie without speaking, tilting her head gently towards the dormitory. Julie reacted quickly, gathering the girls and then setting off down the corridor in single file. When they entered the dormitory she saw two Polish soldiers with papers in their hands counting the girls while Sister Schmidt showed them the official registration cards for each of them. The Lieutenant was polite and formal. He spoke to the Sisters in Polish and then, when satisfied with his understanding of their situation, nodded and left.

Sister Schmidt sighed and turned to the expectant faces, 'We are to remain here and keep the doors and windows closed. The Germans attacked Poland this morning and the Polish army is now fighting back. Let us go to the chapel and pray.'

Thorner Strasse, Posen, 2 September 1939

At dawn small arms fire began again, this time joined occasionally by the sound of automatic weapons. Nearby, there was an explosion accompanied by the sound of glass breaking in the street. The whole building seemed to shake for a moment. The lights flickered and then went out.

As they filed into breakfast, Sister Schmidt recognized, for the first time, the sound of distant artillery and the dull percussive thump of exploding shells. She sensed that the tide of battle had swung decisively and became tense and withdrawn.

At breakfast they sat in silence, their ears attuned to every external sound, bang, or thump, until, at seven o'clock, they heard the remorseless thud of rifle butts on the heavy oak entrance doors. Nobody moved or spoke. Sister Olga stood apprehensively and crossed herself before leaving the room. Sister Schmidt linked hands with the girls around her and soon they were all joined in prayer.

When Sister Olga reached the doors she listened for a moment to the cursing male voices outside, removed the bolt and unlocked the outer door to the street. She found two young Polish soldiers eyeing her warily. They nodded and then walked past into the stairwell. Their manner was very different to that of the Lieutenant the previous day. They seemed nervous – unsure how to treat her. When the girls were assembled in the dormitory the soldiers went through the rooms, opening cupboards and turning out their contents. 'We are searching for weapons.' one of them explained half-heartedly as the girls looked on.

When they felt they had done their duty they stood for a few minutes talking and exchanging cigarettes, wasting time to avoid other duties, while the girls watched them in silence. Eventually Sister Schmidt approached them and drew their attention to additional hiding places they might have missed, recesses that might also be searched, and after this unwelcome additional effort they seemed to lose all further interest and left.

By nine fifteen the shooting in the streets had become more local and so Sister Schmidt insisted they all remain sitting in the inner sanctuary of the dormitory, away from the windows. At nine thirty, Sister Olga again answered to the sound of blows against the outer doors and shouting in the street. As she released the bolts, soldiers forced the doors, flinging her to the ground. They hesitated, eyeing her with rifles levelled as she tried to raise herself. Then they ran into the building shouting for those inside to lay down any weapons, while she was grabbed by the arm and led after them by an auxiliary policeman.

When Sister Olga entered to the dormitory she found a group of ten soldiers surrounding the girls, who were huddling together on the floor, while a Corporal barked questions at Sister Schmidt, 'We've had information there's a machine gun here. This is your last chance - hand over the weapons.'

'We have no weapons.' Sister Schmidt said coldly.

'We know they're here. We've had information.'

'Then *find* them...there are no guns here.'

The Corporal looked aside at Sister Olga and grabbed her arm, drawing his pistol and holding it to her temple, 'This is your last chance, we know about the weapons.'

'Then search the orphanage.' Sister Schmidt said angrily.

He drew back the hammer of the pistol. 'You have ten seconds.'

Ursula and Erika broke down sobbing, while Helene clasped Waltraud's head tightly to her chest. Viktoria began tugging at the hem of one of the soldier's greatcoats, her eyes pleading and tearful. The soldier glanced down at her and their eyes met for a moment, and then he looked back at the Corporal uneasily, letting his rifle fall to his side, 'No, this isn't the way...not here...they are children for Christ's sake.' He walked over to the Corporal and reached for the pistol. The Corporal eyed him for a moment, and then holstered it impatiently.

Sister Schmidt cleared her throat, her voice dry and unemotional, her face stony, 'Corporal, please make your search? We have nothing to hide.'

He looked at her with steely eyes, his nostrils flared, 'Really? Well, we shall soon see.' He began gesturing wildly at the girls, 'Against the wall...hands above your heads.' He grabbed Helene's arm and flung her towards the wall, and then grabbed Viktoria by her plaits, dragging her across the floor screaming. Sister Schmidt quickly gestured to the other girls who stood and went to the wall, raising their arms. When they were lined up, the Corporal walked behind them, slapping any girl who seemed to falter sharply on the back of the head. He looked over to Sister Schmidt, 'Keep them there.'

He gestured to his comrades who began searching the orphanage, breaking and overturning what stood in their path or was not fastened to a wall, filling their pockets with anything of value,

30

breaking what could not be carried away and tearing down the clothing in the wash room. When, after twenty minutes, they returned to the dormitory, they turned over the beds until every one lay on its side, the mattresses, pillows and bedding strewn across the floor, the bedside cabinets kicked over. Sister Schmidt looked on, uncaring of the damage, almost relieved to see them exhaust their fury on material possessions, if this meant the girls remained unharmed.

It was as the final bed was being thrown on its side that Birgit fainted. Julie had been exchanging glances with her for some time and trying to encourage her, but as she began to fall Julie and Erika both raced to catch her. The Corporal saw them from the corner of his eye and turned, drawing his pistol again and cocking it. He stood over the girls shouting, 'Pick her up…put her against the wall - now.' He kicked Birgit's arm sharply, trying to rouse her.

Sister Schmidt became enraged and stormed towards him, her voice thunderous, 'What is your unit, your regiment? I shall write to your commanding officer. You are a disgrace to the Polish army. Now get out!'

The Corporal turned and looked at her, momentarily lost for words. He holstered his pistol, gesturing at the girls with disdain, 'They can stay where they are. We're finished here anyway…for now.'

When they had left Ottilie went to pick up a Bible but Sister Schmidt shook her head. 'They will be back…' she said fiercely, '…and we shall have spared them the need to do all this again. Leave things as they are.' She sighed, 'And now we must eat what we can. The next stage will be looting… if I know anything about war.'

Sister Olga shook her head, 'But what happens when the food is gone.'

Sister Schmidt was unflinching, 'It won't be long now. They must be being beaten badly to have been in such an ugly mood, which means the *Wehrmacht* isn't far away. We can only hope they are here before the *Beast* emerges in these people - that won't be long either.'

It was as they nervously gorged on what remained of their food that five soldiers, an officer, and as many civilians, began breaking down the outer doors of the orphanage. They entered with rifles, knives, cleavers and axes in hand, shouting for the snipers to surrender.

They sounded like a rioting mob, their progress marked by breaking glass and furniture being toppled. Finally as they approached the closed doors, Walraud and Ottilie began to cry in blind fear of what remained heard but unseen. When boots eventually burst open the door latch, and the mob surged forward, spilling into the refectory, the leading soldiers seemed stunned by the sight of a meal in progress and drew themselves up sharply. Sister Schmidt eyed the civilian element with apprehension. She knew the significance of their presence, and the implication that it was now time to settle old scores.

'Are you Sister Schmidt?' a Captain demanded breathlessly.

'Yes.'

'Where's the machine gun?'

The group surrounded the table more closely, the civilians visibly trembling and anxious to start killing, edging toward the girls' throats with their knives, some of their clothes already spattered with dried blood. The girls remained clasping each other's hands as the Captain looked on hesitantly - the balance swaying between the urgings of the mob and his sense of lingering morality. Julie felt a blade touch her neck, closed her eyes and began to pray for their lives. She heard a whisper in Polish at her ear accompanied by the pungent odour of alcohol. She gagged for a moment, her heart pounding.

'Fire has been opened from this building!' the Captain barked again as shooting erupted nearby.

Sister Schmidt rose from her seat and turned to face him. A bayonet was thrust to her chest. She looked at it with studied indifference and met the officer's eyes. 'Please understand we have been searched three times now...' As she spoke a number of aircraft flew low overhead drowning out her words. '...but please search again and you will find all the shutters upstairs closed and no guns. This is a Catholic orphanage - these are children...orphans!'

One of the soldiers from the previous search spoke up, 'We found nothing Sir, she's telling the truth.' Two other soldiers who had been with him agreed and the bayonet was withdrawn.

The man standing behind Julie, a red headed man in his early forties, now stepped into her view as he broke ranks, brandishing a cleaver and jabbing with it toward Sister Olga, 'But shots have been

32

fired, I saw them fired. We should kill them. We can't leave them here. They can't be trusted.'

The Captain rounded on the man, 'This is the third time you've come to us with this ridiculous story. You are wasting our time.'

'The man began to shout directly into Sister Schmidt's face, 'You old witch. You fucking crone. We should have killed you long ago and the rest of these Nazi bitches.' He pressed his blade firmly against Sister Schmidt's throat. Viktoria let out a muffled scream and leapt back in her chair which caused the man to hesitate momentarily. As he did so the Captain struck him across the face with his pistol, leaving a long gash in his cheek, while a soldier quickly took his cleaver and held him.

'This is a Catholic orphanage and I am a Polish officer.' he said angrily. He gestured to the soldiers who now removed the civilians from the room. As the red headed man was bundled out he turned, 'We'll be waiting...we'll be back.'

When the Captain stood alone with the Sister and the girls he became more sombre. 'We are withdrawing from the city tomorrow...we are surrounded.' He gestured toward the doors, 'I won't be able to protect you after today - I'm sorry.'

Sister Schmidt seized his hand, 'Then I shall pray for you tonight.'

He nodded politely, 'Thank you, but I think it's too late for that.' And then as he was about to turn away he added with a note of melancholy, 'I too have daughters; perhaps you can pray for them.'

Later when the girls went to wash they found all the pitchers, pots and bowls overturned and the taps dry. The mob had torn down their remaining clothes from the improvised washing line, trampling them under foot and then urinating on them, a broken vodka bottle scattered across the floor. To Sister Schmidt it seemed that all she had feared was now coming to pass and for the first time she appeared to the girls to be losing her strength and her confidence.

But it was as they put the dormitory back in order that the hardest blow of the day was struck. Helene first noticed the theft; the small silver locket which had belonged to her mother was missing from her overturned bedside cabinet. Then other girls found similar losses: Erika, Ottilie, Viktoria, Dorle and Agnes, all missing the one small token from their parents which had been left with them when they had been orphaned as babies.

Later they lay in their beds, Helene inconsolable and weeping desperately, Viktoria sobbing into Erica's arms, crying out for her mother – while Julie, Birgit, and the other girls listened in the darkness, unable to think of anything they could do, or say, which might relieve their misery.

Thorner Strasse, Posen, September 3, 1939

When they awoke the next morning the mood was bleak and a feeling of desolation hung about all of them. It was Sunday when ordinarily the girls would have been devoted to the services of the Church at least three times and would have been washed and fed before seven o'clock. However, it seemed that after the intense fear and savagery of the previous two days a new and ominous stillness had fallen on the city. From dawn until dusk the girls cowered in the dormitory, daring to speak only in whispers, waiting for hostilities to be renewed, waiting for the sounds of the mob in the street, the breaking of the windows and doors. But the silence in the city now infected their nerves almost as badly as the shooting had, and their blindness to events outside only fuelled their sense of dread.

Their food was now either gone, or useless for lack of water to cook with. Sister Schmidt had found a few pitiful cups for extreme needs, scavenged from the toilet cisterns. But otherwise they simply sat and hoped, hungry, thirsty, and terrified.

But it was their silence that struck Sister Schmidt, as though the tension had left them mute. Communication was by touch or gesture, as if their silence might make them invisible, or that the slightest conversation would be audible from the street.

When darkness came they returned to their beds, tense and exhausted. It was then that the distant incessant rumble of artillery began to penetrate the walls and rattle the windows. Somewhere a battle was being fought - somewhere to the northwest, and it made them all apprehensive about what the morning would bring.

Few of them slept that night and it was only when Viktoria began to snore as loudly as the artillery in the early hours of the morning that their collective anxiety suddenly found an outlet in

34

uncontrolled fits of giggling. But even when some of them could sleep, their anxieties fed into their dreams, waking them up suddenly with a cry, or a jolt of fear.

Thorner Strasse, Posen, September 4, 1939

The following morning, well before dawn, the girls lay in bed anxiously. Birgit climbed into Julie's bed and Julie whispered a story her mother had told her as a child about a girl who was imprisoned by the Moors but then rescued by a Spanish nobleman after many feats of daring. Other girls fidgeted and tossed and turned.

As the light in the dormitory increased the girls continued to listen intently. But, however much they strained their ears, the only sound they could distinctly pick out was birdsong from the street. Once or twice they thought they could hear the distant drone of a plane, but nothing more.

When Sister Schmidt arrived at six o'clock she clapped her hands busily, 'I want everyone washed and smart today before breakfast.' She did not explain why, but in their fevered imagination her words now implied that everything might be alright and their mood swung wildly in relief. When the girls were standing in line in their dressing gowns with their wash bags, Claudia, a usually quiet and reserved girl, spoke up boldly, 'Is the German army here? Is it over?'

Sister Schmidt smiled, 'I hope that this is now an open city; I don't think that the Poles will fight here. We may see German soldiers today, or tomorrow, but they are coming - praise God. Sister Olga has gone to find out what is happening and find some water – she won't be long. As soon as she is back we will wash.'

It was midday before Sister Schmidt ventured on to the bright sunny pavement herself, locking the battered orphanage doors behind her. Sister Olga had not returned and the streets were still entirely deserted apart from a few sparrows cheerfully playing in the branches of the trees. Soon, however, she heard the deep rumble of vehicles and the clatter of boots in Glogauer Strasse and so she edged her way forward cautiously.

When at last she saw a lorry carrying troops pass the end of the street her pace gathered and her heart pounded – they were German, they were here – finally! She allowed herself a momentary smile of relief and hurried on towards them, but it was there, almost at the junction of Thorner and Glogauer Strasse, that she found the body of Sister Olga in a shallow doorway, sitting up, her head resting on her chest. To her side a dark pool of blood had spilled into the gutter and congealed – an empty pitcher still clasped in her hand. Sister Schmidt bowed her head, tears in her eyes and knelt, reciting a prayer for the dead and kissed her on the forehead tenderly.

When she stood back she heard the sound of hobnailed boots approaching at the double and found a section of German soldiers gathering around her led by a plump Corporal in his mid-thirties. He looked down at the body and crossed himself.

'Will you help me?' she said barely audibly, 'Sister Olga is dead and I wish to take her back to the orphanage - it's only a few doors away.' The Corporal straightened himself, detecting something cultured and authoritative in her German and sent back for a stretcher.

'Where are you from?' she asked him as the remainder of his section took defensive positions.

'Magdeburg...I'm a reservist', he said looking down at Sister Olga with compassion. 'There's been terrible slaughter here. Have you lost many people from your orphanage?'

The Sister shook her head. 'She was looking for water - and for you. We thought it was safe. It was my fault.'

'It's horrific.' the Corporal said lowering his rifle butt to the ground, 'In the countryside the ditches are full of them: dead German farmers, their wives, children, and here, butchered in groups...massacred in their homes. You must have heard the killings across the city. I can't feel anything for the Poles now, not after this.'

The Corporal looked on while Sister Olga was placed on the stretcher and covered with a blanket. He said a brief prayer with Sister Schmidt and then his section moved forward toward the orphanage. When they arrived they took Sister Olga to the chapel, laid her at rest before the altar and then went with Sister Schmidt to the dormitory to see the girls. The effect of Corporal Hauser's appearance in the dormitory was electrifying. He introduced himself and looked about him at the hungry, thirsty and expectant faces. 'You are all German?'

'Yes.' the Sister replied.

'I'll put two men on the door until we can be certain the area is clear. I'll speak to my Captain about what can be done to help and I'll get some food and water sent here.' He smiled with a sense of pride,

'You are now liberated. No further harm can come to any German. You are in Germany again now - the Polish occupation is over.'

With these simple words the pent up emotions of the girls erupted in joy and they danced and hugged each other to the evident delight of the Corporal whose rank had never prepared him for such a singular act of liberation, or the consequences of it. Sister Schmidt looked on with torn emotions, knowing she would have to break the news of Sister Olga's death to them, but lost for words as to how to do so.

Julie grabbed Helene's shoulders, 'I'm going home. I'm going home. I can't believe it!' and they too began to hug each other.

That night, as the girls lay in bed, some praying for Sister Olga, others weeping quietly, Julie and Helene sat on Helene's bed together contemplating the future. 'Can Sister Schmidt do this alone?' Julie said under her breath.

'Yes. If there were infants here I would say no – we used to have very small children, but Sister Schmidt can cope as we are.'

Julie reached out and took Helene's hands. 'I've been thinking I might stay a little while – to help.'

Helene looked startled, 'But surely you want to go back? I'd want to go back to my family if I were you.'

Julie shook her head, 'It's not like that, Helene. As I said, it's just my father and me. I have my uncle, but he's really a stranger to me after so many years abroad. No…I'm wondering if I can be more help *here* now, just for a few weeks - until my father gets back. I haven't had a *real* friend since I came back to Europe, at least not since I was a child - and that was different of course. I just want to stay a little longer…to stay with you as long as I can. I don't want to lose you…your company…not just yet.'

Helene clasped Julie's hand tighter and smiled, 'Don't be silly!' and then she looked at Julie more tenderly, 'You are serious aren't you? Please say it's true?'

'Yes, I will speak to Sister Schmidt tomorrow… but of course I am an extra mouth to feed - she may say *no*.'

Julie uncrossed her legs and slipped off the bed as if making to return to her own bed, but Helene still kept a hold of her hand and drew Julie back to her gently, 'I shall really miss you when you've

37

gone. You do understand that, don't you? You will write…and come and see us? You must promise?'

Julie nodded and then smiled, Helene's eyes dwelling on her with a warmth and tenderness that Julie last remembered seeing in the eyes of her mother. She felt Helene's grasp gradually slacken and her hand slip through Helene's fingers, and then walked back to her bed, looking around to see Helene still watching her, smiling, relieved by the thought that they would not now be parted for many weeks.

Sister Olga was buried the following afternoon in the German Catholic cemetery across the city. Although mass was said by a priest who came to the orphanage chapel, they could not attend the interment. Corporal Hauser's commanding officer, Captain Weil, addressed them all on the matter and apologised for the lack of available transport and the continuing risks from rebels in the city. Afterwards he took Sister Schmidt to her office where they sat drinking some ersatz coffee he had brought with other supplies for the orphanage. 'I wonder how much you know of what's happening in the world?'

Sister Schmidt shook her head, 'Very little about what's happening at the moment Captain Weil. All I know is that I am very pleased you are here – and very grateful for these supplies. And you must be very pleased with the progress of the campaign – I hear Warsaw is already besieged?'

'Everything comes at a price Sister…' he said frowning slightly, '…the British and French have decided to fight - to honour their undertaking to Poland.'

Sister Schmidt shook her head, 'But that's absurd, Poland has been attacking her neighbours for the last twenty years - Ukraine, Russia, Lithuania, Silesia - they've been butchering the Ukrainians and White Russians and persecuting us with impunity. *And* they marched into Czecho-Slovakia *with* Germany last year. What possible principles can the French and British be fighting for – to keep Teschen Polish!'

Captain Weil shook his head, 'If it was about principles they would have challenged us when we re-occupied the Rhineland. No, I think they are just feeling things have gone as far as they should.'

'And so what will happen now?'

38

'There will be a bit of posturing. But the French and British don't want a general war and neither does Germany. I hear there's even talk of letting the Poles keep a rump state around Warsaw and Cracow under a Polish Government - like the Grand Duchy of Warsaw Napoleon gave them. It'll allow everyone to claim a victory of sorts. The Poles will have their state and we'll get back what was stolen from the Reich after the last war.'

Sister Schmidt smiled, 'Well, Captain, as you say, nobody wants a general war. But what will happen here now – what will happen to us in Posen.'

He shrugged his shoulders, 'You will return to the Reich again. The army will hand over control to the government as soon as the fighting is over and the Führer will appoint a Gauleiter to run things – a Party man.'

She knitted her fingers together tightly, distracted for a moment. 'Tell me Captain, where were you born?'

He smiled, 'Munich.'

'Ah, a beautiful city. So, are you also a Catholic?'

'Yes.'

'Then may I ask you…for my own peace of mind; is it true what we've been hearing about the difficulties between church and state in Germany…should we be concerned about what might happen here?'

He sat back, 'Is there something concerning you?'

'The Pope's encyclical, *With Burning Sorrow*'. The Poles have been circulating it widely – even I was sent a copy anonymously. I wanted to know if you feel the concerns of the Holy Father had been addressed?'

Captain Weil broached a crooked smile, 'The church needed reforming Sister – and that was in '37. The Party had to act. But it's all forgotten now – the rotten apples have been dealt with.'

'But the hostility of the Party - is it still there?'

'Polish propaganda Sister…you mustn't concern yourself.'

Sister Schmidt sighed, 'I just hope we can go on as before.'

The Captain stood, collecting his cap and placing it on his head, a broad reassuring smile on his face. 'I am a Catholic and an officer. I give you my word; you must not worry on account of the church. Have faith in God and put your trust in the Führer Sister

39

Schmidt. To most of us in Germany now, the two of them seem to be working very well together.'

When Julie found Sister Schmidt later she seemed distant and listened to Julie's request to stay for a few extra weeks without expression. Finally she put her hands together and seemed to awaken from her trance. She breathed in deeply and smiled with her accustomed warmth. 'Before Sister Olga passed away we spoke about how sorry we would be to lose you. I know she would want you to stay - as I do. As for your help while we find someone to assist me, well…that too is a gift. Bless you.'

As they spoke there was a knock at the door. A young man in a grey suit entered, apologised for the interruption and pointed to his camera, 'I wonder if we could have a photograph – to go with the magazine article in 'Signal'?'

The Sister nodded then leaned down to Julie, 'That fine young Corporal is getting his credit for our liberation. I'm told he's even getting a conduct medal – and nobody deserves it more.' She seemed absorbed in thought for a moment, 'Do you know Julie, I wasn't sure how this would end but now I see the German army here, these smart decent young men, and order being restored, I am reassured. Perhaps after all we can look forward to Posen being the city it once was - under the Kaiser. I pray for the dead of course, but for the living, for the girls, I now feel a great sense of hope.'

Julie watched life in the orphanage return to some semblance of normality over the next few weeks. Helene and she began to take on some of the tasks which Sister Olga had formerly carried out in the kitchen and laundry and Julie even began to give piano lessons to Ursula, who had always shown an interest in the instrument and had now revealed her own ambition. Helene and Julie became inseparable, talking as they worked together and finding a spark of humour in each other's company which they had not known before.

Outside the streets also regained some sense of urban normality, particularly as the population had been swelled by thousands of soldiers who idled away their hours sightseeing, sitting in cafes and chatting pleasantly to any pretty German girl they might encounter. The kiosks and shops also became busy, the trams ran again, the streets were cleaned and the parks restored to their civic gentility. The blackout was lifted and the lamplighters resumed their rounds at dusk and dawn.

Then, early one October morning, Sister Schmidt came to the school room with Captain Weil and a rather grave looking man in a thin trench coat and a small moustache.

'Looks like Charlie Chaplin!' Julie whispered to Helene who tried to suppress a giggle.

'We must all go to the street and line up...' the Sister said sharply, '...the police want us to try and identify any of the men who came here before the liberation.'

Julie and Helene stood with the other girls, looking at each other with an expression of foreboding, before filing down the corridor towards the entrance in silence.

It was blustery and grey when they reached the street and threatening rain. They stood on the pavement facing the road in a long line while passers-by stopped to watch the spectacle with curiosity. When they were ready Captain Weil shouted a command and ten men, lashed together with rope, were brought from the back of a lorry and stood in front of them. They looked shiftily about, as a number was pinned to their lapel by a soldier. Each girl was given some paper and a pencil with which to write down the number of anyone they recognised.

Julie looked at the men's faces and saw the same fear in their eyes that she had felt when the mob had surrounded the dinner table. It made her feel suddenly uneasy - unsure of what was happening. Her hand fell lamely to her side. The policeman noticed, came over to her and looked at her sternly, his voice impatient. 'Do you see no-one?'

She looked again and caught the eye of the red headed man who had held the knife against Sister Schmidt's throat and who had been pistol-whipped by the Polish officer. The policeman saw her moment of recognition and stepped forward impatiently, 'Who?' he said looking over his shoulder fiercely, 'Wait - I'll touch each of them in turn. Tell me when to stop?'

Julie shook her head, 'There's no need...number five, the man with the scar. He came with a knife and held it to Sister Schmidt's throat...he said he would kill us all.'

The man grew agitated and swore under his breath. He was silenced with a slap across the face from the policeman who eyed him with deadly satisfaction.

41

Sister Schmidt looked down the line and caught Julie's uneasy glance, 'There is no shame in the truth, Julie.'

The policeman collected the papers from the girls, nodding with approval at the results. Then he returned to Julie, 'This man, Gackowski, the red head, he killed Sister Olga – the other prisoners say so. He was part of a group...they killed a lot of Germans. You were fortunate...'

Sister Schmidt approached the policeman while he stood with Julie watching the prisoners being re-loaded. 'Perhaps you could tell me what happens next?' she said, 'Will you need statements?'

The policeman smiled gesturing at the papers in his hand. 'The girls have spoken clearly enough.'

'So what will happen to them?'

The policeman shrugged his shoulders, 'They will be shot.'

'All of them?'

'Of course...they were part of a group.' The policeman looked at his watch and then nodded to Sister Schmidt, 'Thank you. You have been...helpful. Heil Hitler.'

When they returned to the schoolroom Julie sat with her head in her hands. Birgit pulled up a chair, 'I named three of them - it wasn't just you.'

Julie raised her head, 'You could see it in their eyes couldn't you. They knew what was going to happen to them. I didn't want to be responsible for that. And as for that policeman...why didn't he tell us – he could at least have told us the *truth*.' Julie shook her head with exasperation. 'We were just witnesses...*why* are they so determined to make us responsible for what happens to those men? There should at least be a process.'

Sister Schmidt surprised them and they turned to see that she had been listening. 'Julie, this is war. To fight a war effectively you need to hate. Truth is not capable of nurturing hate because to know truth you have to see it...and hate is always blind. So truth is now our enemy too. All you can do is remain true to yourself and to God, not to others - not to National Socialism. God is love, God is truth – seek Him and you will find Him. That is enough.'

Chapter 3

Eric Scholl had been told by telephone in Moscow the previous month that Julie was in an orphanage in Posen – that she was safe. The message, dated 31st August, had been taken by his secretary Elisabeth Fromm and read to him. But now he held the note in his hand he read it compulsively - again and again. The caller had been a Catholic nun from an orphanage. That at least conveyed a sense of safety and security, but then there had been 'Bloody Sunday', the 3rd of September, and the press had spoken of thousands of Germans slaughtered by Polish mobs.

He picked up the picture of Julie on his desk tormented by the knowledge that he had not been there for her - that he had either been too ill, or too weak-willed to defy the Minister when he had ordered him to Moscow. He shuddered at the thought that Julie might have come to harm believing that he had abandoned her. He put the picture down and pressed the intercom, determined to go to Posen on the afternoon train and find her, but as he did so the door opened and Frau Fromm entered with a bundle of papers.

'The Minister, Herr Funk, wants to see you immediately. He has a Colonel Hopp with him. He told me to give you all the copies we have of the draft memorandum on strategic reserves and war materials.'

Eric stood wearily, put on his jacket and straightened his tie, 'What does the Minister want with me? I've only just got back…I've been away for two months. Can't he wait?'

When Eric entered the Minister's large wood panelled office he found himself in a different world - of luxuriant carpet, fine pictures, opulent furnishings, the air spiced with the lingering odour of good tobacco and furniture polish.

Funk himself was a short tubby man, with whom Eric had enjoyed good relations, but he was not like Schacht - the previous Minister. Funk was functional, a Party appointee, while Schacht had always been at the top of his game intellectually – independent

43

minded, sharp tongued, alert to new ideas and, so it appeared, had ultimately paid the price.

Eric glanced at Colonel Hopp and noticed he was *Sicherheitsdienst,* SD, a member of the Security Police. He nodded and Hopp nodded back without expression.

Funk seemed ill at ease. His normal manner was ebullient and informal, but now he seemed wary of his other guest and sat upright, anxiously fidgeting with his papers, wanting to appear on his mettle. 'Has anyone else seen your draft memorandum on strategic reserves?' he asked sharply.

'No, it's a draft. I had it sent back by diplomatic bag before I left Moscow. I thought you should see it first.'

'And have you discussed it with anybody?'

'Only in the very broadest sense – General von Brauchitsch asked me for a précis of our situation a few weeks ago through Colonel-General Halder.'

'And you gave it?'

Eric looked at Hopp warily, 'I provided some facts and figures. He didn't indicate any specific angle. He asked about raw materials, how long we could maintain certain levels of war production, so I gave him our best current estimates.'

Funk seemed discouraged by the reply, 'But you are a ministerial advisor, that should have come through my office. You worked for the Spanish and Argentine governments, they must have had similar protocols and procedures.'

Eric reflected for a moment, 'Perhaps if you explain the problem I could be more specific.'

Colonel Hopp sat forward. 'The generals are getting cold feet. They're trying to undermine the Führer's position by raising practical objections to further offensive operations – raw material shortages, lack of resources, that sort of thing. There's a meeting between the Führer and the generals on the 5th of November. Sources close to von Brauchitsch suggest he may intend to cite a number of authorities to support his objections to an offensive campaign in the west – senior and reputable authorities from inside this Ministry.'

'But these are military considerations, Colonel.'

Colonel Hopp shook his head, 'No – they are political considerations for the Führer alone. There were similar discussions in August last year. There was a memo from the Chief of the General

Staff, Beck, about preparedness for war. It was sent to the Führer. After that von Brauchitsch was told that interference in political affairs by the army was strictly forbidden.'

Funk leant forward, 'So you see, the army is playing politics and we need to keep out of it.'

Colonel Hopp continued, 'The security police have been asked to consider whether the provision of this information to the army may have amounted to an attempt to subvert the fighting spirit of the armed forces. And I suppose to answer that I would need to know your motives in supplying this information?'

Eric shifted uncomfortably on his seat, 'Colonel, I'm an economist. I have no motives. I provide information in good faith.'

'Have you ever briefed the army before?' Colonel Hopp asked pointedly.

'No.'

'Then why are you adopting a different approach now – bypassing established channels of communication – the Minister and Reich Chancellery?'

'Colonel, I wasn't aware the approach was improper. I assumed that senior generals in the army acted in the name of the Führer and were outside normal chains of ministerial command...I suppose I thought the General had already referred his enquiries to Herr Funk.'

'But you didn't think to refer back to the Minister to check.' Colonel Hopp replied testily.

'I was in Moscow at the time negotiating a trade agreement. It was difficult – there were time constraints.'

Colonel Hopp sat back and studied Eric for a moment. 'Then I can assure my principals that you will, in short order, issue a report which endorses the Führer's strategy?'

Eric looked at Hopp, 'I will need to know more about the strategy to be able to write a new report.'

Colonel Hopp looked at Funk and raised an eyebrow. Funk took his cue, 'We have to demonstrate that Germany is capable of sustaining an offensive campaign in the west – as and when such a need should arise.'

'The General Staff in Zossen lack the Führer's vision; they're clutching at details.' the Colonel added coldly.

'Colonel, I'm not a strategist. My function is to provide factual evidence to support choices within the realms of what is possible.'

'We conquered Poland in three weeks. Everyone said that was impossible - but we did it.'

'Colonel, we lost over five hundred planes. We had barely any reserves of ammunition left – you need to read the reports. Blitzkrieg isn't a tactic, it's an economic necessity. If the Poles had sat back behind their rivers, as the French advised them to, we could have been worn down through simple economic strangulation. The Führer was rearming for war in 1943 not now. ' He paused sensing the Colonel's growing irritation, 'But I can rewrite the report – make different assumptions.'

Funk sat back eyeing the Colonel and then Eric anxiously, 'That won't be enough – not now.'

Colonel Hopp sat forward, 'You need to provide the Führer with a rebuttal to General von Brauchitsch – a short briefing he can use to undermine his position – no more than a page. You need to take a position.'

'A position?'

Funk sat forward again pointing at Eric with his chubby finger, 'I want the memo destroyed and I want a briefing for the Führer. We'll say you were misquoted, that they were preliminary estimates - after all they have nothing in writing. But we can't afford to have another debacle like Schacht - we have to work towards the Führer.'

'As I said, they meet again on the 5th of November in the Chancellery.' Colonel Hopp added gathering his papers. 'We'll need a draft in three days for approval.'

Eric looked down again at his memorandum under Hopp's withering gaze, 'I can frame the facts in a different context, a short campaign, assume certain assets are seized intact, assume certain more optimistic rates of wastage and loss.'

Colonel Hopp stood, 'Then it appears we understand one another and I shall report your intention to Heydrich; but you must understand Herr Scholl that any further contacts with the army, any further leaks from this Ministry and things will be seen in a different way.' He applied his cap and nodded respectfully.

When Colonel Hopp had left the room Funk seemed to visibly relax, 'A drink?' he said moving over to the cabinet by his desk. Eric

46

shook his head, 'So Eric, tell me about Russia - what are they going to give us?

Eric looked at his notes, 'One million tons of fodder and grain, half a million tons of oil seeds, half a million tons of soya beans, nine hundred thousand tons of petrol and one hundred and fifty thousand tons of cotton. Three million gold marks worth of leather and hides.'

'And what do they want apart from gold?'

'Machinery, machine tools...*know how*.' Eric said with emphasis.

Funk paused, 'You know, Eric, the Russians are playing for time...buying us off. That's what I'm hearing from Schnurre at the Foreign Ministry.'

Eric leaned forward, 'They're moving the big industries over the Urals. We really can't rely on them. Should we even be selling them machine tools?'

'Ach...' Funk dropped into his seat, '...you're overestimating them. The Führer knows what he's doing and we're getting a lot out of this deal – remember that. Anyway, getting back to Colonel Hopp; when can you let me have something – we don't have long and they're bound to want changes?'

'Walter, we've worked together since '37, you know me, I'm not political. But what can I do when the facts speak for themselves?' He looked down at his memorandum with a look of strain on his face, 'It's not even arguable. The Allied blockade cuts off 50% of our normal imports, cotton, tin, nickel, oil. Last year 45% of our iron ore came from France or Morocco. Our civilian rations are already the same as they were in the third year of the last war. We have no rubber for winter boots and the clothing allowance is about to be reduced again. For God's sake we're asking children to send in combings from their hair to make felt - how much more desperate can it be!'

'Things will improve as we conquer new territory...when the Russians deliver on their promises...'

'And if we don't conquer, if they don't deliver, if we get bogged down and have to dig deeper into the meagre reserves we have? We can't continue to punch above our weight. Sooner or later we'll meet a modern army and have to slog it out.'

Funk leaned forward, his voice subdued, 'Eric, you've been away too long, you can't talk like this. Berlin is full of rumour, names

47

of senior officers prepared to avoid war in the west. They are already talking about a Zossen Putsch.'

Eric sat back startled, 'But how? A military coup...after victory in Poland?'

'I don't know. But when Colonel Hopp came here today I didn't expect him to leave without you. Whatever he said, your card is marked, so be careful. You're either with them or against them. That's what he was telling you – you need to take a position. You can't plough your own furrow.'

'But I can dig my own grave like Schacht - is that it?'

Funk nodded.

When Eric returned to his desk he found Frau Fromm with an anxious smile on her face and a letter in her hand. It was from Sister Schmidt reassuring him of his daughter's safety at the orphanage. She spoke warmly of Julie's work supporting her after the loss of one of the members of staff. She said that Julie would be returning to Remagen-Kripp in mid-November to live with her uncle, but had stayed on for a few weeks to help at the orphanage after the liberation. She invited Eric to visit them, or otherwise change these arrangements, if he thought them inappropriate.

Suddenly the strain of the last few months began to tell on his emotions and he felt himself welling up for a moment.

'Shall I book a ticket for the 3.30 train?' Elisabeth said, anticipating his decision.

Eric shook his head and gestured impatiently at the draft reports. 'I have to re-write this first - then I'll go. But it's a few days' work so I'd better get started, but my God, what a relief! And for it to arrive today – of all days!'

Elisabeth stepped closer to his desk and her voice dropped, 'Herr Scholl, that Colonel...'

'Colonel Hopp - what about him?'

'He came in here after your meeting – while you were still in with Herr Funk. He was asking about you. He asked about Posen and why Julie was in an orphanage there.'

'And?'

'Nobody except me knows about the orphanage. I don't talk about your private life to the other staff. The only place he could have found out about it was the letter that arrived today, or the note I took for you in August, and I had that locked in my drawer.'

Eric said nothing but their eyes met and registered their inner thoughts eloquently enough. He began to shuffle the papers on his desk, 'You were right to tell me Elisabeth...thank you.' She smiled and went back to her desk, leaving Eric glancing at the letter again anxiously.

Thorner Strasse, Posen, 23 October 1939

Julie paused for a moment on the corner of Thorner Strasse to take in the sunshine. It was a beautiful late autumn day. The air was cool and fresh and the sky was a dazzling cloudless blue. The smell of fresh bread rose from beneath the cloth covering her basket and reminded her of the first time she had taken this walk with Helene. It seemed like an age ago, and then it occurred to her that it was barely six weeks since she had arrived as a refugee, in the middle of the night, desperate to get to the border. She tried to imagine life back in Berlin again, away from Helene, Birgit and the orphan girls, and the freedoms she enjoyed in Posen. She remembered the oppressive expressionless world of the music school, the loneliness she felt in Berlin, and wondered how she could ever return the life she had known after living in the orphanage.

As she stepped across the street, still deep in thought, an elegant open top Audi staff car swept past and pulled up outside the entrance to the orphanage. Two officers got out from the back. They talked for a moment between themselves on the pavement, looking up at the building and referring to a notebook. She noticed out of the corner of her eye that they were both wearing highly polished knee-length boots, black dress uniforms and bore SS flashes on the lapels of their tunics. One of them wore his cap slightly askew, giving him a roguish appearance, while the other appeared to be his junior, more earnest and 'correct' in his manner.

Julie passed them unnoticed and then paused in the entrance, unsure whether to acknowledge them or even how to do so. Finally she turned with a small awkward curtsey and asked them if she could be of assistance.

The tall dark haired senior officer smiled and stooped slightly, 'Excuse me, Fräulein, but is this the orphanage of Sister Schmidt - the one we read about in *Signal*?'

'Yes, Sir.'

'Will you show us to her office? My name is Wilhelm Koppe, I am Higher SS and Police Leader in Reichsgau Wartheland and this is my adjutant SS Captain Kellerman. We don't have an appointment.'

She smiled and noticed the two officers exchange appreciative glances at one another and blushed self-consciously. She turned and led them up the few steps and along the polished corridor to Sister Schmidt's office, knocking briefly on the door before opening it and showing the officers in.

Sister Schmidt stood smiling, 'My brother was in the Black Brunswickers gentlemen – killed at Tannenburg. How can I help you?' Julie closed the door to the office, shook her head knowingly, and went scurrying to find Helene and tell her.

When Sister Schmidt arrived in the dormitory later, as the girls folded and put away the freshly ironed linen, she seemed in a state of unusual excitement. 'I have today received the most extraordinary visit, from no less than the head of the SS in Warthegau, Obergruppenführer Koppe. I have told him that I can do no more than ask you the question he asked me! It seems there is to be a ball at the Bazar Hotel, a grand civic ball in two days' time to mark the visit of many important people to the city. However, it appears that with fewer than 4,000 Germans left here there are not enough young women to grace the dance floors. We have been asked if we will participate.'

Julie smiled repressing her laughter and suddenly her amusement became infectious.

Sister Schmidt also smiled but caught herself, 'Now, now! I shall ask you again. Who would like to take up this offer?'

Julie put up her hand still smiling and then, with growing confidence, they all did. 'But we have no dresses, no gloves, no jewels? It will be like Cinderella!' she said to giggles from the younger girls.

'I am told they have people with all these things at their fingertips – I have only to make a phone call. And I have been assured by Herr Koppe of the very highest conduct by his officers who will escort you to and from the ball. But ladies, you must be ladies! No

50

giggling Viktoria; and Waltraud, you must decide if you are really happy to go - not just because the others are going – we can be together here if you would prefer it….and so…we must prepare!'

It was only later that Sister Schmidt came to Julie with a more troubled expression on her face and took her out of the hearing of the other girls. 'I'm afraid, Julie, I made a bit of a mess of things today with SS Captain Kellerman. He handed a lot of forms to me and I've signed your new residence card here under the name Daase. I don't know why, I simply forgot in the confusion of it all and now all the paperwork for your residence here is going to be in that name - including your invitation! It goes against all my instincts, but as I have already muddled things, I see no point in making things worse so close to the event, so are you agreeable for me to leave things as they are…just for a few days.'

Julie nodded, 'I don't want to be left behind...I'm certain of that.'

'No, of course you don't. Then you will just need to leave things as they are…and just remember *who* you are!'

Julie smiled, 'Of course.'

The orphanage now became the scene of great commotion and excitement as the girls practiced their deportment, their dance steps, how to use the correct modes of address, their excitement growing hour by hour and their expectations running wildly.

That night the girls huddled in the darkness in small groups, thinking of romance and love, the young men they might meet and ultimately marry. Julie thought it was wonderful after the experiences of early September and threw herself into their fevered speculation with glee. Helene looked on smiling and shaking her head with every increasingly improbable twist and turn of these romantic flights. It suddenly seemed to the girls that everything was possible in Posen – however improbable - that their dreams might come true after all. To Julie the orphanage was now her world and that evening she could not imagine being happier anywhere else.

Chapter 4

Danzig to Posen railway, October 24, 1939

"The witness, Hedwig Daase, teacher's wife of Slonsk, makes the following statement on oath:

"On Friday, Sept. 8, 1939 a mounted patrol consisting of about 20 men, entered our village. They were looking for weapons and literature from Germany. A military search was also made in our house again. The search was so thorough that everything was taken out of cupboards, drawers, dressing tables, etc., also in the classroom everything was taken out and scattered all over the floor. The leader of the patrol put my husband's new fountain pen into his pocket. A soldier stole six new soup spoons, another soldier stole 180 zlotys, my gold watch, a penknife, some spirits and some honey from me.

The inspection commission was greatly disappointed to find that my husband had already been interned. I had the impression that the soldiers were looking especially for any German men in hiding.

Towards the evening of the same day two auxiliary policemen came in a wagon, drove up before our house and took away bread, hay and honey. At about 11.30 p.m. they both came again, accompanied by a third. I was forced to stay in the kitchen under guard, whilst the second auxiliary policeman took my youngest daughter into the bedroom and the third went into the living-room with my eldest daughter. I heard my eldest daughter screaming horribly. As she later related to me, she was beaten, half-strangled and threatened with shooting unless she gave herself up to him. The resistance put up by my daughter prevented the auxiliary policeman from carrying out his intention. He therefore let her go, she came to me in the kitchen and he went to the official who was with my youngest daughter. Together they succeeded in overpowering her. After that the two turned their attention to my eldest daughter and overpowered her in the same way. They had previously torn down the knickers of both girls. Both men were natives of Ciechocinek."

Case 34:

The widow of the farmer Hammermeister, Minna Hammermeister, 40 years old, was raped by a Polish First-Lieutenant. The unhappy woman was forced to march to Lowitsch, but was eventually rescued there. Observing the results of the rape after her return home, she hanged herself. Hammermeister himself had been murdered by Polish bandits. "

Doctor Rust closed his eyes for a moment. He had interviewed Hedwig Daase, her two daughters and Minna Hammermeister. He had examined them all at different times. But he had not understood the look in Minna's eyes or her behaviour on the day he had seen her. Perhaps he had been too inexperienced after all, only six months out of medical school and too sure of himself, but he had wanted the job, and at the time it was all that mattered. Then he heard that Minna had returned to her farm and hanged herself, and amid all the other atrocities he had recorded, her ordeal, and the ordeal of the Daase family, had suddenly implanted themselves in his conscience. He could not explain to himself why. Perhaps it was because he had seen the torment written in the faces of Hedwig's daughters – young Melitta in particular, and, as he now recognised, in Minna's eyes. He had not understood those other, deeper wounds, or noted them down for the report, nor even asked about them, but they were what had killed Minna, and would, in all likelihood, haunt Melitta and her little sister for the rest of their lives.

He opened his attaché case and thrust in the report with a feeling of bitter self-reproach. When he looked up he saw that the grey haired pock marked passenger sitting opposite was studying him intently. 'Posen?' the man said casually.

'Yes.'

'Business?'

'I'm a doctor…Dr Rust…delivering a report to the new Gauleiter, Herr Grieser, about the Polish atrocities. I've been sent by the Foreign Ministry.'

The man's brow furrowed, 'How old are you?'

Dr Rust hesitated, 'Twenty-two.'

'You've done well for yourself?'

'I've studied hard.'

53

'The Party does seem awash with smart young professionals these days.'

Karl detected an edge to the man's voice and looked at him sharply, 'My father was a Party member from '25, and I'm no *March Violet* if that's what you are implying. I was a student of Dr Hallerman, that's how I came to be working on the report for the Foreign Office.'

The man shrugged his shoulders, 'I made an observation...'

'And you; what is your business here?' The man leaned forward and drew a wallet from his pocket, opening it briefly. Karl sat back uncomfortably, 'Gestapo.'

The man nodded slowly, 'And a member of the Party since '28, so I think we're entitled to ask a few questions of the latecomers who seem to be doing so well for themselves.'

'Of course...nobody would deny that.'

'So, what do you know about this man you're going to brief - Gauleiter Grieser?'

'They didn't tell me very much at all.'

The man sat back and crossed his legs, 'Then I'll educate you since I *do* know the man. Grieser's a veteran...did his service in Flanders 1914. Became an aviator 1917. Ended it all with a chest full of medals – Iron Cross First and Second Class, Cross of Honour and a Black Wound Badge. Then he lost his home in Posen when the Poles robbed us of it, so he fought in the Freikorps in the Baltic States...and he speaks fluent Polish. No, Grieser has fought for what we have today; he's been there from the very beginning - not like that shit Forster, that jumped up bank clerk in Danzig. That's why I've come south, to get away from the stink of Forster's placemen. Grieser knows the meaning of loyalty, of comradeship; he knows how to reward his old fighters.'

'My father was from Kattowitz...'

'And I'm from the shithole of Essen, but I wouldn't look down your nose at any of us. Your *types* may be needed now, but in the end we're still the ones who made it all possible, and we're still the ones who make things happen, not the lawyers in Berlin. You need to remember that.'

The train slowed, noisily shuddering its way through the final set of points before entering Posen. The man smiled unnervingly and gestured at Karl's luggage, 'After you Doctor.' Karl stood, lowered his suitcase from the overhead rack, gathered up his possessions and stooped at the window to watch the station pass into view.

After alighting from the train he stood on the platform and breathed in the cool air. The Gestapo man emerged from the carriage and stood next to him taking out some cigarettes. He offered one to Karl who shook his head and then lit one for himself, 'Well Dr Rust, enjoy Posen.'

'Yes thank you…I'm sorry I didn't catch your name.'

The man had already begun to walk away and half turned, 'No…you didn't. The name's Krill.'

Karl waited for a moment until the man had made some distance and then began to follow him toward the ticket barrier. It was sunny, so he walked in the shade of the platform canopy with his heavy case. He stepped over signs for Poznan, which lay obstructing his way down the platform, while workmen mounted new ones welcoming passengers to Posen. At the ticket barrier he was met by a smartly dressed man in his thirties holding a sign bearing Dr Rust's name, and an elderly porter. The man seemed in high spirits as they walked towards his car. 'You know those signs were only twenty years old – this time they'll be destroyed. The porter told me they found the old Posen signs in a shed by the main signal box - what a temptation to providence! My apologies by the way, my name is Max Heider – Dr Hertz's assistant.'

As they left the station precincts and travelled through the wide city streets Karl was struck by the lack of any evidence of war. The shops and hotels were open and undamaged, the trams running and pavements bustling as they had been in Danzig. The gardens and public spaces outside the Renaissance town hall were clean and well-kept and in the tenement cafés around the main square a mass of military uniforms vied for tables and benches where they could take in the autumn sunshine while consuming coffee and cakes. After a few minutes Karl turned to his companion, 'I am rather amazed by the absence of damage. I hope Kattowitz did as well. It's my home town - at least that's the way I still like to think of it.'

Max raised an eyebrow, 'It's not like this everywhere – Warsaw and the other places they chose to defend – annihilated! There is some damage here but on the outskirts mainly. Their army sat outside the city awaiting orders that never came. Apparently the generals in Warsaw ran for it within three days. Anyway, here, only the synagogue has been completely destroyed – a taste of things to come I suspect, but very popular with the Poles. We are putting you up in the Hotel Lech on the junction of Viktoria Strasse and St-Martin-Strasse, not the Monopol. Don't be offended. The Monopol is a bit faded and full of political types here for the reception tomorrow. Oh, and Dr Hertz has invited you to dinner tonight – a car will be at the hotel at seven o'clock. Is that alright? Should I say yes?' Karl nodded without really thinking, simply glad to be off the train.

The Hotel Lech was as Max had described; a fine building of six storeys with a magnificent entrance and a lavishly conceived interior. Karl found himself the immediate attention of a middle aged concierge, resplendent in a gold braided uniform of doubtful taste but reassuring cleanliness. He directed him, quite unnecessarily, the five metres to reception and rather unctuously assured him that his comfort and any 'extras' could be arranged with the utmost discretion. Karl dropped his cases with irritation and the man backed away.

After he had signed the register the young lady receptionist ran her hand hesitantly over the key rack. Karl noticed that all but two seemed to be in place, suggesting he had the choice of almost any suite. He requested a room facing the street with some kind of a view of the city and she happily obliged.

That afternoon he remained wedded to the text of his briefing from the Foreign Office. Finally, when he was satisfied with his command of the facts he put aside the papers and telephoned reception for refreshment. The girl at the other end seemed thrown by his request and put the phone down abruptly. Karl was unsure of the outcome of this exchange so awaited developments and sat in a large bay window looking out toward the Basilica of St Peter and St Paul and beyond that, to the river Warta. He had, in his father's words, 'arrived' he thought to himself. All those years of study, all those years of struggle and privation and here he was, in a luxury hotel in the old Germany – the Germany of his Silesian father. If only he could pick up the telephone and talk to him now - how proud he would be. *And* he was going to a dinner with a Dr Hertz, a man he didn't know but who thought him worthy of cultivation because he was the Foreign Ministry's representative.

The sun was waning and a chill began to creep through the loose fitting sash windows. His mind turned toward his preparations for the evening, but just as he contemplated a walk to get some air a thin pale young man arrived with a tray and placed it on the table.

'The management regrets that due to the emergency we do not have even ersatz coffee, however we do have tea.'

'I had to come to Posen to try your tea!' Karl replied incredulously. How could this be so different from Danzig he thought, where everything was still available – at a price.

The young man shuffled, 'It's a herbal tea – very much liked, but I am afraid being a Polish owned hotel and the German hotels taking priority for provisions, we cannot offer all we would wish to - our apologies.'

As Karl digested this explanation he was distracted by the approach of a column in the street and the waiter joined him discreetly to get a better look himself. There were about five hundred people, old and young, men, women, and children. They carried cases and pushed prams and dragged small dog carts. Four policemen flanked them with slung rifles and pushing bicycles, while a vehicle slowly followed at the rear.

'Jews?' Karl exclaimed.

'Poles. They are being sent to the east - deported to the General Government...Warsaw, Cracow, somewhere.'

Karl watched in silence for a few minutes, mesmerised by the scene and then turned to speak to the waiter, but he was gone.

At seven o'clock a car arrived outside the hotel and a chauffeur drove Karl the twenty minutes across the city to Kaiser-Wilhelm-Strasse. It was a cobbled residential street similar to many in Germany's leafier city suburbs. Its broad expanse rose gently from near the city centre towards the Royal Castle on a low hill above the city. The pavements were lined with plane trees and its doorways were approached from street level up short flights of stone balustrade steps. The houses were of a reddish stone with magnificent gables and high, leaded, casement windows from which the occasional glow of chandeliers could be seen through half drawn heavy velvet curtains. The modest porches were supported by Doric columns with a plain entablature and cornice. Each house stood some four or five storeys and when the car drew up Karl noted that Dr Hertz's was double fronted and especially imposing. He straightened his jacket, adjusted his bow tie and grasped the heavy bronze bell-pull.

A smart young man answered the door. Karl smiled, 'Dr Hertz?' There was a moment of hesitation and the young man stood aside. 'I will show you to Herr Dr Hertz.'

The hallway was of marble and stone with a high ceiling and a sweeping staircase which curved toward the first landing. The effect conveyed the impression of a baronial castle rather than something more homely which might be expected of a doctor. They proceeded through high double doors to an ante-room where Doctor Rudi Hertz stood, cigar in one hand, the other extended in an exuberant greeting. As they shook hands Hertz struck Karl to be a man of his father's generation. His dinner jacket was rather worn and now hung awkwardly around his ample midriff, but his shirt was crisply pressed. He had a head of thinning grey hair and an easy but authoritative manner which suggested a man with social connections.

After a moment's hesitation Hertz stood back and slapped Karl's arm boisterously, 'I knew your father...it's just come to me, we both studied with Ferdinand Sauerbruch – he was from Silesia, wasn't he...left in the twenties when the Poles marched in. You all came to Berlin – you must have been a boy. How the devil is he? How are those legs of his?'

Karl smiled and suddenly felt a sense of relief at this unexpected familiarity – even one secured by proxy. 'I'm afraid he passed away last year.'

Hertz steadied himself, 'I'm sorry to hear that...a good man...a good doctor and a good friend at one time - before we lost touch. But, my God you, look like him...come through, come through. You mustn't be shy; these are all my confidants – good men.'

They walked through into a large living room where an ornate black marble fireplace with a roaring fire had drawn the other guests into its orbit, all drinking sparkling wine and talking animatedly.

'Ah, my friends, this is Doctor Karl Rust, may I introduce: Max Heider, my medical assistant – you met today, Peter Mensch my administrative head for resettlement, Gottfried Vogler our most senior civil servant - who also runs the private office of Gauleiter Grieser our civil governor, and my old friend and the man who knows everyone here, businessman and amateur historian Gunther Rath – he's here because he knows where the cigars and brandy are buried - eh, Rath!'

The manner of Hertz's guests was cordial and each nodded as they were introduced but remained seated. Karl guessed that although

58

his invitation was for dinner, many hours had already passed between these friends in deep conversation which his arrival had prematurely ended.

Hertz seemed suddenly hesitant, 'My wife...my wife is abroad, so won't be joining us and I thought we would make this a bit of a business dinner – if you don't mind?'

Mensch, a young man, but older by a few years than Karl, seemed least at ease with his arrival. He was thin and gaunt with lank black hair but had sharp eyes, 'So how did you manage to get onto the investigation panel – quite a feather in your cap, or do you have Party connections?'

'Or was it sheer brilliance, eh?' Hertz interjected.

Karl shrugged, 'I studied with Dr Hallerman in Berlin. When he took up the joint chairmanship with Dr Panning he asked me to do some of the casework, examinations, interviews, notes of autopsies, that sort of thing. I suppose I was in the right place at the right time.'

Max Heider leaned forward, 'Can't you tell us more?'

'Only what the Ministry says; there were 5,437 ethnic Germans murdered that we can identify and likely to be substantially more if you take account of the numbers still missing. It was all pretty barbaric, especially in the countryside where the farmers and their families were isolated. I think Bromberg got the worst of it - a thousand Germans were butchered there in a single day, but it was more or less everywhere where German communities still remained. And, of course, it wasn't simply murder, the women suffered in particular...'

Hertz stepped forward and held up his hand, 'He must brief our Gauleiter Herr Grieser first; it's unfair to ask him about it now. Let us eat...'

Over dinner Karl began to take in his surroundings; the house, the servants, the heavy oak furniture and ornate panelling, the heavy velvet curtains and vivid tapestries depicting medieval hunting scenes - all spoke of wealth and taste beyond his own social horizons. In the corner he glimpsed a glass cabinet of fine Chinese porcelain. Over the fireplace hung a large oil painting depicting *Belshazzar's Feast* which he imagined to be an original.

Karl turned to Hertz, who sat, rather diminutively framed against the back of a high oak chair at the head of the table. 'You've done well for yourself, Doctor Hertz. My father could never have dreamed of this - the house, the fine furniture - it's tremendous.'

Hertz put down his fork mid-motion and laughed heartily. 'What about that Vogler, did you hear that? The young doctor thinks I own this stately pile?'

'Well, you do.' Vogler raised his eyebrow conspiratorially, catching Karl's eye. 'A gift to Gauleiter Grieser from the Jewish banker Tauber!' and then pointing to the oil painting, 'Every house tells a story.'

Mensch suddenly stood up next to Karl, swaying slightly and resting his arm on Karl's shoulder. 'To Tauber - the great philanthropist!'

There followed a mock toast much enjoyed by all except Karl who continued to steady Mensch from his seat. As they sat Mensch resumed in Karl's ear, 'Of course not all of us are so well favoured as the good doctor here…I wish I knew his trick!'

Hertz seemed to dwell on this quip and after a few moments threw his napkin on his empty plate and gulped some more wine. 'I did my bit for the Gauleiter and he appreciates it.' He slapped Karl's arm. 'We medical men, eh, the stories we could tell! I got him out of a few scrapes I can tell you.'

Karl smiled back at Hertz but sensed a dark undercurrent to his aside.

'So when can I expect my address to be the Gorka Palace?' Vogler said, joining the general ribbing of their host.

'There will be plenty more houses and farms up for the taking soon.' Mensch interjected more soberly, 'From Rogaline Palace east to Konin. Koppe is mounting another of his 'Special Pacification Actions' – sending the cattle trucks east.' He rolled a napkin ring toward Vogler provocatively. Vogler banged his fist on the table in exasperation. As he did so Hertz grabbed Karl's arm, 'Sorry, this is unfinished business from earlier, not a word - please!' Karl nodded while Vogler responded with undisguised fury, 'Does the Gauleiter's private office know about this action? Which towns? Who's been told?'

Mensch waved his hand impatiently, as if already exhausted by the subject, 'It's an SS operation with *Einsatzkommando 16* and local 'irregulars', you know the *Selbstschutz*, and I only know because I queried where we were going to put two thousand German settlers from the east arriving on Friday.'

Vogler smouldered for a moment but Mensch was now fortified with wine. 'Oh come on Gottfried, Grieser will always be playing catch up while SS Obergruppenführer Koppe is taking orders from Himmler instead of working through Grieser's civil administration. Grieser needs to put Koppe back in his box. Forster works well with SS Obergruppenführer Hildebrandt up in Danzig. Why can't Koppe toe the line here? It's your territory not mine. You should lay down the law, and the law is your boss Grieser, nobody else – put some iron in the glove for God's sake and save us all a lot of chaos.'

Both men sat back sensing that enough had been said and what remained should be implied for the sake of friendship.

'And so you see Karl, the machine is not working!' Hertz added sombrely.

'And why?' Vogler snapped, looking at Mensch.

Karl shrugged, helplessly framed between the antagonists.

Hertz now tried to defuse the tension and generalise the conversation and so talked over his other guests until they were silenced. 'Do you know how many people...senior party people I mean, are *in charge* of the Führer's 'Eastern Plan', Karl?' Hertz looked over to Mensch who had re-joined the table after a brief foray for brandy. 'Go on, tell him.'

Mensch smiled, 'Ah my *Party* piece again!' He sat and gathered some walnuts from a fruit bowl and drew a deep breath, 'First there is the Führer whose thoughts are disseminated by Bormann, *but* there is also Himmler, Chief of Police, *Reichsführer* SS and Head of Reich Commissariat for the Strengthening of German Nationhood *and* Alfred Rosenberg, *Reichsminister* for the Eastern Occupied Territories *and* Hans Frank, Governor General of Occupied Poland *and* Fritz Sauckel, Plenipotentiary General for the Allocation of Labour in the East *and* Albert Forster, *Gauleiter* of Danzig West Prussia *and* Arthur Grieser, *Gauleiter* of Reichsgau Posen. *And* that of course ignores Göring, Minister of the Free State of Prussia who has his own view on everything! So there are nine of them in charge of the East and each one has unfettered power to shoot, deport, enslave, imprison and tell us what to do.' He now rolled nine of the nuts toward Karl in quick succession, 'Now see how many you can catch.'

61

Hertz shook his head, 'And how do you follow nine different policies simultaneously…madness!'

'And then there is Koppe.' Vogler's voice was dripping with scorn, 'Wilhelm Koppe, SS Obergruppenführer, Higher Police Leader of Reichsgau Wartheland and Himmler's man: ambitious, ruthless and on the way up….except Gauleiter Grieser is in the way.'

Max Heider leaned forward to gain Karl's attention. 'And it's not just the Poles and Jews being deported that are the problem. The Russians are sending us tens of thousands of ethnic Germans over the next few months from their slice of the Baltic and eastern Poland. They arrive with only a suitcase and what they can carry. They are old, they are sick, they are mothers with young children and what can we do? We give them papers, a flat, or a house, or a farm and say – *get on with it.*'

Max seemed to stir something in Gunther Rath, a thickset man, with heavy eyebrows, red cheeks and an evident love of good food. He had been watching until now, alert but keeping his own counsel. Karl had observed him a few times during the meal and felt that, by nature and appearance, Rath should have been the life and soul of the evening, but nothing had lured him from his private thoughts until now.

'I'll tell you something gentlemen…' he tapped the table heavily with his finger, '…the whole area around Posen floods. Do you know that? It's a fertile soil, but it's heavy and demanding on man and beast. These farmers, the Germans and Poles alike, they know it. They have known it since the time before Mieszko, the first Christian Polish King in the Tenth Century, when their forefathers drained and first worked the marshes and tamed the Warta and Cybina rivers. Those marshes became the fields we see today and the breadbasket of Poland and then Wilhelminian Germany.

'Yesterday I went to do business with one of those old families, a farmer, an old friend, a Pole named Moszumanski – one of the most honest and hardworking men I know. But…he was gone. His family, his wife, three girls and two boys…were gone. His parents…were gone. His labourer…was gone. They were put on the road with two hundred others from the village and marched off to the east. And then I met this thin weedy man and sickly wife; he came out of the farmhouse with a pitchfork – his wife and two children in the doorway. I said to him, after I told him I meant no harm, '*Where do you come from?'*, and he said *'Tallinn, Estonia'*. So I said, *'Perhaps we can do business together. What will you plant in the spring?'* He just broke down. His wife said he was a gentleman's tailor. He didn't know *anything* about farming, or why they were there.'

Hertz raised his fork with a slice of apple strudel on it, 'The message of the story being…eat well and eat quickly!'

Rath slumped back rolling a cigar between his fingers and preparing to light it, 'So I must put on my finest for the Posen Ball tomorrow; is that right, Hertz?

Heider took a light from Rath for himself and then interjected: 'Is it true Himmler and a few other bigwigs will be there? Come to *clarify* some of the issues between Grieser and Koppe no doubt?'

Vogler took one of the walnuts from the table and examined it. 'Yes, Grieser's got a big policy team together to take on Koppe and the SS economics mob. It could be a long night…Karl, you may not even see Grieser for this briefing of yours, but hang around, I'll let you know what's happening when I can.'

Karl travelled back to his hotel with Gunther Rath well after midnight. Rath was excited by news of the Lech Hotel's shortages and assured Karl that his car contained ersatz coffee and enough else to 'see them right'. He drove slowly to compensate for the brandy and his mood seemed to have lightened, 'You're not a fanatical Party man then?'

Karl hesitated instinctively, it was simply not a question you asked in Germany and it took him a moment to remind himself that here in Posen attitudes still seemed very different, 'Not a fanatic, but I am a member - I have to be to practise medicine. It was my father who joined me up. He followed Hitler from the Beer Hall Putsch in '23. We lived in Kattowitz when the Poles seized it in '21. He joined the resistance as a doctor and was caught when they broke the siege. They smashed both his ankles with hammers while the French peacekeepers looked on. Then they took our house and threw us out. He was a Party member from '25, but hardly active - how could he be. He enrolled me in the *Jungvolk* when I was ten and the Hitler Youth when I was fifteen. He was a cripple for the rest of his life. It made him difficult to live with. He was obsessed with restoring the borders of Imperial Germany. It's a pity he never saw it.'

63

Rath drove in silence for a moment, 'So was that treason in there my friend - all that talk of incompetence at the top?'

'No…just people trying to make things work - that's what it sounded like.'

Guther's voice became caustic, 'Exactly! I'll tell you for nothing, if it wasn't for the likes of them the Nazi princes wouldn't defy gravity for long. It's the civil service that keeps it all going. The Party's a fucking mess! I tell you eastern Germany, Warthegau and Danzig West Prussia will starve unless they get a grip. That lot can't keep it going for ever, however good their administrative skills.'

It was after one o'clock when Karl finally reached his bedroom. He left Gunther negotiating in Polish and talking animatedly about his 'black' inventory to the night porter, who made frantic notes and gabbled down the phone to the manager.

He sat for a moment in the bay window of his room, looking down at the yellow glow of the gas lights in the street. In the distance a dustcart moved slowly toward the Basilica, the breath from carter and horse condensing and slowly rising in the icy moonlight. He wondered for a moment where the five hundred who had passed below his window would be now and whether they had included the 'honest' Polish farmer and his family. He remembered too his father, crying out in agony from the back of a cart on just such a clear moonlit night, as the family turned their back on Kattowitz and returned with their few possessions to poverty in Berlin in 1921.

Chapter 5

It was only with the arrival of the hairdressers, manicurists, costumiers, sundry boxes of jewels and shoes, that the excitement with which the girls had anticipated the ball began to be supplanted by reality and nervous apprehension. They found themselves in the hands of strangers, their hair *coiffured* into the most exquisite designs, their rough nails trimmed and filed and varnished as they had never seen them before, their faces made up, eyelashes curled and mascara applied. So too their bodies became adorned within new undergarments and shapely dresses in which they suddenly emerged from their drab everyday existence as glamorous young women. When they stood that late afternoon, looking into the dormitory mirrors, they barely recognised these new exotic creatures who stared back. Julie and Helene noticed a palpable sense of nervous excitement at this change. Until today they had all been as one, fellow orphans, part of a family. Now they stood as individuals, each markedly distinct from the other, their particular physique, hair and skin tone professionally styled to emphasise their individual physical grace and charm.

Finally Julie put on the shoes she had been given and began to walk stiffly and uncertainly, 'Oh my Lord! We need to practice in these before tonight!' she said, exaggerating a few dance steps. And with this they all put on their shoes and joined her, dancing, falling and tumbling into the furniture. Suddenly the nerves and tension were gone and in its place the innocent laughter and excitement of their adventure seemed to return. And to Julie there did seem to be a magic about what was happening to them; that for once in their lives, perhaps the only time in their lives, the girls would experience what it was to be young and beautiful and glamorous and dance, not with each other, but in the arms of a handsome attentive young officer at a lavish ball.

Later, when Sister Schmidt came into the dormitory and they stood in line, her feelings of apprehension were no less real. She examined each of them with Prussian zeal, looking for imperfections but finding none. Finally she stood back, 'Ladies...' she said in an almost lamenting tone, '...you are the most exquisite creatures that ever graced a ballroom and were it not for the honourable undertakings of the SS I would not let you out of my sight for one moment - you are all truly beautiful. However I shall be most unhappy if you return with proposals of marriage, still less, if we are besieged by love sick young men in the coming weeks, but otherwise, I wish you a joyful evening.'

As Julie waited with Helene for the cars to arrive and ferry them to the ball Helene gestured at her pale blue ball gown and smiled anxiously, 'I still can't recognise myself in the mirror you know. I keep making myself jump!'

'Are you nervous?' Julie asked.

'Yes...are you?

'Even more than when I perform in public. I suppose it's the thought of everyone staring at us and of course the young men. I wonder what we'll talk about...what they'll expect us to be like?'

'Do you think they really will behave like gentlemen?'

'Of course, but don't rely on it *after* tonight.'

'What do you mean?'

'The Nazi Party has a fairly basic view of women: church, children and kitchen sink. They don't always seem so fussy about the order.'

Helene looked slightly scandalised, 'But I thought the Führer was popular with women.'

'The Führer is *adored* by women, but *he* isn't the Party, and we still have our place. I suppose if you are happy staying at home having endless babies it must be paradise and German women don't seem to be upset by it. I really don't understand them I'm afraid. I suppose, I've seen too much of the world, it's made me restless.'

Helene bounced back cheerfully, 'Oh, I don't know, Julie; it doesn't sound bad if you've never had those things - a home and a family I mean. Why would I want to work in a factory? Why do I need an education if I have a husband and children to look after?'

'But do you really mean that, Helene? Surely you want more out of life than that? What about you? What about your hopes for the future?'

Helene remained silent for a moment and then turned to Julie with an air of exasperation, 'Julie, what do you think happens to us girls here when we are too old to be looked after anymore, when we have to make our way in the world?'

66

Julie shifted awkwardly, 'I don't know. I don't suppose I thought about it.'

'Then I'll tell you. If we are lucky we find work – a farm, domestic service, somewhere with a bed and food working fourteen hours a day with no time to rest or go and find a better job. Sometimes the Church will find work for us in a shop or factory, sleeping on a floor at night next to the machine or in an outbuilding, or we might find a religious house who will take us in. But the truth is that nobody wants to marry an orphan with no money or family property to bring into the marriage. You have to understand that if you start life as an orphan there are no opportunities, only dreams, and if I met a man tonight who could save me from all that it wouldn't matter about anything else.'

Julie hesitated for a few moments then took Helene's hand, 'Perhaps I could help...find work in Germany for you. My uncle has an inn near the Rheine. It's beautiful there.'

Helene smiled, 'That would be lovely, but it sounds *too much* like a dream - and I can't afford to do that. I have to leave next year and make my own way.'

'I'll write to him...ask him. We could still see each other then.'

'But what could I do? Do you think he would let me live there...I wouldn't ask to be paid...just food and a bed - like here.'

'Of course he would keep you and pay you something, I'm sure. It would only be simple tasks like the ones we do here: linen, cleaning, making beds – my father would help me...if I explained the situation.'

Helene's gaze became distant, 'Yes, I like the sound of Germany. It sounds like paradise. Is it true the workers have free holidays?'

'There are jobs, there are holidays for the worker's children at the seaside, there is order, good food, and families are helped and even encouraged with loans; so, yes, Helene, it's paradise.'

'So why did you leave? Why do you dislike Germany so much?'

'Because life isn't that simple. I don't just want bread and a roof over my head and a husband to look after – church, children and kitchen. I also still have dreams, things I want to do, and so do some of the other girls here. When I played a game with Therese, Erika and Ottilie a few days ago I asked them what they wanted to be when they grew up and they all wanted something for themselves – they wanted a future with the hope of something better, not just a function. Surely if you had the choice - if you could invent a different world, you'd want to have those choices?'

Helene looked at Julie quizzically, 'Are you a Bolshevik?'

Julie giggled, 'No Helene…I suppose I just spent too much time in the sun.'

The Bazar Hotel, Posen, the evening of 25 October 1939

As Karl alighted from his taxi outside the Hotel Bazar he looked up and marvelled. He could see the date 1841 in Roman numerals above the vast entrance, but even then, when Prussia had been at its most extravagant, it was a gem of imperial affirmation. Above its vaulted entrance towered eight Doric columns supporting architecture of the scale and style of the Parthenon, while adjoining wings extended some 100 metres to flanking towers. It had been built to do justice to civic and national greatness then, but this evening the whole structure had been appropriated for the affirmation of a different kind - the restoration of Posen to the Reich. The flags of the SS, Imperial Germany and wreaths in gold and silver bedecked both sides of the entrance along the whole frontage, while in the centre, between the columns, four vast swastika banners were suspended, lit from below by red tinted lights. He had seen this sort of spectacle before in Berlin but somehow, in the unfamiliar surroundings of Posen, it seemed all the more magnificent.

Within the hotel the motivic symbolism was maintained, a vast bust of the Führer assuming the focal point of the grand entrance hall, swathed in ivy bunting, with more flags and banners hanging from the first floor balustrade completing the montage.

Both Gunther Rath and Dr Hertz had promised Karl their companionship in this setting, but he had not counted on the scale of these surroundings, nor the numbers of military and civilian guests. A footman took his coat and he loitered, nervously folding and refolding the cloakroom ticket. As he did so he noted, in particular, a group of fifteen or so teenage girls who entered from the street on the arms of impeccably attired junior SS officers. The officers' blonde hair, athletic physique and bold looks were, he thought, arresting,

68

particularly amongst so many bloated party hacks and bored military wives. Their immaculate black dress-uniforms, silver runic lapel flashes, white braid lanyards and white gloves, seemed to turn the heads of everyone around them, while other men could hardly help but look on, captivated by their delicate and stunningly presented female companions in their graceful ball gowns.

It was clear to Karl that such girls, in the company of such men, would hardly bother to give him a second glance and yet, as he studied them, the young ladies seemed ill at ease, their glances painfully shy and even apprehensive. He watched for a moment as they gracefully moved towards the ballroom doors, none less than what he might call 'pretty', and all exquisitely crowned with glittering tiaras, earrings and sparkling necklaces, which drew the gaze of everyone around them. He looked on as this dazzling procession passed the waiters with silver trays of sparkling wine extended and entered the grand hall with its crystal chandeliers. He wondered where such men found such girls in the middle of Posen!

While Karl was still digesting these thoughts, Dr Hertz seized his hand, and he jumped nervously. Gunther also leapt at him playfully. 'I'm afraid we had to fortify ourselves against these horrors! We're a bit merry!'

'Never mind, you've probably saved me…I was about to fall in love.' he said forlornly.

Hertz looked about him and pointed to a large bejewelled matron, 'What, her?'

'No! Some young beauties that came with the junior SS officers.'

'Ah…'Hertz exclaimed,'…be careful. Himmler's made duelling in the SS legal, so don't chance your arm. I don't want to end up as your second with you fled back to Danzig!'

They entered the ballroom clutching their drinks defensively and found a quiet corner where they might sit and watch the proceedings. Karl tuned in and out of his companions' conversation glimpsing, where he could, those men and young women who seemed to occupy this other world of beauty and glamour to which he craved to belong. He watched discreetly as they took to the floor, gliding and turning effortlessly with the music, smiling and comfortable in their station, while he remained looking in to their world from the grey margins. And then he caught the eye of one young lady in an ivory dress. Her hair was dark and raised into an elegant *chignon*, a few gentle strands falling around her temples. She wore a diamond tiara and earrings which caught the sparkle in her eyes, while her ball gown accentuated a graceful shoulder line, slim neck and trim figure. But it was her eyes that drew him in, sparkling, alive and joyful.

With this almost painful image of loveliness he despaired of himself, turned resolutely away, and began to pick up the threads of his companions conversation.

It was as Gunther clutched at his goblet in a final peroration that this same young woman came hurrying to the table and stood looking at Karl anxiously. He seemed dumbstruck by her arrival, but, regaining his composure, he stood, bowed slightly, and invited her to dance. She nodded and passed a brief nervous smile, before he took her arm, walking her to the floor and leaving his companions open mouthed.

As they began to turn together to the music she smiled, 'Thank you for saving me!'

Karl was trying to stay with her steps and replied slightly awkwardly, 'Saving you!'

'Those junior SS officers…'

'I thought you were with them. I saw you come in.'

'Only for this evening - we were *conscripted* from an orphanage.'

'But where did you get these beautiful dresses, these jewels, if you are from an orphanage?'

'Borrowed.'

'Borrowed?'

'Oh, they trawled the city, found tailors, seamstresses and I think one woman was a dresser from the theatre. The jewels, well, who knows! Our SS escorts had to sign for them so I suppose they must be real. I'm told it's all about local prestige - apparently Himmler's around somewhere.'

'So I'm saving you from the SS!' He smiled, 'My friend won't approve. He says they've legalised duelling.' He paused, 'But, if I may ask, why did you come to me?'

'Because you don't wear a uniform! It does something to people when they wear a uniform, and…' she looked at him for a moment as they turned together, '…I saw you glancing over at me and you seemed to have a kind face.'

70

With this a silence fell over them and they began to dance with an ease and pleasure that seemed to echo their inner thoughts. He looked at her, hesitating to linger on her prettiness and anxious not to make her feel ill at ease, but her eyes exuded a warm gaiety which immediately dispelled his inhibitions and so, when the dance finished, Karl took her back to his table, daring to hope she would not be drawn away. Dr Hertz and Gunther had gone, so they sat alone together. He extended his hand, 'Doctor Karl Rust...'

There was a pause. 'Are you a Party official?' Karl shook his head. 'Then my name is Julie Scholl. And if you are not an official what are you doing here?'

'I'm a doctor. Actually I am here on official business – I'm supposed to give a briefing to Gauleiter Grieser, but I suspect they've forgotten about me. I am from Danzig – well Berlin originally. I have to say you don't seem like an orphan.'

Julie smiled 'You mean dressed like this...hardly!'

'No, not that...just your manner, your accent. You sound as though you've lived abroad and your skin, it's not tanned as I first thought, is there some Spanish or Italian blood there?'

Julie opened her mouth in mock speechlessness. 'My word you are sharp, and actually my mother was Spanish. So tell me more about myself.' she said playfully.

Karl sat back and then took her hand, 'May I?'

She nodded and he delicately removed her white glove. As he did so they both sensed something in this simple gesture which crossed the line between playfulness and an unintended but pleasurable intimacy. He held her hand close to him and examined both sides. It was soft and delicate, without calluses or blemishes, and as he turned her hand again their eyes met and lingered momentarily. 'You are not a worker or an academic – though of good family and intelligence...or artistry. Your hands are strong and nimble. You nails are well kept...but short.' He pursed his lips.

Julie laughed nervously, 'You are so close, I can't believe it!'

As they spoke a young staff officer of the Wehrmacht hovered unseen. He had dogged Julie's steps before and was determined not to be thwarted again. As their conversation ebbed he struck, boldly holding out his hand and brooking no refusal. Karl relinquished her with as much grace as he could muster and returned the officer's acknowledgment with a gentle nod of the head.

71

Julie turned fleetingly as she was led away, 'Thank you again for saving me.'

Gunther reappeared at Karl's side with a fresh glass of wine and watched Julie leave, 'You don't lose a girl like that and get her back you know.'

'I will.' Karl murmured. 'Where's Dr Hertz?'

'Oh, it's his wife – he had a phone call booked to Bern. I notice he told you nothing last night about her so I suppose I shouldn't either, but you are both doctors - professionals. You keep confidences don't you? The truth is she's in a clinic…' Gunther tapped his head, '…been there two years. Hertz says it's degenerative but I had an aunt like her and I think it's schizophrenia - well, from what I saw.'

'How on earth…'

'Don't even ask. I have tried to winkle it out of him. How does he afford it? Swiss as well! But look at the house my friend, look at the house. That's a man with something behind him….or at least a man who knows something about a man with something behind him! Eh?'

Meanwhile Julie was enduring, with polite detachment, the attentions of a young officer who now flattered and fawned on her with increasing fanaticism. Lieutenant Drucker was evidently 'keen' and tried to engage her on any and every topic to keep her attention. Finally he sensed he had failed to do himself justice and sought some association which might otherwise impress. When the orchestra stopped, he gently but resolutely kept her hand, 'Have you met Herr Frank the new Governor General of Poland?'

'No I…'

'I am his military liaison officer. It would be my honour to introduce you.'

Drucker ostentatiously led her to Frank's table where they found a small gathering of acolytes surrounding him. He looked up briefly, half noticing his young lieutenant. When at a second glance his eyes fell on Julie he stood swiftly and bowed, drawing her hand to his hovering lips and clicked his heels, 'Lieutenant Drucker, where did you find such a perfectly enchanting young lady? I'm delighted to meet you. Please introduce us.'

'May I have the honour to introduce Fräulein Julie…' He turned and met Julie's eyes with a look of desperation. Julie held out her hand, 'Julie Daase.'

Frank was ebullient, 'Do you dance? Do you play chess!?'

72

'I play the piano better than I dance, but I do dance, yes.'

Frank looked about him and rubbed his hands. 'You play the piano – so do I; but I admit I play chess better! Come, there's a piano upstairs.'

By the time Frank's procession had ascended the great horseshoe staircase in the central lobby and reached a small recital room on the first floor it had acquired a strength of thirty. Drucker anticipated his master and threw open the doors, raised the lid over the bell of the piano and opened up the keyboard.

Frank gestured at the piano stool. 'I played this a little today. It seems serviceable.'

Julie sat at the keyboard and gently probed the action, 'A Blüthner.'

Frank leaned over her. 'They tell me Paderewski played this very same instrument. So what shall it be…do you know the sonatas of Schubert? Some Beethoven, or Brahms perhaps?'

Julie sat without speaking, conscious of the arrival of still further curious observers, 'Would some Liszt please you, Herr Frank?'

Frank stood back, flattered by her gracious humility, 'Of course.'

Drucker brought a chair and Herr Frank sat, discreetly admiring her delicate figure and natural grace as she settled at the piano.

Two rooms distant Gauleiter Grieser sat glowering at the head of a long oak conference table. At the end of the flanking lines of petty officials and their papers lay the object of his ire, SS Obergruppenführer Wilhelm Koppe, his nominal subordinate in Warthegau, but in practice a seditious arriviste, determined to eclipse him and elevate the SS in his place. And, in the centre of the table sat SS Reichsführer Himmler, pompous and aloof, irritating Grieser with his affectation to be an impartial arbiter in their affairs.

'Find out what that is and stop it.' Grieser snapped impatiently to Vogler, as music began to filter into the meeting room from Julie's impromptu recital. Himmler and his Berlin staff were now audibly whispering amongst themselves, while his own civil servants had grown impatient with the circularity of the arguments and fruitless repetition. Grieser looked at his watch and sensed that the time had come when he might plausibly claim to be needed elsewhere. He

73

knocked on the table loudly, drawing the meeting to order, 'So Herr Reichsführer, gentlemen, I think it is now time to sum up: the civil administration has noted the position of Berlin and the Reichsführer himself and, of course, his representative here in Warthegau, SS Higher Leader Koppe, as regards deportations. We do not accept that position entirely, but will make certain *allowances;* Jews will entirely fall under the jurisdiction of the SS, we have no interests in their disposal except that it is done without delay. Similarly the intelligentsia, nobility, clergy, Jesuits, the mentally ill, politically active Poles and former members of proscribed Polish organisations and the ex-military must go. Those convicted by the military courts will stay and their sentences will be carried out in the city or town in which the offence occurred, or a local prison. However, policy on the deportation of those civilian Poles whose value to the Reich has not been defined in economic terms - tradesmen, artisans, farmers and the like - must remain, for the time being, within my jurisdiction. Those definitions will be determined by my officials on a case by case basis and by no others. There will be no further irregular or 'spontaneous' actions. Any departure from these points must be agreed with my office in writing on not less than twelve hours' notice.' Grieser stood up. 'And now gentlemen we must join our guests at the civic reception and I thank you for your contributions. Thank you. Heil Hitler.'

Himmler stood awkwardly and saluted stiffly along with the assembled officials. The slight was a public one; there would be no closing comments of dissent and no deals, and his local man, Koppe, had overplayed his hand. He had been too reliant on the weight of Himmler's personal attendance to 'carry the day' and Grieser was still clearly unmoved by the implication that he was out of step with Berlin.

As the meeting broke up Himmler's adjutant Wolff beckoned Koppe and Kellerman to Himmler's side. Himmler looked at Koppe with irritation, his voice acerbic, 'You do understand don't you, Obergruppenführer Koppe, that we must all work towards the Führer at the same pace – we simply can't allow these civil governors to slow things down. I've told both Herr Grieser here and Forster in Danzig West Prussia that these provinces must be fully Germanized within ten years. That is the Führer's wish and it is our duty to see that his wish is realised.' Himmler waved his hand dismissively, 'Grieser is evidently not listening. He is distracted by the economics – the agronomics, like Forster. But he must be *made* to listen and if not by you, I will find

74

someone who can.' Himmler smiled coldly, 'Do I make myself clear?' Koppe nodded stiffly. Himmler's eyes lingered on him critically for a moment and then he turned to Wolff, 'We will not be staying for the reception. I'm sure our presence would only distract these officers from other and more pressing duties.' Himmler passed his file of meeting papers to Wolff and then turned to Koppe again, 'You have one month to turn this situation around. *How* you do it is of no interest to me. Liaise with Wolff on matters of detail and I shall await your report.'

Grieser dared not risk being cornered by Himmler, and wanted no technical 'afterthoughts' from their officials, so he strode quickly along the red carpet toward the central staircase. When Vogler emerged from a side door they met awkwardly outside the recital room. Grieser drew himself up abruptly, still hearing music. 'So what's going on Vogler?' Vogler opened the door without speaking and Grieser saw within the figure of Frank, enthroned in a large red leather chair and surrounded by his attentive courtiers. He was wistfully eyeing a pretty, dark haired young pianist in a long off-the-shoulder ball gown who was entrancing Frank and his pliant audience with pianism of breath-taking dexterity. He smoothed the pate of his balding head and tugged on the hem of his tunic.

'Who is she?' he whispered.

Vogler leaned over, 'Frank's adjutant Drucker says she is from the orphanage off Glogauer Strasse – an orphan! Müller told me she's one of a group they hired in for the night for the junior SS officers...her name's Julie Daase I believe.'

Grieser paused for a moment, his eyes studying her every detail, drinking in the spectacle. She turned momentarily and he caught an impression of her brilliant, captivating eyes. His voice dropped to a whisper, 'I can't believe it...she could be Anna.'

Vogler leaned over to see a look of anguish momentarily cross Grieser's face. 'I'm sorry Herr Grieser?'

Grieser said nothing, but entered the room, slowly approaching the outer circle of the audience where he waited. When Julie finished and the applause began he advanced and shook Frank's hand, smiling and issuing some perfunctory remarks, then moved to the piano where he applauded Julie with the others and then drew her to him with sweeping gestures.

He collected himself and began to address the audience. 'Tonight you have heard a German orphan from this city attain the highest standards of artistry at this piano…' He turned and looked at her, their eyes meeting briefly, and then suddenly seemed lost, hesitating and stumbling awkwardly, 'From…from nothing…and from the greatest misfortune she has struggled and triumphed, just as Germany now rises from her own misfortune to rise again with our youth at the forefront of these achievements. I thank Herr Frank for bringing Fräulein Daase to our notice. She shall want for nothing now and we shall embrace her as a leading light in this city. But now, I invite you, on behalf of Posen, to re-join our comrades…'

Frank clasped Grieser's shoulder. 'A moment, Herr Grieser! I wanted to talk to this young lady.' Frank tilted his head. 'You know, Clara Schumann played that *'Toccata'* to show off her prodigious talents and Robert composed it as a study for himself, so it must be exceptionally hard to play as an amateur. So who has taught you to master it? Did you really teach yourself – an orphan?' Julie reddened and fumbled for a moment.

Grieser saw his opportunity and while Frank awaited her reply he locked arms with her, 'Hans, you are terrifying the young girl.' Grieser winked at Julie who looked up with nervous relief at the unexpected protection his intervention offered her.

As they turned away Frank laughed, 'Very well then, I will invite you to Warsaw some time. You can come and play for us. Then we will see what the critics say!'

As they descended the stairs Julie felt an ease and familiarity in Grieser's manner. He seemed disinterested in the normal pattern of introduction and happy to talk of his plans for culture and the arts in Posen. Near the bottom of the stairs he stopped and looked into her bright but slightly anxious eyes, 'So, Fräulein Daase, shall we have our photograph taken to remember this evening, before you return to the orphanage in your pumpkin coach? But perhaps we could dance first - before you re-join your SS friends? That would be a great pleasure to me. Would you be so kind?'

Julie smiled, 'Yes, Herr Grieser, I would like that very much.'

'And shall I send you a copy of the picture?'

'Yes, yes that would be very nice too.'

With this Grieser snapped his fingers and a waiting photographer stepped forward to take their picture. Afterwards they swept into the ballroom, Grieser nodding regally to others as they acknowledged him.

When they reached the floor Julie observed her young SS escort loitering with evident irritation. He eyed her with a malignant coolness that turned her in on Grieser, to whom she now devoted her attention. His hand settled gently in the small of her back, she clasped his hand lightly, and they began to dance.

When the dance finished she saw the young SS Lieutenant begin to approach again impatiently. Grieser saw nothing and bowed graciously but as he did so Julie extended her hand toward him again and smiled invitingly. He stood tall and reassumed his station, looking down at her with a fondness with which she was happy to engage.

'You have a keen step young lady.' Grieser said after a few moments.

'Thank you, you are very kind.'

'You know with playing of that calibre you could make a career. Will you do that?'

Julie smiled but noticed his eyes wandering over her in a way which made her feel momentarily self-conscious, 'Yes, I would like to, but it is difficult. There are so many good pianists.'

'But tonight all doors have been opened. Come and see me tomorrow. We shall arrange something for you?' He looked around him, 'Are *all* these girls with the SS really from your orphanage?'

'Yes.'

'Run by Catholics?' he said disparagingly.

'Yes.'

Grieser shook his head, 'They should get out more. It's a crying shame to be locked away when you are so young and so pretty. So, Julie Daase, what did you make of Hans Frank, 'Stalin's man in Warsaw'.'

Julie shook her head, 'I'm sorry?'

Grieser laughed, 'That's what they call him behind his back. The Führer wanted to give the Poles a rump state that they could *mismanage* themselves, but Stalin vetoed it - can you imagine! So Frank got the rump state instead, and what a poison pill that is.'

Across the floor Karl and Gunther looked on as Grieser and Julie maintained their pairing for three more dances. Gunther passed some cynical remark about power and beauty which Karl ignored, but

77

in his heart he felt deep frustration, even a sense of betrayal. Soon his thoughts were jolted by the exhausted Vogler, who slumped beside him.

'I'm sorry Karl, that's it for the day. You can go back to your hotel a free man.' He drank some wine from Karl's glass thirstily, 'No briefing, no audience and no questions. Total waste of time. When do you leave?'

Karl's tone was dejected, 'Tomorrow afternoon on the four thirty train.'

Gunther put down his glass heavily, 'God that's foul…so Karl, you have some hours to kill tomorrow? So why don't I take you for a guided tour of the city, eh? I have a car, it's my treat, and next time I'm in Danzig you can treat me.'

Karl looked over toward Julie who was finally beating a retreat from Grieser's immediate circle of guests and coming toward them, 'Could I bring a friend?'

'Who?'

Gunther followed Karl's line of vision. 'If you can get her out of the orphanage, it's all the same to me – have you met Sister Schmidt!'

As Karl greeted Julie again Grieser watched them from a distance his face now stern and unsmiling. He lit a cigarette and gestured to his Gestapo liaison officer, Lieutenant Müller, who leaned over the back of his chair confidentially, 'Tomorrow I want you to make enquiries about that girl Julie Dasse. Get Krill on to it first thing. He's a good man for this sort of job.'

Müller stood back slightly. 'Is there something wrong Herr Grieser?'

'Frank put me on to her. She says she's an orphan from Thorner Strasse, but there's something about her that's not quite right.'

Müller nodded, 'I'll get on to it immediately, Sir.'

The ball was now beginning to ebb and so Müller made his way into the lobby where he found SS Higher Leader Koppe engrossed in conversation with his adjutant Captain Kellerman. Kellerman saw Müller loitering and beckoned to him over.

'Well, what is it Müller?'

'It seems we may have a situation, Sir... concerning Herr Grieser and one of the orphans we brought here tonight.'

'What do you mean?'

'He's asked for an investigation.'

'Because?'

'There seems to be an issue about her identity. He says there's something '*not quite right*' about her. He's asked me to put Krill on to it, Sir.'

Kellerman frowned, 'Krill – that's a little excessive for preliminary enquiries isn't it?'

Koppe shook his head, 'Well, I see no objection to it. He's entitled to ask... so, put Krill on it, give him what he wants – bring her in for questioning if that's what it takes...just keep him happy...until we decide how to deal with him.'

As Müller withdrew Kellerman's eyes followed him, 'I tend to watch my back when he's around...there's something of a Cassius about him.'

'Nothing wrong with ambition surely – or is it that he's making *you* feel nervous?' Koppe raised an enquiring eyebrow, but Kellerman remained tight lipped. 'Now, what's this about an SD Colonel...Hopp?'

'A close associate of Heydrich. He's sending a man down from Berlin, Gerhard, he's plain clothes and only a captain but he's got the authority of Hopp's rank behind him - that was spelled out to me very clearly over the phone. He won't say more. He's asking for cooperation at the highest level – which I assume means personal access to you.'

Koppe looked about with irritation, 'Typical bad timing. Well, do what you can to keep him away from me, but I'll see him as and when...just keep me informed.'

As they left the Bazar Hotel, pulling their greatcoats around them, they stood for a moment on the steps taking in the cool evening air. Koppe lit a cigarette and exhaled slowly, his face thoughtful, 'This business with Krill. I want you to keep an eye on it.'

Kellerman leaned forward. 'Sir?'

'Grieser's got a past...something Wolff told me as he was leaving. Come and see me tomorrow with Müller and we'll see if we can't find a way to *play* Grieser over this orphan business. After all,

79

you heard Himmler, he's not interested in how we go about this…so it seems we have a free hand…at least for now.'

Chapter 6

Glogauer Strasse, Posen, 26 October 1939

Karl and Gunther were early and so drove the length of Glogauer Strasse from Posen Central Station to its terminus at the *Messenhallen* - the great trade centre building - to pass some time. As they did so Karl was struck by the scale of this civic artery which seemed to rival even the Ringstrasse in Vienna for its grandeur. Down its broad central span ran the tram lines which took the large crowds to the annual trade fair while either side of the tramways were wide avenues of linden trees which shaded the lower floors and shop fronts of the tenement buildings which rose five or six storeys above the street in ornate Gothic style brickwork.

'I had no idea how imposing Posen was.' Karl said as he peered upward from the car.

Gunther grunted, 'Oh, there's better than this – this is just the functional stuff. This was a wealthy city in the old days and there's the architecture to prove it.'

They parked in Thorner Strasse opposite the orphanage and after getting out of the car Karl stared at the imposing façade for a moment, struck by its monumental grandeur amongst so many more humble and dilapidated houses in the street. He crossed the road with Gunther looking up at the high, arched, leaded windows on the first floor, and above that, to the steep gabled roof and ornate pale stone chimneys. He had visited orphanages during his training as a physician in Berlin and had found them on the whole gloomy and unhappy places, and this exterior did not suggest to him that this would necessarily be any different, so he was pleasantly surprised to be met by the giggling figures of Erika and Viktoria as they passed through the arched stone portal and began to ascend the few steps to the entrance hall. When they reached the girls they quickly drew themselves up and greeted Karl and Gunther with great solemnity before leading them to Sister Schmidt's office and then scampering away again.

Sister Schmidt stood as soon as they entered the room, receiving them with a broad smile and a warm handshake. 'Ah, gentlemen – Herr Rath, how nice to see you again. Julie mentioned that you wanted to see me about a possible sightseeing expedition with…Dr Rust I presume? But perhaps you would also like to see the hidden treasures of our home? I see you have your camera – ah, now I've been waiting for this opportunity for some time. Come, I must go to the school room and perhaps we can talk together.'

Sister Schmidt led them up some steps, down a bright corridor smelling of disinfectant, through double doors and into a dormitory which she said had at one time been a place for dance instruction. At the end of the rows of neat beds the wall was composed of a series of broad mirrors which supported a hand rail. In times past the Sister told them this would have been a place for ballet exercises. Above them Karl observed the finely crafted classically themed plasterwork, which the artisans of another age had thought suitable for the inspiration of the young. Karl raised his camera, but then lowered it again, 'What are those steel pipes – what a shame.'

The Sister raised her eyebrows, 'Ah yes, and so ugly. That was put there to support canvass partitions during the last war - this was a hospital. I worked here briefly…before I found my vocation.'

In the classroom, Karl marvelled at stained glass windows, which again sought inspiration from musical mythology – scenes from Lohengrin, Parsifal and Rienzi. In one corner stood a small grand piano with a walnut case, ornately carved legs, and a music stand with polished brass sconces. On the stand was a battered score heavily marked with blue pencil, 'Ah yes, Julie practices here very often, indeed too often I sometimes think. The girl is *driven*…a perfectionist.' Sister Schmidt observed with a smile.

Karl took more photographs and made appreciative noises, but as they walked about the orphanage he also wondered if this diversion was perhaps by way of a 'no' to his further meeting with Julie. But, after much conversation and many questions about his life in Berlin, he realised the Sister just wanted to assure herself of him, and also revealed another purpose to their discussion; she wanted a photograph of all the girls together – a family photograph. It was half an hour before this task could be completed but when that request was satisfied Julie was found and made ready for their excursion.

Karl had wondered if she might be different, away from the lights and glamour of the previous evening, but she seemed the same bright vivacious character that he had sat with the night before. After introductions Gunther took the wheel and began to drive them though the busy streets, pointing and describing the various sights on their way. He promised them a stop at the Fara Church, the Royal Prussian Academy, the town hall, the Basilica, the opera house, and finally coffee and cakes at Klindworths – which he said were better than anything in Vienna.

While Gunther made himself audible, Karl and Julie found something in each other's glances which they both recognised as more lingering than mere passing acknowledgment. In the confines of the back of the car each sensed the other's nervous expectation that they were embarking on a journey together, not knowing where it might lead, but willing to go on for the simple pleasure they had found the previous evening in each other's company.

Soon Gunther drew the car up outside the Basilica of St Peter and St Paul which gave Karl the opportunity to take Julie's arm and walk with her. Only snatches of Gunther's encyclopaedic discourse about the Archcathedral penetrated their inner preoccupations; '…the oldest church of former Poland…Tenth Century foundations…the burial place of no less than seven Polish Kings.' They nodded appreciatively and looked with dutiful attention, but saw and heard little.

As they looked up at the Dome of the Golden Chapel, Karl's hand slipped from her arm and met her fingers which now meshed with his own. He leaned towards her, 'I have so much I want to say and no time to say it.'

Julie smiled but remained silent, the grasp of her hand communicating her feelings, though her inner thoughts remained in a state of complete confusion. To Julie, Karl seemed such easy company, so unassuming and gentle, and yet what could she do or say now that would change the future that was already awaiting her in Berlin, or him in Danzig – worlds apart. She felt him brush against her arm and suddenly realised how much she missed the simple pleasure of belonging, of being cared for, of being loved – of knowing that she could reach out to someone. She tried to cling to the pleasure of the moment, to the contentment and warmth they shared now, and drew closer to him.

83

Gunther felt he had more success with his companions at the Fara Church whose Baroque splendour emphatically silenced them. As they stood, humbled by the sumptuous splendour and beauty of the gilded columns, intricate plaster arches and vividly painted ceilings, Gunther continued his narrative, 'This is one of the most beautiful Baroque churches in Europe. It was built in 1651 for the Jesuits.' He paused, 'You know it is said that the Renaissance was the transition from the Age of Faith, to the Age of Reason - as the reaction of the individual against the universal...'

Karl interjected in a voice which communicated his marvel at their surroundings, 'A victory for the spirit of criticism over a spirit of unquestioning acceptance?'

'Quite. Each successive ruler over Posen, the Poles, Austrians, Prussians and Germans, brought their own symbols of permanence. The Jesuits who built this only lasted seventy years and then they were expelled.' Gunther sniffed and shuffled, momentarily absorbed in his own thoughts, 'So, now the opera house?'

Karl tugged on Gunther's arm and discreetly proposed a curtailment to the comfort of Klindworths patisserie. Gunther winked at Karl sympathetically and announced that while they partook of coffee he might leave them briefly to see a business associate.

At Klindworths they seized a window table, forestalling other expectant patrons who frowned disapprovingly. The place was heaving and the smell of coffee, confectionery, tobacco and perfume overwhelmed them after the cold purity of the Fara church. Julie took off her coat with difficulty in their cramped surroundings while Karl observed her. As she settled his eyes drank in her simple natural prettiness. And yet gnawing at him all the time was the hopelessness of this liaison.

She reached out and held his hand, 'Do you know how old I am?' She paused only briefly, 'I'm fifteen but only celebrate my fourth birthday next year. So when is my birthday?'

He smiled, 'So we continue from last night. More tests!' Karl thought for a moment, 'Well, 1940 is a leap year...so if you are only four next year you must have been born on 29th February '24.'

Julie clapped her hands vigorously and drew testy looks from neighbouring tables for her trouble, 'But what do my hands tell you?' She held them out.

This time he took both hands and held her gaze 'That you are…a pretty, talented, pianist!' She feigned surprise, but quietly enjoyed his flattery, 'But I am afraid I got that from overheard conversations last night.' He sat back slightly, still holding her hands, 'I wanted to ask how your trip home went. Was that young officer very short with you?'

Julie grimaced, 'They were mostly awful. Honourable! Only just. Nobody really enjoyed themselves, not even Viktoria. They seemed to think we had been ordered there for *them* and had to keep *them* happy. They talked and we smiled. Jutta's SS man tried to kiss her on the steps of the hotel – which was a mistake! Birgit's tried to touch her in the car and she actually slapped him, and Ottilie's officer kept asking her to meet him again. Fortunately Waltraud had a nice young man who seemed very correct and talked about his girlfriend in Bremen all evening. But it was Helene I really felt sorry for.'

'Why?'

'Her officer was already married…and she so wanted to meet a man who would marry her and take her back to Germany.'

'But your officer?'

'Oh, he kept on about how I had slighted him and then started attacking the Catholic Church. I suppose he thought I must be a devout Catholic and this explained my behaviour. I think it was his way of getting back at me. He seemed to think religion is the enemy of National Socialism.'

'But everyone got back safely?'

'Oh yes, but they were in a pretty resentful mood by the end of the evening and I wouldn't want to meet them again – not after they'd had a few drinks! Why do you ask? Have you become so anxious about me already?'

Karl sighed, 'You know I think I have.'

Julie became suddenly more still and serious, 'Karl, can I ask you something - some advice?'

'Of course.'

'It's so stupid; I really don't know how to explain…' Julie paused as a waitress took their order and removed used crockery from the table. '…but I came here from Warsaw in August because I was going to be arrested as a German. At the time my professor told me it was better to carry another student's paper's – Julie Daase – because she was an ethnic German from Posen. When I arrived here I was

85

registered by Sister Schmidt with the Polish authorities under the false name. But then, when the SS men came about the ball, they had the old Polish police list and produced a whole lot of new papers for Sister Schmidt to sign. She didn't say anything – she completely forgot. So last night I thought I would get the Sister into trouble if I told the truth so I kept telling people I was Julie Daase. It was just the young SS Lieutenant at first – that seemed a small enough lie, but then, later, it was Herr Frank's liaison officer, then Herr Frank, and then Herr Grieser! It just seemed to become a bigger and bigger lie.'

'And so you need to tell them quickly what has happened so there are no problems – no suspicions.'

Julie raised her eyebrows, 'But how? What about Sister Schmidt? She began the lie by accident, and what if they take issue? And what about my repeated deliberate lies – to Herr Frank and Herr Grieser? Perhaps I should just go back to Germany quickly.'

Karl pursed his lips. 'Can I contact your father? Could he come and get you and explain everything - with your papers from Germany? At least he could vouch for you.'

'I only wish it was that simple. They say he's with a trade mission. At the end of August Sister Schmidt telephoned the Economics Ministry where he works. His secretary was very helpful and said they could contact him but that it could take weeks before he'd be back in Berlin. He still hasn't responded to a letter she wrote two weeks ago, so I don't even know if he's returned yet.'

Julie suddenly righted herself and smiled, 'Gunther's coming. I don't want him to think I'm in trouble.'

But Gunther's return found Karl hopelessly lost in a sea of conflicting desires and emotions. The interlude had not been as he would have hoped and now the moment had passed - it would remain a fleeting liaison. And, if there had been an opportunity for it to become something else, that moment had passed in Klindworths.

As they drove back towards the orphanage Karl felt them both begin to reconcile to their parting. But strong feelings had been aroused within him by Julie's beauty, her natural warmth and her innocent confidences and he felt suddenly devastated by the idea of losing her.

As they parted outside the orphanage he tormented himself further by assuming an air of detached politeness which he hoped might at least lend the parting some dignity. But when Julie smiled at him affectionately and wished him a safe journey to Danzig his resolve quickly crumbled, making a clumsy note of his address at the Central Hospital, slipping it into her hand with a feeling of desperation, and asking if she might one day visit him.

She looked at the paper, nodded, and put it in her coat pocket. Then they wished each other well again, she thanked Gunther for his kindness and turned, re-entering the orphanage and disappearing into the gloom of the stairwell.

SS Headquarters, Fort Winiary, Posen, 26 October 1939

Koppe sat back in his chair and toyed with a paper knife, looking across his large desk at his adjutant Kellerman and the new arrival from Berlin, SS Captain Dr Fischer.

'And that was the message from Heydrich was it, '*...a free hand...act as we see fit'?*'

Dr Fischer nodded. 'With the proviso that any fuck-ups would remain deniable in Prinz-Albrechtstrasse.'

Koppe threw the knife onto his desk and looked at an open file. 'Oh that goes without saying. So it couldn't be clearer then - we'll go ahead...if we can. The rest of what we have on him is chicken feed anyway: too old, too feeble, or too commonplace. Kellerman – are we all set?'

Kellerman nodded 'Müller's arranged everything at the Monopol and Krill knows as much as he needs to. Yes, we're all set up.'

'And what about our source inside his office; do we have a '*Plan B*' if he doesn't rise to the bait? Does *he* have any leads we might pursue?'

'There's a doctor Grieser's very thick with - for no apparent reason. They go back a long way. If there is dirt he will probably know something – I'll do some background.'

'Old sins cast long shadows, eh! Chase it hard...Now Dr Fischer, let's get back to the reasons you're here; what does the Race and Settlement Department say about strategy?'

Dr Fischer pushed his glasses back up to the bridge of his thin nose and sniffed, 'That we have a duty to think ahead – the consequences of deportations on the scale we propose. The SS wants a

87

deportation ratio of two Poles out for every German gathered in to achieve some sort of realistic chance of maintaining agricultural production and civil cohesion. We agree there are difficulties in moving so quickly, but Grieser is exaggerating when he says it's impractical. In pre-war Germany we talked of the concept of family and motherhood, of law and custom, of duty; for Germany that was necessary, but here, now, there is no German law, the law of Warthegau is in this building, and the law is the SS - whatever Grieser claims. So, if we need to re-colonise we can use methods far more creative than he seems to imagine to fill the gaps left by Poles, Jews and the rest.' Dr Fischer pulled out a file from his briefcase and took out a cutting. 'I mean, for example, just look at what Himmler said in September, '...*that beyond the borders of perhaps necessary bourgeois laws, customs and views, it will now be the great task, even outside the marriage bond, for German women and girls of good blood, to become the mothers of children of soldiers going off to war.'* So the first thing is the optimisation of fertility among our own bloodstock, particularly the Nordic type. That will be a vital component in building the core of the new Europe. But the Führer wants this area and Danzig West Prussia fully Germanized within ten years, so we need a mixed strategy – breeding can only achieve so much. We need twenty years to re-stock with Germans using conventional family models, so we need to be imaginative elsewhere. We have the eastern ethnic Germans of course – the Russians will send us them. We can get some figures on Scandinavians and Nordic types we can pull in and we can take Polish children of Aryan appearance for our own purposes and place them with German families. There are also Germans who could emigrate from the Reich, particularly those who fled there before war from Poland...'

Kellerman leaned forward on his chair. 'And don't forget the religious houses and orphanages here. There's plenty of good material there.'

Koppe nodded and then hesitated, 'Any reason you mention those in particular?'

'We've had some complaints...after the ball the other night...about the continuing involvement of the Church – about the girls we hired in.'

'Specifically?'

'There were some altercations - I've taken the matter up. There's a fair amount of resentment about the way the girls behaved towards the SS officers they were with - a feeling that legitimate expectations were not met. Besides we have a city full of young fit soldiers here with nothing to do, we have 60 German orphan girls in the city *of age*, or near enough, and the Catholic Sisters won't even allow association.'

Koppe looked at Dr Fischer and gestured toward Kellerman, 'There you are – start there. Close them down, re-socialise them, be creative, but get a move on. I want you to tell me how this happens and *show* me how this happens....You have a week to come back to me with a policy paper and demonstrate some practical progress. Liaise with Kellerman if you have questions.'

Chapter 7

Birgit and Helene were sitting anxiously on the end of Julie's bed when she returned from her trip with Gunther and Karl. Her pace slowed as she walked toward them, detecting an anxiety and tension in their expressions which seemed focused entirely on her. She put her coat down and smiled uncomfortably, 'My word Helene, you look so serious. What's the matter…am I in trouble?'

Helene looked pale and frightened, 'You have to go to the office. Julie, it's the police.'

Julie felt a shudder run through her body and clutched the end of the bed frame while Birgit leaned toward her, whispering nervously, 'I made them some drinks. There are two of them - they've been here for hours Julie. What do they want?'

Julie felt unable to speak for a moment, her mind racing and her heart pounding, 'It's probably nothing – a problem with my papers. Sister Schmidt knows about it. Don't worry; it can all be sorted out.' She picked up her coat and retraced her steps back towards the office with Helene and Birgit at her side. When she got to the door she hugged and kissed them both before knocking lightly. She waited, hoping there would be no reply, but Sister Schmidt called out and so she entered. As she closed the door behind her she felt her legs begin to buckle and it was now as much as she could do to stand clutching the heavy brass door knob behind her for support. Two men in brown pinstripe suits sat looking at her with dead eyes. On the table lay the file in which the Sister had placed Julie's registration documents, police residency permit, her ration cards and some spare identity photographs.

The older policeman, in his forties with short grey hair and pock marked face, looked briefly at her picture. 'You are Julie Scholl, also known as Julie Daase?'

Julie nodded and looked at Sister Schmidt, searching for reassurance. The Sister's face was impassive, 'I've told these gentlemen the truth Julie – you have nothing to fear from that. I have told them it was my mistake. I'm assured by Sergeant Krill here that this can be resolved after some elementary enquiries, but you will appreciate that this situation has excited concern. You have met some very important people and now you must explain your papers so that people do not become concerned about you.'

Sergeant Krill got up and took Julie's arm. 'Better to tell us everything at the office where we can make a proper record. We won't be long.' He took Julie's coat from her and passed it to Sister Schmidt, 'She won't be needing this…it's a warm office.'

Krill kept a hold of Julie's arm as they descended the orphanage steps and once on the pavement, out of Sister Schmidt's sight, paused to grab her other hand and handcuff her. She stood looking dumbfounded at her manacled hands while he waved to a car across the street which turned and met them.

The journey to SS Police Headquarters was a blur, her only sensations being of time and motion slowed down. They approached Fort Winiary as dusk fell. She looked out at the large stone ramparts as the car rattled over a short wooden bridge. They stopped while heavy wooden gates were drawn back and then the car moved slowly forward into the shadowy interior where further red and white sentry boxes marked their progress toward the centre of the redoubt. At each one a guard took papers from the driver, looked through the back window at Julie and then waved them on. As she watched this ritual for the third time she felt a growing sense of helplessness, a sense that only something terrible could lie beyond these impenetrable barriers to the outside world.

At the main building, in the centre of the fortifications, a guard stepped forward to meet them, opening the rear door, dragging Julie from the car. She lost a shoe and turned to retrieve it, falling to the ground as the guard lost his grip. He leaned over her, screaming obscenities in her ear and ran a wooden baton through her handcuffs, the other end of which was taken up by Krill. Together they dragged her over the gravel toward the guard room, still clinging to her shoe, begging them to stop, her wrists chaffing under the whole weight of her body. They drew her upright at a doorway and she hobbled into a small room where a bull-faced Sergeant sat smoking with his feet on the desk reading an old copy of the *Völkischer Beobachter* newspaper. He threw it in the bin with a grunt and sat up, taking her details from Krill and entering them in a large ledger while she attempted to replace her shoe with trembling hands. Finally the Sergeant rose from his desk, eyeing Julie with cold detachment and grabbed a large set of keys from his drawer. He unlocked and pulled open the heavy steel door which led into the prison block and stood for a moment, suddenly broaching an unnerving smile, gesturing toward the open doorway with mocking courtesy.

When her eyes had adjusted to the gloom Julie found herself being led along narrow labyrinthine passageways and down spiral steps into a dank cold stinking subterranean cell block. One in a series of low wooden doors was unlocked and she was pushed into a small gloomy chamber filled with the overpowering stench of excrement. Krill stepped inside for a moment, unlocked the handcuffs and pushed her backwards onto a low wooden shelf.

A dim yellow light, recessed into the ceiling behind a metal grille, provided the only illumination in the room and from this she could discern a bucket in the corner surrounded by a pool of dark liquid. What little straw there was on the flagstone floor had long since become foetid and sodden and the mildewed walls, on which prisoners had scratched their names and dates, ran with condensation.

As she sat, a sense of unreality allowed her to continue to think in terms of the outside world for a time, but this didn't last. Instead she began to shiver and her wrists began to swell and throb. She suddenly felt the intense pain caused by the grit wedged under her toenails and embedded in the top of her foot and could dimly see blood against her pale shoe strap. Finally she lay down on the bench and huddled up to keep warm, dazed and disorientated, trying to make sense of what had happened to her and why she was there.

After an hour men's voices could be heard echoing down the corridor and heavy boots approached the door. She stood expectantly but it remained closed and instead she could hear keys rattling in the door of the adjacent cell. There followed the sound of voices, shouts of command and dull impacts. A man protested uncomprehending, first in Polish and then in broken German, at first begging and then sobbing and then screaming in simple animal terror as blows rained down. His agonies soon became her terror too and she began to weep and silently beg them to stop, rocking backwards and forwards, her hands over her ears, trembling.

When eventually the man stopped responding to the blows Julie could hear the guards' muffled voices debating what to do next and then a brief argument break out which seemed to ebb as they left

92

the cell. As they walked past her door Julie saw the spy flap open and an eye peer in on her. Then, after the shuffling of feet, another eye appear, which lingered. The flap then fell back and the sound of their footsteps moved away again, laughter echoing down the corridor as they went.

She now felt blind terror gripping her. She searched for something to focus on – something which would entirely shut out the world around her and stop her going mad. Then she remembered her voyage from Argentina, of the weeks at sea in her small cabin miming her finger exercises on an imaginary piano. In her mind she envisioned this piano in front of her and the score of the *'Toccata'* which still sat on the music stand in the orphanage. The two were now in front of her and she began to play, the music coming to her, strong and clear and crisp, as her foot tapped on the floor and her body swayed slightly in time with the music.

She awoke with a jolt to the sound of boots shuffling outside the cell door, curses and keys turning stiffly in the lock. Her heart pounded and her mouth became dry. The door swung open under the force of a boot and a stocky silhouette stood commanding her in guttural, incomprehensible German. She stood, murmuring her name. The warder stepped forward, grabbed her arm, and led her roughly out of the cell. As they ascended the stairs he tapped his key against the handrail to the rhythm of their footfall, swearing and shoving her in the small of the back when she fell behind.

In the gloomy interrogation room on the second floor two male warders stood behind her while Krill studiously read a file, ignoring her. He lit a cigarette and drank some water. Every so often he would underline something in heavy pencil and tut out a rhythm to himself. Finally he turned on his chair and closed the file, his tone matter-of-fact.

'You came from Warsaw with a Pole according to Sister Schmidt?'

'Yes.'

'Is he still here?'

'No. I don't think so.'

'What was his name?'

'He…he didn't tell me his name.'

'And you studied at the Conservatoire there? Why? Why Warsaw and not Berlin, Vienna, Rome?'

'I was in Berlin at the *Konservatorium der Reichshauptstadt*. I didn't like my teacher.'

'Who was your teacher and when?'

'Gieseking…36…37'

'Everyone's has heard of Gieseking and you seem to be searching for the date. Is that just a name you plucked out of the air?'

'No, I studied with him – you can check with the *Konservatorium*.'

'So why Warsaw?'

'It's technical. I can't explain.'

'Am I so stupid? Explain…'

'I have small hands. I wanted to work with a teacher who could help me extend my playing and overcome my limitations. Zbigniew Drzewiecki was famous for his work with others like me – and on Chopin.'

'So you lived in Warsaw for…a year, eighteen months? And who were your friends, contacts, associates? Who briefed you to come to Posen?'

'Briefed?'

'For whatever mission you were to undertake – to get close to senior Party men here in Posen. Perhaps you would use your charm to obtain information. You tell me?'

'I really can't answer you. I can't tell you anything except the truth…I am a music student. My father works for the Economics Ministry in Berlin. I fled from Warsaw because there were Germans here – ethnic Germans, they were going to arrest the Germans in Warsaw.'

'*Were* going to? Who told you? Were you tipped off? Did you have contacts in the Polish Interior Ministry?'

'No, one of the professors did – a mature student.'

'But you had sources and intermediaries in the Ministry.'

Julie hesitated, 'I suppose you could say that.'

Krill dwelt on her response and made a note while continuing to talk, 'No, *I* did not say that, *you* agreed with me that you have sources and intermediaries in the Interior Ministry - that is what I am recording. And so you arrive in Posen. What do you do?'

Julie bowed her head, 'When I arrived I had to register in a false name with the Polish authorities.'

Krill opened the file and turned a few pages slowly, 'Ah yes. But you could have told the German authorities this weeks ago - after the liberation. The Polish registration card says you arrived on the 29th of August. Why delay? Why continue the subterfuge - even last night with Herr Frank and Gauleiter Grieser. Why not say, *'Can you help me?'* Why deceive them - as a German what did you have to fear?'

Julie held her hands to her face. 'I don't know, I don't know, I panicked. On the list the SS had when they came to the orphanage I was Daase, Julie Daase, and Sister Schmidt didn't correct it so I kept it up for a little longer – she must have told you this. And then it didn't seem the right time to explain. When Sikorski....' Julie halted herself.

Krill's pen hovered over a notepad and he beckoned her to continue…'Sikorski?'

Julie dropped her hands 'Kazimierz Sikorski.'

'Your intermediary? The man who brought you at his own risk to a town near the German border with false papers to lie low until the Germans arrived?' Krill stood abruptly, 'WELL…?'He slammed his fist down on the desk in front of Julie and she leaped backwards into the hands of the warders.

'Yes, he brought me…' Julie spoke through her sobs, '…but it was not like that.'

His voice was calmer, 'You said you didn't know his name? You lied.' He stooped to catch her eye. 'Are you working with the Polish underground?'

'No, please...I didn't want him to get into trouble. He helped me!'

'You arrived on the 29th of August and the Poles issued their general mobilisation orders on the 30th of August. Were you part of the mobilisation? Perhaps you have a lover in Warsaw who took you in.' Krill leaned back. 'Are you a virgin?'

Julie's voice was now low and broken, 'Yes of course.'

Krill pinched his nose, 'You play the innocent very well, but I give you an alternative scenario. You came here under the protection of a Polish agent named Sikorski, you concealed yourself in an orphanage, you lied about your identity, you have evaded detection and you have consorted with Polish officials.' He leant back, 'Do you know the penalty for using false papers provided by the enemy and

95

seeking to infiltrate the German administration? Do you know what it is called? It is called spying.'

Julie shook her head vigorously, 'Please believe me, it's not true.'

Krill picked up his pencil. 'And death is the penalty for spies. But you can save your neck yet, and for that I want everything…the whole network, right back to the Warsaw Conservatoire.'

The telephone rang and Krill picked it up with irritation, 'Yes, what is it?' He stood abruptly, his eyes fixed on Julie. He listened without speaking, occasionally nodding and then held the receiver away from his ear slightly, 'Immediately…Heil…'

Clearly whoever had been speaking had not waited for him to finish. He sat down and stared at Julie coldly. 'Well, well…it seems you have some unlikely friends. Perhaps we will meet again, perhaps not. Take her to Lieutenant Müller at the front gate.'

Müller was a tall, thin, ascetic looking man with intelligent eyes and a reserved manner. Julie initially greeted him with some hopes that he might be there to help her after Krill's reference to 'unlikely friends', but he seemed entirely indifferent to her dishevelled appearance, hobbling walk and bloody feet, and said nothing to Julie on their journey back into the city from the fort. She stared at her black rimmed fingernails and filthy dress, too shattered in mind and body to ask where she was being taken next, or why, and besides, she was suddenly very cold. She struggled to remember whether she had worn a coat to the prison, or whether she had left it on her bed at the orphanage, or in Sister Schmidt's office. It now seemed months ago that she had sat in Klindworths with that coat over her chair, sipping coffee with Karl and talking idly, but then, after reflection, it seemed something that had happened to somebody else entirely.

As they neared the city centre Müller pulled off the road under an archway leading to the back of the Monopol Hotel and stopped in a dingy inner quadrant where the refuse was piled up and dogs scavenged. He helped Julie out of the car and produced her suitcase from the boot. When she saw it she put her hand on his arm, 'Has my father arrived? Is that why we're here? Is he here for me?'

Müller pulled his arm away from her brusquely and led her to a door which he unlocked with a large key. They climbed the creaking dimly lit stairs until, after great effort, they arrived at the top of the building. Here, in the attic, servants might once have lived in small dingy rooms. Now all was empty and silent. At the end of a long corridor they arrived at a door marked 'Herr Meyer.' He pushed it with the side of his boot and they entered.

The room itself seemed to be part of a folly at the top of the hotel - a square tower which might once have accommodated a more senior member of staff. The ceiling was plain but high and the room had windows on three sides which gave it a light airy feel. On the side of the room with no windows a low door led to a bathroom, while in the glazed frontage there were two sofas and a coffee table. Next to the bathroom door was a large bed with heavy covers and an ornate headboard. The room was warm and seemed well used, with a few plants and some books. Müller clicked his heels. 'With the compliments of Herr Grieser...' Julie followed the arc of his hand and saw, on a small occasional table: fruit, gherkins, rye bread, herring rollmops, some wine glasses and a bottle of Riesling.

Müller withdrew, but paused at the door, raising a key in his hand, 'You must understand that technically you are still under arrest. I will lock the door but if you attempt to leave you will be returned to Sergeant Krill at the fort.'

Julie nodded and after he had locked her in she sat completely stunned for a few minutes, listless and unable to think. When eventually she gathered her thoughts she went to the bathroom where she found toiletries and towels. She held some soap to her nose and breathed in its perfume, enraptured by this symbol of civilisation. And then it occurred to her that someone had gone to a lot of trouble to prepare the room and it seemed reasonable to infer that at least some element of her innocence must have been accepted, despite Müller's attitude. She unpacked her bag with a sense of renewed hope and, after washing and changing her clothes, sat looking at the food, still too shaken to eat, but nauseous with hunger.

As Julie contemplated this dilemma and the tempting contents of a fruit bowl she heard muffled footsteps on the carpet in the corridor. A key was clumsily inserted and Gauleiter Grieser entered. He stooped slightly as he passed through the doorway and then flattened the grey hair either side of his bald pate. He was no longer the imposing figure of last night, resplendent in Party uniform, medals and insignias of rank. Now he was a large heavily built man in his forties wearing a charcoal grey business suit and carrying a black attaché case. The only clue to his status was a gold Party lapel badge which shone brightly.

He looked about the room and finally fixed her with a disarming smile. 'May I join you?'

Julie stood and gestured apologetically to the sofa opposite, 'Please...'

He settled into the corner of the sofa, spread his arms out, and then remembered himself, 'Oh, I brought you something.' He pulled out a packet from his attaché case which he handed to her. 'A gift for my exquisite dancing partner of last night.'

Julie took the parcel slowly from his hands. She removed the brown paper and sat for a moment with a silver framed photograph, looking at it keenly. Finally she returned his anticipatory gaze and stood the picture on the table between them. 'I really don't know what to say. You must have gone to so much trouble to have it developed this quickly. Herr Grieser, that's so terribly kind of you.'

He sat back again waving his arm dismissively, 'Oh think nothing of it, but please call me Arthur. I think we can dispense with formality here.'

Julie looked at him momentarily and repositioned the picture so that he might share it more easily.

'So what do you think of your new home? Is everything to your liking?'

Julie sat forward. 'Herr Grieser, *'Arthur'* seems too familiar - you are a very important man.'

Greiser held up his hand raising an eyebrow. 'It's *'Arthur'* or nothing – I insist!'

Julie smoothed her dress, not meeting his eye. 'Herr...Arthur, I have to explain how this misunderstanding has happened...'

Grieser interrupted, 'Julie, you are now under my protection. Müller has explained everything to me. I was happy to help sort things out. I only wish you had asked earlier, before this unpleasant business with Krill.' He suddenly leaned forward, 'I trust you are unharmed?'

Julie half-heartedly held out her bruised wrists, 'Only this and some grazes.'

Grieser stood and walked over to her with a look of intense concern. He stooped, taking hold of her hands, gently bringing them toward him. He studied the chafed wrists carefully, 'You have such delicate hands too...beautiful indeed. I am sorry, that should not have happened - I will take action.' Julie drew her hands from his clasp. He stood back. 'Please understand that nothing can happen to you now. You are, so to speak, a part of my household here and this is *my* flat.'

He glanced again at the picture Julie had placed on the table. 'I did enjoy our dancing. You have such a light step and a natural grace on the floor.' He paused, 'But I am curious; why did you dance with me so much last night? I mean, you could have had any number of young fellows - those SS men for example. They are more your age - why me?'

Julie searched for any explanation that might not offend, 'I think you are a good dancer - you lead very well. Young men don't always have that confidence.'

Grieser digested this for a moment and then gestured to the food and drink. He took a plate and a selection of food for himself and then began to eat and talk with exuberance, 'You know you need mature friends, especially when you are young – and not just for dancing! I've had many special young friends who I've helped – I like to be with young people. A man like me, with my connections - I can open doors. Come with me to Obersalzberg and I would show you how big. Young men…we have to ask; what do they know? A woman is at her best when she is young, like champagne, and men become better with age, like a good red wine. It's crude but that's my experience I'm afraid.

'You know you should hang around with us in the east. In a few years we'll live like princes. Do you know we're going to get the Ukraine eventually? Germany will have vast lands – the breadbasket of Russia at Germany's disposal. Do you realise what that means? Colonisation - like the British in India. The Führer has always admired what the British did in India. Then we will be the masters and *rich*. And you - you are the seed stock of this new dominion - you and your young fellow Germans. You are so lucky. What I would give to be your age now.' Grieser seemed lost for a moment in his vision. 'Everything can be yours if you give yourself to Germany.'

He poured himself a glass of wine and sat next to her on the sofa. She felt uncomfortable and withdrew to the side slightly. He leaned forward patting her knee gently. She could smell the alcohol on his breath, 'Yes, yes of course you want this, but could you live here, away from your concert halls and high culture?'

'In Posen?' she said, anxious at his increasing encroachment.

99

He paused and looked searchingly into her eyes, 'No here…in these rooms, under my protection...as my second household, so to speak.'

She stood abruptly, 'Herr Grieser, I must return to Germany. Please understand my situation. I am alone. I'm very frightened. Nothing like this has ever happened to me before. I need your help. You will help me won't you?'

Grieser stood with a look of remorse and stroked her cheek with the back of his hand. 'What is this? I have upset you? No! I have. You have misunderstood me but it is my fault…my clumsy language.' He moved away, his hand slowly falling down her sleeve as he did so, 'But think about it as an opportunity. You have new contacts, new and influential admirers – Herr Frank, the citizens of Posen; and of course you have me to punch for you all the way. Life can be good for you here.'

After a few moments in which these words hung in the air he reached into his pocket and waved a key at her, 'But you will be here for a few days, until we sort out your papers, so you have time to think. This studio is yours until then and only I and Müller have a key. You're safe here - if you don't try to leave. Do you promise to remain here?'

Julie nodded feeling that perhaps she had misunderstood him, perhaps overreacted, but still sensing an underlying purpose, a menace in his manner towards her.

As Grieser left and the door closed behind him Julie felt suddenly drained. She looked at the bed but after hesitation went to the sofa instead and nervously ate some rye bread. She thought of Sister Schmidt and how determined she had been that the girls should remain together in those dark days before the liberation. Now she was locked in a room alone – isolated, and felt a terrible sense of foreboding.

Chapter 8

Thorner Strasse, Posen, 27 October 1939

SS Captain Kellerman and Dr Fischer arrived at the orphanage under leaden skies in the middle of the afternoon. They entered Sister Schmidt's office after a perfunctory knock on the door and found her talking to a delicate young girl who fidgeted and eyed them nervously. Sister Schmidt was unhappy at their interruption the more so because Waltraud had been crying and was now ashamed and embarrassed in their presence. She begged to be excused and struggled to her feet, offering a timid curtsey to the officers, before scurrying from the room.

Sister Schmidt remained seated behind her desk and gestured toward the only seats not occupied by books, or other bric-a-brac. By the time they were seated she seemed to have reconciled herself to their arrival and ventured a faint smile, 'Captain Kellerman we have met, but…?'

Kellerman gestured at his brother SS officer, 'Dr Fischer. He has joined us recently from Berlin. He's been working on race and resettlement with SS General Darré. That's why we're here.'

Dr Fischer nodded formally, 'Sister, I'm sure I can talk to you in forthright terms. I've been told of your defence of this orphanage and the protection you gave to these children during the liberation and you are from a military family which makes my task today easier I'm sure.'

'Your task?' she said, warily.

'My colleagues and I have been studying the structure of care for the young in Posen…from the point of National Socialist teaching, welfare and education. We are concerned at the apparent restrictions and contradictions of the system – its continuing reliance on outmoded institutions. In particular it seems that while the Church broadly cares for the needs of these children it does not promote many of the values necessary to foster the great leap forward which is so crucial to Germany. In fact the Church seems at odds with almost everything we want for these young people.'

'At *odds* Dr Fischer?'

101

'Have you not followed political developments in Germany in recent years?'

'No - not at all.' Sister Schmidt said crisply, 'We have *no* politics here.'

'But you are aware of the hostility of the Vatican to National Socialism – that we banned the Catholic Youth Organisation in December '36. And now we are here in Warthegau we must be consistent and make sure there is one clear and unambiguous path for the young to learn about National Socialism and live in a manner consistent with its teachings. That means, in practice, that the Reich will no longer surrender its youth to the Church in Posen either, particularly as the values of the Catholic Church are so evidently counter to the principles of our nature, of our Aryan blood. *Mein Kampf* is now our infallible guiding star. Sister, you will need to come to terms with the fact that times have changed – that your work here is done. We are closing the orphanages and opening schools across the city where these girls and boys can grow and develop together in a healthier atmosphere. Leave *us* to forge the future with these young Germans. Leave us to impart them with our more, how shall we say, *practical* values.'

'I see nothing impractical in the teachings of Christ. They are the very foundation of modern civilisation.'

'But civilisation is older than the catechism. And we now have alternatives which serve the people better. We have moved beyond the need for magic shows - incense and transubstantiation and that nonsense.'

Sister Schmidt looked askance, 'Then let us *be* practical; that girl you saw leave when you arrived, what will become of her?'

Dr Fischer shook his head, 'I don't understand?'

'Her only strength is her faith, beyond that she lives in the shadows. She was brought to us by the police after she had been assaulted in the street by drunks – I need hardly explain what I mean by that. If you take away her faith, her support, what is left to her but despair?'

'There is *strength through joy*.' Kellerman quipped acidly.

Sister Schmidt shook her head with irritation, 'You offer me slogans! This is too serious for that, Captain Kellerman.'

Dr Fischer leaned forward, 'Her support will be a belief in the future, in the Führer, in the destiny of the German people. Sister, we live in a new age now, God is dead.'

Sister Schmidt's voice was indignant, 'Dr Fischer do you *know* your Nietzsche?' He remained silent. 'Then I will continue the quotation, *'...but considering the state the species Man is in, there will perhaps be caves, for ages yet, in which his shadow will be shown'.'*

Kellerman passed a pained smile, but Fischer persisted, 'This is no *cave*, and there are no *shadows*. These girls no longer need *you*, they need to be prepared for the New Order in the east – and that requires a National Socialist teaching and thinking. It requires preparation for their role as mothers and wives – the wives of soldiers.' He waved his arm dismissively, 'Nothing you can say will change that unalterable fact.'

Sister Schmidt looked witheringly at Dr Fischer and turned with a smile to Kellerman. 'But Captain Kellerman, these girls know nothing of National Socialism, there were no youth organisations in Posen, no League of German Maidens and certainly no Hitler Youth – the Poles would never permit it. As for *Mein Kampf!* I don't think I have ever seen a copy – after all it was banned here until '35 and we have few books. Of Germany itself they know the language, the traditions and something of the culture and of course the history of our religion, but this has been a turbulent time, they need a sense of continuity and stability. I must stay. You are a Catholic are you not? Can there at least be a delay – a period of transition?'

Dr Fischer became incensed, '*I* have explained the position. In any event the church will pass into obsolescence soon enough.'

Sister Schmidt's expression became thunderous, 'The Church is an anvil which has worn out many hammers, and I've seen no hammer yet that will shatter it. You Dr Fischer...I don't think so.' But her anger ebbed as quickly as it had risen and she became more reserved, unhappy at her loss of composure, 'And you still don't answer the question about souls like that young girl...souls that need to be nurtured in the love of Christ.'

Dr Fischer was now animated, 'But National Socialism is the doing of God's will. God's will reveals itself in German blood. True Christianity is revealed by the Party...'

Kellerman held up his hand forcefully and Dr Fischer only desisted from arguing further under protest. 'We are closing all the orphanages and religious houses of instruction. You may leave with a clear conscience - if *that* is what bothers you. We will take them over that's all – it's policy here now. I will come back in two days with an overseer to take care of things until new staff arrive from Germany. You must be ready to leave at midday.' He stood, putting on his coat and gathering up his cap, 'You have your Orders Sister...and I have mine.'

Sister Schmidt looked down at her desk. 'I read the Pope's encyclical in which he accused the Government of hostility to Christ and His Church. I had hoped for better – especially after meeting the ordinary fighting soldiers...I'm sorry that you have not found it in your hearts to change since then.' Captain Kellerman noticed her hands were shaking as she rearranged the papers on her desk, 'But perhaps some good comes of ill; please thank Herr Grieser and Captain Müller for reuniting Julie Scholl with her father – that at least was good of you.'

Kellerman looked at Fischer, 'Yes, I'll let Müller know.'

As they regained the street Dr Fischer began to chuckle. He looked at Kellerman who would not return his glance and looked irritated.

'They still peddle their old superstitions - astonishing! But is she right; are you a Catholic?' Fischer persisted.

Kellerman shrugged and looked around combatively, 'The Führer was a Catholic - he was an altar boy. So...what's your point? Why intellectualise? Why demean the uniform?'

They had parked their car in Glogauer Strasse, and walked up Thorner Strasse in the gathering gloom toward the junction. As they did so they passed two anxious looking pedestrians – a mother and her daughter. After a few paces Kellerman stopped, turned, and quickly retraced his steps until he stood in front of them. He began questioning them aggressively, gesturing at the Star of David, 'You are Jews and it is dusk. Why are you out after curfew? And what are you doing on the pavement? Can you explain what you are doing on the pavement when you should be in the gutter?'

As Fischer drew level he saw that Kellerman had drawn his pistol and was cocking it. Mother and daughter, dressed in filthy old rags, and gaunt with hunger, scurried into the gutter but Kellerman blocked their way. Fischer could see the mother clasping the young

104

girl's head to her chest. She began to plead with Kellerman in Polish. Kellerman gestured with his pistol at the ground and both of them lay down in the gutter. He let the gun fall by his side and spoke more softly, 'Quiet please! Shhh.' The mother looked up at him, her face pale, her cheeks hollow, momentarily meeting his eyes. He took a step back and shot her. She fell to one side motionless. The little girl started to cry, clawing at her and calling for her. Kellerman looked on impassively and pulled the trigger twice more. The girl stopped crying and then, as she lay motionless, her blood merging with that of her mother, seemed to sigh gently as the air seeped from her lungs. Kellerman nudged the young girl with his boot and holstered his pistol. He looked at Fischer for a moment with cold detachment and then walked on.

When they reached the car Kellerman paused with the door open and looked across the top of the roof at Fischer, his voice harsh and belligerent. 'Does that settle the theological debate Doctor? Did I need to quote Nietzsche?' He paused, his voice laden with scorn pointing back towards the bodies, 'How can God possibly exist... if I can do that!'

The Apartment of Herr Meyer, Monopol Hotel

It was dark outside when Grieser re-entered Julie's room. He placed cold chicken and milk in front of her on the low coffee table and stood looking at her. 'I'm sorry if this situation seems awkward, but you know I can't really be blamed for this arrangement...you here, in my flat. What else could I do to help?'

Julie was nervous but contrite, 'I know you have tried to help me. I lied to you. You have been kind and understanding and...I am sorry about my behaviour earlier. I'm not used to being alone...with strangers...well I hope you understand my feelings. Everything that's happened to me just seems so unreal - like a nightmare.'

'Oh, I understand; new dilemmas, new situations, new experiences. It's a question of how you see life.' He sat opposite and polished a tumbler with his handkerchief before pouring himself some schnapps. 'But before you eat, I want to know if you have thought about your future - your alternatives?'

'I'm sorry Arthur, what do you mean?'

'Your alternatives; the meaning is clear.'

Julie looked at him nervously, 'Not...not really. What alternatives are these?'

He sipped some schnapps, 'To blossom and flower and grow old, to follow the well-worn path of mediocrity, never exploiting the powers you have, never grasping the future that's there if you only reach out for it.'

Her mouth felt dry, and she suddenly noticed the scent of aftershave which had not been there earlier, 'And what is the alternative?'

Grieser waved his hand, 'Ach, before we get to that. First I have something for you.'

She watched him take a red leather box from his attaché case. He held it reverentially. 'This was my mothers.' He passed it to her and she received it with apprehension, understanding its significance all too plainly. She flipped a little metal catch and opened the lid. Inside lying on a bed of silk was a diamond necklace on a gold latticework with two matching diamond earrings. 'It's beautiful.' she said flatly.

'The only necklace that would not be eclipsed by those eyes.' He gestured at the jewel case. 'I think you have to understand Julie that this is what you mean to me.'

She closed the case quickly and held it out. 'I cannot take anything from you Herr...'

'Arthur!' he interjected softly and then shrugged, putting the box down in front of her. 'Now where were we? Your alternatives...'

Julie turned her face from his lingering gaze, 'My options?' she said after a long pause.

'You know your options; it is for you to take. From me you can have what you want, you know that.' He looked at the photograph on the table again, 'Last night when we danced you made me feel so young, so alive. If you have the power give me back my youth, my vigour, can you not use that for your own benefit as well?'

Julie placed her hands on her knees so that he would not see her trembling. 'I am still young and this is all...'

Grieser scoffed gently, 'You are not a child, you are a woman, and like all women you perhaps suffer from an excess of pride. Perhaps when you held me last night and we felt each other's power you did not expect me to present a moral dilemma to you so quickly, but that moment *has* arrived. Perhaps being young you don't like to make decisions yet - is that it? Do you want me to take the decision for both of us? Is that the kind thing for me to do?'

Julie stood up and began to pace the room with her arms folded, 'I can't think about anything until I have spoken with my father. You talk of moral dilemma. I also have hopes and dreams. How can you know what they are?'

'Because in all women they come back to the same thing; the rest is merely a self-delusion with which you embellish your lives. But in the end it is nature that drives you and me.'

'And what about love? What if I can't feel for you as you feel for me?'

'Love! That's childish talk. Where in nature do you find love? You need to see things differently – as they did in ancient times: security, strength, the possibilities for the next generation, strong blood lines - those are the real values, that's the real choice. With me you need never struggle, never question, never toil and want for money. You can live in comfort. My wife won't bother us. Nobody will talk of the sacred oaths of marriage soon anyway, that Christian bondage is over. We will just be left with the knowledge and power of my experience and the vigour and beauty of your youth.'

Julie looked at him blankly and after a long silence he seemed to become resigned to her obduracy. Finally he nodded at the jewel case, 'Take it from me anyway; it belongs on you. Perhaps some other man will have the pleasure of seeing you wear them.'

He reached for his case and withdrew a train ticket. 'And now I know your mind on this issue, I can break my other news to you, which is that if you wish to leave tomorrow you can and I will have your papers ready in the morning. Berlin called this afternoon. Your father will greet you there.'

She clasped her hands together. 'Herr Grieser…Arthur…'

Grieser finished his schnapps, eyeing her with exasperation, and then went to the door. As he grasped the handle he turned, 'You know the secret of reaping the greatest fruitfulness and the greatest enjoyment from life is to live dangerously. Do you know that?'

Julie shook her head, 'No, I didn't. I'm afraid I leave it to others to make those choices.'

He nodded thoughtfully, 'Very well. Go on, drink your milk and eat your chicken; you have a long journey ahead of you.'

Julie nodded, 'Thank you. I'm sorry I could not...I am still too young to understand your feelings.'

He half smiled and then left without a further backwards glance, locking the door behind him.

As she heard his footsteps receding down the hall she said a short breathless prayer to herself and clutched the train ticket to her chest. She sat waiting for her heart to stop thumping and her hands stop shaking and then drank the milk, tearing apart the chicken greedily, suddenly conscious of her hollowness. When she had finished she began to feel tired, her limbs leaden and heavy. She tried to rise from the sofa and go to the bed but struggled, her eyes becoming unfocussed. Then she slipped awkwardly to the floor, struggling to reach the table for support. She lay for a few minutes, half-conscious, her eyes staring out across the carpet, and then there were shoes in front of her and she blacked out.

When Julie awoke she was numb – even to her nakedness. Then, imperceptibly, feelings and senses began to filter through. She turned her head slowly to see Grieser's face, at first blurred and then boldly staring at her. He also lay naked, his hand gently stroking her abdomen. His voice was quiet and calm. 'In the end you answered my question and your own. Perhaps it *is* easier this way. Perhaps you are too young and too confused about your feelings to know them yet, I understand. You leave others to make these choices and I am happy to bear that responsibility.' Julie struggled to raise herself but fell back. He kissed her belly and moved himself slowly down the bed still watching her eyes which now followed him with terror. He raised himself on his knees and forced her legs apart placing his head between them and then she felt his tongue probing her vagina. Gradually his face pressed further into her until his breathing became intermittent as he penetrated deeper. After a few minutes his arms reached up to her breasts which he began to fondle and stroke. She lay, breathless, watching him, feeling him, unable to cry out or move.

After a while he raised himself, smiling at her, 'Did you enjoy, did you? You almost taste like Anna did. Did I tell you how like her you are?' She looked at him through pleading eyes as he lay next to her again, stroking her hair. 'So let me tell you about your future; I need a girl like you around me, young and fresh, fertile - to give me back my vigour. When I saw you - all those men admiring you as you

108

played the piano - I knew then, I had to have you; I had to father your children. With your fire inside me I can do anything.'

He worked his finger toward her vagina and toyed with her clitoris. 'Your fertility is what gives you your power over men and only your pregnancy can restore that equilibrium. We shall have a large strong family – that is your future...your destiny.'

He began to move over her and she turned her head away from his gaze in revulsion. She felt him fumble with his penis between her legs and then begin penetration. A dull pain grew inside her. His body crushed her and she fought for breath. After a few minutes, as he entered the last throes of orgasm, he turned her face forcefully toward him, searching for something in her eyes as she shuddered under his violent thrusts. As he ejaculated he let out a strangled groan of pleasure and forced himself momentarily deeper inside her until she cried out. He held her, looking down, elated, while she returned his gaze in a grimace of agony. Then he gradually shrank from within her, holding her head in his hands and kissing her forcibly, his tongue probing deep into her throat and choking her.

Finally he lifted himself from her and lay to one side, staring at the ceiling, breathing heavily, absorbed in his thoughts, and then slowly sat up. He looked down at her tearful eyes, 'That is the essence of the sacrifice - your blood, my seed. Do you understand? You belong to me now. Nothing can come between us.' He smiled, stroking her cheek, 'Besides, nobody will want you - not after I have claimed you like this.' Then his hand fell still and his expression became more severe, 'But, until we are sure you are carrying my child, I can't leave things to chance can I?' He rose from the bed, 'So we will have to keep you calm and safe until you get adjusted to things.'

He went naked to his jacket and removed a long black box and laid it open next to Julie. He took out a syringe and charged it from a small bottle. Julie watched the injection into her arm with remote detachment, 'We can start all over again. I promise I will do it right this time – not like Anna.' He put his hand on her abdomen and kissed her. 'This time...there will be no second thoughts...I promise.'

Julie blinked slowly and then closed her eyes and held them shut as a tear trickled from the corner of her eye, hoping the injection might be the end of everything and that she would never wake up.

109

Chapter 9

Hertz had been wary of the invitation to attend a conference chaired by Obergruppenführer Koppe. His dealings with Gauleiter Grieser were too complex to risk mixing with his powerful enemies in the SS, but he had been sent a policy paper which he had been unable to ignore and to which he now had to contribute as the civilian doctor overseeing resettlement.

It was after an hour of discussion about migration from the Baltic States that Hertz stumbled on a paragraph about the future of the Catholic orphanages and schools. He looked around him at Koppe, Kellerman, and Dr Fischer, and tapped the desk, 'This paragraph about the schools and orphanages. I'm sorry but I hadn't picked up on it when I was preparing for this meeting. Surely this is the sort of thing we should refer to the Reich Ministry of Science and Education, even if they don't have direct jurisdiction. They should be giving us advice surely. Why is the SS involved?'

Dr Fischer looked across the table, 'It's not a matter solely of education - well, not in any formal sense - it's about how we tidy up anomalies, and the orphanages are an anomaly. That's partly why you're here, because you've got local knowledge. It's not a critical issue for the Race and Settlement Department but we won't put up with the church infecting our young people, so we're closing everything down.'

'And not a moment too soon!' Kellerman added with steely satisfaction.

'So, the Danish and Scandinavians...' Fischer resumed.

Hertz slumped in his chair, 'No, I don't want to move on, I want to understand what you are saying. In paragraph 32 for example; '*...there will be only one kind of secular institution for the education of girls and boys in mixed classes for the propagation of National Socialist ideas and values*'.' That's not the traditional way here, not at all. We can't accept co-education across the board. It'll cause a backlash. And then there's the footnote about the need for social interaction between ethnic Germans and the garrison '*...in the light of recent events*'. I see you are suggesting a managed process involving selected elements from the SS who might engender a better understanding of National Socialism through social and recreational interaction. *German values*? Soldiers have one thing on their mind by way of *recreation* and yes, that includes the junior officers of the SS. I am a Catholic doctor and a supporter of the orphanages; I want to know about moral safeguards for conduct and behaviour.'

Kellerman interrupted, his voice contemptuous, 'We thought you might have some ideas. You worked locally. You know the mentality of these orphan girls...I would imagine. The reports I had, when a few of our young men met them, was that they were terrified, frigid, full of Catholic piety. They even slapped a few of the young officers who chanced their arm. Not the healthy confident young maidens we have in Germany who seem happy to get together for a bit of '*Strength through Joy*' on summer camp.'

Fischer interrupted dryly, 'We thought we would run a bit of a trial at the old Royal Prussian Ballet School - try to get a bit of social interaction going between some elite members of the garrison and the local girls there - and see how it goes.'

Hertz shook his head in disbelief, 'Yes, clearly there has to be interaction, but last time it ended in acrimony and I can't imagine how the girls would respond to a further encounter. You don't seem to grasp how different the Germans in Posen have become from their brothers and sisters in Germany. We've been ruled by the Poles for twenty years – twenty years of repression: of German culture, language, economic and political freedoms. It will take years not months to reverse that and the Catholic Church is still *the* force in these children's lives not National Socialism. No! I have to say this is a shameful proposition – send them to Germany if that's the issue, why not?'

Dr Fischer shook his head, 'Because it isn't the only issue. We need to build the community not deplete it.'

'And they need to understand their place!' Kellerman barked with impatience. 'They were the precious little things who came to the ball and proved so dull and frigid. Our young officers were treated with hostility, like the marauding elements of a foreign army. Our men expected gratitude and got a slap in the face for their trouble.'

Dr Fischer interrupted, 'The young men of the SS can spend their recreation there mixing freely with the girls and getting to know them - some wine, some food; it will do them good. We just need you to look after their general well-being.'

Hertz tapped the table, his voice raised in indignation, 'To these girls any mature encounter with the males outside the family is anathema unless it's properly supervised. As for relationships; to these girls it's about permanence, about physical and mental capacity and understanding, commitments solemnly entered into, sacred bonds…marriage! And some of these girls are just fourteen – interacting with grown men and with alcohol present. I don't think so – it's scandalous, abhorrent!'

Koppe stood impatiently, 'Surely they can't be that different from the girls back home. They'll get used to things. It's like breaking a horse – they'll kick off a bit but after that…Gentlemen, I'll speak with Dr Hertz alone now if I may.'

Fischer and Kellerman stood, saluted stiffly and left, while Hertz began to shift uneasily in his seat. Koppe walked over and sat next to him. Hertz sensed that he had walked into the very trap he had so long avoided and steeled himself. Koppe took out a cigarette case and offered one to Hertz who shook his head nervously. He lit one for himself, glancing at Hertz as he did so. He sat back amid a plume of acrid smoke. 'You know morality is the herd instinct in the individual - it's not something noble.'

'I believe it's wrong. I can't deny it. Anyway I thought Germans were inviolable.'

'Nobody is proposing anything immoral.'

'Have we really moved so far beyond the concept of *good* and *evil*?'

Koppe smiled, 'I'm not St Augustine! But I am glad we could finally meet and get to know each other. I've heard so much from others about your views - they intrigue me.'

'Why?' Hertz said warily.

'Because you are a paradox.'

'How so?'

'You work for Grieser in a relatively minor role but you receive from him a level of patronage that is, how shall we say, stratospheric. It makes people talk. Your friends wonder not so much where the money comes from as why it comes. Oh yes, Dr Hertz, I've been exploring the past and your finances - the palatial residence, the servants. So, you are blackmailing the Gauleiter - or what else?' Hertz

112

met Koppe's eyes and Koppe smiled. 'But what I really want is for you to tell me about Danzig. I keep hearing that this special relationship goes back to Danzig, when you and Grieser were setting out together. What happened there? What do you know about him?'

Hertz shook his head, 'I have no idea what you are talking about. We are good friends. So we prefer to work together...he's helped me.'

'Does the name Anna mean anything to you?'

Hertz slumped and put his head in his hands, 'I know nothing.'

Koppe rose and went to his desk where he drew a file from a drawer, 'But my job *is* to know; that's my reason for existing. For example, I know that your wife is in Switzerland. I know she's in a mental hospital there in Berne. I know you moved her there to escape German *methods*. So what happens to her if your funds are cut off, if corruption, or even the investigation of corruption, interrupts the flow of money?' Koppe walked slowly back across the room still reading the file and sat opposite Hertz again. 'If the Swiss send her home she becomes eligible for the T4 programme as an untreatable schizophrenic. You know what that means. You've been to the Villa in Tiergartenstrasse, you know Dr Bouhler. And of course, all this ignores your violations of the currency laws - the use of foreign bank accounts, illegal payments to officials. That's a serious crime Dr Hertz - a capital offence.'

Hertz looked up, pale and anxious. 'What do you want?'

'A good story about Grieser; one that puts him within my grasp and sets me free to do the Reichsführer's bidding.' Koppe stood up and placed his hand on Hertz's shoulder, 'Now I suggest you go home and mull it over; then see Kellerman. He will take a statement, a long statement I hope, full of intriguing detail and compelling facts. And, if we don't have the evidence to bring Grieser into line within forty eight hours, then we'll just settle for you...and of course your wife.'

Hertz gestured at the policy paper in front of him, 'And in return? Would you abandon this whole idea about the orphanages? Is that it…?'

Koppe shook his head, 'I don't need to barter with you Doctor, and don't *ever* presume to lecture the SS about policy.'

Koppe picked up the paper and took a pen, scribbling next to the footnote in the margin, *'To be confined under supervision. For the use of unmarried junior SS officers only.'* He signed the page and

113

stood back admiring his work, 'So now you know what we are about. And remember Dr Hertz, we need more mothers, more children, not lectures on morality – and I shall leave it to you and Dr Fischer to ensure the young ladies understand what is expected of them.' He thrust the paper back in Hertz's chest and walked back to his desk.

Royal Prussian Ballet School, Thorner Strasse, Posen 29 October, 1939

Irma Grese had been reassigned, but nothing had been explained that made any real sense to her: a travel permit, a ticket, some meagre expenses and a single page of orders with a couple of names; that was all she'd been given – and of course, a tight lipped 'good luck' look from her barrack leader. She had loathed Ravensbrück and hated the prison service, but nobody had seemed to be listening until two days ago. Then, out of Central Administration had come a posting to oversee an orphanage in Posen run by the SS, and so it seemed that her requests for transfer back to nursing had been met half-way, a grudging acknowledgment that, at eighteen, she was not cut out for the more brutal methods of the service.

However, she was not reassured when she arrived in Thorner Strasse and saw the Royal Prussian Ballet School. The building reminded her of the asylum in Luchen and as she twisted the heavy iron ring to open the entrance doors, passed under the stone archway and into the gloomy stairwell her expectations were not enhanced. In the corridor outside Sister Schmidt's office she found a window that perfectly reflected her image and so she adjusted her grey tunic and reapplied her SS cap over her tightly pinned blonde hair.

She was of medium height, with a shapely figure, a pale complexion and dark eyes, which combined to flatter her field grey SS Auxiliary uniform. She had affected the use of a riding crop in the camps, which she now placed under her arm as she entered the office. Sister Schmidt seemed startled by her appearance and half rose in her chair before sitting again. 'I assume you are my nemesis - are you with Captain Kellerman and that odious man Fischer?'

Irma was immediately impressed by Sister Schmidt's hostility and smiled, 'I am the overseer, but yes, my orders came from them. I've just arrived from Ravensbrück.'

'And *you* are going to oversee the needs of these children!' Sister Schmidt exclaimed, 'A prison wardress!'

Irma sat down without invitation, her voice laconic and unmoved. 'I go where I'm sent and do what I'm told. But if it's any consolation I wanted to be a nurse not a wardress – that's what I did before. Maybe I'll be discharged – I have complained. Perhaps the papers are waiting here.' She picked up an apple from a bowl on the desk. Irma pointed to a camera, 'Are you a photographer? My brother's really keen.'

'No.' replied Sister Schmidt haughtily – 'A doctor left it. It is to be returned. I have left a note for you about it.'

Grese shrugged, looking at her watch, 'Anyway we have five minutes and remember no speeches!' She bit into the apple with undisguised relish and stood up, insolently pointing to the door, 'Introduce me to the girls then!'

Sister Schmidt was familiar with Irma's type; she was in her experience the very worst kind of peasant, vulgar, crude and rough. There would certainly be no appealing to her better nature, and if Christianity had entirely passed her by it was probably for its own preservation. She set about explaining the workings and routines of the orphanage in icy mechanical detail, '…But I am told more girls are coming in a few weeks. They are all orphans. They are all studying, but above all, they are all pious, God fearing and know nothing of your politics. I pray that you will try to support them as I have done.'

As they stood, eyeing each other, the girls entered the room and assembled. Sister Schmidt turned to them, 'Children, this is Overseer Grese. Today she becomes to you what I have been…'

Irma leaned toward her, 'That's enough.'

Sister Schmidt looked at her askance, 'But I'd hardly started!' Then Sister Schmidt saw Dr Fischer entering the room and her face hardened, 'A dog returns to its vomit.' Irma caught the comment, smirked, and decided she rather liked the old witch after all.

While Sister Schmidt was escorted from the orphanage by Dr Fischer, Irma lit a cigarette and sat on a desk. She looked at the girls and they stared back with incomprehension. Finally Viktoria held up her hand, 'Are you allowed to smoke in here Miss?' she asked innocently.

Irma blew a smoke ring and remained silent. Erika drew closer and inspected her riding crop. 'Do you have a horse, Miss?'

115

Irma looked around her, 'Well, if you find it, there are five *Reichsmarks* in it for you!' She smiled and gradually the girls began to surround her, fascinated by their new keeper's uniform. She removed her cap and Erika and Viktoria examined the skull and crossbones badge with morbid curiosity. She shook down her long blonde hair, 'So, you're all orphans – that's tough. But don't think I'll go easy on you just because you had a bad start in life. It'll get a lot harder for you - but look at me and learn. I'm alright. Be good and I'll look after you. Cross me and….' Irma took the riding crop and cracked it over a desk, a broad smile crossing her face as she did so. The girls jumped, giggling, and so Irma did it again. Then Helene stepped forward and extended her hand, 'I'm the Head Girl.'

Irma looked at her warily, 'My Kapo[1], eh?'

'I'm sorry?' Helene said earnestly.

Irma stood with a twisted smile on her face, 'It doesn't matter. I suppose I'll need a bit of time to get adjusted.'

---

1. Kapo - a term used in concentration camps to describe a prisoner voluntarily accepting authority over others.

Chapter 10

When Greiser entered the room that evening Julie was seated on the sofa. She looked up at him sleepily. She had dressed after a fashion, but her hair fell about her face and was unkempt and her feet were bare.

He walked over to the sofa and kissed her languorously on the lips, his hand smoothing its way up her leg as he did so. She did not react as he worked his finger into her vagina, probing her mouth with his tongue as he did so. When he stood back she closed her eyes and shuddered slightly. He stroked her cheek with the back of his hand, smiling, and then went to the bathroom.

When he returned he sat next to her and opened his briefcase, producing some schnapps while she pulled down the hem of her dress clumsily, struggling to coordinate her movements, her head bowed, unwilling to acknowledge him.

He threw his head back and took a large swig, immediately pouring himself another from the heavy earthenware bottle. He sat forward, holding the glass between his hands, staring into the clear liquid, 'You know we married when I was just a *nobody*. The very worst thing that can happen - to grow old with someone who is still by nature a nobody, petty, cheap, and small minded.

'Last time I was in Obersalzberg I asked the Führer for a divorce – we have to do that you know, to set an example. I was refused. I hate her – more now you and I are starting a family together – much more. All the time I'm with her I'm thinking I could be here.

'I have been imagining it you know; the large villa in the country, the children – lots of strong healthy children…Ah yes…' he said, noticing the red leather box on the coffee table, '…unfinished business.' He opened it, removed the necklace, undid the clasp and stood behind her, laying the necklace around her neck carefully and then securing it. She felt his hands move around her shoulders to straighten it. They lay there for a moment as he kissed her neck and then he walked back to his seat to admire her. 'So beautiful, especially with your eyes…only diamonds could do justice to those eyes.'

Grieser's breathing now became heavier and he moistened his lips with his tongue before kissing both breasts through her dress. She stared at him with glassy dispassion and felt him run his trembling hand through her hair. 'We'll get you off this morphine. I'll see about the dose. You'll enjoy the physical side more then - I promise. He began to unbutton the front of her dress but her hand met his at her waist and she tried to hold it. He smiled, momentarily confused by the gesture, 'What are you doing, Julie?'

Her voice was weak and breathy from the drugs, 'No – please no…I don't want to.'

He gently put her hand to one side and began to unbutton the dress and again she took his hand and held it.

He withdrew and sat motionless. 'But, Julie, there is no shame for you in this. You don't have to think this through. I've made those judgments for you – to help you deal with your conscience. You need only do what I tell you.'

Julie sat shaking her head, her voice laboured, 'No; you can't do that.'

Grieser got up and paced the room slowly, perplexed, 'But what have you to gain? If you refuse me I will beat you…as I must beat you now, but I don't understand - there is no path back from where you are – you are mine now. You belong to me…I have claimed you – I told you that at the time.'

His mood now became vengeful. He looked around and finally went to the corner of the window where a duster with a long cane handle stood. He broke off the head and lashed out with it against an empty chair. Then he gently lifted Julie to her feet and walked her to the end of the bed. She stood impassively as he undressed her, folding and placing her clothes on the bed with care, and then finally, when she stood naked, removed his mother's necklace. He laid her over the base of the bed pausing for a moment, 'You should have something in your mouth to bite on.' he murmured. When he had completed these preparations and was satisfied with her position he began to strike her with the cane, slowly and methodically, counting as he did so.

She did not cry out; the morphine protected her to some extent, but she felt the blood trickle across her back and her thighs. When he had finished he looked at his work and shook his head, throwing the bloody cane to one side. He fetched a bowl of water and a flannel and began to wash her, tenderly dabbing at the bloody weals. Her head

118

hung from the side of the bed and she wept quietly as he worked. He sighed deeply, 'Creation is not yet at an end you know. Biologically man is at a turning point, a new variety of man is beginning to separate out, a mutation - precisely in the scientific sense. The old type will sink into a sub-human race; the other, the god-man will rise above him, but the moment he accepts his limitations, then he is lost. Gods and beasts; that is what our world is made of.'

He kissed her back and then soaked the flannel. Julie saw the water turn pink. 'You see Julie, politics today is completely blind without a biological foundation and biological objectives. Only National Socialism has recognised this. It draws its criteria and its objectives from a complete and comprehensive recognition of the essential nature of life.' He paused, 'What you cannot see is that the new man is here, God is inside *us* – the power I draw from you - your life force, and the power I have to murder and create.'

Julie raised her head momentarily and looked at him half conscious.

'That's better.' he said smiling and putting the bowl to one side. He stood, his eyes wandering over her naked body, and began to undress.

The orphanage, Thorner Strasse, Posen

As Irma paced around the long dining table each girl presented her empty plate for inspection. Many of the girls also glanced around surreptitiously to follow her progress, wondering what might happen next. The previous evening Irma had gently placed the core of the apple she had been eating on Waltraud's shoulder without her noticing and then accused her in the most exaggerated terms of slovenly eating habits. It was the first time any of the girls had seen Waltraud actually giggle and they marvelled at Irma for having done it - and for the invisible bond she seemed to have with Waltraud in particular. Irma had also shown them her capacity for gestures of friendship which they had not known before, talking to them casually as if they were equals, and helping them with their chores when they struggled. But while Helene saw Irma's kindness, she also noticed another darker side, a fierceness that concealed her lack of education, of understanding about their school work. She noticed the careful way

119

Irma avoided ever having to read to them as Sister Schmidt had done so fluently in the evenings and how untidily she wrote in the register. And so Helene now carried much of the burden of the schooling and reading out loud herself. It made her miss Julie's presence all the more. She had even taken to sitting quietly with the letters Julie's mother had written her and which had been left behind in her bedside cabinet, reading them to feel her presence again and to be close to her.

When they had finished their meal Irma led their prayer: *'Thank thee for this bountiful meal, Protector of youth and friend of the aged. I know thou hast cares, but worry not, I am with thee by days and by night, Lie thy head in my lap, Be assured, my Führer, that thou art great. Heil, Mein Führer!'*

It was Irma who saw Dr Fischer enter the refectory first, 'Stand', she shouted, and the girls rose rigidly to attention as one body. He beckoned them to him, Jutta and Therese under his arms facing their friends. Irma sat on the corner of a table out of sight licking the soup ladle and half listening.

'Tomorrow begins a new chapter in the history of the Reich and of its eastern provinces and you, the orphaned girls of Posen, will write it. How you may ask can a young German girl serve the Reich in such a momentous way. The answer is in your fertility and your blood - by becoming the mothers of children, the children who will grow up as farmers and warriors in the eastern territories of the Reich.

'Your Catholic education is now over and we must begin afresh. Your books are now an unhappy footnote in your past. Your faith in the destiny of the Aryan Nordic peoples and in the Führer is your strength and *your* destiny.' Irma stood uneasily and put down the ladle to listen. She had heard this sort of shit spouted by the Party officials in her village, the ones with wandering hands and limp dicks, but now this seemed different, and while Dr Fischer ushered his two charges back into the fold, she began to feel that there was a purpose to what he was saying - that he really intended to carry things through.

Fischer smiled, 'A few weeks ago you were all treated to an evening with the handsome young officers of the SS here in Posen at the Bazar Hotel Ball. Many of you will have fond memories of these fine young men I am sure.

'I am aware that Sister Schmidt subsequently refused to allow you the opportunity to foster any deeper relationships with these men. I am also aware that your lives have been deprived of much of the colour and joy to which we are accustomed as Germans - particularly young Germans.

'We have therefore decided that tomorrow night we shall throw open these doors to the young officers of the SS and provide wine and food and allow you all the freedoms and opportunities which their company will provide…without any intrusive supervision. This will give you the chance to reciprocate their kindness and to thank the SS for your deliverance from the Polish yoke.

'And in this context I must make one final point, which is that you must put aside any personal thoughts or feelings on this occasion but consider first giving yourselves to these young men who have come to Posen as your liberators…I wish you every joy.'

With this Dr Fischer smiled, nodded toward Irma and left the room.

Irma sallied forth from her position near the table to be met by Helene's reproachful, anxious, searching gaze. She looked away, unable to face her, and gestured them back to the table, where the girls sat again in bewildered silence, staring into their glasses of milk.

That night, after Irma left the dormitory at nine fifteen, shadowy figures congregated around Helene, who sat on her bed with a look of apprehension and foreboding. Viktoria spoke first, 'What does this mean Helene? What are they going to do - let those men in here to get drunk and…what are we supposed to do?'

Helene struggled for a moment, 'It's clear what they mean. We are expected to give ourselves to them – allow them to do what they like and be happy with it.'

Agnes shook her head, 'But why? I don't want to see them. I didn't like them.'

'Me neither.' said Jutta with agitation.

'I won't.' said a voice from the darkness and they looked around to see Waltraud standing back slightly, 'I will never allow that to happen again - never. I would rather kill myself.'

Gabriele buried her head in her hands, 'But when they come they will bring drink, they will expect us to drink, and then we can't say no.'

Ursula shrugged, 'We have no choice. We must escape.'

Helene shook her head, 'Irma has the keys. She would stop us. And besides, where would we go. Nobody would take us in.'

Edda looked around, 'If we stay in a group, like we did in September…'

'There's nobody to protect us now, Edda,' Helene said heavily, 'If we fight back who knows what they will do. You saw how they looked at us after the ball.'

Birgit grabbed Helene's arm, 'But how many! How many will come? What if there are…thirty of them! What will they do to us?'

As she said this Waltraud began to weep with an intensity that infected everyone with a sense of the terror she had already known. Finally Helene felt Ottilie pawing at her, imploring her to do something and leapt to her feet, her face etched with helpless panic, the weight of their expectations shattering her fragile veneer. She stumbled between Klara, Ottilie and Birgit and ran down to Irma's office bare footed, with Agnes and Klara pursuing her. She began beating on the door with her fists, crying and shouting for help. Soon the remaining girls followed them, pleading though their sobs for Irma to protect them - to save them. Only Waltraud remained in the dormitory - alone in the darkness that had never left her.

'What is going on?' Fischer exploded beating the office desk with his fist. Irma remained rigidly at attention. 'I left three hours ago and everything was in order!'

'They became hysterical that's all – crying, sobbing, so I called Dr Hertz.' Irma said coldly.

Hertz gestured toward the door, 'They're in a state of complete terror…this madness has to be stopped. What the hell did you say to them?'

Fischer ignored the question, 'And you have calmed the situation Hertz?'

'Yes…but I have already made my position clear. These girls are completely naïve. They are also terrified!'

Fisher slapped the table and eyed them both. 'Then it's time they became a bit more worldly, time they discovered a bit of fucking joy. You are postponing, that is your prerogative as a physician. This changes nothing. And if I have to break them in one at a time down at the barracks then I will, the ungrateful bitches.'

Hertz was silent for a moment and then lunged forward his finger stabbing at Fischer's chest, his voice harsh and emphatic. 'This is rape – you're turning this into a brothel for the SS. You're treating them like nothing more than cattle – it's an outrage. They are ethnic Germans for Christ's sake, it's criminal! I'll go to Himmler if I have to…I'll expose you all.' He faltered, his words lingering in the air for a moment, sensing he had gone too far.

Fischer was silent. He eyed Irma, 'Overseer Grese, what do you say?' Irma looked impassively ahead and maintained the position of attention.

Fischer picked up his coat and belt brusquely, 'I take full responsibility in law for the health and well-being of these girls. My conscience is the Führer. Your conscience, Doctor Hertz, is a matter for the authorities – I *shall* make a report.'

Hertz looked at Irma as Fischer's footsteps receded…'And what would you say if you had a voice? Do you have a voice…?

She looked at him sharply but the tenor of her voice was strangely distant and solemn, 'I would say they are still children…in a dark place…without a mother.' Then, after a pause, she abruptly picked up her cap, centred it in the mirror and opened the door, 'They've been quiet for the last hour. I'll go and see them.'

Chapter 11

The home of Dr Hertz, Kaiser-Wilhelm-Strasse, Posen, 31 October 1939

It was nearly two o'clock in the morning. The fire was dying in the hearth. Hertz sat motionless with a bottle of schnapps by his side and an empty glass in his hand as the shadows lengthened around him. Late the previous evening, after returning from the orphanage, he had been visited unexpectedly by Grieser. It had been pleasant enough at first. They had talked a little about Danzig - the old days when they were setting out together, but then he'd moved the conversation on and the true purpose of his visit had become apparent.

The subject had not been Koppe, or his rivalry with the SS. Nor did he seem to know that Hertz himself was being blackmailed into betraying him. The subject was morphine and when he had finished the blinkers had finally been torn from Hertz's eyes, robbing him of the last vestiges of moral pretence, finally confronting him with the reality of his pact with the 'old fighter.'

He looked into the glowing embers and cast his mind back, trying to identify the point at which he could be said to have definitively started the journey which now ended here, but he couldn't. Instead his memory plucked out events which had simply nudged him along, clinging to his comforts, his compromises and his little self-deceptions, until he now found himself surrounded by wealth and opulence beyond his wildest dreams, but also inhabiting a world bathed in a darkness from which he could see no means of escape.

His eyes drifted up from the fireplace to the large oil painting of Belshazzar's Feast – the King and his thousand lords. He looked for a long time at this scene of power, idolatry, wickedness and lechery and then recited what he remembered of the Old Testament quietly to himself. *'And in that night came forth the fingers of a man's hand, And the King saw the part of the hand that wrote, And this is the writing that was written, "Mene, mene tekel upharsin". Thou hath been weighed in the balance and found wanting...And in that night was Belshazzar the King slain, and his kingdom divided.'* He put down his glass, rose from the chair and went to the writing desk. He took out some heavy embossed writing paper from a drawer, placed it carefully on the blotter, dipped the nib of his pen into a well of green ink, and began to write…

SS Headquarters, Fort Winiary, Posen, 31 October 1939

Koppe stood to welcome Captain Gerhard, leaning across his desk with an extended hand. Dieter Gerhard was an athletic looking man with blond hair, a square jaw, and penetrating confident stare. He took Koppe's hand and shook it briefly but firmly.

'I trust you had a good lunch?'

Captain Gerhard nodded with reserve and looked at Kellerman pointedly.

'I thought my adjutant Captain Kellerman would join us.' Koppe said gesturing at the seats set out in front of his desk.

'I'm afraid that's out of the question. Only you have been cleared for this briefing.'

Koppe nodded to Kellerman who clicked his heels and saluted before leaving the room, closing the double doors behind him discreetly. Koppe sat back eyeing Gerhard with some impatience, 'And how can I be of assistance to Colonel Hopp?'

'You have an orphanage in Thorner Strasse - the former Royal Prussian Ballet School, run by a Sister Schmidt?'

Koppe hesitated, disconcerted by the subject matter, 'Yes. I believe we do.'

'There's a girl there by the name of Julie Scholl.'

Koppe shrugged, 'I'd have to consult our records department.'

'That wasn't a question, it was a statement. She was arrested on the 26th of October by a Gestapo officer, Sergeant Krill, and brought to Fort Winiary. She was then removed from custody in the middle of her interrogation by an SS Gestapo liaison officer, Lieutenant Müller. Why? On whose authority?'

'I would need to talk to Müller - these are matters of detail.'

'But where is she now? Nobody seems to know.' Koppe began to grope around the papers on his desk while he thought of a response, but Gerhard became impatient. 'Lieutenant Müller is under your direct command. He's your liaison officer for the civilian governor Gauleiter Grieser - you see him every day at your morning briefing - so I'm told.

125

If you don't know where he has taken Julie Scholl perhaps he can tell us. Call him in please.' Gerhard gestured at the telephone.

Koppe put on a display of bluster, 'I'm sorry Captain Gerhard but you don't enter my office and start to issue summonses for my men. You put such requests in writing and allow proper opportunities to recall officers from their assignments. And where did you get your information about Julie Scholl's arrest? I have no information.'

'I pulled your files as soon as I arrived this morning.'

Koppe stood indignantly, 'On whose authority? Colonel Hopp doesn't have that right.'

'No, but Gruppenführer Heydrich does and he's my authority, and above him the Führer – do you wish to see my credentials and my authority?' the Captain replied curtly.

Koppe sat slowly, extending his hand and taking the papers. He read them in detail and then looked up, 'What does it mean '...*in a matter concerning the security of the Führer and Fatherland.*' and what does Julie Scholl have to do with it?'

Gerhard sat back, 'They are linked - but not directly as far as we understand it. Julie Scholl is the daughter of Eric Scholl a senior ministerial advisor to Herr Funk the Economics Minister. He produced a memorandum in early October which we believe he leaked to anti-Party elements in the army. Its effect was to subvert the fighting spirit of the army by appearing to conclude that Germany lacked the resources to fight a sustained aggressive war. Just over a week ago he was interviewed by Colonel Hopp. He undertook to revise the findings of his preliminary report to accord more fully with the strategic plans of the Führer and strengthen his position *vis-a-vis* the army leadership's arguments.'

'And?' Koppe said shrugging his shoulders.

'At the interview Eric Scholl said he had provided a few figures verbally – nothing of substance, but we know who some of the Zossen conspirators are. He gave them more than he let on – a copy of a memorandum…and he's still leaking information. So, we need some leverage, and we need to know if he is an innocent dupe, or an active participant in a plot. In short, we need to pursue your lines of enquiry – his daughter's Polish connections – to enable us to apply the maximum pressure to her father. I'm here to take her back to Berlin.'

Koppe stood handing back Gerhard's credentials, incapable of any coherent argument which might deflect him from his request. 'If I can deliver her to you tomorrow morning will that be acceptable?'

'You will tell me nothing more than that?' Captain Gerhard said impatiently.

'I need to liaise with Captain Müller - he will need to be found.'

Captain Gerhard reached for his briefcase, 'I am at the Bazar Hotel. I leave for Berlin on the midday train. I will be here at ten in the morning to take custody of the girl. Ensure her file is also available.' He stood, 'And Obergruppenführer Koppe, please don't underestimate the seriousness of this matter. Julie Scholl is now crucial to our investigation of her father and, through him, the anti-party elements of the High Command in Zossen. You can expect any further unforeseen difficulties - any irregularities in Posen, to attract very considerable censure.'

Koppe nodded, unsmiling, their eyes meeting briefly in recognition of what was actually being said.

The area of Nowe Miasto, Posen

Dr Hertz approached 'Villa Schroda' that afternoon on foot as the light began to fade. It was chilly and there was a misty rain falling, but he did not want his car to be seen, least of all by the person on whom he was calling. He wanted to give no opportunity for evasion, so he walked the last half kilometre through the pitted lanes.

The house was extensive, imposing, and occupied a generous isthmus of land between two small lakes which provided both seclusion and security.

A bored sentry stopped him without much formality and looked at his papers. The large trees made the guard post especially gloomy so he shone his torch at them squinting, 'You are a doctor? Doctor Hertz? Has Frau Grieser called for you?' Hertz nodded and with this the barrier was raised and he walked on.

He was greeted at the front door by a Polish manservant who showed him in to a large conservatory at the rear of the house, assuming that he was expected – a state of affairs which Hertz did not try to correct. As they entered a nanny shepherded out two young children. The servant stood for a moment, 'Frau Grieser, a doctor.'

127

'A doctor! I called for no doctor – for the children?' she said in some confusion, but then turned and caught sight of Hertz. She stood immediately, startled and venomous, 'Get out.' she snapped to the servant, clicking her fingers and gesticulating toward the door. He bowed awkwardly and scurried out of the room.

'Why Dr Hertz... why are you here? You promised me never, never, to set foot in my home again.'

'May I sit?'

'We have nothing to say to each other...I want you to leave now...immediately.'

'It's about your husband...it concerns *you* too, and your family.'

She hesitated for a moment and then waved at the sofa impatiently. When he was seated, she sat opposite him, eyeing him coldly. 'You have five minutes.'

'I apologise, but there really is no one else I could turn to. It's a matter of some delicacy.' He looked over at her with a faint smile trying to engage her, but her expression remained waspish. 'As you know your husband and I have worked together for many years and recently...'

Frau Grieser snorted, waving her hand dismissively, 'You are tied to each other yes, but you are not a friend of the family, not a friend of mine, and I know exactly what you are to my husband, so make this brief.'

Hertz smiled, 'No, indeed, I'm not your friend, but as I was saying, I recently met with your husband.'

'Is he ill then?' she said sarcastically.

Hertz held out his hand, 'You asked me to be brief.'

Frau Grieser lit a cigarette and exhaled impatiently. 'Go on, get on with it then.'

'Very well – I'll go straight to the crux of the matter. SS Obergruppenführer Koppe and your husband have been arguing for weeks about policy. Your husband is refusing to surrender certain powers to Koppe that the SS regard as vital to them. It all came to a head when Himmler was here. Your husband humiliated Himmler in front of Koppe - in front of the heads of the civil administration.'

Frau Grieser shrugged her shoulders 'My husband tells me nothing of his work. Why should it matter to me?'

'But it should at the very least concern you.'

128

'My husband has always got the better of Koppe – and Himmler for that matter. He's the personal appointee of the Führer and the Führer is always loyal to his Gauleiters. So what does Arthur have to fear from Koppe, or that jumped up chicken farmer Himmler - what's changed?'

'The method.'

'What do you mean?'

'Koppe is looking to compromise your husband - to blackmail him. He's asking me questions – about Danzig. He's having your husband watched.'

Frau Grieser's hostility waned and her eyes became alert, 'Be precise.'

'Did you know that for some weeks now he's been having relations with a young woman?'

Frau Grieser laughed, 'Hitler won't remove my husband for having an affair. He already asked him for a divorce and he said *no*. Did you really come to tell me this tittle tattle? Is there something else? Or do you want money – you can't need more, he's already stuffed your pockets with enough surely?'

'It's not an affair…'

'Then it's of no interest to me. We're married; I'm the mother of his children – that's where it ends.'

'Not if Koppe finds out her identity.'

'Finds out what exactly?'

'That she's the daughter of a ministerial advisor working for Funk; that he's sedating her - raping her.' He knitted his fingers together tightly shaking his head. 'Arthur took her from the orphanage in Thorner Strasse a week ago, she'd been helping there after the liberation, and now she's under lock and key somewhere in the city. He's keeping her a prisoner.'

She became still and distant, her mind reeling, 'But this is insane! Why would he do it?' She rose abruptly from the sofa and went to a drinks tray where she began to pour herself a brandy. She paused, looking out of the window, 'And how do you know all this - how do you know it's forced? How do you know it's not consensual – she wouldn't be his first mistress to take drugs?'

Hertz's voice dropped, 'Because he came to me last night. He asked about dosage. I realised then, when he explained the problem, what he'd been doing and who it is.'

129

She looked at him sharply, 'And you supply the drugs?'

'Yes…but not for this - I swear I had no idea.'

'So you too are now on the hook.'

He looked at her, his voice almost pleading, 'She's only fifteen. He's obsessed with her. He won't listen to me. I tried to talk to him but he's beyond reasoning. You need to help me stop this now – otherwise…otherwise it will be like Anna all over again and we can't let that happen. I *won't* let that happen.'

Frau Grieser smiled acidly, 'I wondered how long it would be before you brought her into it. And what if she is another Anna, what can I do? What could I have done then?' she said bitterly.

Hertz steadied himself, 'Do you know where he keeps her?'

'And why should I tell you that.'

Hertz's face reddened and his voice became harsh, 'Because it's only a matter of time before the SS find out about her. Because when they do you're finished, your whole fucking family!' He gestured wildly around the room at the fine furnishings and pictures, 'All this…!'

She looked at him, startled by his ferocity, and steadied herself. 'So, what do you propose?'

Hertz stood, 'Get her away, quickly, out of Posen Gau, up into Danzig. I know people there. If we can clean her up, give her time to heal…it gets us all off the hook.'

'And you guarantee she won't make accusations later against my husband?'

He clasped his hands together, 'Yes.'

'And why should I believe you? How do *you* guarantee it?'

Hertz sat again, 'Because your husband can do something in return…which *will* keep her silent. I promise your husband will hold all the cards. There will be no scandal.'

'And so tell me; what could he do that could guarantee this?'

Hertz placed his hand on the table and leaned forward, 'The SS are taking over the city orphanages, the children's homes and religious houses. They're taking all the older girls in particular and placing them in the old Prussian Ballet School off Glogauer Strasse. I want your husband to stop them. What they propose there is monstrous. I want to save the orphans. I want your husband to take them over as the civilian governor and stop the SS. It's already within his power - he merely needs to act.'

Frau Grieser looked at him warily, 'Is that *it* then? That's the deal?' Hertz nodded. She turned and took a large sip of brandy, studying him for a moment. She went to a writing desk and stood behind it, 'My husband's affairs are nothing new - you know that better than any of us. I'm not shocked by an affair, but this, the insanity of it...We don't share our lives any more, still less our bed, but I do expect *discretion*. And you are right of course; we must act - clean up the mess before he wrecks everything.' She hesitated, 'He keeps a flat at the top of the Monopol Hotel – in the name of Meyer. I make no enquiries and ask no questions – it's where he takes his whores. She might be there. He keeps a spare key in his desk drawer here.' She took the key and clasped it in her hand, 'Tonight I'll pick you up at eight o'clock outside the opera house - Arthur's giving a short presentation there - we'll go on to the flat from there. It's only a guess you understand.'

Hertz shook his head, 'But I must go alone. I don't want you there.'

'She put the key from the desk into her bag which lay on an occasional table near the door, 'It's that or nothing. I must see her with my own eyes. I have to face her. Then you can do as you wish.'

When Arthur Grieser arrived at Villa Schroda late that afternoon he sensed an unusual stillness in the house. The children were nowhere and the servants had been sent to their quarters. There remained only his wife, sitting and waiting. When he entered the living room he saw the malevolence of her gaze and went to his desk without speaking. And then, as if a spring had been released, she erupted. 'How could you?' she shouted, standing and waving her arms, her voice hoarse with emotion and her face contorted, 'Can you imagine my humiliation? To stand here in my own drawing room and be told by Hertz - that parasite - that you have some drugged up little whore in the Monopol – I mean I know you have a taste for the juvenile but not at the cost of our family and our position. Why *force* a German for God's sake when you can have a Slav, or an ethnic, who won't matter a damn?' She paused placing her hands on her hips, 'I suppose she was just too much like Anna was she? Innocent, petite, dark haired, bright eyed...is that it?'

Grieser took a large measure of brandy from the decanter and sat silently with his glass. He looked at his wife with cold indifference,

131

his voice low and rumbling, like thunder across the room, 'You really want to know - eh? Do you really want the truth about Hertz?'

'After today don't you think you owe it to me?'

Arthur sat back, 'Very well then…it makes no difference to me – not now. The truth is Anna died from an abortion - she didn't die of an overdose. It was an abortion and I made her have it.' He grew quieter, 'It was Hertz who tried to sort it out, covered it up. It was Hertz…the good doctor…he paid the family off, arranged the post mortem, the certificates; that's why he can't be ignored. He can sink us. I can't touch him.'

His wife grew quiet and closed her eyes with an expression of exasperation, 'So did he tell you Koppe is on your trail – that he's trying to corner Hertz to find out about Anna - that you're being followed.'

Arthur slumped, 'No; he didn't tell me that.'

His wife sat down on the sofa exhausted, 'They'll get to this girl of yours and they'll get to Hertz. Tell me what our options are Arthur – this is your mess.'

He flipped a pen through his fingers. 'You helped me before, will you do it once more…this one last time?'

She glanced at him coldly, 'For the family, for the children, for the life we have, yes. For you…no.'

Grieser swivelled on his desk chair, picked up his glass and swallowed another large measure of brandy. 'Then go with the good doctor - go to the flat with him…play along with it. Then, when they're out of the way, the SS will have nothing. It has to end here.'

'End h*ere!*' she said rising from her chair and fixing him with an expression of icy contempt, 'It ended years ago Arthur…it ended in Danzig in '37…with Anna.'

Chapter 12

The Monopol Hotel, Posen

It was eight fifteen by the time Frau Grieser and Dr Hertz arrived in the grubby quadrangle at the back of the Monopol Hotel. They sat motionless in the car for a moment, the engine turned off. 'Can I have just five minutes with her?' Hertz said in a subdued voice.

She flung open the car door and looked at him fiercely, 'No. I must see this girl for myself. I told you, after that, you can do what you like.'

They climbed steadily up the stairs to the attic passageway and began to walk along the threadbare carpet towards the end door, pausing for Hertz to catch his breath. As they entered they both saw Julie's profile under a muddle of blankets. Frau Grieser paused and Hertz saw a flicker of something in her eye, an expectant tension which unsettled him. 'Is she dead?' she asked when there was no movement. She held back while Hertz walked over to the bed. Julie murmured as he drew back the blankets. Hertz leaned over her, 'We've come to take you away – you're safe now.' He went through to the bathroom. 'I'll wash her face – she'll need to be brought around slowly.'

As Julie began to focus, aware of the presence of a woman, she saw Frau Grieser pull some gloves from her handbag and hurriedly put them on. Swiftly taking up one of her husband's heavy schnapps bottles she entered the bathroom from where Julie heard a dull impact and the thud of a body hitting the floor.

When Frau Grieser re-emerged she locked the door and came over to the bedside, looking at Julie intently. She held her head in her hands and looked into her eyes. Her voice was cold and steely. 'You look terrible.' she said running her gloved hands roughly through Julie's hair. 'My husband never fails to disappoint me with his selection of the worst types of humanity for his pleasures. Let me look at you. Can you walk? No? Too bad.' She took a handkerchief and poured some water on it, gently dabbing Julie's face.

'Who are you? What are you doing here? Julie asked feebly.

133

'I am the cleaner, I sanitise my husband's life of all his little accidents.' she said in a bright mocking tone. She rolled up the sleeve of Julie's nightdress and looked at her arm. 'Ah what a mess! How you must have suffered. But that's all over now.' She smiled, wiped over the scars on the inside of Julie's elbow carefully and then went to the coffee table where the syringes and morphine lay in open cases.

'These are Dr Hertz's. Did you know that? He's the midwife of your misery.' she said inspecting the ampules of morphine. 'Oh, and that's him in the bathroom – just in case you haven't been introduced. And when they find you together your corpse will be his too.' She began charging the syringes, but as she did so her eye was caught by the red leather case containing the jewellery her husband had given Julie. 'His mother's diamonds – the little shit!' she said viciously, but then turned to Julie, 'He loved you then – well, he was always an incurable romantic.'

As she charged the second syringe her eyes also alighted on the silver framed picture of Julie and her husband taken at the ball. She picked it up from the coffee table and studied it with growing irritation before tearing the picture from the frame and placing it in her bag. 'He's really gone too far this time, but this is it, you are the last.'

She picked up the syringes and walked over to the bed, putting the spare syringe on the bedside table, 'You need to sleep – it will do you good.' She took Julie's arm with the syringe poised, but Julie pulled away and edged across the bed. Frau Grieser grabbed her roughly and dragged her back, 'Don't be stupid...you can't fight with me, it's over...everything.'

She held Julie's arm again, lining the needle up carefully with a vein, but then Julie's other hand, which had been reaching out, silently groping for the other syringe, found it and held it tight. As Frau Grieser leaned over her a little further, Julie plunged it deep into the side of her neck and injected raggedly. Frau Grieser grabbed at Julie's clenched hand and they struggled for a moment, the steel needle gouging and then tearing her throat as she twisted and writhed to free herself from Julie's desperate grasp. Soon the needle pierced a vein and blood began streaming from the gash. Julie quickly lost her bloody grip, sending Frau Grieser tumbling to the floor. Julie fell after her, trying to clutch at her again, but she pulled away, crawling towards the bathroom door, blood trailing behind her. She grappled wildly with the key trying to unlock it, clutching at her neck. Finally the door fell open and she dragged herself a little further, but there, just inside the bathroom, the morphine took effect and she slumped, unable to go further, falling slowly and silently into unconsciousness.

When Julie roused Hertz with a dousing of water he was initially incoherent. She slumped down next to him on the bathroom floor, the surge of adrenaline which had saved her, now rapidly fading. 'She was going to kill us both.' Julie said pointing with a trembling hand at the gloves and the syringes. Then he seemed to gather his thoughts and become aware of his own injuries. He sat for a moment with an air of desolation staring at Frau Grieser. 'What a mess...'

He turned to Julie and suddenly noticed that the back of her nightdress was covered with a mass of long thin bloodstains from the beatings she had been given. He bit into his fist, suppressing a cry, and then buried his head in his hands. 'I knew what he was capable of...I should have stopped him.'

It was ten minutes before Hertz seemed to have any grasp of their situation and the need to escape. Eventually, after washing the blood from Julie's hands, he searched for her clothes and began to dress her, and after what seemed an eternity he was able to lead her toward the door. As he did so he caught sight of the red jewel case and put it in his pocket. As he opened the door to the passageway a door slammed deep in the stairwell at the end of the corridor. He looked at Julie who he supported clumsily over his shoulder, whispering to her insistently, trying to cajole her, 'Help me? Walk just a little way. You *must* walk. Walk for God's sake!'

The heavy footsteps in the stairwell now resonated loudly, marking a steady relentless path toward them. He pulled Julie along as far as half the distance to the stairs and then veered into one of the empty rooms. There he waited behind the door, the footsteps growing in their menace and bowing the floorboards under Hertz's feet as they passed by the other side of the thin stud wall, and then, gradually receding, they stopped at the door to Herr Meyer's room. Hertz could hear a key being inserted, confusion at finding it unlocked and then Grieser calling out – inaudibly, cautiously. Hertz shut his eyes, his heart pounding, and sank to the ground.

A terrible commotion erupted and Grieser thundered down the corridor, pushing open doors of the empty rooms as he went, calling Julie's name; but by the time he passed the room in which Hertz cowered with her he had gained such momentum that he failed to see

135

them, and in a moment he was down the stairs and gone, leaving nothing more than a lingering hellish echo.

Hertz guessed it would only be minutes before he returned with the Security Police, and, if they were found now, Grieser would consign them both to the guillotine with impunity, freed from any scandal, simply on the basis of Julie's attack on his wife. He desperately dragged Julie down the stairs after him, expecting at each landing to meet the heavy frame of Grieser, knowing they could be trapped at any moment with the arrival of the police below them.

Finally, breathlessly, they emerged into the darkness, convinced that voices would confront them. Instead there was only a dog which eyed them warily before trotting away with a bone. Hertz looked about for a moment, listening and catching his breath. He drew Julie into the shadows of the quadrangle, edging his way towards the archway which led to the main road and then, stumbling forward, he passed under the arch, across the road and into the city park, where they melted into the safety of darkness.

Gunther Rath was maintaining his car in the lean-to garage next to his house the following morning when Hertz came in quietly, startling him with his sudden appearance. He wore a trilby hat crudely concealing a bandage and there were traces of blood on his shirt. Hertz dispensed with pleasantries. 'Does that thing go?'

Gunther lowered the bonnet slowly. 'It depends how far you want to be taken?' He leaned forward gesturing at the blood-stained collar, 'Trouble?'

Hertz shuffled nervously, 'Come with me now…to my cabin on the outskirts of town. Bring enough petrol for Danzig. A girl's life depends on it.'

Rath smarted, 'Danzig, that's everything I have!'

Hertz pulled out the red leather jewel case, 'Here, take that. No idea of its value.'

Gunther opened it, looked at the makers label, nodded with approval and snapped the lid shut. 'Get in. I'll gather my cans.'

When they reached Hertz's cabin by Lake Strzeszyn, they parked out of sight in a clump of trees and made their way cautiously inside. By now Julie was fully conscious but still breathing with difficulty. Gunther looked at her with disbelief, 'Christ what's happened to her - is she even fit to travel?'

136

Hertz busied himself, producing a stethoscope from his leather bag and listening to her heart, taking her pulse, her blood pressure and then examining the pupils of her eyes. At length he stood, 'Yes, she can travel, but she's been kept on morphine - too much morphine, it depresses the heart and respiratory system. She could have a seizure, but we have no choice - she must go.'

They carried Julie to the car, laying her on the back seat and covering her with a blanket. 'Take her to Dr Karl Rust - he works at the Central Hospital in Danzig, but be discreet for God's sake - he's the only man we can rely on. He fell in love with her I think…what's left of her.' He produced a slip of paper, 'If anything goes wrong, don't call me, call this number, and there is this - give him this roll of film, but tell him under no circumstances to develop it. Someone will come, perhaps not soon, but they will come and collect it. It's all we have left…'

Gunther slapped him on the shoulder, 'Are you sure you're alright, my friend?'

Hertz looked at him blankly, 'I should have done something. I was too late. I failed them. I failed them all.'

Posen Central Hospital, 1 November 1939

When Frau Grieser awoke the following morning her eyes first alighted on the doctor reading the chart at the end of the bed and then on SS Obergruppenführer Koppe, who gestured him away. He pulled his chair to her side and leaned forward confidentially. 'They tell me you will make a full recovery.'

She looked at him, pale and exhausted, 'Why are you here? What's the time?'

'It's seven thirty in the morning. You're lucky to be alive – we found you just in time. Any more blood loss would have killed you. I need to know what happened - that's why I'm here?'

Her brow furrowed, 'Didn't Arthur find me?'

'No, we did. We came to arrest Julie Scholl at about nine forty five and found you instead. Where is she?'

She seemed lost in thought for a moment, 'I know about your plans for my husband and I have nothing to say.'

Koppe sat back, 'Berlin has sent a man for her. We're not playing games anymore. We need Julie Scholl...or my deal with your husband is off.'

Frau Grieser looked at him askance. 'Deal! You're not in a position to deal with him – not now.'

He reached down impatiently into a briefcase and pulled out an envelope from which he took out a wad of photographs and laid them on the bed in front of her. He stood for a moment hovering over one of them, his voice quietly disdainful, 'I can see why you would have preferred to let him go elsewhere. After all, who would consent to this - the poor little bitch?'

Her eyes skated over the images for a moment and then veered away with disgust. 'You bastard – you already knew?'

Koppe nodded, 'Of course, but we only spoke to your husband last night – too late as it happens to prevent this. So why go to the elaborate step of trying to kill her?'

'She was a liability and so was Hertz.'

'And what did he know that suddenly made him so dangerous?'

'Ask him.'

'Oh, I'd like to speak to Hertz, but he's dead. It seems that he went home, went to the basement, made himself a noose, and hanged himself.'

Her brow furrowed, 'But I don't understand – why? He got what he wanted.'

Koppe leaned back looking at his watch and realised that he needed to twist the knife a little to move things along. 'You know he loved her. I suppose that's why he gave her his mother's jewellery – that's gone too. I think he hoped to wean her off the morphine, or that was his fantasy at least - perhaps when she fell pregnant, perhaps awaiting a sort of enlightenment. He was most uncharitable about you, of course, but that is the lot of the middle aged *hausfrau* – I *have* read the transcripts...you owe your husband nothing. I can at least be a friend to you - set things straight - so your family can go on being *respectable*.'

She glowered at him, her nostrils flared, but her voice remained weak, 'A friend - how?'

'Why did Hertz come to see you? We need to know - it may lead us to her.'

She sank a little in the bed, sullen, 'Hertz wanted Arthur to close down the SS programme at the orphanages.'

'Why?'

'He said they were monstrous, bestial…or something like that. He said he had to take a step back. He wanted to force Arthur to do something. Then later he said…he said that he had made a *Faustian pact'* with him.'

Koppe removed the photographs from the bed and stood, returning them to his case, 'So where would she go? Danzig - or to the west?'

'Danzig; he worked there – lived there. He would have known people, but if he's dead she could be anywhere.'

'So, Danzig – his old territory. But there was a girl called Anna in Danzig wasn't there - a girl called Anna? What was that all about? What did Hertz *have* on your husband?'

She looked at him with steely eyes, 'He still hasn't told you then?'

Koppe leaned forward, 'You've seen the pictures. Look at yourself Frau Grieser. What is it you think you're preserving – your husband's dignity? From now on you owe everything to me. I can finish your family whenever I like…or we can help each other. So, tell me about Anna?'

Frau Grieser seemed to fade and closed her eyes for a moment, 'I never met her. What I know I got from Arthur. The rest I got from Hertz last night in the car.'

Koppe nodded. 'So…what did you hear?'

She looked at her hands and fidgeted with the sheets, 'Arthur worked with Hertz in Danzig. Hertz had moved up from Posen looking for work. He became a city doctor - he was *on the make.* They became friends – made a lot of money together. Then one night in July '37 Arthur called out Hertz to help him with a girl called Anna who was sick. Apparently Arthur knew her through the Party youth organisation - the *Jungmädel.* Her parents were living in poverty; the father had been crippled in the docks. They lived in the worst area of Danzig, with the pimps and prostitutes. Her mother was an alcoholic…thought Arthur would see them right. At first it was just clothes and shoes for the girl and little treats – days out to Party youth events where she could get away from the squalor. Arthur seemed to have taken the family under his protection – become the 'father' their daughter

139

couldn't have - and so if they needed money for food and medicine he gave it to them, and if Anna's mother wanted money for drink he'd help out; but then one day, when she was in the middle of one of her bouts of drinking, he took her daughter away and didn't come back for a few days. The mother looked the other way after that, and *kept* looking away so long as Arthur kept paying their bills. Then, six months later, he found out the girl was pregnant. Arthur wanted Hertz to help get rid of it but he refused, so he took her to someone in the back streets – but the old crone fucked it up. By the time Arthur called Hertz again it was too late, her blood was poisoned. But *good old* Hertz squared it with the mother, sorted the post mortem out for Arthur - got him off the hook - saved his career. He even paid off the abortionist. So, there you are - that's it – that's the story. They get money every month.' Frau Grieser brooded for a moment, 'You know he even made us pay for her fucking headstone.'

Koppe sat back, 'And so Arthur kept Hertz close.'

'Arthur told me why Hertz was *special* years ago. I just thought Anna was one of his 'affairs' that had got messy, that she'd taken an overdose, that Hertz had helped cover it up, but I didn't like it hanging over us. I wanted nothing to do with Hertz – he was so obviously a leech. Then last night Arthur got drunk and told me the rest of it – that she was pregnant…thirteen years old…that he'd forced her to have an abortion. After that we both agreed Hertz had to go. He said we had no alternative, not with you on our backs.'

Koppe sat back. 'And that's the whole story.'

'Yes – the whole filthy story; except of course that our marriage is over…I'm going back to Germany. I'm taking the children.'

Koppe stood. 'And so, you would kill her…kill them both…for the sake of your status and reputation - for no other reason?'

She turned angrily, struggling to raise herself in the bed, her voice hoarse, 'Not for Arthur, or the fucking Party…for the family, for the children! Now get out.'

He looked at her coldly and she suddenly understood her insignificance to him, her powerlessness - that she was nothing to him. He gathered his things, put on his greatcoat, applied his cap, and left the room without any further acknowledgment or parting gesture. As Koppe walked down the corridor he heard a glass smash against the door behind him. The waiting Captain Kellerman looked at him with a raised eyebrow. Koppe shrugged his shoulders, 'It seems the marriage is over…anyway, she got the message. She won't be a problem.'

Kellerman suddenly remembered himself and handed Koppe an envelope. 'This just came in by despatch rider from Dr Fischer. We *are* running late Obergruppenführer; we're due to see Müller at nine and Captain Gerhard at ten.'

'Yes…but we still don't have Scholl – where the fuck is she.' Koppe opened the envelope and stood for a moment reading the contents. When he finished his hand fell by his side and he cursed momentarily under his breath. 'It appears I can now explain Dr Hertz's death after all…and it seems Julie Scholl has taken off with a man called Gunther Rath to Danzig. I want them found. They took pictures at the orphanage.'

'Pictures?'

'It appears that Hertz took some pictures in the old Prussian Ballet School after an incident there. I want Overseer Grese and Dr Fischer out of there – I don't want them anywhere near the orphanage, or Captain Gerhard – and I want the girls out of the city tonight.'

'And what do you want us to do with Rath and Scholl when we find them.'

Koppe looked at him sharply, 'I want them killed, and I want the film destroyed.'

SS Headquarters, Fort Winiary, Posen

Koppe slumped heavily into his chair and stared over the desk at Captain Gerhard. Kellerman sat a little back from the desk to one side of Koppe. The Captain raised his eyebrow at the empty chair next to him, 'It's eight minutes past ten. Where is Fräulein Scholl?'

'We don't have her.'

'And Müller?'

'Müller is missing.'

'Are they together? Is this some sort of joke?'

'We are still pursuing lines of enquiry.'

'Did you know this yesterday when we met?'

'I had no knowledge.'

'Who ordered Müller to interrupt the interrogation by Krill?' Koppe turned and looked at Kellerman, but Captain Gerhard continued, 'He could not have acted alone. He would have acted on senior authority. You, Obergruppenführer Koppe, are the senior authority. Did *you* order it?'

Koppe opened a silver cigarette box on his desk, took one out and lit it. 'I have already told you that I have no specific knowledge of her.'

Captain Gerhard smiled and shook his head, 'Alright then, let's move on. Do you know a Dr Hertz, lately of Posen?' Koppe nodded uneasily. 'It seems that two days ago he wrote Eric Scholl a letter. He sent it via the Race and Settlement Division, *'by hand of messenger only'*, so we failed to intercept it, but Eric Scholl's secretary did tell us something of its contents, of the events here in Posen...concerning his daughter. And now he's gone missing – officially on the wanted list. I just begin to suspect, Herr Koppe, that all is not well here in Posen. I think the Colonel needs to escalate matters.'

Silence fell over the room. Finally Koppe stubbed out his half smoked cigarette. 'You must do as you see fit, Captain Gerhard, but first allow me a few more hours to try and find Captain Müller. It is possible there's an explanation.'

'Possible, but not probable – wouldn't you say. And Julie Scholl...what about her?'

Koppe looked around to Kellerman, 'Our investigations are continuing – but until Müller is found I'd really rather not speculate.'

Captain Gerhard stood and gathered his things, 'If you do not contact me by three o'clock this afternoon with news of Captain Müller...'

Koppe interrupted impatiently, 'Yes, we understand...your position is clear.'

Gerhard paused, 'Oh, and I went to the orphanage on Thorner Strasse early this morning – where Julie Scholl was staying. It was locked. I should like to go in and look around – talk to some of the girls. Perhaps you will arrange it?

Koppe stood, his face ashen, 'Yes...tomorrow, when we have sorted this out.'

'Tomorrow it is then.'

After Captain Gerhard had left, Kellerman leaned forward, 'But what about Müller – he's not reliable. Not if it's between Berlin and us. I told you, he's ambitious and we can't keep him out of sight for much longer. He'll talk.'

142

Koppe sat back stony faced, 'Müller, the orphans, Scholl; they're all part of the same problem now.

The Office of the Gauleiter, Imperial Castle, Posen

Gottfried Vogler sat and looked at Grieser unhappily, 'You need to explain what's going on. Peter Mensch, Head of Resettlement, is completely in the dark.'

Grieser shook his head and appeared to look at some papers on his desk, 'If Koppe chooses to tell you that's one thing but you'll get nothing from me.'

'But I'm your most senior civil servant. Koppe is SS. I need to hear things from you. I need to brief others. People are already talking - your wife is returning to Germany after a *car accident* and you've surrendered your prerogatives on a dozen different areas of policy overnight – policies you argued through with Himmler only a few weeks ago. What's changed?'

Grieser gestured toward Vogler with a pencil. 'You don't need to know.'

'The SS, the *Einsatzgruppen*, the *Selbstschutz*, they're roaming at will. It's chaos…'

'Policy on pacification is now with the SS.'

'Yes, but with your name on the orders – *who* is giving the orders?'

Grieser looked up, 'So, Herr Vogler, apart from *that*, what news? Give me your briefing.'

Vogler shook his head with exasperation and looked at his notes, 'Your liaison officer Müller has gone missing – absent without leave.' There was a silence and Vogler looked up fleetingly to see a steely glint in Grieser's eyes. 'And there's a man down from Berlin, a Gestapo Captain, Gerhard. The rumour is he's looking for that girl who played the piano at the civic ball. I can't remember her name I'm afraid.'

Grieser looked up sharply, 'Julie Scholl.'

Vogler nodded and made a note. 'Oh, and Koppe has asked me to book a meeting with you. Apparently you met her – spoke to her at some length. I think he's keen to hear what you have to say before the officer from Berlin sees you – just in case there's a local angle.'

143

Grieser sat motionless, 'Yes, I met her - just once. A pretty young thing as I recall.'

Chapter 13

Danzig, West Prussia, 3 November 1939

Karl approached Danzig Central Hospital that morning through the narrow cobbled back streets, bracing himself against the icy wind which was howling off the Baltic Sea. He drew his collar tighter and quickened his pace as he approached the entrance, but still cast an admiring sideways glance at the heavy Baltic-German towers and Hanseatic gabled houses with their heavily ornamented façades. He had grown to like Danzig with its heritage and traditions, but it would take him time to adjust to the winters with their dry searing cold and the bitter sub-zero winds.

Although he was a junior doctor at the Central Hospital and Sister Kohl, who awaited him, was nominally his subordinate, she had a matriarchal manner that discouraged any pretentions to rank or authority among all but the most venerable consultants. It might be Karl's responsibility to oversee 'C' Wing, but they were her wards and today her time was being wasted. As he swung open the doors to the wing she stood waiting for him, her stern face framed within a starched headscarf, watch pointedly in hand and an eyebrow slightly raised. She greeted him with her own special blend of testy politeness and while Karl gestured apologetically he maintained his momentum, unwilling to dwell in hostile territory. 'Shall we do the rounds?' he said, as she turned to keep in step with him.

When they reached the sister's office she passed him a clipboard which he flicked through impatiently, but she anticipated him, 'One admission last night: female, about fifteen to sixteen, name unknown, nationality unknown. Could be a Pole, could be German, or a Balt. They found her slumped in the entrance with a lot of minor injuries, but also some more serious symptoms of prolonged drug addiction. She had a very low respiratory rate. We had her on oxygen for three hours during the night. The injuries were of a sexual nature.'

Karl paused, 'Of a sexual nature?'

After a long nursing career working in a major seaport, Sister Kohl was incapable of being shocked by anything she encountered.

145

'She had been severely beaten with a rod or cane, raped and sodomised – we assume it was rape due to the other bruising. But it is the puncture marks that are the enigma. We think, or rather the duty doctor thought, morphine, given the symptoms, but who can afford that now…with the war? Even then it would be unusual in a common prostitute - especially one so young.' The Sister looked at Karl, hesitating to abandon her objective discourse.

He caught her look of indecision, 'What is it?'

'Well, she has such an intelligent face, the eyes as well. I think she may have *been* someone.'

As they approached the girl's bed Karl took the chart from the end and studied it. Her head was turned away from him so he walked to the other side and sat on a chair to look at her, gently brushing away the hair which obscured her face. Suddenly he leapt up, pushing the chair aside, his head shaking with disbelief, 'Sister, I know this girl!'

The Sister looked over, 'You do! Well, who is she and what's she doing in this dreadful condition?'

He spoke haltingly, 'She's from Berlin. I met her in Posen a month or so ago. She's a music student.' Karl stood back looking at the pale gaunt reflection of what had been something radiant and vivacious. 'I can't understand it - she was healthy, safe!' He began to move toward the nursing station and the telephone, 'We must call the police.'

The Sister, informed by her long experience of what must be done and the proper order of things intervened, 'Doctor, I venture to suggest that we should record a few facts first and call the registrar.'

Karl composed himself, 'Yes, yes we must - of course.'

The registrar, Dr Guttman, approached after twenty minutes with two members of the Security Police following close behind. Karl took him aside. 'What are they doing here?'

Guttman shrugged, 'We always report admissions to the police first thing, even if there is no name.'

'Is this Julie Daase?' one of the policemen asked the Sister sharply.

Karl approached them, 'I am Doctor Rust and this is my patient. Of what interest is my patient to the SD?'

'The SD decides what interests the SD.' The policeman looked down at Julie and moved her head from side to side impatiently. 'Can she be moved?'

'No.' Karl said forcefully.

'Is she injured so badly?'

'She's German, her name is Julie Scholl. She cannot be moved. She is semi-conscious.'

The SD man pushed Karl back, 'In your opinion. And in the opinion of our intelligence department in Posen she is a Pole who poses as a German and incited others to kill ethnic Germans on the 2nd of September, and that's where she's going back to now – to face justice.'

The SD man nodded at his colleague and they stripped back the sheet, pulling Julie from the bed. They began to drag her toward the doors of the ward, her feet trailing lazily behind her, 'We know how to deal with people like this.' the officer snapped.

Karl placed himself between them and the doors, but Guttman grabbed him, 'Karl they will arrest you too if you do that.'

Karl and Dr Guttman followed them to the doors of the hospital where other plain clothed Security Police waited by a car. He seized Karl's arm, 'I will phone the SS Chief Hildebrandt. I know him - he'll help.' He ran back inside the hospital, but Karl understood that this was too little too late. Julie's semi-conscious body was now braced between two men in the back of the car and with a perfunctory salute between the policemen the car pulled away.

The Office of the Gauleiter, Imperial Castle, Posen

'What is going on, Koppe?' Grieser said shaking his head and gesturing towards his telephone. 'The business at the Hospital in Danzig this morning - I've had Gauleiter Forster's office and Hildebrandt his SS Police Leader on the phone. They say we mounted an operation without consultation. Is this true? And what about this Captain Gerhard from Berlin, what's he doing here asking about Scholl?' He pointed his finger at Koppe accusatively, 'We had a deal!'

Koppe opened a cigarette case and tapped one on the cover briefly before lighting it. 'The SD men were from Kolmar District - in our area, but deniable as a rogue operation. They were intercepted by Forster's men in Karthaus.'

'Karthaus! That wasn't on their way home, it's west of Danzig. What's there?

'Marshes, woods, nothing much - a remote execution site perhaps.'

Grieser's expression hardened, 'And so what happened?'

'They ran into a checkpoint - a simple piece of bad luck. When the Danzig SD became suspicious about the girl and the Kolmar boys started getting aggressive, the officer in charge rang back to Hildebrandt's HQ - the cat was out of the bag.'

Grieser looked at Koppe hard, 'But why try to kill her? What could she do to me now Hertz is dead, apart from make a few wild allegations? Don't you realise how much this has stirred up Forster's curiosity. I'm told he's even taken her to his home.'

Koppe dwelt on this news for a moment, clearly unaware of this development, 'And why should he do that?'

'She was recognised by a doctor at the hospital. He named her father as Eric Scholl and Forster is now asking some very direct questions. He's guessing there's leverage in it.'

'Leverage?'

'We loathe each other; you know that – right back to the Danzig Senate days. If he can damage me he will. He says he won't refer the matter to Berlin *immediately*, but wants to meet with you to find out what is going on before he makes a decision. He'll no doubt have a price in mind.'

Koppe sensed Grieser was getting the upper hand, so now changed the subject to one less palatable to him, 'Hertz wrote a letter to Julie Scholl's father in Berlin before he killed himself. Did you know that?'

'A letter! For Christ's sake! And?'

'And now Eric Scholl's gone missing - officially on the wanted list. Captain Gerhard is now looking for him *and* his daughter.'

Grieser leaned forward, 'Well, let's just hope for your sake Fräulein Scholl isn't handed over – not if there's a letter to support allegations.'

'Gerhard also wants to speak to your liaison officer, Lieutenant Müller.'

Grieser became wary and sat back, 'What about?'

'He wants to know why Müller took her from Fort Winiary – on whose authority. He wants to know where she is…what's happened to her. We've been looking for *him* for the last twenty-four hours, but we only found him this morning.'

'So, what did he say? Will he talk if Gerhard gets hold of him?'

'I doubt it. He'd been shot in the head twice at close range and dumped in the Warta River.'

Grieser looked Koppe in the eye, 'He won't be missed. I was going to get rid of him anyway.'

'A fortunate coincidence then?' Koppe said raising an eyebrow.

'For both of us.' Grieser retorted, meeting his gaze.

'You do know Berlin is threatening to escalate things? The last thing we need now is for a bunch of policemen to descend on Posen rummaging through our dirty laundry. They want Eric and Julie Scholl, that's all. I'll go up and see Forster and do a deal on Julie, if that's what Forster wants, but if Eric Scholl turns up here with a letter from Hertz, you had better be sure of your story.'

Grieser leapt from his chair and thumped his fist on the desk, 'You took me on, you set her up, you leaned on Hertz, you sort it out! I won't be held to account for the unintended consequences.'

Koppe stood, put on his cap and leaned forward over the desk heavily, meeting Grieser's gaze head on, 'Perhaps not - but what about Anna Abetz - what about the unintended consequences of that little liaison? She was how old…twelve, thirteen?' Grieser became still, withering under Koppe's gaze. He sat down again and began to shuffle some papers. Koppe took a step back and picked up his attaché case, 'Don't delude yourself *Arthur*; your wife told me everything.'

149

Chapter 14

The Country Residence of the Gauleiter of Danzig, West Prussia, November 1939

The dream in which Julie had been so pleasurably immersed merged almost seamlessly into reality. Her mother faded and instead a young nurse gently washed her face with a soft flannel. Her eyes gradually focussed on her surroundings and she found that she was in a comfortable homely room with a good fire blazing in the hearth and family photographs adorning the walls.

Her bed felt luxurious and comfortable, a thick duck down duvet pulled slightly back across her abdomen, the pillows soft and pliable. Her heavy cotton nightdress was scented delicately with lavender. A bowl and ewer sat on a dressing table to her side and at the end of the bed some clothes lay over a chaise longue which stood in front of a large bay window. Outside she could see trees and lichen and hear seagulls in the far distance. She reached out to assure herself that this was not an illusion, grasping the nurse's arm for reassurance. The nurse smiled, 'At last! You are awake. My name is Beata. You are safe now - under the protection of Albert Forster, the Gauleiter here in Danzig. This is his home. I will fetch his wife to speak to you.'

After a few minutes a blonde woman in her early thirties, of slim build and wearing a light blue frock entered the room. She stood smiling, leaning against the closed door, 'So, Julie, welcome. I'm Gertrud.' Her voice was pleasant and soothing and she seemed greatly relieved that her guest was now conscious. She advanced and took Julie's hand, looking into her eyes reassuringly. 'I don't want you to worry about anything. Albert and I and my children Inga and Peter are delighted to be able to welcome you. We've heard so much about you from Dr Rust.'

Julie tried to raise herself, but sank back again into the pillows exhausted, 'Thank you so very much. You are so kind.'

Gertrud gently pulled back a lock of Julie's hair from over her eyes, 'Do you remember anything?'

'Everything is very confused.'

Gertrud patted her hand and then clasped it more tightly, 'That's understandable. Now you must concentrate on getting better.'

Julie's eyes began to wander, her voice still weak, 'Dr Rust?'

'Yes, we brought him here from the hospital. Albert needed him to explain a few things and you needed a doctor. He's been very good – and very concerned about you.'

'How long have I been here?'

'Five days. And, in a few days more you can get up and meet the children. We also have a piano - I am told you play very well. There is a lovely garden...'

At that moment there was a tap at the door and Karl entered. He paused and they looked at each other, unsure of the ground on which they now found themselves.

'The nurse said you were awake.'

Julie drew up the duvet weakly and bowed her head, 'I don't want you to see me like this.'

Gertrud stood and stroked Julie's head, 'Karl is your doctor, Julie.'

A tear began to fall slowly down Julie's cheek, quickly followed by another. Karl stepped forward to her bedside, took her hand and knelt, looking up into her downturned face, 'Julie, nothing that has happened to you could take away those few happy hours we spent together. Soon you will feel better. You have been through a terrible time, but it's all finished. You are bound to feel fragile. I'm just so happy to see you again.' But Julie withdrew her hand and turned away, slowly shrinking into the covers, weeping softly. He stood for a moment, looking down at her, but she remained in this way, gradually drawing the covers more tightly around her, unwilling to face him.

When the nurse had resumed her station Karl and Gertrud left quietly and walked together down the broad staircase into the hall. He seemed upset by what he had witnessed and had become withdrawn. 'Were you close friends,' Gertrud asked eventually.

Karl's voice was subdued. 'It was brief. I only knew her for a few hours. But yes, we were friends...'

'And you fell for her?'

Karl looked at Gertrud, taken aback by her directness and unsure how to respond, but she smiled disarmingly, 'Karl I could see the look you gave her and I can also see how upset you are. It's a perfectly innocent question.'

Karl hesitated awkwardly, 'I hadn't realised. Is it really that obvious?'

Gertrud nodded, 'I'm afraid so.'

'Then yes...I fell for her - very much.'

When they reached the bottom of the stairs and stood outside the drawing room Karl hesitated, 'Gertrud, can I ask you to help me - to help Julie?' Gertrud raised an eyebrow inviting him to continue. 'There is a chance, possibly a chance that much of what she has experienced will be lost because of the drugs she was given. I don't know how conscious she was through it all. I just think it might be better if we pretend we don't know everything – the nature of her other injuries - for her self-esteem if nothing else. And...'

Gertrud smiled and took his arm 'You are afraid it may turn her in on herself - away from you?'

Karl ran his hand through his hair, 'I saw a sense of shame just now – a sense of hopelessness. If she won't let me help her it will make things so much more difficult for her recovery. We must make her believe we still see her as the beautiful young woman she was - not what she sees herself as now. She has to believe as little has changed as possible and if we can be part of that then so much the better.'

'But is it true? Do you feel the same about her?'

He looked down. 'Yes, she is the loveliest person I have ever met.'

She pressed his arm more urgently, 'But Karl, if you say all that, if she begins to build her hopes around you, and then finds out she is pregnant, won't that be twice as bad for her when you have to let her go?'

He turned sharply, 'I would not abandon her for that – *especially* that.'

The double doors to the drawing room opened abruptly and Albert Forster emerged. Inside the room Hildebrandt, his SS and Police Commander, sat with some papers scattered on a low stone table. Albert looked at them both, aware that something had passed between them that was lingering uncomfortably, but astute enough not to enquire. 'Doctor Rust, I need you again. Darling, will you spare us?'

When they were seated Hildebrandt passed Karl a photograph. It was of a middle aged man's naked body slumped against a birch

152

tree. He seemed to have been shot several times in the head. Karl grimaced, 'It's too disfigured - I don't recognise him.'

Hildebrandt said nothing, but passed over another photograph, 'Do you know this car then?'

Karl peered at the picture closely, 'Yes, that looks like the car Gunther Rath drives. He's a businessman from Posen. I met him a few times.'

'We think the face, what's left of it, is that of Gunther Rath. They found the car in a forest about fifteen kilometres away.'

Karl looked at Hildebrandt, 'Gunther, Julie and I all went out together on my last day in Posen. We were in that car – I'm sure.'

Forster thrummed on the table with his fingers, 'So we probably have the answer to how she got here. Was there nothing on the body?'

'They stripped the car and the body; the clothes were shredded…everything.'

Forster looked at Karl expectantly, 'Is Fräulein Scholl talking, or is it too early for that?'

'Too early - I will try tomorrow perhaps.'

Hildebrandt began to gather the pictures, 'We'll need some answers, Doctor. Who knows, perhaps you may be next on their list?'

Forster put his hand on Karl's arm. 'You'd better remain here - just until things are clearer.'

When Karl saw Julie that evening she was sitting up in bed reading. 'A good book?' he said reaching for a chair.

' *'Gone with the Wind'* – Gertrud lent it to me. I needed to take my mind off things.' She put it down on the bedside table. 'Gertrud tells me you've been sitting here next to me a lot of the time - that I've been drifting in and out of consciousness. I'm afraid I don't remember any of it. Did I say anything – did we speak at all?'

'No, you murmured a little. I promise you were a model patient.'

Julie's head fell forward and she looked down at her hands, 'I'm sure I don't feel like one. Part of me doesn't understand how you can look at me at all…not anymore.'

'Julie, you have to understand; to me those hours in Posen with you were the happiest I can remember spending with anyone - anywhere. To me you are still the Julie Scholl I met in Posen – the girl

153

I danced with, the girl I went sightseeing with. This terrible ordeal you've been through, these injuries, it doesn't change who you are to me, does it?'

Julie looked up, 'And you really feel that way…you really believe that, despite everything?'

Karl nodded, 'At this moment you are the most important person in the world to me. I just want things to go back to the way they were – for you to be well again.'

She clasped her hands together and her saw her lips tremble. 'I can't see that things can ever be the same as they were…not now…not ever.'

He leaned down slightly and caught her eye, 'Let's talk a little…we've never really talked have we?' Karl said gently.

Julie's eyes settled briefly on a family photograph on the wall, 'I suppose you could tell me about your life – your childhood? I'd like to hear about that.'

Karl settled back in his chair. 'So where would you like me to begin?'

Julie's spirits seemed to revive a little, 'Tell me about your parents.' She tried to sit up but struggled to contain the pain from her back and slumped again. Karl caught her eye, but she shook her head, 'I'm alright…honestly. Tell me about your parents.'

Karl smiled gently, 'Well…my father was a family doctor in Kattowitz, in Silesia. He met my mother when she was a nurse there at the hospital. They lived there for many years. In those days, before the last war, we were part of Germany, but after the war, when the Polish attacked us during the uprisings in '21, we left and went to Germany.'

'How old were you?'

'Oh, that was when I was four. We literally loaded a cart at gunpoint and headed for the border with what we could carry - along with all our German neighbours. My father couldn't walk – he'd been wounded, so they loaded him up as well and we went to Berlin.'

'So what did you do then?'

'My father studied further medicine at Berlin University Medical School so that he could teach, but his legs were always a problem to him and he had to give that up. Afterwards he did a little private practice. My mother did some part time work, and she practically raised me – and she was very strict. But no, my father died last year. My mother is in Ulm.'

154

'And you studied medicine too?'

'Yes, at the same university as my father. But I'm afraid I let him down a little. He was very disciplined with himself and expected me to be the same, but I liked the humanities too much! I was always wandering off to go to the cinema, or drinking with the art students - they seemed a much more interesting bunch. They were happy days. We didn't take long to find the cabarets and bars near the *Zoo*, along the *Kurfürstendamm* and *Friedrichstrasse*, besides the museums and theatres and the *Unter den Linden* and *Lustgarten*'

'And then?'

'Well, when I graduated I worked with a Dr Panning and Dr Hallerman on the report about the massacres of German civilians in Poland at the beginning of the war. They needed an assistant...and that's when I met you.'

Julie looked at him mischievously, 'We didn't meet exactly. You were abducted! I remember distinctly your expression. I have never seen a man look so bewildered. Had you ever danced before?'

Karl's lip twisted slightly, 'Yes, but never as well.' He stood, 'And now as my patient I have the duty to ask for your hand.'

She smiled, 'But I hardly know you!'

He raised an eyebrow, 'I need to take your pulse.'

She extended her arm and he pulled up her sleeve a little way. As he did so their eyes both fell on the large yellow bruise and scarring. She let out a brief cry and turned away sharply.

He stood with his finger gently pressed against her wrist looking at his watch and then, after a minute, rolled down her sleeve. She looked round at him, passing a brief uncertain smile.

Karl bent down and reached into the bedside cabinet producing a stethoscope which Julie applied through the buttons of her nightdress. He listened and she waited expectantly. Eventually she caught his eye and he removed the ear pieces with seeming impatience.

'Is there something wrong, Karl?'

He smiled wistfully, 'I was listening to your heart...it's really quite enchanting... and *very* strong. You are definitely getting better. So tomorrow we shall let the nurse go and we will walk and talk together in the garden - the air will do you good.'

Her lips twitched and she tapped his hand in a mild rebuke, 'Where exactly did you study medicine Karl?'

155

He looked at her with an expression of wounded pride, 'In the cabaret in the *Kurfürstendamm* – I'm sure I told you a few minutes ago. I was their most distinguished pupil!'

As he stood to leave she reached for his hand again, 'Karl, I have nothing to give Beata for her kindness. If she is going to leave tomorrow is there something you could do for me? My father will send money I'm sure and I can pay you back, but I want to give her something from me.'

'I will bring her some flowers. I will make sure she understands they are from you.' He hesitated and they both sensed something hovering between them. He clasped her hand more tightly, 'Sleep, we will talk more tomorrow.' And then, as his grip loosened, he bent down and kissed her hand, slowly and tenderly.

When he reached the door to leave he turned and saw that her gaze had followed him and she seemed suddenly more tranquil, 'Thank you', she said, in a steady and now more confident voice.

By the following day the weather had turned grey and windy and so, after Gertrud had helped Julie find some clothes from amongst her collection, she joined Karl in the living room.

She gestured at her new dress, 'I can't tell you how wonderful it is to be in proper clothes again. Gertrud's been incredibly kind. We spent ages looking for things that would fit, but fortunately we seem to be a quite similar size and shape. She keeps everything - there's just so much to choose from. I'm sorry…it took us so long.' Julie seemed to fade suddenly, as though a trigger had been operated somewhere in her mind.

Karl leaned forward, 'I need to know how you are feeling, Julie? You seemed better yesterday evening. Today you seem a little nervous, a little fragile. Have you been crying?'

Julie looked away and rocked on her chair, clasping her knee, 'I still have moments of anxiety, little things which make me feel I am back there - in a dark place. Sometimes it's just a sense that something terrible is going to happen that comes from nowhere. It can be anything – like this morning…' she stopped rocking and put her hands over her face suddenly overcome.

Karl leaned forward, 'I am here for you…you can't do this alone…I can help?'

156

Julie's hands fell into her lap, 'Help? Who can help me?' she said, the tears welling up.

'Something to make you feel calmer.'

Julie drew a handkerchief quickly from her sleeve and wiped her eyes, 'Don't give me anything – you must promise. Don't try to give me anything to help me. I can manage.'

'Of course not. If you can cope without medication it's better.'

Julie sat up, her face suddenly alert and sharp, determined to change the subject. 'Karl what has happened to my friends in Warsaw? The nurse said the city is in ruins - is that true?'

'The Poles decided to fight for the city. I'm sorry, yes – it's true.'

Julie's face fell, 'But I had good friends there who gave me a home - Albert and Maria Beck. Their daughter Sophie showed me the city – we cycled everywhere together.' She sighed heavily, 'You know Karl, it was like Paris – like an eastern Paris. The Mayor laid beds of flowers everywhere. It was so charming, so beautiful in the spring and summer - it was like a garden. Sophie and I used to go for picnics by the lakes in the park and spend whole days there, reading and talking.' She hesitated 'How was all this possible? How could it all end in such terrible destruction?'

'The Poles seized a German radio station, we counter-attacked – we had no choice – it simply escalated.'

'And the Poles say we attacked them – but does it really matter who cast the first stone, Karl, when the end result is so terrible for all of us.'

'Julie, nobody wanted this war, but surely now, as a German, you feel the same as the rest of us about it – that at least it restores to Germany land that was rightfully hers – ends the Polish occupation...the persecutions?'

'No Karl, how could I feel the same knowing what's become of Warsaw? I lived there, studied with them...drank coffee with them – I *had* Polish friends. And sometimes I don't think I am German at all – not in my head.' Julie paused, 'Surely there must have been a better way.'

'But you do understand the causes – the grievances?'

Julie's eyes became distant, 'No, I didn't learn the history. I was in Argentina from '31 to '36. I missed all the background – the *justification* for it all. I just arrived and it was there, the new Germany,

157

the Olympic Games, the flags and banners. I remember when we landed at Hamburg, finding it difficult to understand the way intelligent people could say the most peculiar things – the complete lack of understanding of other opinions, the lack of empathy…'

Karl's voice suddenly seemed jarring, 'Germany had to defend itself Julie. We had to right the injustices.'

'But was it worth all this suffering – for the Germans and the Poles?'

Karl leaned forward, 'Julie, after the war they took one-eighth of Germany, most of our iron and steel industry, one tenth of our population was put under foreign rule, our colonies were shared out among the victors and Germans were made to pay for the war while France, Belgium and Denmark took what they wanted. Of course the Führer made this war possible, but Versailles made the war *necessary* – absolutely essential. And as for the Poles…what I witnessed…the massacres…after what they did to my father!'

Julie's voice was almost imploring 'But won't this war destroy us too?'

'Julie, when you see the German army, you must understand how superior we are in every respect, but most of all we Germans *believe* in the war – the allies don't. Nobody wants to fight for Poland. When the Russians took their share of Poland in mid-September the British and French didn't even bother to declare war. We cannot lose.'

'No Karl! Please listen to me – I don't mean our ability to win; I mean our ability to keep our Christian morality, our sense of humanity?' she paused, 'I sometimes think that the German is either a Christian or a Barbarian, he does either with full commitment but he is never both. I'm simply afraid we will all become Barbarians if this war goes on – that it will drag us all down.' She paused looking into the distance, 'Are you a Christian?'

Karl hesitated for a moment, 'I'm an agnostic, but my father would say that by birth I'm a Protestant.'

'As a man of science I suppose that makes sense, but are you also a National Socialist.'

'Of course.'

'Then you have placed your faith in the Führer. The Führer has become God.'

Karl nodded, 'Yes…I suppose he has in a way.'

158

Julie sat still for a moment, her expression distant. 'I'm tired. Can you help me back to my room?'

Karl suddenly sensed a formality in her voice, that she had withdrawn from him, that he had alienated her. He asked himself *why* he had allowed himself to be drawn into politics, into religion. Why?

He took her hand, but she did not meet his eye and as they went up the stairs slowly, resting every ten steps or so, she remained absorbed in her innermost thoughts and so he remained silent. When they got to her room she turned as she opened the door and took his hand firmly, 'Karl promise me you will never try to become a god?'

Karl smiled gently but with slight perplexity, 'Julie, I'm a doctor, my place is among mortals. My place is where I am right now.' They stood for a moment in silence and then she turned away without acknowledging his smile, entered the room and closed the door. He stood for a moment, confused by their exchange, suddenly overwhelmed by a sense of insecurity about her and unsettled by her feelings, her sense of detachment from the causes he so fervently believed in.

When he returned to the living room he found Gertrud sitting alone, waiting for him. They both sensed unhappiness in each other, but it was Gertrud who spoke first, 'You must be very cross with me? I'm so sorry about this morning. I suppose she said something did she?'

Karl looked at her, confused for a moment, and then realised that she had taken his sullen expression to be a reproach aimed at her. 'I'm sorry Gertrud, you'll have to explain? My mind was elsewhere. I do apologise.'

'The clothes, the dresses - it was pure chance she reached for them – they were all together you see at the end of a rail and my back was turned. I had no chance to stop her. And then I turned and she was in tears.'

'Why?'

'Karl, they were my maternity dresses.'

Karl sank slowly onto the sofa, 'I thought she looked as though she'd been crying.'

'She made me promise not to say anything but...I'm still afraid for her Karl. There was nothing I could say – nothing I could do. She simply sobbed.'

159

'No, I don't suppose there was. She must be terrified.'

Gertrud said nothing, but after they had sat in silence for a few minutes stood anxiously and began walking towards the door, 'I'll go and see her. I must make sure she's alright. I'll stay with her, Karl. Don't worry, I'll stay with her and make sure she doesn't...come to any harm.'

Chapter 15

The Office of the Gauleiter of Danzig West Prussia, Danzig Rathaus (town hall).

Koppe stood eyeing the oil paintings in the lobby of Forster's palatial Danzig town hall offices for long enough to sense the chill that accompanied his arrival. At length, Albert Forster's SS Police Leader Hildebrandt appeared and he was led through tall heavy doors into a gloomy wood panelled office with mahogany furniture. After a cursory salute he seated himself in front of Forster's large desk. Kellerman was soon admitted from a side door and sat to one side with Hildebrandt.

Forster reclined in his high backed green leather chair, a pen poised between the fingers of his hands, 'My first question to you is this; why has Grieser completely reversed his position on resettlement? We were united about this when we met in Berlin in September. As I recall it was the only thing.' He leaned forward and tapped the desk with his pen, 'We don't want these people; we can't use these people. There's a ship in the harbour full of ethnic Germans from God knows where and with God knows what skills and we have nothing for them. They will deplete our already stretched resources - it's unacceptable. As I remember it was unacceptable to Grieser. Now I find you have gone to Hitler with a complaint about me.'

Koppe clicked his fingers at Kellerman, who passed him a folder, 'But the agreement with the Soviets is to settle 135,000 Germans from Russian occupied Poland and 100,000 from the Baltic States.'

Forster waved impatiently, 'Old men, women, children, urban workers …creating the new breadbasket for Germany! You take them - all of them. We need farmers - not more mouths.' He paused, his tone becoming more determined, 'They will only disembark from that ship when Grieser gives me an undertaking in writing that he will absorb them directly; I accept no responsibility.'

'I can give that undertaking - if I choose to.'

Forster looked sideways at Hilderbandt and then fixed on Koppe, 'That's a lot of authority you've recently acquired, doesn't Grieser have a say in these things anymore?'

161

'Your policy on the Polish expulsions is causing comment in Berlin. Himmler is unhappy about the racial implications. You should not be treating the Poles and the Germans the same - the Poles must go.'

'If I looked like Himmler I would spend a little less time talking about race. And it's causing comment because you are headlining it to them and masking your own production failures in the process. My policy on expelling Poles is clear and practical; if a man or woman declare themselves to be German I'll give them the benefit of the doubt so long as he or she signs the papers, keeps producing, and remains passive.'

'You keep old Party fighters out of the best jobs; you promote your own friends. The Party men have been passed over - they are unhappy. Your loyalty to the Party is being questioned. People say you lack ideological commitment.'

Forster smiled, 'Correct me if I am wrong, Hildebrandt, but in the forests around Piaśnica since the 21st of October we have shot, how many...as I recall, two thousand Kashubians, twelve thousand Poles, Czechs and Germans and one thousand two hundred mental patients. I've done more than enough to prove my *zeal* here. But, I am also a practical man; I will Germanize, but not at the cost of food and other production - the war comes first.'

Forster collected himself and now directly assaulted Koppe, 'And what are you doing mounting Security Police actions in my Gau?'

Koppe looked at Kellerman who interjected, reading from a document which he hastily pulled from his briefcase. *'The Polish woman Franziska Wolska had a military patrol fetched by a boy and led them into a house belonging to the minority German Rohrbeck: father and son were shot.'* That was in Posen on September 2nd. We believe she then used false documents in the name of Julie Daase to evade justice - hiding in Warsaw and then in Danzig. We want her back.'

'Let's not play games, Julie Scholl is safe. There's no Daase, or Wolska!' Forster said with disdain.

Koppe looked at Kellerman and shook his head slightly. Kellerman returned the document to his briefcase.

Hildebrandt sat forward, 'There seems to be a lot of confusion at your end over Julie Scholl's identity. We don't feel the same doubts.'

Koppe bridled, 'With respect, this girl you call Julie Scholl also claimed to be Julie Daase, and there are many people between myself and the investigating officer. I am not privy to all the facts, but I trust my men. I am told she is Polish. Give my people a chance to talk to her. What is she to you anyway?'

'An enigma; the source of many questions but apparently no answers. And have you heard her speak?' Forster scoffed, 'Since when did Polish peasants learn impeccable German - is there a school somewhere! Your men are idiots. Even Grieser's man Vogler admitted her name is Scholl. And we also know her father's identity. Perhaps you would like us to settle the matter once and for all with him – I'm sure Funk would let him take a little leave for his daughter's sake.'

Koppe's expression erupted into a wry smile. 'I'm sure that won't be necessary. But there must be an accommodation we can reach – a trade perhaps. We want her back. We need to speak to her.'

'Is this official?'

'I'm hoping not.' Koppe said enquiringly, 'At least, I can't imagine you would pass up this opportunity to make a trade – Gauleiter Grieser wants this matter resolved as quickly and quietly as possible. I merely wish to ensure this business with Scholl doesn't go any further and create a distraction.'

'And you really want to ease Grieser's relations with Berlin - after that business with Himmler? I would have thought you'd only be too happy to see him in the shit.'

'Since then we've reached an accommodation.'

Forster smiled, 'Yes, I can see that. So, what exactly is her significance to you?'

Koppe shrugged, 'She attacked Frau Grieser – hospitalised her. We want to deal with it discreetly.'

'An affair?'

'More complex than that.'

'And by *discretion*, what do we mean? Sending the Kolmar SD to the Central Hospital in broad daylight to drag her off under the noses of the medical staff – is that it? And then what; a trip to the forest and a bullet in the back of the neck? Seems a little excessive, even if she did injure Frau Grieser – and of course that's ignoring Julie Scholl's own injuries which are extensive and so far unexplained.'

Koppe held up his hand, 'And will remain so. That's the deal. You trade – you forget she was ever here and you forget what you know. It's that simple. I'm sure Gauleiter Grieser will be happy to agree any reasonable terms to secure his continued good standing with the Führer and keep this domestic matter out of the public gaze.' Koppe sat back, 'But, I can see you need more time to consider your position. Perhaps a week to think things over? So for now I'll assume this is an on-going situation – no need to refer to Berlin. Is that agreeable?'

Forster nodded, 'For the time being.'

'Very good. So, that being the case, I'll thank you for your time. I'll report back. And, just to show some goodwill, we'll let you have the undertaking you require regarding the ship's cargo.' Koppe stood, nodded to Hildebrandt and then saluted Forster. 'You have been most helpful.'

After Koppe and Kellerman had left, Forster sat in silence with Hildebrandt for a few minutes, both trying to attach motive and meaning to Koppe's behaviour. Finally Forster threw down his pen with irritation.

'They didn't even try to lie convincingly did they? Just rolled over in front of us - but why? Why expose Grieser like that?'

Hildebrandt, turned slowly toward Forster. 'Because you'd answered their question.'

'What question?'

'They needed to know how much we knew. As soon as you admitted you didn't know Scholl's value they were satisfied. They didn't care if we had Scholl for now; not really, so long as we hadn't made all the connections - and they're not going to help us do that by telling us what Grieser is *really* nervous about. So we need to make the right connections - if we do that, who knows what terms we could impose. I suppose for now they're still hoping to get whatever it is back without paying us for Scholl.'

'What do you mean - get *what* back?'

Hildebrandt stood 'When they killed Rath they stripped the car, tore it apart and turned him inside out – shredded his clothes – you saw the pictures. Obviously they think he brought something with him.

164

They didn't find it on him, or on Julie Scholl, so it's still out there somewhere, some piece of the jigsaw which links Julie to the bigger picture. So, I'll keep looking. He must have stayed somewhere.'

Forster sat back, 'This is a big game…high stakes. But it's madness, what could be worth all this humiliation for them? I wonder if even Scholl knows how all the pieces fit together.'

Hildebrandt shrugged, 'As you say, it's a big game.' He picked up his briefcase and walked slowly across the room still deep in thought. As he grasped the door handle he turned, 'Incidentally, would you have done a trade – handed her back to them - if the price had been right?'

Forster sat back raising an eyebrow, 'You'll never know...'

Hildebrandt smiled, '…Until it happens.'

Private Country Residence of the Gauleiter of Danzig West Prussia

Albert Forster was the last to join the breakfast party that bitterly cold December morning. He kissed his wife fondly as he made his way to the head of the table where a plate of cold meats, eggs, bread and conserves had been set out meticulously. The kitchen girl stepped forward, poured his coffee, and left. Julie was seated opposite Karl and they exchanged friendly glances, but she remained reserved and consumed by her inner thoughts. With the help of Gertrud, the previous afternoon, Julie's hair had reassumed its former healthy sheen, but with the additional embellishment of some of her jewelled clips which secured her *chignon*. She had also been given a new dress which now showed her to be at no disadvantage in Gertrud's presence. But Karl still saw a nervous agitation in her eyes and her former gaiety and sparkle remained eclipsed by a darkness which seemed to haunt her.

After coffee and some gentle banter with Karl, Albert sat back and looked at his wife and guests more soberly, 'I'm afraid there was some more news this morning - about the *Graf Spee*…difficult to take in. She was sunk yesterday - scuttled outside Montevideo. That arse Goebbels was on the radio two days ago hailing a victory. Now Berlin says Captain Langsdorff has shot himself. A beautiful battleship, beautiful! She came to Danzig in '38 on the way to Memel. Impossible somehow to imagine her gone! The U-boats will avenge her though, Dönitz will see to that...give them six months.'

Gertrud looked at Julie and whispered, 'Goebbels! A horrible, horrible little man, and that wife - impossible!'

Forster looked reproachfully at his wife, 'So Julie, you are feeling better every day Gertrud says.'

'Yes, thank you Herr...

'Call me Albert. It's Albert or nothing - I insist.'

He smiled, but as he did so Julie suddenly rose from the table gasping for breath, 'I'm terribly, terribly sorry, I must...I must get some air.' She threw down her napkin and fled from the table leaving her chair askew.

After a few moments those remaining recovered their composure and Karl stood, 'It's to be expected I'm afraid. I'll go and see her - my apologies.'

In the garden Karl found Julie sitting hunched over on a bench by the frozen lake. He placed a coat over her, knelt down and put on her gloves. 'Did you really feel ill, or did you have a sudden anxiety attack? You looked terrified.'

Julie raised her head, her lips trembling. 'It's the slightest thing, just a phrase, the way Albert spoke. They were the same words *he* used...' Julie looked down at her feet.

Karl put his hand on her shoulder and spoke softly, hardly daring to press her to say more, 'The same words..?'

'*'Call me Arthur...I insist.'* he would say. They were the words Grieser used...'

Karl moved to embrace her and they stood together, rocking backwards and forwards for a while, Julie convulsing with tears of desperation, rage and shame.

After a few minutes Gertrud found them and took Julie back into the house, her hand cradling her head, gently issuing words of comfort. Karl stood there desolate; paralysed by rage. When the blood had drained from his eyes and he felt able to contain himself he sought out Forster. He found him at his desk in the library, 'Well isn't that enough? Isn't her evidence enough?' Karl snapped eventually. Forster looked at him with sympathy and then got up and paced over to french windows overlooking the lake. He paused for a moment with his back to him, 'Karl do you know the *real* meaning of the New Order?' Karl sat, brooding. 'Then I will help you to understand the term. The New Order means order below. It means abject submission. It means moral abnegation. It means unthinking obedience by the masses. And for the Party the New Order means *'the will to power'*, which in practice means the law of the jungle and chaos.' He turned and faced Karl, 'Do you ever hear the Party hacks talk of *'working towards the Führer'*? That's a more insidious term still; it means interpreting his will, excelling, being more fanatical and more determined than the next man to realise some abstract notion of his. That's why, very often, we have four, five, six people assigned to realise each new idea - to see who emerges at the top, to encourage the others to be more ruthless in pursuit of the ends. And when that task can be achieved without moral restraint, it's a race to the very bottom, to a form of moral bankruptcy that may, in time, destroy us all.' He paused, 'And then, on the way to the bottom, they sometimes meet someone like Julie.' He walked back to his desk and leaned over it towards Karl, 'Let me ask you a question, Dr Rust, as a medical man, knowing her condition; would you put her in the witness box?'

Karl hesitated, his mind struggling for a moment to find the necessary equilibrium. Finally he replied barely audibly, 'No.'

' *'No'* not now', or simply *'no'*?'

Karl wavered for a moment, 'Not now.'

Forster returned to his seat and looked at him sceptically, 'Then let me make it simpler. Would you pit her against Grieser, in open court, with a tame Party man like, say, Freisler on the bench as judge?'

Karl clasped his hands together tightly; his voice exasperated, 'Then where is her justice?'

'We listen, we watch and we wait.' Forster reached for his cigarettes on a side table, 'But I must make myself clear, it's not my place to bring down Grieser just for Julie Scholl's sake - noble though that cause is. The prize must be big enough and the chances of success...well...they have to be very high for a man like that.'

After this exchange Karl spent many hours alone walking around the lakes which ringed the house, inured to the cold by his anger, trying to fathom and dissect Forster's motives and reasoning. Suddenly his world seemed shaken; a whole raft of assumptions about

167

Forster's guiding principles and those of the Party, undercut by his simple, crude, base analysis. And yet, inwardly, he struggled; National Socialism was not about these cynical careerists - they had always existed, even in the Hitler Youth; it was about the national collective will and the Führer, who towered above all such men. The movement was simply too big, too potent, too proven in its ability to effect real change to be a charade. He hardened himself against Albert's reduction of the Party and became irritated by his own weakness, his failure to stand his ground. And yet his *desire* to believe now began to unsettle him. He sensed something, an artifice, a hollowness in his zeal. And try as he might to deny it, something in what Albert had said had hit home, just as it had done when Rath berated the 'Nazi princes' for their incompetence after his dinner with Dr Hertz, and Julie had pleaded the case for humanity after the destruction of Warsaw. Karl was suddenly reminded of the Fara church and Rath's monologue about the Renaissance. He reflected that he too would need to move beyond the comforts of unquestioning faith, even if he still 'believed', and adjust to some harsh new realities.

Later that afternoon, having buried these inner thoughts, he found Julie with Inga and Peter in the playroom upstairs. They were all sitting on the floor happily completing a jigsaw puzzle and Julie seemed unexpectedly relaxed. She looked up, 'Aren't they adorable? Gertrud has asked if I will stay and be their nanny.' The children cried out excitedly in approval. 'She says they will give me an allowance.'

Karl extended his hand and helped her up from the floor. When she stood their eyes met as they had the evening of the Posen ball, lingering with pleasure and happiness, a tenderness and warmth in the clasp of her hand, and Karl was quietly relieved to see the change in her. The children stood up and tugged at her skirt, 'Can we play the piano, please?'

As they walked with the children down the corridor toward the stairs their hands touched and their fingers entwined for a moment. They both remembered that moment when this had happened before in Posen and Karl leaned towards her, kissing her temple without further conscious thought. It was the kiss which had been denied him that day and it was a kiss which exorcised that memory. And now there was no sense of the futility of their feelings and no confusion of thoughts. Suddenly there was every reason to believe in a future together. Inga

168

ran mischievously ahead and Julie turned to Karl for a moment, the joy once again behind her smile, before running after her.

Later that afternoon, Julie sat with Karl in the living room awaiting Gertrud, who had gone to find some playing cards. They looked at each other in silence for a moment unsure of themselves. Finally Julie spoke, 'Gertrud said you were afraid I might have changed. Do you think I have?'

'I was worried you would be different, that something might have been stolen from you: your confidence, your feelings for people, the look you used to have in your eyes.'

She thought for a moment, 'I'm better today. Today has changed everything. Until now I was afraid. Now I can look forward a little. Don't worry about me. I will get better. Just…don't go away - please? Not 'till I'm myself again and we have had time to get back to where we were. The nights are still difficult and the days too, but I'm not where I was. I can cope better.'

Julie got up and rested her hand on Karl's shoulder, 'I'll be back in a moment.'

Karl sat perplexed, trying to understand her veiled meaning and the sudden change in her. Then it came to him and his head sank into his hands, 'Of course, of course…thank God!'

When Gertrud returned with the playing cards she looked at Julie's empty chair. 'Will she be long?'

Karl looked up, 'No, but Gertrud…have I understood things correctly? Do we still need to hold our breath?'

She clasped his arm, 'If you mean the *change* in her this afternoon then yes; we can breathe again. Isn't it wonderful? And what a relief…for all of us.' She suddenly noticed his eyes glistening behind his broad smile and she too suddenly felt the exhilaration of their relief.

'I would have stayed with her…whatever had happened. You do know that don't you?'

Gertrud sat down and began shuffling the cards, 'I know that now Karl.'

169

Chapter 16

Country Residence of the Gauleiter of Danzig West Prussia, Christmas Eve 1939

'It's so much more like a family Christmas with you here, Julie; you can't imagine how nice it is to have proper company at a time like this, just family and friends – not those dreadful *duty* visits we used to have to put up with from the hangers-on in the Party. At least Albert can afford to have his Christmas functions in Danzig now, especially when we have so many things to do around the house.' Gertrud tied another ribbon to the tree and stepped back to admire it. She looked around at the children expecting them to be looking too and stifled a smile. It appeared that while she had been working on the tree, Inga had been equally dedicated to decorating her brother - with as many baubles and other decorations as possible. He had sat happily enough as she tied them to his golden locks, watching his mother from the far side of the room, but now he was almost unrecognisable.

Julie unpacked another box of decorations and took them over to Gertrud, 'Albert seems very close to them which must help. Peter misses him so much when he's not here, it is difficult to please him sometimes. I don't think *we* can ever replace his *daddy,* can we, Peter?' Peter shook his head accompanied by a cacophony of clinking baubles.

Gertrud laughed, 'No, certainly not, and you're right, he won't be bought off either the little beast! But that's the thing I like in Albert, however terrible the day, however stressful, he keeps his work in a separate place and we never talk about it. He comes home and the children come first for twenty minutes at least - always the children and then me.

 'I only remember once that he came home in a rage, when Rauschning published a scurrilous work about Hitler and took a huge sideswipe at Albert in the process. I lost my favourite Chinese vase that day. How are you getting on with Karl?'

Julie looked coy, 'Oh, he is lovely. Sometimes it's just enough to be with him, walking and thinking of the future – of course, I don't tell *him* what I am thinking. Sometimes we talk for hours, but other times it's enough to know he's there in the same room, reading or listening to the radio. But…it's too early to make any commitment isn't it? When the war is only beginning?'

Gertrud stood back from the tree to admire it. 'Oh, Albert thinks the Führer will finish the war by the end of next year. I mean Poland fell in three weeks and the British and French have done nothing in the west. And now we can sort out the west as well, especially with the Soviets on our side, sending us everything we need. It will all come to negotiations, you'll see.'

Julie shrugged, 'It just seems that it's getting more complicated. I thought there would be negotiations after Poland fell.'

'Only men understand these things Julie. I try to avert my eyes.'

'Did Albert get any response from the Economics Ministry about my father? I'm really concerned about him now. It's been too long.'

'Well, not really. But I will ask him again. Don't worry.'

Stephan the manservant entered and cleared his throat. Gertrud turned, 'Ah, some Christmas post!' She picked a few letters from the tray and then looked at the large bulky envelope which lay at the bottom of the pile. 'My word, it's been redirected by the Central Hospital - it's for you!'

Julie looked at it, studying the various postal marks and then turned to Gertrud uneasily, 'It's from Posen. I don't know the writing.'

Gertrud looked over her shoulder, 'Would you like me to open it?' Julie nodded and passed the envelope back to her but then she too paused. 'Should I give it to my husband?' Julie shook her head. 'No, it might be something quite innocent.'

'It's a very crudely written address.' she said as she gently prized open the flap and peered inside. She pulled at a thick wedge of tatty paper and put it down on the table in front of her, 'Old letters, a lot of old letters addressed to you and a music score!'

Julie looked around sharply, 'My mother's letters - all my mother's old letters. Oh, what a relief! It broke my heart when I thought they were lost.' She took the folio of music, turning the pages slowly. 'It's my copy! My mother bought it for my birthday. They're from the orphanage. That's incredible, but how did it find me? Who could have sent it?'

171

Gertrud looked into the envelope, 'There's nothing - no note.'

Julie smiled, with a mixture of confusion and relief, clutching the letters, 'This is the best Christmas present I could ever have been given!'

'Come on then, I'd love to hear you play – but what a mystery.'

When they reached in the library where the grand piano stood, Albert was seated at his desk working. He seemed pleased at the interruption and greeted his wife with a warm embrace and a kiss on the cheek. 'Albert, would you mind very much if Julie played this music? It's just arrived quite out of the blue from the orphanage she stayed at in Posen. Are you terribly busy?'

He gestured towards the piano, 'Not too busy to hear Julie play.' Then he stood speechless as Inga led Peter into the room, his head laden with every conceivable decoration, but now also including a small candle, while Inga maintained a smile of sweet innocence.

Albert and Gertrud sat on the sofa smiling playfully with the children while Julie looked at the familiar score for a moment. It still bore Gieseking's strident exhortations in blue pencil from the *Konservatorium* in Berlin and her own fainter reminders. Each one brought to her the memory of a lesson, of the hours she had spent in exercises and in moments of sheer frustration. 'It's so long since I played, it will be very rough, I'm afraid.'

She looked over to the sofa, 'Albert, could you turn the pages for me?'

Albert gladly abandoned the sofa to his still giggling children, and stood over her looking at the score, 'My word, Schumann's *'Toccata'*, what a lot of notes! With repeats, or without?'

She smiled defiantly, 'Oh with - let's be brave.'

Julie played, faltering occasionally, but pleasing her hosts sufficiently to attract their spirited applause when her hands quietly came to rest.

Then Albert glanced over Julie's shoulder at the music stand where she had placed the envelope in which the old letters and the music had arrived. He studied it keenly and looked inquisitively at Gertrud, then Julie. 'It is odd though isn't it - and there was no note?' Gertrud shook her head, 'I opened it, there was nothing.' Julie nodded in agreement. Then he seemed to collect himself, continuing in mock reproach. 'And you will start to practice again won't you. I won't let

172

you waste your talents; we *shall* have a few recitals after dinner? That will go down well with Herr Krebs and the good wife.'

Gertrud studied the decorations on her son's head, 'Well Albert, since it's nearly Christmas, shall we light Peter's candle – let *his* be the first!'

Peter yelped and leapt from the sofa, running towards the door pursued by his sister, while Albert playfully brandished a box of matches and cantered after them.

Gauleiter's Office, Rathaus (town hall), Danzig, January 1940

Hildebrandt entered Forster's office quietly from the rear door without Albert's secretary noticing and gesticulated to him behind her back as she took dictation. When she had left he sat down and opened his briefcase.

'You know people underestimate my network at their peril Albert – top men, I've not worked with better. They went through the Chamber of Commerce archives and looked up possible merchant connections Rath may have had in the city – people he did business with. We traced a tobacco importer and he knew a few of Rath's old friends in the city. My men did some leg work and now have the address where Rath stayed before he was killed; 43 Stettiner Strasse - here in Danzig, on the western side of the city. Our people say the occupants knew Rath, an old business associate. He appeared one afternoon and asked for a bed for the night – said he was doing a deal and needed somewhere for two or three days. He implied it was black market, so no questions were asked. He made one telephone call and then, the next day, he didn't come back. He left a bag with two items: a roll of film – we have a man developing it now - and this...' Hildebrandt took out a long red leather case and handed it to Forster.

Forster unclipped the metal catch and opened it, examining the gold and diamond necklace and earrings in the light, 'Genuine?'

'I had Dieter Yorck look at it. He says it's worth good money, very good. Quality diamonds and twenty four carat gold.'

Forster snapped the box shut and put it in his desk drawer while Hildebrandt studied his notes. 'The envelope was posted two days after Rath's death. It was someone who had access to the military postal system. It means that they would have had to know where she'd

173

been dumped – the Central Hospital – and where Rath was staying. I suspect that was the telephone call - to let someone know things had gone wrong. Perhaps the film will explain more, but I'm sending Epp south to do some digging of his own. If we can find the sender of the envelope things might start to make sense.'

'Well, be bloody careful, I don't want them coming back at us with accusations.'

Hildebrandt paused, 'And there's one other thing; your wife asked me to trace Scholl's father. She said you were running into *road blocks*. She asked me as a friend of the family. I agreed not to say anything to you.'

Forster sighed heavily, 'Well, I don't blame Gertrud for asking. Julie is…well…one of the household now. I've been stalling for two weeks.'

Hildebrandt stood and leaned on the back of his chair, 'The pictures should be out of the lab' by seven this evening. I only put one man on them - for discretion's sake. Shall I come around later?'

'Yes – after dinner. And perhaps then we'll get to know where all this leads.'

Hildebrandt's car arrived at the house that evening at speed. Albert hastily got to his feet; Hildebrandt was not a man to be hurried, his strength was his imperturbability under pressure, but something had clearly rattled him and Albert didn't want unnecessary questions from his guests. He nodded to his wife as she played cards with Karl and Julie, and went into the hall.

Hildebrandt stood grim faced as he was relieved of his coat by Stephan and then began to reach into his attaché case. Forster shook his head toward the Library, 'In here, we won't be disturbed.'

When they were alone Hildebrandt placed a large manila envelope on Albert's desk. It was sealed with wax and ribbon and bore a security marking. He withdrew to a chair and watched Albert intently.

Forster eyed the envelope, 'I take it this is not just for show?'

Hildebrandt shook his head, 'Open it!'

Forster broke the seals and then laid the pictures out on his desk methodically but with a look of increasing irritation. He stood back looking at them blankly, 'Is this some kind of practical joke?'

174

Hildebrandt reached into his pocket and put a roll of film on the desk heavily. 'According to my expert this film has never been exposed – never been in a camera. It was a new film...there are *no* pictures.'

Forster sat down and put his hands over his face for a moment collecting his thoughts, 'I thought this was going to be *it*.' He lit a cigarette and drew heavily, 'But we do know there is *something,* even if this was a ruse, to put Koppe off the scent. His men wouldn't have torn Rath and his car to pieces looking for nothing. They obviously still believe there's something out there and so must we.'

'I agree, but the necklace is all we have for now. I can't see where we go from here, unless something else falls from the sky.'

Forster picked up the envelope again, feeling its weight, 'Then I won't take this further now – too difficult – and as you say we have no leads. But who knows what the future will bring.' He threw the packet down. 'I'll play the Führer's game – await events.' He stood up and went to the drinks cabinet. 'Now; if you're going to speak to Julie about her father, we'd better have some Danzig goldwater first.'

'Schnapps! Why not. But no; I can't speak to Julie about her father.'

Albert paused, 'Problems?'

'I need time. There's something going on about him. People are asking me why I'm enquiring. I'll get back to you, but a sixth sense tells me I need to tread carefully.'

Albert shrugged, 'Very well then, keep me informed.'

After they had sat drinking for a while Forster turned on his chair and studied Hildebrandt thoughtfully. Hildebrandt chuckled, 'I knew your curiosity would get the better of you eventually.'

'Well, why *did* you do it – the dramatic arrival, the security markings – not your style?'

'It's a matter of appearance. You still have powerful enemies in Danzig and Grieser has plenty of friends – friends who would like to see you gone. We must assume that Koppe gets to know and see almost everything – and if this is a bidding war it does no harm for him to think we're making progress.'

Albert leant back and stared at the ceiling. 'But what is it, Richard, what could be so threatening to Grieser, that he would risk everything – open conflict with us? And why is Koppe backing him?'

175

Hildebrandt shook his head, 'If Koppe is helping Grieser it's purely self-serving – you heard him – he's reached an *accommodation*. But while we still have Scholl we still have a place at the top table. She's our trump card – you'd just better be certain she doesn't get restless feet and go wandering off, or rather, I wouldn't give much for her chances if she did.'

Country Residence of the Gauleiter of Danzig West Prussia, 20 April 1940

Karl entered the library after breakfast to find Albert on the telephone. He beckoned Karl silently forward and pointed to a chair. After a few minutes he replaced the receiver and they sat looking at each other. 'You asked to see me?' Karl said.

'Yes, I thought we would do this away from the breakfast table.' Albert reached into his pocket and sat forward with a letter in his hand. 'It was in the morning post - I picked it up accidently. I'm sorry, but I thought you might want to look at it on your own first – to collect your thoughts.'

Karl looked down and recognised the unmistakeable imprint of his 'call-up' letter for military service. 'My gift from the Führer on his fifty-first birthday! Still…' he said flapping the envelope in his hand, '…I've never been to either Denmark or Norway.'

'Ah, that's all over now! By the time you are trained it will be Paris not Oslo for you – Paris! But Julie will be upset wherever you go, I'm certain of that.'

'Of course, but it's my duty isn't it. The Fatherland needs soldiers, and soldiers need doctors.'

Albert pointed at the phone, 'You know I was just talking to Berlin – just chatter you understand. Do you know that Germany is suddenly awash with bacon, hams, chickens, eggs – from Denmark? They can't import feed for the livestock anymore because of the British blockade, so they're slaughtering them and sending them to the Reich – at rock bottom prices too. Who in Germany is really going to complain about the war when they are stuffing themselves stupid with the best food for a decade? And what is clever? In August the rations were reduced – to the same level they were at in the third year of the last war and everyone was furious as well as hungry. And now of course everyone loves the war – can't wait for the next instalment! You wait for France to fall. Can you imagine what they'll say about the Führer when he starts importing the best vintages and delicacies from there too! Of course the problem soon will be knowing how to distinguish the gastronomic from the strategic objectives!' Albert sat back and slapped the desk, laughing quietly to himself. Karl looked down at his call-up papers again and tried to think of what he might say to Julie. Albert saw his preoccupation and became more earnest, 'I'm sorry Karl, but it will be over sooner than you can imagine.'

'And Julie can stay?'

'Of course – but you must remain discreet about her presence here. We must try to keep this business away from Berlin. Who knows what influence may have been brought to bear there – what stories may have been told.'

Karl nodded, 'Of course, you have been very kind.'

Later Karl found Julie in the kitchen preparing some food for the children with Gertrud and slipped the letter in its envelope in front of her. She pushed it aside without speaking, and turned away for a moment to conceal her despair.

Gertrud looked over and shook her head, 'I'm sorry for you both. Julie, go for a walk with Karl, it'll do you good.'

As they emerged onto the front steps Karl held Julie closer as their breath froze in the morning air. They walked as they had walked so many times, around the lakes and woods, which were now bathed in the cool brilliant sunshine of the late morning. 'I knew it would happen eventually, my being a doctor especially - we are needed at the front. But now the time has come I can't find words to say goodbye. I can't think of life outside, especially in the army. It all seems so remote, Denmark, Norway. Albert seems to think I'm going to end up on the Western Front…he even mentioned Paris!'

'Oh, please don't talk about it. We have until tomorrow. Let's pretend this is just another day.'

Karl nodded, 'But will you stay here until I return? Albert said you can and Gertrud seems very happy with your company.'

'Of course…if I can. I *will* wait for you somewhere.'

'And you won't go back to Argentina - with your father?'

'No Karl, I think we belong in Germany now. But it is true, even here we have few *real* family and friends. I should like to have a large family one day. There are so few of us Scholls left - just my uncle in Remagen and some very distant relations in Spain.'

She felt his hand reach down to hers and their pace slowed, 'Julie I know you are still only sixteen and I know this is all very sudden - that there is a proper order for things, that I should write to your father, but there is no time. I just know in my heart that when this is over...'

Julie stopped, turned, and held her finger to his lip. She stood impishly on tiptoe and pecked him on the lips, 'Yes.'

He stepped back slightly and held her hands, 'You know the question?'

Her eyes sparkled and the radiance of her smile told him that she had understood everything; that a part of her had already been waiting in hope, and her heart was already his. They were motionless for a moment, their minds racing. He cupped her head in his hands and began to gently kiss her lips, each kiss lingering more tenderly, more passionately, until she drew him to her and they stood enfolded - lost in each other.

When they returned to the house Gertrud noticed the difference in them; the fragile hopes they had carried for each other as they had stepped outside had now blossomed, and she instinctively knew that the ease of gesture and smiling confidence which now united them could only have come from a declaration of the love which she had witnessed steadily grow. She embraced them both, 'And tonight we will have a special dinner for you Karl, to say a very sad goodbye... and, I think, seeing you together like this it's a special night for you too, Julie, am I right?'

Julie bowed her head slightly, her expression still brimming with happiness, 'You are right, yes. I am very happy, despite everything, I am very happy.'

Gertrud and Albert did not deny their guests anything that night. Albert had drawn on all his reserves of guile to obtain everything they could want and they ate, drank, and toasted happily until nearly midnight. Finally, when all was done and they sat in the living room with liqueurs and *real* coffee from Spain, Albert produced his guitar and began to play with the most enjoyable light-heartedness and dexterity. As he did so Gertrud quietly regaled Julie with her tales of visiting Hitler in Obersalzberg. 'It was the 7th of August '39, the most boring night of my life, no really, I'm serious! Hitler always talks

178

and generally repeats himself three of four times – he's *so* dull. We women are just decorative of course and don't even *think* of smoking, *that's* for men! It is very petty bourgeois - lots of affectations and hand kissing and lots of fawning and God, the late nights! You know, his regular guests used to try desperately to keep visitors from raising his war service - kicks under the table that sort of thing. If that failed, we could be there 'till 2-3am. I almost preferred the sort of company we kept when Albert was a Franconian bank clerk!'

Julie smiled, delighted by Gertrud's outrageousness and also quietly flattered by the confidence she seemed to place in her.

Gertrud was now happily under the influence of her second Grand Marnier. 'He was friends with Julius Streicher for ages, but they fell out. Big bull of a man - never understood what he had to bring to the Party and such a vile mouth. Called Albert 'Röhm's other *chauffeur*'! Nothing wrong with Albert's little *chauffeur,* of course! Perfect in fact…always took me where I wanted to go!'[2]

Albert sat down next to them sensing his wife was in need of moral support. As he did so Julie realised that she didn't really know him at all. The public face of Forster and the Albert who had just strummed so joyfully on the guitar seemed two entirely different people. He rubbed his hands with relish, 'Heard an excellent story today, from Dieter of course, it's the honest truth *he* says. Anyway as you know you can't listen to the BBC, so there's this mother of a Luftwaffe pilot who's shot down. She thinks he's dead and arranges a funeral. But before she does she gets three different letters from neighbours and friends to tell her that he is not dead at all - he was captured by the British and his name was read out on the BBC. So, like a good German, she reports them to the police and all are arrested. Then there is this other mother, her son is in a U boat. It's reported sunk with all hands so she arranges a funeral, and again she receives letters from friends and neighbours telling her his name was on the BBC, and he was captured. But she doesn't know what to do; does she cancel the funeral and thereby arouse suspicion and betray her friends, or does she go ahead, knowing he is alive. Anyway, she holds a family

---

[2] Streicher, the publisher of many semi-pornographic and anti-Semitic newspapers, had accused Albert Forster of being a homosexual in the late 1930s. Ernst Röhm had allegedly been found in bed with his chauffeur on the night of his arrest and murder by the SS during the 'Night of the Long Knives' in 1934.

conference and they agree a strategy. So the next day everyone attends his funeral and then go to a party to celebrate his capture. Only in Germany! It's true I tell you, perfectly true…more bubbly?' Julie smiled, still quietly fascinated by the many dimensions to his character.

It was one fifteen before the party broke up. Karl and Julie ventured for one last time into the garden. It was unseasonably cold and their feet crushed the crisp frosty grass beneath them as they walked in the moonlight. The night sky, undimmed by lights from the house, was dazzling in its intensity. They kissed and held each other, unwilling to break the spell that now fell over them in the pale glow of the moon. It seemed that they walked in silence for hours before succumbing to their exhaustion and then slowly went back into the silent house. Somewhere a clock struck three. Julie paused in the hallway, 'I just wish you could ask my father and I could tell him about you. That would make my happiness complete.'

They ascended the stairs quietly and stood facing each other on the landing, unsure how to part this last time. Then they suddenly embraced, passionately, desperately; holding each other as tightly as they could. His lips lingered as he kissed her forehead, breathing in the sweet smell of her hair. 'Soon…let it all be over soon.' she whispered softly. They kissed tenderly one last time and then returned to their rooms, to sleep fitfully until dawn.

In the early morning, after breakfast, they all gathered to wish Karl farewell. He knew he would be unable to maintain any pretence with Julie as he had done the last time they parted in Posen but wanted to appear, as far as possible, composed - if only for the memory he would leave behind with her. Anticipating this, Albert and Gertrud said farewell to him in the library on their own, leaving Julie and Karl to endure their own more painful parting in the privacy of the living room. It was an act of discretion he found strangely affecting.

By the time he stepped into the living room, the car was already waiting outside to take him to the station. He found Julie in front of the fireplace, unable to face him. He put down his bag and walked over to her, but she remained as she was. He placed his hands on her shoulders and kissed her on the neck tenderly. When she turned she tried to collect herself and wipe away her tears. Her voice was distraught, 'I can't live without you Karl. Promise me...promise me you will come back.' After a moment staring into each other's eyes he stood back, his hands resting on her shoulders. He fixed her resolutely 'I will come back, I promise you. And I will write every day and you must do the same.' She nodded and he kissed her once more, closing his eyes as he did so. Then he let go and turned quickly, understanding that to look back was unendurable to them both and knowing that, whatever lay ahead, his pledge to her would remain.

Chapter 17

The weeks that followed Karl's departure were initially barren of news. Gertrud and the children became Julie's constant companions and she immersed herself in their company to fend off her anxieties. Then, after three weeks, his first letter arrived and after this Julie always greeted the post, her mood wavering between wild excitement and sullen dejection. But Karl did write often, as he had promised, and sometimes, where gaps emerged, letters would arrive together, bringing her much distraction and relief.

Julie soon realised that however strong the feelings had been between them, the army's claim on Karl was now stronger and more immediate. What he described of his initial training, and his comrades, made her realise that the bonds he was making would only strengthen and deepen, while their own would become strained by distance and the passing of time. Most of all she could see from the letters that he was becoming a soldier and an officer - his language more concise, his opinions more trenchant, and his desire to fight, unflinching.

However, once posted, he was reluctant to say more than a few words about his circumstances, or where he was. And so, in her fevered imagination, what little action there was in the 'phoney war' on the Western Front inevitably involved him and the possibility of his being wounded, or killed.

Early in the morning on the 10th of May 1940, Gertrud came to Julie's room in a state of high excitement and stayed with her while she dressed. 'It was on the radio this morning; the blow in the West has fallen: Holland, Belgium, Luxembourg – we're moving forward. The Führer has spoken and says this battle will decide the next thousand years.'

Julie sat at the dressing table subdued, her mind racing with fear and apprehension, while Gertrud began to brush her hair. 'A thousand years…what use is that to anyone? I want to know about tomorrow…next week. Where will we be then…and where will Karl be?'

Gertrud met Julie's eyes in the mirror and smiled, 'It will all be over by the end of the year, Julie. It won't be like before - at least that's what Albert says. We shall be sightseeing in Paris by the summer. These modern conflicts are over in weeks not years. I mean, the British abandoned Norway with hardly a fight and how many weeks did that take?'

Julie sighed, 'If we are in Paris by the summer and Karl is back here and out of uniform, then I will be truly happy.'

'And you promise you won't fret over him?'

Julie shrugged, 'How can I Gertrud?'

'Because life must go on Julie, and there is nothing to be gained – nothing. And…we also have the children to think of.'

'Yes Gertrud….I know you're right, but I can't help thinking about him – where he is, the dangers he is facing.'

'Thinking is one thing, Julie, I know you'll worry, but don't let it rule your life. Wait for news. Please say you'll try.'

'Yes, I promise.'

'Good! Then until we know more, until there is real news, let's change the subject completely. *Now*, Albert asked me to talk to you. We're having a dinner party in two weeks' time for Herr Krebs and his wife and a few of the city bigwigs. Frau Krebs studied the piano you know but gave it up. When I mentioned you she wondered if you would like some of her old music scores - she offered to bring a few of them with her.'

'That would be *very* kind. How generous of her. But I sometimes wonder what happened to my collection of old scores – I do miss them. Some were my mother's. I took so many clothes out of my suitcase to keep them with me and then, apart from the *'Toccata'*…it was lost. It's probably still there at the orphanage.'

'Oh, I don't think so Julie - not now, I'm sure I heard Albert say it had closed. He sent someone down there to see them after you came here – discreetly of course.'

Julie turned and looked up at Gertrud, 'That's really terrible – someone has closed it. Why? It was the only home most of them had ever known. The girls will be completely lost – and they were such good friends. We went through the whole liberation together. Sister Schmidt was like a mother to us - a good woman. I can't imagine how she would have felt. And I wonder what will have happened to Helene. I promised her we would remain friends. I promised to keep in touch. I thought perhaps, one day, I would find her.'

'Time moves on, Julie. Orphanages are very old fashioned now. There are lots of much more progressive ideas in Germany.'

'But they didn't need to change it. It was a happy place.'

'Well – what's done is done! Now Julie, Albert wants to know if you will play the Schumann *'Toccata'* at our dinner party - and perhaps some other music. He wants to impress people.' Gertrud was pinning Julie's hair in place and assumed an expression which suggested her continuation was a condition of acceptance. Julie's eyes narrowed in mock defiance, 'Oh yes. You win! It'll take my mind off things a little, but nothing will stop me worrying about Karl – however hard you try, Gertrud. Are you *sure* Albert won't be disturbed by my practice? I shall have to do lots of work on the *'Toccata'!'*

'Well...actually...that won't be such a problem as you might imagine. You see I've had the piano moved to the sitting room. It's all ready for you. He says you can practice until the smoke rises from your fingers.'

Julie looked at her long delicate nails and held them up to Gertrud, 'I will so miss them!'

Gertrud looked on sympathetically for a moment, 'I'll get my nail scissors!'

Office of the Gauleiter of Danzig West Prussia, (Rathaus) town hall, Danzig, 28 May 1940

Albert Forster looked at the bundle of papers in front of him and waved his arm at them, 'I rather thought we had put this all to bed, Hildebrandt; is this necessary?'

'It potentially concerns your relationship with Fräulein Scholl and that of your wife.'

Albert sat back, 'Alright, go ahead.'

'Well as you may remember I sent Epp down to dig around in Posen some months ago. He's made quite a few trips since then, but couldn't make any progress – nobody was talking. Then, last week, he met, through an intermediary, a man called Gottfried Vogler who works as Grieser's Chief of Staff on the civilian side. Vogler it turns out knew Hertz and Gunther Rath very well. His story though, was not about his boss Grieser, it was about Koppe. A lot of what he said only confirms what we suspected; Koppe had got wind of Grieser's dirty

184

little business with Julie Scholl and no doubt has some evidence which means Grieser has been completely neutralised – Koppe even sent Grieser's wife packing to Germany. No, the real story is about Koppe and Eric Scholl.'

Forster leaned forward, 'Julie's father?'

'It seems that a Captain Gerhard of the Berlin Security Police arrived in Posen asking about Julie Scholl around the time she came to Danzig with Gunther Rath. He had a private meeting with Koppe, a one-to-one, and asked to meet a Gestapo man called Müller – Grieser's liaison man with Koppe. It seems Gerhard wanted to find out about Julie Scholl's activities in Posen and Müller had pulled her from an interrogation for no apparent reason. We assume of course that whole interrogation was to soften her up as bait for Grieser, but it seems Koppe was reluctant to share his little intrigues with Berlin. It also seems that this Gerhard was connected right to the top and Koppe was shitting himself that Müller would let on. Anyway, two days later Müller is found in the river Warta with his brains blown out. It seems someone didn't want to rely on his sense of discretion – either that or Grieser took revenge. So, when Julie Scholl could not be found and Müller turned up dead Gerhard lost his temper and summoned the big boys down from Berlin - except the boys never arrived. Instead he got a call - nobody knows who from - and went back to Berlin himself, with nothing but the file of papers from Julie Scholl's initial interrogation to show for his efforts. And now, when I try to trace Julie's father, Eric Scholl has disappeared too. His secretary is privately saying he went down to Posen looking for Julie, but one of my sources in Heydrich's office says that he's in a cell in Tegel prison awaiting trial – that he was lifted off the streets without ever getting to the station.'

'And Gerhard didn't ask any more questions about Julie - about where she was? He didn't think Müller's death a little coincidental.'

'He was *recalled.*'

'That's bloody odd isn't it? Not the usual practice. If they wanted the father they would certainly want the daughter. So, what are the charges against Eric Scholl?'

'Heydrich's office won't discuss it officially. But there's talk he fell out with Funk and leaked some figures to the army. If he goes to trial he'll go before a People's Court and since that's held in closed session I doubt we will even know the sentence, let alone the charge.'

'Two judges and three Party members?'

'They'll get the verdict they want. And my enquiries have generated their own questions, so I'm keeping my head down for now. I can't push any harder.'

'So why didn't Koppe raise this at our meeting – we even admitted we have Scholl. Why not tell Berlin she's here – get her arrested and carted off to Ravensbrück? I mean, what possible threat could she be to Grieser if her father is now an enemy of the Reich.'

'This is the interesting part: Epp asked Vogler, *If Koppe knows Scholl is in Danzig why not tip off Captain Gerhard?* ' But he said there was a group, Koppe, Kellerman, Dr Fischer, and a female overseer called Grese. They met the day after Scholl escaped and Hertz hanged himself – he knew because Koppe had arranged a meeting with Grieser and cancelled it at the last moment due to an *urgent* matter he had to attend to. Then the Race and Settlement Team was disbanded and the orphans from Thorner Strasse – the Prussian Ballet School where Julie stayed - were shipped out to Gnesen. There was talk of an incident there but nobody knew what it was. The critical thing is that Vogler thinks Captain Gerhard was leant on from the top to drop the hunt for Julie Scholl. He was all for taking Posen apart to find out what had happened to her and then he walked away, and he thinks it was Koppe who called Berlin, and used up a lot of favours, to get Gerhard recalled.

'Epp's view is that it is *Koppe,* not Grieser, who wants Julie Scholl to stay in place here – that he wants her isolated.'

'Meaning?'

'Our guess is there's someone or something that's intended to find its way to her, something in transit, a film perhaps, like the one we recovered from Rath's accommodation. But whatever it is, it will come to Julie Scholl, she can't go to it. And Koppe seems to be more worried about what Berlin would do if this missing evidence turned up there than he is about us. Koppe still assumes we'll do a deal – that's his calculation.'

'He's a shrewd operator.'

'But is he a shrewd judge of character?

Albert didn't answer but remained stern faced for a moment, 'And what does Grieser think?'

'Grieser doesn't think, apparently - not any more. He signs the papers, drinks, eats, shits and masturbates a great deal - I would imagine.'

A wry smile crossed Albert's face. 'So you think this is all about the orphanage where Julie stayed - an *incident* - not about Grieser raping Julie Scholl at all? You think Koppe was trying to lead us off the scent when he said Grieser was his principal?'

'Grieser's not worth it on his own. Koppe's pawned the family silver for this. Whatever he's doing he's negotiating for himself, and the orphanage must be the key, it's the only thing the players all share in common. Look at it this way; Dr Hertz - the duty doctor at the orphanage - kills himself after freeing Julie; Rath is dead, murdered after bringing her to Danzig; Julie is almost murdered after the hospital stunt, and Müller is shot at close range and dumped in the Warta River, presumably so he doesn't speak to Captain Gerhard about who gave the order to lift Julie from the interrogation.'

Albert sat back, 'So where are Overseer Grese and Dr Fischer now?'

'Grese has been promoted twice within Ravensbrück since then, and Dr Fischer is at Dachau doing some sort of research.'

'Out of reach.' Albert murmured.

'So what will you tell Julie Scholl?'

'Her father has to be accounted for some time.'

'She can't go to the trial – if there is one.'

'Then we have to lie, don't we.' Albert closed the file, 'I'll have to let Gertrud in on some of this. But we'll wait until after it's over before we tell Julie – so it's too late for her to do anything. Then we only need to deal with the consequences.'

Hildebrandt stood, 'So that's as far as I've got.'

Albert toyed with a pen on his desk. 'Good work. But you know I'm almost relieved – for Julie's sake. At least we know now – it was the uncertainty that was difficult to deal with.'

Hildebrandt eyed him warily, 'You should be careful...these domestic arrangements of yours. Remember, she's your hostage...don't become hers.'

Chapter 18

Country Residence of the Gauleiter, Danzig West Prussia, June 3, 1940

Julie and Gertrud descended the stairs that evening with a radiance that left Albert feeling elated with pride at his wife and covetous of Julie. He kissed Gertrud on the cheek and Julie on the hand. Then, standing between them, their arms entwined, he entered the living room.

The guests had already arrived and were assembled, enjoying champagne and canapés. They seemed to Julie very much as Gertrud had described: middle aged, middle rank, and middle brow. Ferdinand Schörner was tall, slim, bald, and rather self-effacing, but with a striking moustache which lent him an air of military distinction. Dieter Yorck was in his sixties, with a shock of white hair and a mature beard which lent him the character of a minor prophet. Kurt and Anneliese Alfarth were in awe of their surroundings, timid and rather too self-deprecating to be interesting. After a few moments in their company, Julie seized the chance to meet Frau Krebs. She was in her late thirties, of distinguished bearing and with an intelligent if slightly severe expression. Her younger and sternly handsome husband stood to one side, passively observing as Julie and his wife talked.

'I particularly wanted to thank you for the music Frau Krebs; I can't tell you how much enjoyment it will bring me. I hope I shall be able to return the kindness later by playing for you.'

Frau Krebs smiled gently, 'I used to like playing, but my heart went out of it when we came here.'

'Oh, and where do you come from?'

'We were in Vienna – such a beautiful city, so much culture. Hermann is a policeman so we must go where we are needed.' She paused and extended her hand, 'My name is Edie by the way and you are Julie? Tell me, Julie, are you especially keen on any German composers? I am told you like Schumann.'

Julie nodded, 'And Schubert.'

'And others?'

'I like all music of merit.'

This answer seemed to trouble Edie. 'You know, when I was a girl my mother took me to see Mahler at the Philharmonic – 1910, I think. What a disappointment. Those symphonies, all terribly brilliant and clever don't you think - to take all the elements of German symphonic tradition and native genius and then turn them into a Wurlitzer. How he must have marvelled at good Austrian manners when we applauded his efforts. I suppose they had *merit*, but as what? Clever mimicry, confections, parody – even perhaps an attempt at Jewish humour? So, you see, *merit* is a strange word. Ah well, now we have Strauss – and he *is* a genius!'

Edie looked at Julie and noticed an expression of distance, perhaps concealing dissent. She glanced toward Gertrud, indicating a desire to move on, 'Well, enjoy the music, I shan't need it back.'

When they were about to go to dinner Dieter accosted Julie with a mischievous smile. He took her hand and assumed a noble bearing, 'Before I submit myself to judgment by the Lord may I sin one last time?'

Gertrud looked over and shook her head, 'Dieter, stop it!'

He stepped back and with an affected anguish, 'It is amazing how complete is the delusion that beauty is goodness. Pray child, are you good?'

Julie stood her ground, her lips quivering with a suppressed smile, 'I am not sure it is for me to judge.'

Thereupon he locked his arm with hers, 'Then I shall take you to dinner and find out!'

Over dinner it seemed that Kurt Alfarth had the greatest command of the situation on the Western Front and Julie listened anxiously while pretending to be focussed on an anecdote of Ferdinand's, '...just two weeks ago we started, it's unbelievable; Holland overrun, four fifths of Belgium, the French with their backs against Paris and a million men – the French and British – trapped and encircled on the Channel. If you see the army in action, the tanks, the Stukas, the artillery; the same tactics again and again just blasting them aside. The French have no answer. I tell you it will be days.'

Dieter leant over from his place next to her, 'I was in the last war, you know. Do you have anyone out there, a brother perhaps?'

'A fiancé.'

'Are you worried?'

'Of course.'

189

He patted her hand, 'No ring yet?'

'No.'

He smiled, 'That's the way it was then, too.'

'Will he be alright do you think – as a doctor.'

'You know more people died of Spanish flu after the last war than died in it. Don't worry, he will be alright.'

Anneliese leaned forward, 'Albert says you came from Warsaw - that you escaped. Was it very frightening?'

Julie hesitated, 'Yes, I suppose it was.'

'I remember Warsaw…,' Dieter interjected, '…a Russian city then and looked it. The architecture of Catherine the Great and nothing that you might call Polish about it - more like Paris.'

Ferdinand interjected, 'But you could say that about the whole Polish claim to some kind of statehood. I mean look at it: Austro Hungarian in the south, Prussian in the west and north, Russian in the east and railway networks to match. *If thou judge a man by his deeds'* then what have the Poles built for themselves – where is the state? Everything of substance or permanence is the product of others - I'm thinking of St Mary's Church in Cracow, Wawel Castle, Lemberg Cathedral, St Johns Church in Thorn, the old Gothic Cathedral of St John's in Warsaw,' Dieter looked at Ferdinand, surprised at his evident command of the subject, 'You're a scholar?'

'I studied medieval architecture at Munich…a long time ago.'

'Then you may also know that Copernicus and Hoene were of German origin. I have seen Poles try to claim them as Polish.'

Hermann spoke across them both, 'I look forward to them claiming Field Marshall Kluge, Von Hindenburg and Merten as their own! They were all sons of Posen. No, Poland was meaningless – the bastard creation of Versailles. The rump of Poland is Cracow and Warsaw – the old Grand Duchy. That's where the Poles belong now and from ages past – the General Government – and they will now have to make do with Frank rather than some senile old Polish general.'

Albert looked across, 'They may be Slavs, Hermann, but the Führer would rather have taken *them* as allies than the Soviets, but they wouldn't deal, they believed they could keep it all because of those idiotic British and French guarantees - and now they've got nothing.'

190

Dieter tapped Julie's hand again, 'I always seem to start something!'

Julie smiled, 'Have you worked with Albert long? What do you do?'

'Oh, I'm an administrator – well, a curator really. I deal with antiquities, cultural artefacts. The army is always coming across things and they tend to get sent through my office for classification, valuation, and cataloguing. But I'm afraid Albert got into a lot of trouble about his appointments – we're not really *old fighters*, you see. Most of Albert's appointees are just people who are good at their jobs - not Party men. I've been in this line of work for thirty years, but the Party wanted their own man – an amateur, an SA man from Hanover. Albert said *no*. He's been the Gauleiter here since 1930, but not in power so to speak, that only happened last autumn. After all, this was the first part of the Reich where National Socialism really took hold and Albert's very keen on putting the principles into operation...He just isn't so keen on the more thuggish element. Oh, I must be boring you.' He paused, 'Do you want to hear a story?' Julie nodded and then noticed the other conversations around her ebb, as Dieter looked about him, drawing in his audience, 'A man from Cologne told me this - true, I promise. Well, you know how many uniforms there are these days - lots of them are new and unfamiliar and people just salute and go on their way. Anyway an RAF pilot bales out of his plane and lands near the city. He takes off his thick leather flying jacket so he will look smart in his uniform and puts on his cap and starts to walk into the city to surrender. It's a Sunday, so it's very quiet on the streets. When he gets to the suburbs he sees the police and they salute him from across the street and walk on. Then some soldiers pass him and click their heels, salute and pass on. It starts to rain so he thinks he'll try his luck at the cinema. As it happens, all RAF men get ten Marks 'just in case', so he hands it over to the cashier and asks for a two Reichsmark seat, but she gives him back nine Marks explaining that men in uniform go half price. After the film he walks around 'till midnight looking for a police station and eventually finds one. Whereupon he complains about how difficult it is to get arrested in the heart of a German city. The police don't believe him so they summon the cashier from the cinema just to see. *'Did you sell this man a ticket to the performance this evening'*, they ask her. *'Certainly she replied, half price like all men in uniform'*. Then, proudly noticing the initials on his uniform,

191

she says '*It isn't every day I can welcome a Reichs Arbeit Führer. Me; I know what RAF stands for.*'

When the chuckling had died down Gertrud clapped her hands, 'Oh, go on Dieter, tell another?'

He thought for a moment and then smiled mischievously, 'Well…it goes like this; after the recent bombing raids on the German coast the air-raid protection chief in Hamburg advised the people to go to bed early and try to snatch two or three hours sleep before the bombings start. Some take the advice, most do not. Well, the Hamburgers say that those who take the advice arrive in the cellar after an alarm and greet their neighbours with a *Good Morning*. This means they have been to sleep. Others arrive and say, *Good Evening,* which means they have not. A few arrive and say, *Heil Hitler!* which means they have always been asleep.'

Julie began to smile and others around the table who had been surreptitiously listening gave muffled laughs, but Edie Krebs looked on, stony faced. 'In Vienna you would be arrested for telling that story.'

Albert caught the sudden frisson of tension among his guests and broke from his conversation with Anneliese, fixing Edie with a disarming smile. 'But, Frau Krebs, we are not in Vienna, and we are not in Berlin, we are in Danzig, West Prussia, and this is my home.'

'Well, of course, Gauleiter Forster.'

Hermann Krebs remained unmoved by his wife's evident discomfort, dabbing his lips with a napkin, eyes wandering around the table, but remaining silent.

After dinner, as they smoked and sipped their coffee and liqueurs, Julie played some light music which she had found in the library. Finally, when these salon pieces were exhausted, Albert stood and announced that she would play Schumann's *'Toccata'* at his special request. Then Julie began to play - with passion and verve, and all sat spellbound as her fingers raced and fluttered over the keys. Hermann in particular watched intently as her body swayed and rocked with the pulse of the music. It was a gaze not lost on his wife.

When Julie stood to acknowledge their applause she could hear Edie's astringent voice articulating in a manner calculated to carry, 'You know, Clara Schumann probably played that piece very much as Julie played it, she too was diminutive, though of course Clara

Schumann was a touring virtuoso by the time she was eighteen. I'm not sure Fräulein Scholl will ever quite match that…with the war you understand.'

Julie stood and waited for the applause to die down, pretending not to have heard, but quietly humiliated, 'And now, a little something to finish - a *Serenade in E flat.*' Then, as she sat, she caught Edie's eye and registered her icy hostility.

When she finished her audience murmured in appreciation and then clapped again. Hermann looked at her, his piercing eyes fixing her until she could not do otherwise than return his gaze. His face remained severe and unsmiling. He approached her boldly and bent down, his lips hovering a few inches above her hand in stiff respectful acknowledgment. 'You are to be congratulated…' he said, finally broaching a smile, '…such a lovely turn of phrase.' And then he added quietly, 'My wife loves talking about culture, but please do not be offended, she claimed some modest talent once and it tends to make her rather insufferable on these occasions.'

'Thank you those are… kind words.'

He studied her with a disconcerting intensity, unwilling to let the moment pass, 'And if I may be of personal service please do not hesitate to call on me at *any* time.'

Julie stepped back and glanced at Gertrud, who registered her look of unease and discreetly joined them, at which Hermann quickly took his leave.

It was one o'clock in the morning before the guests finally dispersed and Julie could sit alone for a moment with Gertrud. She recounted her brief but awkward exchange with Hermann Krebs to Gertrud's shameless delight, *'Insufferable…'* oh I wish I'd heard that, but my word Julie, fancy making eyes at you in front of his wife like that. No wonder she was in such a foul mood – you can hardly blame her!'

Julie blushed putting her hands to her cheeks, 'Surely not…how embarrassing!'

'Julie, really, only you could have missed the tension between them. From the moment they arrived Edie was on edge - as soon as she saw you were unaccompanied, young, and desperately attractive. She has probably had a lifetime of keeping him in check. No, Julie, it didn't matter what you did, your card was marked.'

193

'But who is he Gertrud? He has such a strong presence. I found him rather intimidating and slightly unpleasant to be honest. Surely he's not *just* a policeman?'

Gertrud raised an eyebrow, 'Oh, Albert doesn't always tell me *everything* about our guests and when he doesn't it's generally best not to pry. You have to be careful, Julie, sometimes it's better not to ask *exactly* what people do, not here, not in the *wild East*.' Gertrud stood and held out her hand to help Julie up from the chair, 'And now it must be time for bed? Ah! Just one final thing; Albert asked me who wrote that delightful piece you finished with – the *Serenade*. He thought it would sound well on the guitar.'

Julie stood, 'It was just some good music Gertrud, sometimes it's better not to ask *exactly* what the music is, not here in Danzig West Prussia.'

Gertrud's face erupted in a knowing grin and they began to walk to the stairs. Her voice was joyously conspiratorial, 'I'll tell Albert it was Chopin, by the morning he'll have forgotten he was serenaded to bed by a Jew!'

The following morning a letter arrived from Karl and Julie settled herself in the living room to read it. As she poured herself some coffee Gertrud emerged from the library to join her.

'Is there anything wrong Gertrud?'

'Could that letter wait a moment – I'm sorry.'

'Of course.'

Gertrud sat, looking uncomfortable, 'I have to go away for a week, perhaps a little longer. Could you look after Inga and Peter for me? I will arrange for extra help from the staff for you. You know how I hate leaving things to strangers where the children are concerned.'

'Gertrud, I would be happy to, but…is it your health?'

'No, but that's where I would prefer to leave it. It's a family matter, Julie. Albert wants it to stay that way.'

'Certainly.'

Gertrud still seemed unsettled and Julie could see that she was struggling. 'Will you stay with us Julie? I mean…until the war is over? I'm not sure I could get used to living without you. I think I would feel very lonely here.'

Julie paused, 'There's something wrong, Gertrud, what is it? Why are you suddenly talking like this?'

194

Gertrud looked away, distracted, 'You are like a sister to me. I need a friend here and you have been that to me, but suddenly I'm afraid I'll lose you. I want you to promise me you won't go.'

Julie sat back, 'Oh Gertrud don't be silly. I can never repay you for what you have done. I do miss my father, and I miss Karl, too. I suppose I'll have to live with the war like everybody else. I shall be happy so long as I hear from both of them again soon, and I hope, whatever happens in the future, we will always be friends. Of course I'll stay if you'll have me. But what *is* it you came to tell me?'

'No, not now Julie. I might have said something but I find…I can't…sorry.'

Gertrud stood and kissed Julie on the forehead before walking back into the library. Julie could feel that something had passed between them in that moment which had affected Gertrud deeply, but could not understand what it could have been. She sat unhappily with this enigma for a few minutes and then turned impatiently to Karl's letter. It was dated the 24th of June 1940 and was written in small neat writing on good French writing paper,

"Dear Julie, Today I walked around Paris with Walter, my trusted guide and friend from basic training. There were no buses, cars or taxis and the Parisians who fled our advance have yet to return, so it is like a city of ghosts. I walked down the Place Vendome and thought of Napoleon. We then pushed on through the Tuileries, and it was pleasing to see so many children playing. I thought of you and Peter and Inga and wished so much you were here, they would have loved the merry-go-round, and swings. It was such a hot day and we stopped to admire the view up the Tuileries to the Champs-Elysees, with the silhouette of the Arc de Triomphe on the horizon. Then we went through the Louvre and across the Seine. The fishermen were busy and it reminded me of my childhood, when my father and I would sometimes surprise mother with some fish from the local river. Then we went down the Seine to Notre-Dame. The sandbags had been taken away from the central portal but inside was a disappointment as the original rose window and two transept windows were gone. But from the river we had seen the Gothic façade in all its glory. Finally Walter and I went for a beer at the Balzar, next to the Sorbonne. It was a magical day.

You would be amazed at our situation here. We are in a château outside the city. We are treated like kings and we eat the most

195

superb food. Today we had caviar, roast duck, crepes, fine wines and good cognac from the Champagne region. I have bought some wonderful soaps and perfumes for you. I hope they will arrive soon. ...I miss you so much....PS. Just as I was going to take this to the Field Post I had news that I am to be given some leave - at last! I will have 7 days! Can you imagine how this has tormented me? I have thought of every conceivable combination of ways to see you but since it is two days by train to Danzig – at least – and two days return I wondered if we might meet in Berlin? That would mean two extra days together. Would it be safe for you now? Perhaps Albert might have a view...?"

Julie got up and walked briskly to the library door. She knocked gently and when no answer came she entered.

Albert was not at his desk but at the end of the room on the sofa cradling Gertrud in his arms. She was murmuring to him inaudibly. Then, without a word, their eyes met and in a kindly way he shook his head. Without being seen by Gertrud, Julie turned, embarrassed at her intrusion, and retraced her steps.

These events sent Julie into despair. For the first time she felt alone. While Karl now grew in stature in her eyes, she remained as in aspic, dependent on Gertrud and the children for her entire existence. But she knew she was not *their* entire world - how could she be, she was a guest, a stranger, an outsider. Such thoughts fed on her insecurities. Was Gertrud really so close to her, or was this pity for her? Would Karl want to know her after experiencing the pleasures of Paris? Suddenly she felt she had to get to Berlin to see him - that it was the only way to be sure of him. She suddenly felt could no longer remain, that she must break free and breathe again.

Julie and Gertrud dined alone that evening. As they did so Gertrud glanced at Karl's letter which lay open next to her on the table, while Julie looked on expectantly. Finally Gertrud put down her knife and fork in a state of exasperation, 'I just can't see if he's saying he won't come to Danzig unless you go to Berlin, or whether it's really about how much time you spend together. Will he come regardless?'

Julie sensed that Gertrud was being evasive and suddenly felt irritated that a woman who shared her own life with the man she loved could be so determined to overlook her own desire to share a little of the same pleasure. 'But I *want* to go to Berlin. I *want* five days with him and I want to try and find my father. I want them to meet each other.'

'And what about the children?' Gertrud said curtly, 'I have to go away - or have you forgotten?'

Julie wilted, 'I am sorry Gertrud. How can I explain this - except as an affair of the heart. And I am ashamed to admit that I hadn't actually thought about your trip.'

Gertrud stood abruptly and went to the cigarette box on the mantelpiece and lit one with a heavy marble lighter. Her inner tension was now all too visible. She never smoked at dinner and hated the brand her husband kept in there for guests. Julie stood and extended her hand in a gesture of reconciliation. 'Shall we go to the living room; we don't seem very hungry do we?' Gertrud's expression softened and they walked through to the sofas in front of the fireplace.

Gertrud sat staring into the flames drawing anxiously on her cigarette. 'Julie, you're still only sixteen, and I'm thirty. Sometimes it's easy to forget that – I know I do, frequently.' She smiled gently. 'I had no idea what to expect from you when you arrived. At first I just felt pity – as we all did; lying there, day after day, sometimes shivering or weeping, sometimes crying out in your sleep. We could only guess what you must have gone through. And I have to admit, I didn't understand Karl's feelings towards you in the beginning. He was so attentive, so beside himself with concern for you and to me you simply looked like a helpless waif. But later, when I spoke to him about you, I understood. It wasn't pity, it was devotion. He would have stayed with you whatever had happened – however things had turned out, simply on the basis of the person he'd known and fallen for in Posen. But that's the difference isn't it, between men and women, they can afford to be like that. For them everything can be so clear cut. For us it's not that easy. I simply can't look at you as an outsider anymore, not even simply a friend. How could I when the children are so close to you and love you so much. You have become more of a sister to me and I don't think Albert really understands that – the bond between women, the trust we hold in each other.'

Gertrud sighed, 'The simple truth is that I won't lie to you, but neither will I dishonour my husband. And the fact is that Albert brought you here because it is the one place you could be truly safe, never expecting we should become so close. But Albert is also the Gauleiter – a position of trust bestowed on him personally by the Führer and I am his wife. So I am torn between you, and I don't

197

always know how to deal with it, and sometimes I can't follow my conscience.'

Julie took Gertrud's hand, 'Sister Schmidt used to say there was no shame in the truth – but then we lived in an orphanage. Here it's much less obvious where the harm lies, isn't it. I can't expect you to tell me everything – I understand that. I'm just glad to have found this friendship and I'm sorry you've suffered so much over this. But I do understand, Gertrud. I will never speak to anyone about us, about our lives, our conversations, our confidences – I promise. I am happy enough that you see me as a sister.'

Gertrud clasped her hand more tightly, 'Then listen on Julie, please! Your past…it isn't behind you, it's all around us…*that* is what I have been wanting to tell you.' Gertrud nervously lit another cigarette. 'Albert says people are watching and waiting – that you are still in danger. And remember, last November you were going to be murdered by men who came to Danzig with orders to silence you. Hildebrandt saved you only by chance. What has changed since then, Julie? Do you think they have forgotten you? Do you think you would leave this house without it being noticed? Do you think they wouldn't follow you to Berlin?'

Julie brooded, 'So you're saying I'm trapped?'

Gertrud tapped the ash off her cigarette with such agitation that it broke in two. 'For your protection you must stay.'

Julie clenched her fists in impotent rage and beat them on her knees, her voice pleading, 'But I don't understand. What have I done? Why won't they leave me alone?'

Gertrud sat, quietly looking on with compassion and shaking her head, 'I don't know, Julie…I really don't know.'

Julie tried to steady herself and then stood and went to the sideboard, removing the bundle of music Edie had given her. She undid the string and began to look through the scores.'

Gertrud looked on perplexed, 'What are you doing?'

'You know, Gertrud, the thing that really frightens me is not dying or even being murdered in my bed, but being alive; the choices I should be making now about the rest of my life. I can't live my life like this. I'm young. I should be learning, studying…discovering who I am. So, I must grab what I can with both hands.' She shrugged, 'And while I am here Karl is changing - building on his experiences and seeing new things. His expectations of me won't be fixed on what I was, or what he was. When he comes back he will expect me to have grown too. How can I do that if I'm still trapped like a child?'

'And the music...?'

'I've been thinking about when the war is over. If I can't be like him and travel and become more interesting, then I can at least offer Karl an accomplished companion in other ways – he used to like the company of artists in Berlin. I shall build my repertoire and my technique until I can take to the concert stage.'

Gertrud put her arm around Julie, 'But you won't leave here?'

'No. Karl wouldn't dream of putting me in danger and I'm sure he will come, even if it is only for three days...So when do you go?'

'I'm going to Switzerland on Tuesday.'

Julie sat back astonished, 'Switzerland?! You *are* ill.'

'No, no, no!' She paused, searching for a suitable expression, 'It's where we keep our *insurance.*' Gertrud withdrew her arm and held Julie's hand, 'You see, the whole National Socialist movement was built on old street fighters at first; the veterans, the Steel Helmets, Free Corps and the SA - not people like us. Then, later, the movement didn't need them so much, it needed other men like Albert, Darré, Rosenberg, Göring, Schacht and Frank, to manage things. They got rid of Röhm and a lot of the SA radicals, but the gangsters are still there and a lot of them are resentful that they've been passed over. We need to have protection – so Albert can do his job without rivals stabbing him in the back.

'I suppose in the Reich you don't so much cultivate friends as *lock them in,* so they know the consequences if you go down. It's a Darwinism of sorts – a means of influence and survival. And so that's why I go; to lodge papers, photographs, old letters, statements.'

Julie shook her head, 'Is that why we have never invaded Switzerland?'

Gertrud laughed, 'Well if we did it would be the end of National Socialism!'

'And what about your friends?'

'Who - the sort of people you met the other night? No. There's just you.' She sighed, 'You can trust no one. Everyone is watching and listening. Everyone is an informer. Do you know how many letters and tip-offs Hilderbandt gets each day - dozens; some German denouncing his neighbour, his employer, his wife! The Hitler Youth spy on their parents, their parents spy on each other and the neighbours spy on them. Don't ever assume the person you're talking to means you well – they generally don't…and if they don't betray you now, there's always tomorrow.'

'But how do you cope, knowing that everyone is a potential informer.'

Gertrude smiled, 'I cope because apart from my good husband and my children, I have you.' Gertrud stood, 'And now I can relax again. I'm sorry it came out like that but I had to clear my mind – I had to say *something* to you. And now, let's go and make some coffee and forget about the whole thing.'

The following day Julie's heart leapt when Karl telephoned from Paris. She ran to the phone and seized it from Stephan breathlessly. But Karl was not as she expected. His tone was melancholic and subdued, distant, but still tender. This combined to set her mind racing with fears that his feelings for her had changed, that he had called to tell her he wanted to end their engagement. Then, quietly and solemnly, he explained that his mother had died and that he had obligations and duties as her only son which he could not, with any honour, ask others to undertake. She listened silently but could barely feel anything for his loss, or find words of condolence. Her hopes shattered, she understood even before he uttered those few deadly words, that he would have to give her up and go to Ulm for the funeral, and those precious few days together she had mapped out for his leave now vanished from within her grasp.

Finally he seemed distracted and apologised for having to go so soon. After a few gentle words of consolation, and words of affection, the line went dead. As she stood, tears welling up, she tried to remember those last precious phrases he had uttered. Had he said he loved her? Had he said he missed her as much as she had said she missed him? Did he sound upset that they would not be together? It seemed her senses had become deafened by her own intense misery and she could suddenly remember nothing.

She put the receiver down and sank to the floor. Those three days she could have lived for, but the emptiness that now lay ahead, the knowledge that she might not see him for six months, was impossible to live for. She felt bereft, her will to go on sapped, and she wept.

When Inga and Peter found her they sat with her silently on the floor, nestling close to her, holding her hands. She put her arms around them and kissed them each on the head. They could see and feel her misery and huddled closer. She shut her eyes and after a few moments felt her mother's calming presence, too.

When the clock struck noon the children stood and raised her up, slowly walking her towards the piano. Then they sat on the sofa expectantly, watching her. Julie stared at the keyboard for a moment and laid her fingers silently on the keys before falteringly beginning to play. And when, after a few minutes, she looked across at the children, they were smiling again.

Chapter 19

When Julie entered the conservatory for breakfast on the morning of Gertrud's departure she found the room filled with the scent of a multitude of flowers which Albert had arranged with great secrecy the previous afternoon. Albert had one hand on Gertrud's arm and was reading from the paper, *'Churchill's Answer – Cowardly Murdering of a Defenceless Population,'* his eyes scanned the paper, 'They've rejected the Führer's peace terms. They've bombed Bremen, Hamburg, Paderborn, Hagen, and Bochum. It talks of big civilian losses.' When he saw Julie he put the paper down. 'Do you have more news from Karl?' he said smiling. Julie noticed Gertrud look sharply at Albert, but he persisted tactlessly, 'Is he enjoying Paris?'

Julie spoke with an unusual acerbity, 'I'm sure he is, but his mother has died so he won't be coming to see us. I suppose it's a duty he must perform. It's a shame. Perhaps *next* year we shall see him.'

Gertrud turned to Julie, speaking quietly, 'Are you alright?'

Julie shrugged 'I've been a fool. I'm always fretting about Karl, about my father - it's so pointless. I'm not going to allow myself to dwell on things I can't do anything about - it upsets Inga and Peter. While you are away I shall be entirely theirs. I'm not going to think about anything, or anybody. They know where to find me when they have some time on their hands.'

Albert put the paper firmly to one side, 'Gertrud says you're not writing as much to Karl as you were. You mustn't lose heart. He needs those letters – ask any man who fought in the last war. They are what gives them hope, reminds them of who they are fighting for. Don't give up.'

Julie persisted in her coldness, 'I know my duties, Albert, and I take them seriously, but sometimes I can't think of anything to say and what I have said has been repeated in so many different ways. I'm afraid he will become tired of me. He's probably already wondering what he's got himself into. He must be meeting a lot of much more interesting people now he's got time on his hands in France.'

Albert pointedly changed the subject. 'We wondered if you would like Gertrud to bring back something - some books, or music?'

Julie's ill temper seemed to subside quickly into melancholia. 'That's very sweet of you but I still owe Karl for the flowers we gave to Beata. I couldn't in all conscience take more from you than you've given me already. I'm sorry, but I can't accept. Thank you.'

Albert and Gertrud exchanged glances. Then Gertrud remembered a half forgotten invitation, 'Oh, you will never believe who wants to come and see you while I'm away. Thank goodness I remembered!'

Julie looked up, suddenly engaged, 'Someone I know?'

'Edie Krebs!'

Julie giggled nervously and her mood seemed to lighten, 'But why on earth...she loathes me!'

'It seems she has found the score of some music for piano duet. She wants to come and play it through with you...on Saturday.'

Albert smiled, 'I will look after the children for a few hours – perhaps take them to Zoppot! Yes, I think Zoppot's far enough!'

Gertrud held his hand, 'Oh Albert, the children would adore that.'

Julie thought for a few moments and then tugged on Gertrud's arm discreetly. 'Thank you Gertrud, I'm sorry. It will do me good.'

Julie left Albert and Gertrud to their final farewell and took the children into the living room, where Peter and Inga contented themselves with Snakes and Ladders. She returned to the bundle of music Edie had left her. She had devoured the volume of Beethoven sonatas, but had not really delved further. She now flicked through the pages of each score looking for some indication that Edie might have studied the work. She wondered what her tastes might be, her abilities - whether something of her personality might be revealed - but found little.

It was near the bottom of the pile that she came upon a leather bound edition of Schubert's *'Impromptus'* with what she took to be the family monogram on the cover. On the inside of the title page she found an inscription and a short hand written poem: *'To my darling Hermann. This music I play for you alone. Edie, 20th February 1924, Penzing, Vienna.'* There followed a love poem inscribed before the Impromptu in G flat major:

'Thou art my soul, and thou my heart,
Thou all my joy and sorrow and art,
Thou art my world for life adoring,
My heaven art thou, wherein I am soaring,
My guardian angel, my better self!'

Julie carried the open score to the piano and placed it on the music stand. She played the music at sight, trying as she did so to equate the fierce character with whom she had sparred at dinner with this soulful, intimate, tender music, and the loving inscription. When she had finished Inga looked up, 'Julie, that is beautiful. Will you play it again?'

Julie picked up the handsome volume, 'Inga, I will play them all. And when Edie comes I will play them to her as well.'

The following Saturday was hot and airless. Julie greeted Edie wearing the lightest summer dress she could find and tried to appear, as far as possible, as though nothing had passed between them when they had last met. For her part Edie seemed more attentively courteous than Julie had nervously hoped for and had dressed likewise for comfort and coolness. They complimented each other on their appearance with a generosity that also seemed to set a different tone. They stood for a moment admiring the garden, went up the steps into the cool hallway, and then sat for a while with a pot of iced tea in the living room. 'You said you came from Vienna. I'd so love to go there, especially to see the music festivals and the opera. Is that where you were born?'

Julie's question seemed to elicit fond memories which Edie appeared happy to share. 'Oh no, I was born in Trieste; when it was part of Austria-Hungary of course. How things change. It was really lovely and I was such a happy child – my sister too. We moved to Vienna when I was seven or eight I think.'

'To Penzing?'

'How ever did you know that?'

'The address was in some music I found…in the scores you gave me.'

'Really? Something I gave you? Remind me - I must have forgotten.'

Julie went to the piano, opened the score of the *'Impromptus'* and began to play the one in G flat. She caught Edie only once from the corner of her eye and noticed that she sat motionless, bolt upright, her eyes closed her hands tightly clasped – the knuckles white and strained.

When she had finished she took the score back to the sofa and passed it to Edie with the page open at the inscription. 'Are you sure you meant me to have this?'

Edie looked at it for a moment and her whole demeanour changed, sadness crept over her face and bitterness seeped into her voice, 'You played it as I would have played it all those years ago to Hermann when we were courting. How sad that makes me feel, to look back, to hear you play with the feeling I once had…but I couldn't play to him like that now.'

Julie sat expectantly, but Edie said no more and after gazing for some time into the empty fireplace she collected her thoughts and picked up the score she had brought, 'Some Mozart duets then?'

Julie brought two chairs from the dining room and they played happily for an hour, the music bringing their hands and thoughts together as a single stream of sparkling music. Occasionally they would stop and work together on a difficult passage, or Edie would stumble apologetically over a phrase, but as time wore on they warmed to the companionship the music brought them.

Finally Edie sat back smiling, 'And now I am exhausted! I had forgotten how hard it is to concentrate. But what fun. Please, Julie, can we do this again? It brings back such happy memories.'

Julie smiled, 'Of course, but can we talk for a while. Gertrud is away and I would really like your company for as long as you can spare. I want to know all about Vienna - about Trieste! I'm afraid I don't have many visitors and you seem to have led such an interesting and cultured life. I'm afraid the truth is that when you talked about Mahler the other night, I had no idea about his music. I don't really know very much about anything apart from the piano.'

Edie seemed to reflect on this admission and when they were back on the sofa studied Julie, as she poured some lemonade, with an expression of growing remorse. 'I must have seemed very *discourteous* last time we met…no, that's a silly pompous word - perhaps rude is a better one. It was stupid of me, but that is the effect it has you see; when you are married to a man like Hermann and you see a pretty young woman. Sometimes I think he does it deliberately – knowing I'll humiliate myself. I suppose younger women must feel sorry for him – I must seem a harridan. Perhaps that's why he does it.'

Julie passed her a brimming glass and sat back. 'You seem perfectly nice to me and I don't feel the slightest bit sorry for Hermann. I thought your dedication and the poem was so tender, so loving – he's a lucky man. I have a fiancé now - a doctor. I hope I can always feel about him as I feel now. Is that realistic do you think, or does time always change things? Have your feelings towards Hermann really changed so much?'

Edie sipped the lemonade. 'I used to play that music to him. It used to affect us both. We were so in love. No, I don't think time alone changes us, but everything else around us does – people, events. We inevitably have to evolve as individuals…make choices. Sometimes we decide to leave those choices to others. I know I did. I worshipped Hermann for so many years, like a god, but then he took us both on a journey…'

'A journey - how do you mean?'

Edie pondered for a moment, 'When I met him he was the man of the moment - in Vienna at least. Everywhere we went he knew people, charmed them, made connections. He seemed to be indispensable to the Austrian Nazi Party in the twenties and thirties, to always be saying the right things to the men who mattered. He was driving so hard and so fast in the late thirties it was intoxicating – it was like a dream – dinners, balls, the meetings, the rallies. We seemed to be caught up in a whirlwind. And then we had the *Anschluss* with Germany and suddenly Hermann was struggling. He had been building power for others you see, not for himself. New men arrived from Germany and Hermann was pushed aside. So, he joined the SS and was rapidly promoted – after all he was a brilliant lawyer. But it was when he was sent to Poland to work with Frank that it seemed to fall apart. I don't think he ever really understood how far people were prepared to go – how much would be demanded of him. That's when he changed, and when he came home on leave he'd become someone else, someone much darker…someone I couldn't possibly love any more. That was when we reached the end of our road.'

Julie remembered Gertrud's admonishment not to ask about Hermann, but now Edie seemed so open about him and she felt emboldened, 'But Edie, what does Hermann actually do – what happened in Poland that changed him so much?'

Edie's eyes suddenly flashed at Julie and she immediately recoiled, 'I am sorry Edie, please accept my apologies.'

Edie's expression softened again, 'Not your fault. It's enough to say that we grew apart and Hermann became someone else. And now Hermann is my bitter, bitter, regret.'

'Were there other men you might have married?'

Her face became slightly mischievous, 'Oh yes! Many tried to court me. Good men, who *remained* good. But when you are young you want excitement, the challenge, and so often you overlook what's right. When I caught Hermann I was exultant - he had turned so many girls' heads you see. He was a man with a dazzling future…the world at his feet. And now I look back at the choices he made – that I let him make – and all I can see ahead of me is a lifetime wasting away…childless, alone, away from my family and friends.

'When he was posted to Danzig he told me we were going to live on the Baltic Riviera, Zoppot – the famous spa town with an open air opera, theatres, festivals and galleries; so I brought my good dresses, hats, and jewellery. You can't imagine what a shock it was when I arrived and saw the reality – the emptiness of the place. Julie, I might as well be on the dark side of the moon.'

Edie sighed deeply, lost for a moment, 'Do you know that Albert has given us a grand old merchant's villa in Zoppot? Generous you might think, except that it wasn't his to give and I *loathe* it. I couldn't invite you or anyone else in and do you know why? It's stolen! Not just the house but everything in it: the linen, the cutlery, the furniture, the pictures – family pictures – still on the wall, staring out at me. Julie, I am an Austrian from a good family and it makes me feel like a thief. It makes me feel dirty…and I was once so proud.' Edie became quieter, looking around the room, 'But this rotten business, it's brought us all low, hasn't it. We've all been sullied…corrupted…bought and paid for.'

Edie stood and held her hands over her face for a moment. 'Please forgive me. I'm not myself today…hearing the music again… but thank you for being patient with me. It's been a long time since I could talk like this.' She paused anxiously, 'I can talk to you, can't I?'

Julie stood and they embraced, 'Of course you can.'

'And we can still play next week?'

207

'It really was the happiest hour of music making I've had since the Conservatoire days and you are such a good player.'

Edie stood back, 'You think so? Still - after so many years? I'm so pleased.'

As they stood together on the entrance steps, yet again bathed in hot sunshine saying their goodbyes, Edie abruptly hugged Julie with an intensity that seemed to go deeper than friendship or affection. Then, suddenly, she turned and walked to her car seemingly unable to face her any longer.

As she pulled away, her face stern and unyielding again, Julie wondered about the passions which seemed to lie so near the surface of this tormented woman - the love she had felt as a young woman, now dissipated and wasted in anger, betrayal and bitter regret. She wondered for a moment about that 'journey' Edie had spoken of and where it had taken her. And then, as she stood pondering, she felt a chill running though her body - a voice echoing through the numb darkness of her own recent past. It, too, spoke softly of choices, of a journey, and then she understood with a brutal clarity what Hermann had become to Edie.

When Albert returned from Zoppot that afternoon he sat with Julie and the children and they had some ice cream together in the conservatory. It was too hot, so Albert opened the doors and the children spilled into the garden.

After a few minutes he laid down his spoon and dabbed his lips with a napkin. 'You saw Gertrud crying a few days ago – when you came into the library?'

Julie turned, 'Yes, I'm sorry. I didn't mean to intrude.'

'But you had just had what must have seemed a strange conversation. I think she broke off in the middle, didn't she?'

'She was upset. I sensed there was something, but she said it was a family matter.'

'You are, so to speak, a member of the family. She was crying because I had asked her to lie to you. When she tried, she found she couldn't. That's the woman I married and I respect her for it.'

'Why had you asked her to lie?' she murmured hesitantly.

'I had my reasons, but my wife persuaded me they were…dishonourable.'

'Is it about Karl - my father?'

208

'Your father…there's a rumour he was arrested and tried in the People's Court…that he's been sent to Dachau concentration camp.'

Julie buried her head in her hands, 'Oh God! I knew something was wrong. Why? What's happened?'

'We don't know. There are rumours. I wanted to delay to spare you the uncertainty, but we simply don't know.'

'But he's an economist, he has no politics?'

'He fell out with his superiors – that's the rumour. He had a point of view - that's enough sometimes.'

Julie clasped her hands together, 'Could there be a mistake? How long will he be there?'

'I really don't know.'

Julie sat in silence, stunned and withdrawn, while the children's voices echoed from the garden. They remained like this for a few minutes before Albert finally rose from his chair and put his hand on her shoulder, 'I'm sorry.'

Julie looked up at him. 'He answered the call. He came back to rebuild Germany - he loves Germany.'

Albert looked down at her sombrely, 'Sometimes even that isn't enough.'

Inga came to the doorway and called Julie into the garden. She stood sharply and turned to face him, her eyes glistening with tears, 'Thank you for being honest…and for allowing Gertrud to be honest too.'

Julie turned and ran into the garden with Inga, while Albert's gaze followed her, troubled by the confusion of motives and feelings which now unexpectedly gripped him.

It was the following Friday when Julie was drawn to the window of the living room by the sound of a car arriving at the house. As Julie stepped outside Edie smiled at her from the passenger's door gesturing at a multitude of suitcases and hat boxes which occupied the rear seats. The driver remained in the car and began to read a newspaper.

'I'm going.' Edie said boldly, as she linked arms with Julie and they went inside.

'I don't understand.'

'I'm leaving Hermann and going back to Vienna,'

'But why?'

209

Edie sat in the living room, while Julie stood by the fireplace looking down at her with an expression of disbelief. 'You reminded me of who I once was. After our time together last Saturday I felt unable to go on - I had to get away. It made me realise what a dreadful state my life is in. That little bit of happiness with you at the piano – it reminded me of who I really am. I suddenly realised I was *waiting* - and for what? Hermann won't suddenly go back to being the man I married. It's too late for that. I can see that now.' Julie sat next to her still stunned. 'And now I am finally taking back my future – I still have one, even now. I mean look at me! I'm still young enough to *be* someone. I'm going to go to Vienna, play the piano again, go to concerts, the theatre, the cinema, see my friends – go to Drucker's for cakes! And then I will decide what to do next.'

'Are you going to divorce?'

Edie looked suddenly less elated, 'I don't know. Hermann's not willing to let me go in that way.'

'Does he know you are here?'

'No, I didn't say I was coming. I don't want him to start looking for excuses – someone who *influenced* me. But I had to come and thank you. You woke me up. I was sleepwalking and now I'm going to set myself free.' She looked at her watch, 'But I have a train to catch, so I must go.'

When they stood by the car again Julie hugged her, 'It's ironic really; I had just begun to think you might be *my* saviour – that we might be close friends!'

Edie stood back holding her hands. 'I'm sorry, but you're still young. I'm thirty seven. I'm afraid that soon it will be too late for me. I have to go back and try to make sense of things again…pick up the pieces.' She half turned and then hovered for a moment, 'Julie, there is one final thing I have to say to you and that is about Hermann.'

'Yes?'

'Just be wary of him…he may come to you some day and talk to you about me, about our marriage. He may flatter and charm – he's very good at that. He may ask your advice. But never try to help him, or feel sympathy. Just stay clear. And I'm sorry to say this, but he's no good - he brings unhappiness, especially to women.'

Julie nodded, 'I promise.'

With this Edie got into the car and wound down the window. Julie leaned in and kissed her on the cheek, 'I wish I was coming with you. I had such hopes for our music making.'

Edie looked at her, beaming with pleasure again, 'In Vienna someday soon? I'll find you after the war and we will spend a glorious few days together. Look at me, after all, who would have thought it just a week ago?'

With that the driver started the engine and began to pull away. Edie leaned out of the window, looking back at Julie as the car gathered speed 'Good luck!' she shouted, and then was gone.

The silence that now descended on the house seemed different from the silence that had preceded Edie's arrival. It was bleaker. It made Julie feel desperately alone again, robbed of the culture, sophistication, and friendship that Edie had fleetingly brought into her life. These were the shards of light on which her enclosed world had briefly relied for its colour – and now they were gone.

Chapter 20

It was in late April 1941 before Julie saw Karl again and by then the passionate expectations of the previous April had been dimmed by distance and a year of exhausting apprehension. Even Gertrud feared that the feelings Karl had nurtured for Julie in 1940 might have been lessened by experience and the harsh realities of military service.

So it was with much relief that Karl returned that Tuesday evening in Albert's car from Danzig station and embraced Julie as she might only have dreamed he would – wrapping his arms around her with a long impassioned and unselfconscious kiss, before taking her hand and walking into the house. They all went into the living room where Albert had arranged drinks and canapés to celebrate his return. Karl was now a captain and a medical officer serving in the 25th *Panzergrenadier* Division. He sat relaxing in his new uniform and began telling them of his life over the previous year, Julie's eyes adjusting to the image of this new man and listening to the stories of his training and of the campaign in France with devoted attention.

'But the most difficult thing to witness I suppose ...' he said towards the end of his recollections, '...were the civilians. There were whole villages and towns that had been simply flattened. Some of them had been beautiful, like Leuven; others had stood for nine hundred years and then in the span of ten minutes the Stukas or artillery would obliterate it – that was a place called Tongres. And afterwards the people would just sit, listless, completely lost. That could be hard to watch. But then when we reached Paris...Well, if only you could have seen us marching past the Arc de Triomph. It made me think that perhaps the French had looked at Warsaw and decided they didn't want Paris to go the same way – that perhaps Warsaw had been a terrible lesson.'

Julie sat watching him, entranced by this tanned young man. He was bolder and fitter than she had remembered him, broader shouldered and more confident, his face weathered by the sun. And now Julie fell in love with him all over again, but even more ardently, and impatiently waited for them to be alone.

When Gertrud and Albert left them, they sat together holding hands on the sofa and slowly began to relax into each other. He breathed in the scent of her hair and it was as he had remembered it. He met her eyes as he lightly stroked the nape of her neck and kissed her gently. She moved closer and he kissed her chin. She closed her eyes. His hands began to slowly move down the contours of her body. Tentatively he caressed her breast, and soon they became entwined in an impassioned embrace, their lips and hands roaming freely as their pent up feelings were finally released.

As she returned his kisses with a growing intensity he felt himself harden and held her firmly, 'We can't, we can't go on – we must stop!' Julie was flushed, her eyes dark and passionate; she reached up and ran her fingers through his hair, her voice softly elated and shimmering with the pleasure of him, 'You have a soldier's haircut…what happened to all that lovely hair?'

Karl breathed deeply trying to regain some control. 'Julie, we must stop! What if Gertrude comes back.'

Julie sat back, clinging to his hands, 'She promised me…!'

Karl shook his head smiling, but then looked down at her hands more thoughtfully, 'Did you ever doubt that I would return?'

Julie shook her head, 'At first I believed, but then, each time I hoped, something happened, so I tried to prepare myself. I began to believe you would never come. I was worried that you had changed. I'm sorry if that came through in some of my letters.'

He sat back, 'I even contemplated taking a plane ride with the Luftwaffe to get here. I thought they could drop me in the lake!'

She laughed but he seemed unhappy recalling his feelings. 'I even thought of desertion. I couldn't help myself. I was tormented. I kept thinking I might be killed - I might never hold you again, kiss you and feel you close to me. Sometimes I would sleep with your letters on my pillow because I imagined I could smell your perfume. It was the only way to touch you. Even on the day of my mother's funeral I could only think of you. It was driving me mad to know that I could be with you – that it was my choice to be there and not here.' He paused and noticed Julie looking at him, 'Am I making you feel uncomfortable?'

'No, how could you ever do that?'

213

'Perhaps I shouldn't say these things.'

'Karl, you are an extraordinary man – even in uniform.'

'Ah yes, the uniform! You told me once you didn't like what it did to people…at the Bazar Hotel. Does it make you uncomfortable now? Should I change before dinner?'

Julie shook her head, 'No, you look very handsome, but fancy remembering something I said so long ago! Anyway your uniform is only your authority; it's what you do with that authority that matters. You save lives…to me that's a wonderful gift…What else do you remember from that evening?'

'I remember every word…every gesture. Some nights in France, under a hedge in a bivouac, or in camp, or in the château, I would go to sleep reliving the moment you arrived at my table. I remembered the music and the dancing. I remembered removing your glove…'

Julie suddenly felt an intensity of love for him that pained her and she held him tightly to her, 'And to think that all the time I had pictured you in a café, or bar, with a pretty girl on each arm. And you were there…thinking of me. I'm sorry. I think my letters probably made me sound so suspicious.'

Later, after dinner and toasts of welcome, they continued their conversation in the garden, strolling slowly round the lakes, but by now Karl had become pensive and his thoughts ran far into the future. 'You know this is going to be a long war Julie.'

'I heard the news.'

'Oh, it's not just Yugoslavia and Greece – that's a sideshow; it's Great Britain standing alone with her empire, and America in the background. It's about moving east and everyone is wondering what next?'

'Moving east?'

'In *Mein Kampf* the Führer said the great mistake of the last war was to fight on two fronts. And now I think we're about to make that mistake again. I'm afraid Germany will destroy itself and invade Russia before finishing Great Britain.'

Julie looked up at Karl, but his eyes were far distant, 'The Soviet Union?'

'Possibly…probably. And if so, what becomes of the future?'

214

Julie hesitated, surprised by his sombre tone, 'But Karl, you were so positive before. I remember you talking about the fighting spirit of the army, the morale. What's changed?'

'I suppose I've changed. I've seen things. I understand things better.' Karl looked up at the moon which had suddenly emerged from behind a cloud, bathing them in pale light. 'I remember one night my section was called out to a crash site – a British bomber. The local villagers had laid out the bodies of the crew. I was ordered to recover the identity tags and papers from the bodies. And then I noticed they were from all over the world – New Zealand, Australia, South Africa, Canada, and only the pilot and navigator were British. It made me think; if these people were prepared to come half way around the world to fight Germany, to die for the British Empire, then it changes everything.'

They walked on in silence and then Karl turned and took her head gently in his hands and pressed his lips against her forehead. He spoke softly, looking into her eyes, 'Look Julie, I know you would never betray your vow to me, but really, am I entitled to ask you to wait for so long when I can offer so little? There are months now when we have not spoken. Now even your perfume can send me into endless fits of despair. I know you've felt like this too. In your letters you sound so wounded sometimes - by your fears and suspicions. Would it be better…I mean would it be less selfish of me…'

Julie stood back shaking her head, 'Don't say it, Karl…don't say it! I have not come this far to give you up now. I am seventeen. The vow is final. I will not let you go…unless you force me.'

Karl closed his eyes with a feeling of relief and then locked arms with Julie and they walked around the lake again in silence.

When they re-entered the house Karl went to his room leaving Julie to sit with Albert and Gertrud. Julie noticed mischief in her expression and it irritated her. After a few moments she stood up again, agitated by Karl's absence and unsettled by their earlier conversation. As she turned she saw that Karl had crept up behind her and that in the palm of his hand lay a small black box.

Julie looked around, first at Albert and then Gertrud, whose face now beamed with an irrepressible smile, and finally at Karl, who dropped to one knee. 'You will understand, I had to ask…to make sure…and now of course I must ask you to marry me - after the war.

215

Please, will you take this ring and wear it until then, as a token of our love and betrothal?'

Julie took the gold ring and held it for a moment, looking at the cluster of diamonds, a single ruby at their heart, with tears in her eyes. He stood, took it gently from her and carefully slipped it onto her finger. She raised her hand, Karl kissed the ring and they embraced. As they did so Karl whispered in her ear, 'And when I buy the wedding ring we will go to the same jewellers in Paris; I swear to it.'

For the remaining two days together they were inseparable, except for those sleeping hours when they parted briefly after long nights talking and walking. And then at dawn they would rise to catch every moment of the growing light of day together in the conservatory, often sitting but not speaking for minutes on end, content to be in each other's arms, thinking of the future.

On the afternoon of their last day Albert asked Karl to join him in the library while Gertrud took Julie and the children for a walk. He had claimed an interest in Karl's campaign in France and on this pretext Gertrud had separated them for the one and only time during his leave.

They sat in the two leather chairs separated by a small coffee table.

Albert lit a cigarette, 'So you are to be Julie's husband – congratulations! She's a remarkable girl. And all this business in Posen, you can put that behind you can you?'

Karl nodded, 'I have no illusions about what Julie's suffered, but she has recovered, probably better that I had hoped she would.'

'And never speaks of it?'

'No.'

'And you feel no desire for retribution against Grieser?'

Karl shook his head, 'There's nothing to be done is there - that's what you told me. I suppose it's as much as we can hope that they leave her alone.'

'And what about Koppe? Does Julie ever refer to him? Did you ever meet him when you were in Posen?

Karl's brow furrowed, 'I think Julie met him briefly at the orphanage once. Why?'

216

Albert stood and went to his desk taking a thin file from a drawer. When he was seated again he passed Karl a photograph, 'That's Koppe.'

Karl studied the picture and shook his head, 'No…never seen him before.'

Albert fixed Karl with a more severe expression. 'I'm going to show you a confidential briefing from a man called Epp – it *is* confidential. Tell me if anything here means something to you.' Albert passed the two page report to Karl who studied it, shaking his head from time to time. When he finished he passed the papers back to Albert.

'No. None of this makes sense. You must understand, Albert, I was there for only three days.'

'I hoped you might have an idea? I was wondering about Julie's interrogation. Did she say anything about her father?'

'Julie was questioned about her false identity - about the Polish friends she had. They didn't even ask about her father.'

'Of course, this is an old report.' Albert paused, 'Did Julie tell you that her father has now been sent to Dachau – or that's what we're hearing?'

'No…' Karl said, disconcerted.'

'Don't you think that's a little odd?'

Karl hesitated. 'We agreed not to talk about her father - it upsets her. You have to understand, she has a certain way of dealing with things. I sometimes think in her mind there are lots of boxes where she puts things away. It's how she copes…how she's survived. But what was his crime?'

'He seems to have fallen out with Funk. It seems he was talking to the wrong people - or something like that. We don't know exactly.'

'What did Julie say when you told her…I can't believe she hasn't said anything to me.'

'She cried a little - as I said, she is a remarkable young woman. I would say exceptionally strong. But everyone has their limits and so I suppose we have to deal with what comes next. Karl, I've seen the camps. If he's there for five years and does hard labour he'll be finished. His only hope will be leniency, a job in some administrative role. I think you need to understand he may die tomorrow, next month,

217

next year. We probably won't be told. Sometimes people are - usually not. Not many people live through re-socialisation.'

'Will she be able to write - to communicate?'

'It's forbidden - inmates can't communicate with the outside world. Besides you miss the point; Julie is his daughter. The SD don't generally content themselves with the accused; where the head of the family goes, the wife and children usually follow – the principal of *Sippenhaft* runs deep. The miracle here is that they haven't come for Julie yet.'

'And you think that's deliberate?'

Albert smiled, 'Karl, you need to understand that what Julie got caught up in was a *honey trap* – a power struggle between the SS and Gauleiter Grieser. Grieser has no axe to grind with Julie - she's no threat to him now. In fact Julie would never have been harmed if Koppe hadn't placed her in Grieser's flat – at his mercy so to speak. We just think somewhere down the line there's another dimension to this and it exploded in Koppe's face. Now he's trying to gather up the pieces. Except that some of the pieces, some incriminating evidence against him, is still out there, floating about and waiting to land. Koppe seems to be betting that when it does it will find its way to Julie.'

Karl shook his head, 'But she knows nothing about Koppe. She was at an orphanage and then she was imprisoned by Grieser - that's all that she knows and for most of that time she was drugged. Anyway, how does it help Koppe if Julie gets the evidence? Pardon my frankness but aren't Warthegau and Danzig West Prussia at each other's throats? Weren't you and Grieser sworn enemies – even going back to the Danzig Senate days? Aren't the rival police and security elements still at loggerheads after the hospital debacle? If the evidence against Koppe finds its way to Julie surely he'll also expect it to fall into your hands.'

Albert smiled, 'But Karl, that's precisely what Koppe is relying on. He's relying on us to blackmail him. He knows we won't waste the evidence on simply destroying him or Grieser. What good could that do us? We'd only see Koppe replaced with another SS hack with local ambitions. No; we can be relied on to play the game because it's in our interests. Julie is the key.'

'And Berlin?'

'You read the report. Someone is covering for Koppe, but I'm not sure everyone is *in* on the reasons why - hence Colonel Hopp and Captain Gerhard's little adventure.'

'And so where does this leave Julie?'

'Under my protection.'

'Until this evidence turns up - and if it turns up?'

'Then we shall see. And if we can keep it away from her - if she hasn't seen it - she can't be a threat can she? Then we can trade directly – leave her out of it - and you will both be in the clear.'

Karl ran his hands over his face wearily and smiled. 'Thank you, Albert. I can't say how much this means to me. I don't think I had understood even the basic elements of this.'

'So you will keep a look out for me? Make sure she doesn't stumble on anything she shouldn't?'

Karl extended his hand and Albert shook it, 'Of course - if it keeps her safe.'

It was only later when Karl met Julie again in the hall that he became suddenly conscious of the significance of his conversation with Albert. Julie hugged him passionately and her curiosity about his conversation with Albert seemed easily satisfied, but it was a lie. And only now did he realise that to collude with Albert to protect Julie, was also to deceive her, and this sense of having been tainted by Albert's intrigue lingered uncomfortably.

That evening they walked in the garden. Julie seemed to be struggling for some time before she felt able to say what she was thinking, 'Karl, the evening you arrived, when we sat together...'

'How strange, I was thinking of that too.'

'Karl, I don't know how to say this any other way but I wanted you. I wanted to give myself to you so completely that evening.'

Karl kissed her tenderly and they went and sat on a bench by the lake. 'I wanted you too. I still want you...but not a snatched moment - I don't want that...not for us. I want to take you somewhere...Paris, Vienna...somewhere magical. I don't want to make love to you and then leave you, not knowing when I will see you again. I couldn't bear that.'

219

Julie smiled, 'No. I don't think I could bear that either. But I wanted you to know how I feel about you. That when it is all over, I dream of the moment when we can finally be together…'

'In Paris…in a luxury hotel. We shall order room service, and not be seen for days.'

Julie laughed gently, 'Paris sounds wonderful.'

'We can buy the wedding ring then, perhaps even get married there.'

'Oh Karl, if only!' She looked skywards, 'Lord, please stop the war.'

Karl stood, 'Just Russia now. Once that's over I shall insist the Führer calls it a day. We're getting married…no more war! I shall insist.'

Julie sprang to her feet smiling, 'Of course….'

When they parted the following morning she cried, but not with the desperation of a year earlier. The ring in its own way now united them, and fended off some of the anxieties that had previously tormented her. After they had embraced and kissed for the last time, he drew her hand to his lips and kissed the ring. He met her eyes, 'I won't stop thinking about you…and I won't stop thinking of Paris.'

As he walked towards the car he turned briefly, smiling, 'I'll send you a Russian doll for the children - if we visit Moscow!'

She waved and tried to look positive, but inside she felt the pangs of apprehension, knowing he was possibly destined to fight again, and dreading he might be killed.

As the car pulled away she leaned down to look at Karl one last time, 'Don't be long! I'll pray for you every night. Come home soon.'

As Karl lost sight of Julie these were the words which lingered with him and he became more sombre. She hoped for a swift victory - even knowing her father was in Dachau and that victory for the Reich would probably only seal his fate. He found the innocence of her belief in an outcome to the war which was quick and happy, both moving and desperate and yet, he loved her more for clinging to the notion of it.

Chapter 21

As the weeks passed, news began to filter through from the breakfast and dinner table that the army was indeed building in the east as Karl had alleged. And then, at breakfast, on the 22nd of June 1941, Albert sat with a look of quiet satisfaction on his face and opened a report which lay to one side. He looked at Julie tapping it gently, 'Well, it seems Karl's prophesy came true! Perhaps he should be promoted.'

Julie looked at him shaking her head gently, 'I'm sorry Albert, I don't understand.'

'Russia, Julie - the Soviet Union! We invaded this morning. The world will hold its breath. The army say six weeks and it will all be over, that the whole rotten edifice will come crashing down.'

Julie was quiet as Albert talked excitedly with Gertrud about the prizes that awaited Germany in the East – Caspian oil, coal and wheat from the Ukraine, and the treasures of the Hermitage. As he did so she remembered Karl's analysis which had been simpler; that this would be the end of Germany, that this would mean a long hard war on two fronts against overwhelming odds. She wondered too if that would have been her father's analysis.

Life in the Forster's household now assumed a settled pattern; Gertrud and Julie would attend to the children, sew and mend in the mornings, and in the afternoons they would walk through the grounds, perhaps make pastries, or cakes, play the piano, and work with the children at their lessons. In the evenings after dinner they would play cards, listen to music, or to the radio, or read. They also began to plan extravagant changes to the house which Gertrud might make when the war was won. They planted vegetables, taking trouble to extend their variety and create a special garden for the children. They also re-worked clothes with greater and greater inventiveness - creating new from old, and made pickles, jams and wines.

But the outside world continued to crowd in: 1942 was a year of tactical victories but strategic defeats as Germany extended itself to the limits of its manpower and resources, and its enemies prepared to strike on land as they already were by air. During this period Albert continued to see only hope in the news from the front, and Julie continued to receive letters from Karl in Army Group Centre, which told of their being drawn still deeper into Russia and a longing for its final collapse.

The first blow to Albert's hopes fell in February 1943, with the surrender of Von Paulus at Stalingrad, when ninety one thousand Germans and twenty four generals were taken prisoner by the Russians. In May, came news of defeat in North Africa, and in June, Anglo-American landings in Sicily. By late July, Albert learned that the German army had been defeated in what was hailed as the largest tank battle in history at Kursk, losing one hundred thousand men. Then, in September, the Allies landed in Italy.

By January 1944, Albert had become withdrawn, his manner abrupt. The children were subdued around him and he rarely ventured home during the week. On the 27th of January, the siege of Leningrad was lifted by the Russians and the news from Germany spoke of cities bombed relentlessly by night and by day. In June, when so often the Germans in Russia had seemed to turn the tide against the Soviets in a summer offensive, the coast of France was invaded by the Allied armies and the Russian front began to crumble.

As Albert's optimism faded and the possibility of defeat began to inform his thinking he became stoic, even apologetic, about the failures that he saw might now overwhelm them.

By late May 1944, Karl's infrequent letters had stopped, and by late June his engagement ring slipped loosely around Julie's finger as the realisation that he might be dead or a captive of the Russians began to grow into a seeming reality. Finally, in early July, Julie sought out Albert in the library. He looked up as she entered, 'Gertrud said you wanted to speak to me?'

Julie sat, her eyes tired and apprehensive, 'It's been three years. I've seen Karl once. There's nothing on the radio except military music and no news in the papers. His letters used to be, at the very least, a few weeks old, but they still arrived. Since May I've heard nothing. Albert, please tell me what's happening – I've never come to you like this, never! I need you to be honest with me. I can't live on my nerves anymore.'

Albert's face was tense and drawn. He had not been eating or sleeping properly and his hands shook slightly, but he smiled in a sad

222

almost nostalgic way as he studied her, 'Tonight we have a dinner. We'll discuss it then in the open with others. The time for optimism is over and now the reckoning begins. We will all need to face reality Julie…all of us.'

His head drooped and he returned to his papers. Julie stood up and walked slowly to the door. But when she turned to thank him, she saw that he remained as he had been, anxiously scribbling notes, lost in his anxieties, and for the first time she thought he seemed a broken man.

She sat in the living room, found Karl's last letter and, as was her practice at such times, read it again from the envelope inwards. The letter was dated 10th May 1944.

"Dearest Julie, I am in Vileyka at the moment and life is very uncomfortable. Much of the town is in ruins and there is little shelter and no running water. The partisans are constantly harassing our supplies. A couple of men went out the other night to draw provisions in the town and were taken. Even inside the perimeter it isn't always safe. The partisans are like ghosts and everyone is tired and jumpy. The unit is short of almost everything. We re-use what we can but there are limits! The other day I went to a man who had shot himself after we had carried out some anti-partisan actions and executions. I suppose he had reached the end, but it was sad because he had a wife and two children back in Göttingen. He died a few minutes after I got to him. The Soviet soldier is now much tougher than he was and better equipped and we are finding their tactics are improving. They are also fanatical, like savage animals, and everyone is now more afraid of being taken prisoner by them than being killed. Meanwhile you would be hard pressed to find anyone here who would make it onto the newsreels back home. The replacements are either second rate, or have been patched up and sent back. Many are underweight, or have previously lost fingers or toes to frostbite, or need glasses just to see the enemy! I can only hope they don't bother us too much until we are back up to strength. Recently things have been very quiet which has meant a bit of time to write to you – I hope you are getting my letters? The talk is that the Russians are elsewhere preparing something big…"

Julie put the letter down, '…or were about to attack you.' she whispered to herself. Was that the unwritten conclusion to the sentence which Karl had spared her? She put the letter down, went to the piano

223

and started playing, but her doubts and anxieties now seemed uncontrollable and she found herself struggling to focus, unable to find any pleasure in the music.

That evening the gathering was a formal and subdued occasion. SS *Obergruppenführer* Richard Hildebrandt, and SS *Sturmbannführer* Hermann Krebs arriving in uniform, while Dieter Yorck, and Ernst Jünger donned dinner jackets in what seemed a strangely macabre gesture of continuing normality. All were unaccompanied, leaving only Gertrud and Julie to provide female company.

When they were all seated in the living room Albert stood up and the group fell silent. 'Thank you for accepting this invitation. This is not a working dinner in any sense - there are ladies present, but I have asked each of you because you are all thinking men and we have reached a moment of crisis. You've all heard something of the news from Russia, but not everything I am sure. And now I want to use this evening to tell you our situation without reserve and to canvass your views after dinner with the benefit of that knowledge.

'So; a situation report arrived from the Führer's headquarters in Rastenburg this morning. I've spent the day digesting it. It's nothing less than catastrophic. A Russian offensive to destroy Army Group Centre began on 22nd June. The operation has been an unqualified success, not only re-taking the last areas of Russian territory held by us, but bringing about the total collapse of Army Group Centre as a whole. Of thirty four divisions fielded in the area twenty eight have been annihilated, or rendered ineffective. The High Command estimates that 400,000 Germans have been killed or captured and a gaping hole has been torn in the German front leaving the road to Berlin open. Army Group North and Army Group North Ukraine are now cut off from each other. They in turn have had to withdraw in the face of offensives.

'Of course in Normandy we also face losses and the allies continue to destroy German cities at will from the air. But it is Russia where we now face strategic collapse. And Julie, I promised you news of Captain Rust. I know something but not all. Your fiancé was still serving with the 25 *Panzergrenadier* Division in Army Group Centre when the Russian assault began. They were surrounded and tried to break out, the Division striking west towards Dzerzhinsk. They were gradually separated into smaller groups, some of which managed to cross the Bobruisk-Minsk railway line and then turn east, bypassing Minsk to the north. The groups eventually reached the safety of the German lines at Molodechno. I don't know if Captain Doctor Rust was among them. As you can imagine, everything is chaotic and information about casualties is sketchy. That's all I can tell you for now – I'm sorry.'

Over dinner Julie became acquainted with an articulate and cultured SS Major, Ernst Jünger, who said he was attached to Hermann Krebs 'office' as he insisted on terming it. She needed the distraction, as her mind was now absorbed by the morbid notion that Karl must be either dead or a prisoner of the Russians which might indeed, from all he had said, be worse. Ernst also seemed preoccupied with her situation, but in another direction entirely, 'You know it's exactly people like you who should be going back to Germany. If you can go, *do*! It's not just the Russians, it's the Polish underground army - they've grown in confidence.' He put down his knife and fork and turned to more directly command her attention, 'I mean think of this; on 1st February SS Major General Kutschera was shot down outside SS HQ in Warsaw – in Warsaw! He only had 150 metres to cover from his home to SS Headquarters, he always used his car, but they killed him! If *he* isn't safe there, then no one is. And that wasn't the end of it, since then they've murdered over seven hundred Gestapo men. Now they even put up the names of the condemned Gestapo and SS men on city walls during the night so they know what they're in for – it's a terror campaign I tell you. And then down south last night, in Cracow, they wounded SS Obergruppenführer Koppe. They say he's lucky to be alive. You have to take them seriously.'

Hermann Krebs leaned forward, slightly the worse for drink, 'The Führer will turn things around. We *will* wipe them out. This business in Russia – we can bounce back.'

Forster began to jab the air with his finger, 'Will we…will we? You won't get them back, those half million men. They'll be marched off to die in Siberia – like the Poles before them. And what about the materials, the steel, rubber, oil and the copper – the guns and tanks we've lost? Hermann, we're like the gambler who keeps returning to the table for one last spin of the wheel, when the odds should tell him to walk away, that he's finished with the big game.'

225

Gertrud clasped her Albert's hand and whispered into his ear. At this he bowed his head slightly, 'My wife reminds me that a chain is no stronger than its weakest link. I believe that is a metaphor which silences me for the moment.'

Dieter clearly felt it was time for some disarming anecdote and winked at Julie in a way which finally displaced some of her misery and brought her out of the pervading gloom of the evening, 'Would anyone like to hear a joke?'

Gertrud smiled and shook her head, 'Oh Dieter, not another of your anecdotes!'

Dieter looked about him at the stony faces and his playful expression seemed to wane, 'Alright then...' he said dryly, '...this is doing the circuits in the Berlin air-raid shelters, it's a riddle; an aeroplane crashes with Hitler, Göring, and Goebbels on it. All three are killed. Who is saved?'

Albert sat back in his chair, 'Germany.' he said morosely. Dieter nodded without smiling. Julie met Gertrud's eyes - it was a miserable evening and they both wished it would end.

When they rose from the dining table Julie walked toward the living room to play for their guests. As she passed through the hall Hermann Krebs, who had seemed to be loitering all evening in the hope of speaking to her alone, caught her arm gently and asked to spend a moment with her. Gertrud hesitated as she passed them, unsure whether to stay, but walked on. He was no longer the sternly handsome figure Julie had first met in 1940. Instead he seemed subdued and anxious, his face bloated by alcohol, his eyes bloodshot – a rather pathetic figure and difficult to reconcile with the description Edie had once given of him as a dazzling Viennese lawyer with the world at his feet. She noticed his hands were shaking slightly as he stood searching for his words, 'May I ask if you have heard from Edie at all?'

Julie shook her head. 'No, did you expect her to be in touch with me?'

'I had hoped. She won't respond to any of my letters or calls. I don't know what to do?' he said with exasperation.

'I knew her very little I'm afraid. We only met briefly.'

226

'But she changed in that weekend…that weekend you met and played music together. I need to know what was said so I can understand what has happened.'

'Nothing was said. We played music together. She was very happy to play the piano again. She became nostalgic, that's all.'

He caught her eye and smiled slightly, 'So you do understand something. If she said she was nostalgic what was it for – Vienna, our past together? You *can* help - please?'

Edie's words suddenly came back to Julie - her warning, and she began to understand that Hermann was probing her, attempting to lure her into an indiscretion. Julie remained expressionless, 'No. I can't remember. It was four years ago.'

'But will you speak to her. If I give you the number; will you call her and tell her how I am? She needs to come back. *I* need her.' He began fumbling though some scraps of paper which he had drawn from this tunic pocket.

'I'm sorry, I don't know either of you well enough to become involved. I'm sorry Herr Krebs.'

Julie turned abruptly realising that anything she said now could only invite further difficulty and began to walk toward the living room. She felt him keeping in step with her and turned to face him, 'Do not press me further, please! We played the piano - I cannot answer for the rest.'

He hesitated for a moment, not angered by her refusal as she had feared, but unsure of himself - inarticulate. He returned the bundle of papers untidily to his pocket while a contrite smile fleetingly passed over his face, but said nothing more.

When they entered the living room she noticed how silent their guests were. Gertrud looked at her and rolled her eyes. When she began to play they seemed to husband their thoughts and take comfort from the familiarities of their culture, in the nostalgic memories of *Kinderszenen*. When she finished with the first movement of the *Moonlight Sonata* nobody roused themselves and applause appeared, for the moment, out of place, so Julie closed the lid of the piano quietly, stood, and left with Gertrud, unnoticed and unacknowledged, leaving the men to resume their deliberations in their own time.

They went to Julie's room where they talked anxiously about what little they now knew of Karl's circumstances. Eventually, when

227

they realised the hopelessness of their speculation, Gertrud brought the subject around to Herr Krebs.

'So what did he want?'

'His wife I suppose – but Edie had warned me about him. I didn't offer to help.'

'Julie, you do know he's a drinker?'

Julie shook her head. 'No, Edie never mentioned it, but he smelled of drink when he arrived. He looks unwell.'

'He was a great lawyer in his time - in Vienna. He worked with Seyss-Inquart after he became Minister of the Interior in '38. But I suppose if you want me to point to a man who fell out of favour with the Party and didn't have the right friends, or the right level of *insurance*, then that's him. He's been trying to *excel* ever since.'

'Gertrud, you once told me never to ask, but what does he do?'

Gertrud shook her head. 'He drinks alone at night. It helps him sleep. Or at least that's what Hildebrandt told Albert. He lost his grip though under Frank…in the early part of the war. A lot went on then – nasty things. He was also in Warthegau, I think, before he came up to us. He told Albert he'd worked with *Sonderkommando Lange* there. They say he changed after that. He was never cut out for the work they gave him. He was a cultured intelligent man and a Catholic, and it destroyed him.'

'But what was it? What did he do?'

Gertrud's expression became strained and she shook her head, 'It really doesn't matter, Julie. He just did a job… like everyone else.'

By one o'clock the following morning Forster and Hildebrandt sat alone in the library. The bottle of brandy they had opened at eleven was empty, but they had found it impossible to get drunk and so sat smoking, their shirts open and feet resting on the furniture.

'Koppe wounded!' Hildebrandt said morosely.

'Might have been justice for Scholl if he'd been killed, after what he put her through.'

Hildebrandt looked at him sharply and changed the subject, 'She played well tonight.'

'Are you surprised? Three years of virtual house arrest does wonders for technique…a fortune in tuning fees.'

228

Hildebrandt looked upwards into the smoke, 'Did you ever tell her about the visit of Captain Gerhard to Posen, or Koppe – anything about Epp's report?'

'No, I kept it simple. She doesn't ask about her father. I think she assumes no news is better than bad news. She seems happy to be under my wardship and of course, she gets on with Gertrud. I think she prays for her father - that's about it.'

'Will you send her back to Germany? Did you hear Ernst going on about the risks of staying?'

'Yes, but I'm not sure.'

Hildebrandt exhaled the smoke from his cigar slowly. 'What do you think happened to the missing evidence – it never landed did it, and I always expected it to.'

'You think I've kept something back?'

Hildebrandt turned to Albert, his expression more severe, 'You know Albert, the SS is beginning to do a lot of exhumations - it's revisiting a lot of old files. You must understand where our friendship ends and my duty to the broader SS begins. Even we are beginning to plan for the possibility of defeat.'

'Are we still talking about Julie?'

'Eric Scholl is dead - so is Vogler.'

Albert's eyes wandered, 'So they've started?'

'I've been approached about how to deal with the situation up here.'

'Who?'

'Kellerman - now that Koppe is wounded.'

'What will you do?'

'My duty as an SS officer of course.'

'Should I be concerned?'

Hildebrandt took his boots off the table and sat forward. 'You got sucked in - we both did. We need to take a step back. The game's over. There are bigger issues at stake now.' Hildebrandt stood and buttoned up his tunic, 'This little indulgence with Scholl - it's finished. You need to give me the files and anything else you have.' He put on his cap. 'You'll have to let her go.'

Chapter 22

Country Residence of the Gauleiter of Danzig West Prussia, November 1944

It was late November 1944 when a letter finally arrived for Julie in a tattered Field Post envelope, nearly seven months since Karl's last communication. She looked at it for some time and trembled as she opened it. It was written on thin army notepaper, but the envelope was not in Karl's writing, and so her immediate thought was that this would be a comrade, or a brother officer, who might be reporting Karl's fate. She held the paper in her hand for a moment, knowing that to unfold it might mark the end of hope, that in a moment Karl might finally be dead to her. Gertrud came into the hall and saw her. She understood the letter's significance immediately and put her arm around Julie and they walked together into the living room and sat.

Julie unfolded the letter carefully, daring herself to read the contents. The writing was small, but neat and clearly legible,

'Dear Fräulein Scholl, Your fiancé Hauptmann Dr Karl Rust is alive and safe in a military hospital in Germany...' Julie's hands fell into her lap and she wept with relief for a moment before reading on aloud in a quaking voice to Gertrud, who sat, leaning forward anxiously on the sofa, *'...I am writing this on his behalf. He is well, but was wounded by shrapnel in the retreat from Minsk. The shrapnel has now been removed and he is recuperating from surgery. He hopes to re-join the current brigade when it is upgraded to divisional status at the Baumholder training area and there is a belief that the new division may then be moved to France. Herr Rust wanted you to receive this letter without delay knowing your concerns. I have been asked by his comrade, Feldwebel Walther Bruch, also in this surgical ward, to add that he has never served with a more able and dedicated medical officer and that his injuries were suffered while remaining with wounded men and in defiance of orders to withdraw. Signed: The Ward Orderly.'*

Julie put down the letter and looked at Gertrud with a mixture of relief and apprehension, 'What injuries?'

Gertrud picked up the letter and read it quickly, 'Well, clearly serious, but not enough to prevent him returning to active service.'

Julie put her head in her hands, 'You know, Gertrud, I almost wish they had been serious enough. I wish it was just all over. The truth is I'd rather have him back injured than not at all. I know that must sound awful, but that's the way I feel.'

Later they walked arm in arm in the garden. It was still bitterly cold, their breath condensing in large white plumes against the dazzling blue winter sky, the frozen gravel breaking up noisily under their feet. Gertrud lit a cigarette and began to smoke nervously. Now and again they could hear distant rumbling.

'Guns?' Julie asked.

'Albert says *no*, they aren't close enough yet.' Gertrud halted and turned to Julie with a look of desperation, 'What will become of *us* - the women and the children? Where is the future now?' Julie remained silent, 'Albert is so distant, so quiet. I've never known him like this. He keeps erupting from his inner thoughts saying *'I must tell the Führer that all is lost – that we can't go on.'* but I know we will go on, somehow. He's going to East Prussia he says, or Berlin; anyway, he's going to tell the Führer it's all over. But I can't believe him - not now.'

Gertrud sighed and they began to walk again. 'When we married in '34 Hitler and Hess were our witnesses at the Chancellery – did I ever tell you that? Then I became just another Frau – 'Frau Forster'. And do you know, it occurred to me the other day that I can't remember a single discussion in Hitler's presence where a woman featured as the subject...isn't that odd? No opinions sought, no obvious relevance, just auxiliaries in the great struggle, to be awarded medals for motherhood. It's all been terribly patriarchal hasn't it?

'And you know, when I look back to the '30s, to the rallies with their sense of hope and expectation, it's those bright young girls with their pigtails, starched white shirts and beaming smiles I want to weep for - the Young Maidens – tens of thousands of them, with such idealism in their hearts and love for their Führer...and then to betray it, and for what - for this!'

231

Julie drew Gertrud closer, 'I was with young SS officers in '39 in Posen at a ball. I was partnered to one of them. Back then they seemed like bronzed gods – terribly intimidating. They were just as intoxicated by it all, just as convinced. I wonder where they are now.'

'Rotting in some Russian bog I would imagine. The boys in the bogs of Russia and the girls under the rubble back home – it reminds me so much of that fairy tale, *'The Pied Piper of Hamelin'*. He got rid of the rats with the enchanting sound of his pipes, he also restored the town's pride, but then, when he left, playing the pipes as he went, he took the town's children too…a whole generation, and they were never seen again.

'I saw Hitler once you know after one of those big Party speeches with Putzi Hanfstängl, his foreign press advisor. First I remember seeing him on the podium, his face contorted with rage about the injustices meted out to Germany, his hands gesticulating with such expression, the crowd hysterical. And then a few minutes later he was there, in the back room, calm as you like with the script in his hand, saying plain as anything to Putzi, *'That went well'*, or *'No, that didn't work'*. It was all theatre, all put on. But the effect on others…that was real enough.'

Gertrud threw down her cigarette and crushed it with an expression of bitterness, 'Julie, I love you, the children love you, but you must get out. You must go to your uncle in Remagen – get away from here. He will take you in won't he - he's a good man?'

With these words it was as though a gigantic spell had been broken. Suddenly it was as if everyone around Julie was beginning to emerge from a trance and think for themselves, of survival, of the individual and not the destiny that had consumed them for eleven years. Julie had sensed this moment might come but had expected Albert to be its instigator after his fit of bleak realism at the dinner. 'What did Albert say exactly?'

Gertrud paused awkwardly, 'He says it's no longer safe for you to stay - but then says you can't go either. He can't think it through, Julie - he's all over the place. I'm trying to spare the children, but he's beginning to upset them. No, *we* must make the decision; you must simply go to Germany and disappear until everything is finished…Albert thinks it will be over by March.'

'Gertrud, shouldn't you tell him?'

Gertrud turned almost pleading, 'No, but you *must go* - and I don't want to tell him - he's too confused. I think you have the chance to go now and you should grab it with both hands.'

Julie was startled by the anxiety in Gertrud's voice. Until now she had glibly claimed to 'avert her eyes' when asked about the events unfolding in Russia and her husband's work, but now she seemed very clear about what lay ahead of them and very frightened. Julie stopped walking and turned to face her, 'I will Gertrud; I will go - if that's what you want. I suppose I knew this moment would arrive. I've known it for some time. But I find it difficult. You are my closest friend – my older sister - and I feel about the children almost as though they were my own. It's difficult to imagine life somewhere else without you all. And, to be honest…I'm frightened too… frightened of the future…frightened for you and the children.'

Gertrud looked down and toyed with some gravel with the tip of her shoe, 'Well don't be.' She fixed Julie with a sad smile and put her arm around her and they walked on in silence.

The following morning Albert went out at dawn without seeing anyone. When he had gone Gertrud prepared food for the journey in a small parcel. The children had not been told that Julie was going for fear Albert would hear of it and so their reaction to the news was immediate and intense. As a final farewell Julie played some of their favourite music until she realised that this was seen by them as a way of delaying her. So, after one final request, she closed the lid of the piano for the last time. And then, as if recognising the symbolism, she took the heavy cloth cover and placed it over the instrument. The children looked on forlornly at these 'last rites' and Inga began to cry.

A car had been arranged by Gertrud for noon. After Julie's suitcase had been placed in the hall she ushered Julie upstairs and into her private dressing room. She seemed weighed down by the parting, but also tense, 'I could not decide until this moment whether to give you this, but I realise now that we have no further use for such things. I want you to have at least a chance. I'm afraid it's all over for us. I don't see a future - not anymore.'

Gertrud dropped to her knees and pulled out the bottom drawer from the body of a wardrobe. Lying beneath, in the void above the floorboards, were two plain manila envelopes. 'These are the files on your case. It's what Hildebrandt managed to compile over the years since '39. I found them in our safe. There are some later additions, but the substance is there. The second envelope – well, you can use that to rebuild your life, but guard it carefully. I always knew, one day, it would be for you to use and not us.'

Julie took the two envelopes, 'But what can I do with this? Who will use it?'

Gertrud took her arm and they walked back down stairs, 'They will be something for after the war. I really don't know, it's your past not ours. Just don't open the files until the war has ended – hide them well. You must promise me? Perhaps there will be a moment for justice to take its course – who knows.'

As Julie packed the envelopes in her suitcase Gertrud took an identity card from her purse and gave it to her. 'I couldn't get this from Albert, he would have been too suspicious, but Richard Hildebrandt was more helpful; he's been a good friend to me over the years. He's arranged a female escort to take you back as far as Berlin. He said it would be better that way. She'll meet you at the station.'

Julie looked at the card, 'So finally, I am Julie Scholl again.'

Julie kissed the children once more and gave Gertrud a long warm embrace. They felt each other's tears as they kissed goodbye. 'I don't want to lose you Gertrud.' Julie stood back still holding Gertrud's hands, 'I can't lose you and Peter and Inge, I can't. I've lost too many of the people I care for. Promise you'll find me when it's all over …promise you'll write to me at my uncle's inn?'

Gertrud looked away nervously, 'I don't know Julie…I really don't know. I'll try – of course I will. We are sisters after all.' She turned and smiled bleakly. 'But you still have a chance, Julie…you and Karl…you must live for that, not for me, not for the children…don't cling to what we had…please. I couldn't bear the responsibility for that.' Gertrude embraced Julie and then turned away, taking up her case and walking out onto the steps, the children following behind her.

As Julie got into the car she felt her anxieties mounting and as the car began to pull away she looked out at the children and Gertrud waving and grabbed the door handle, holding it fiercely. Then, as they passed out of sight, her grip loosened, knowing in her heart that the security she had enjoyed with Gertrud was no longer there for her and that, as Gertrud had said, it was all over for them too.

234

When the car arrived at Zoppot station Julie's female escort was nowhere to be found so she fought her way through the ticket hall, confused and frightened by the voices and the crowds of people struggling to get away. Finally she reached the platform for the Berlin train and began to edge toward the front of the crowd, anxious and uncertain. She wondered how to fight her way on board with her heavy case and looked about for a friendly face, but everyone was preoccupied with their own difficulties. Finally, after ten minutes, she found herself exchanging casual remarks with a short, slim, pretty woman of about twenty-four with blonde hair which had been pinned back severely to accommodate a cap which was tucked into her belt. She wore a heavy grey uniform of sorts, the tunic and skirt for which seemed crudely tailored. Her knee length boots were scuffed and bore traces of mud, but aside from this unflattering uniform, she seemed very pleasant, if a little 'slow'.

As the train pulled in the woman gestured at Julie's case and offered to help her on board. Together they fought aggressively for the door and finally pushed aside the other competition with the aid of the suitcase and secured window seats in a compartment. They both felt stunned by their achievement and sat eyeing each other with childish satisfaction.

'Thank you so much. My name's Julie.'

Her companion seemed entirely indifferent to the formal pleasantries of their meeting, 'Hello. Yes. Suitcases are useful, but heavy, eh!'

Julie studied her pretty face and well-kept hair and wondered what a girl with such 'film star' good looks could possibly be doing in this drab uniform. Finally her inquisitiveness overcame her, 'I'm sorry, but I'm so curious, what do you do?'

'I'm your escort.' the woman said with mischievous satisfaction and smiled.

Julie looked at her askance, 'However did you find me in the crowd?'

'I was given a copy of your photograph by Hildebrandt. I thought we would save introductions for the train and I couldn't resist the temptation to play along. My name's Irma Grese.' She extended her hand and they shook gently.

'What's your job?'

235

'I'm an SS auxiliary – prisons mainly – admin, that sort of thing.'

'Surely you didn't volunteer, I mean, I imagined them to be big, tough looking women...you just don't look like that at all.'

Irma smiled 'Yes, I don't suppose anyone volunteers if they can go elsewhere. I tried doing all sorts of things: worked in a dairy, a shop and then a hospital. I really wanted to be a nurse but my education wasn't good enough. I stayed two years at the hospital. Then the labour exchange sent me back to a dairy in Furstenburg. In '39 I tried to get a nursing post again – I was sure the war would help - but I got sent to Ravensbrück instead. I complained of course but they had me by then and wouldn't let me go.'

'So what are you doing in Zoppot?'

'I was ordered to collect you. How long have you been away from Germany?'

'Five years. I'm looking forward to going home.'

'Home!' Irma shook her head and laughed coarsely, drawing disapproving looks from the other passengers, 'It doesn't exist anymore. You can't imagine. Everything is flat – *Magdeburgisieren* - everything is gone!'

Julie sat back, startled by Irma's outburst. After a few minutes she began to thumb through an old copy of *Life Magazine* which Gertrud had given her as a parting gift. It contained a picture of Gertrud's meeting with Hitler at Obersaltzberg in August 1939. Julie looked at her smiling face and then recalled Gertrud's drunken admission that what followed was the most boring night of her life! She flicked through the other pages, but as she did so she noticed her neighbour looking over her shoulder at the magazine and their eyes met. He was an elderly gentleman in his late sixties, dressed in clothes that would once have conveyed the impression of money and good taste, but which now hung about his shrunken frame, worn and frayed and tired – like the man himself. He nodded at a pre-war picture of Nuremburg, with its narrow streets and ancient wooden framed houses and tears came to his eyes, 'She's right…it's all gone. Everything is flat. It's unimaginable! Nuremburg, Cologne, Hamburg, Aachen, Berlin, Lubeck; they are all gone. I tell you Germany has lost its soul. It's hopeless. Germany is finished.'

The next hour of the journey passed in relative silence. Later the other passengers watched with ill-disguised envy as Julie

236

unwrapped the food which Gertrud had prepared for her. Irma leaned forward to take a closer look, 'My God, where did you get all that?'

Julie suddenly felt embarrassed and isolated. She could not share her food with everybody but she could at least offer Irma something to deflect the growing resentment in the compartment. She proffered her napkin and Irma greedily took a slice of black bread and sausage.

Julie watched Irma savouring the food and then delighting in the coastal scenery. She seemed to find a childlike pleasure in being on the train – as though she were on holiday and free, leaning forward to watch the world go by, and occasionally tapping Julie on the knee to point something out.

Later, when the evening had begun to close in and the blackout had been completed, Julie got out a pen and paper and began to write to Karl in the dim glow of the carriage light. Irma eyed her and when she had finished leaned forward out of the hearing of their companions. 'Would you do a letter for me?'

Julie offered her the pen and paper but she shook her head. 'My writing's not good like yours...I'd like to send my sister a letter. I haven't seen her since '43. I went home and my father and I had a big fight. I'd like to explain to Helene why. Could you write for me if I tell you what I want to say?'

Julie nodded and found it agreeable to help Irma in the same way the orderly at the hospital had helped Karl. She felt it would be a favour returned in some roundabout way. When she had finished, and had addressed the envelope, she put it in her bag, but Irma held out her hand for it, 'It's alright, I'll post it for you.' Julie said cheerfully.

Irma withdrew her hand, 'Well, I suppose so - that's kind, very kind. And if you are ever in Wrecken, look up my sister. She's a great person - really good. If you ever do see her, send her my love, I miss her. We were all very close after my mother died. Not now; not any more. I've changed a lot because of the war.'

Julie looked at her, 'I'm so sorry about your mother. I lost my mother too. She died in childbirth with my brother. But I have lived with orphans, in Posen in '39. They were some of the best friends I ever made. They took me in and sheltered me, just before the war started – and when it's finished I'm going to find them again.'

Irma studied Julie for a moment then averted her eyes.

After a few minutes Julie stood, 'Can you watch my things?'

Irma looked about at their sleepy companions, 'Surely.'

When Julie got to the end of the congested corridor she found the toilet door open and went in, but as she tried to drop the catch it was pushed open again under the force of Irma's weight. She entered, pushing Julie against the basin and locked the door. They stared at each other. Irma spoke with a quiet intensity, 'The orphanage was off Glogauer Strasse, wasn't it - the old Ballet School?

Julie nodded, 'But how do you know?'

'Because I was their overseer - I replaced Sister Schmidt.'

'I don't understand; what were you doing at the orphanage?'

'I was working for two SS officers, Kellerman and Dr Fischer. They kicked out the hard faced nun. I'm part of the group you see: me, Fischer, Kellerman, Koppe and a few others - we're all there on the file. And now the SS wants things tidied up and I got dragged back from Auschwitz to get you.'

Julie slumped against the sink. 'Why? What have I done?'

Irma looked away and shook her head, 'It doesn't matter now…let's say you're *half* a witness. You knew them, you were there - you can name them.' Irma dug deep into her skirt and pulled out a roll of film. 'And this is the other half - the film from the orphanage - it proves everything.' She thrust it into Julie's hand, 'It's all I have, so keep it safe.' Irma leaned against the toilet door and lit a cigarette, 'The war is ending. I'm supposed to deliver you to Bergen-Belsen. There'll be a couple of SS men waiting to help out at Stettiner Bahnhof. So get off anywhere before, but not there.'

'You're going to let me go?'

'Yes.'

'But why? Why are you doing this?'

'Same reason I sent you the music book and your mother's letters, same reason I helped Dr Hertz.' Her face hardened, 'This is for me. You'll understand that when you see what's on the film - so don't fuck it up. They're trying to cover their dirty filthy tracks - don't let them! It's all there – the whole story.' Her voice became quieter, 'I loved those girls too.'

They fetched Julie's case and stood by the carriage door waiting for the train to halt. As they did Irma suddenly looked at Julie, 'You did say your name was Scholl?

'Yes.'

'Your father's name Eric?'

'Yes! How did you know?'

Irma hesitated, 'They met in '39, Obergruppenführer Koppe and your father. I was there when he came to the orphanage.'

Julie grasped Irma's arm, 'What do you mean? My father never went to Posen. He was put in prison in Berlin and then sent to Dachau. He fell out with Funk.'

Irma looked at Julie coldly, 'No – that was the official version. The truth is he arrived on the last train from Berlin after getting a letter from Hertz about Grieser. He came looking for you late that night. Kellerman challenged him first. We were loading up the girls onto trucks and he just seemed to appear from nowhere. Koppe bluffed and said you were in a villa outside the city and put him in his car. They drove him to the forest near lake *Kiekrz*. Kellerman said Müller refused to shoot him in cold blood so Koppe had to do it…then he shot Müller too… no witnesses you see.'

Julie's voice was broken, 'And this was November '39? But I was told he was alive…that he was in prison…I've prayed for him all these years. Are you sure…it was *him*?'

Irma's voice dropped, 'Your father was never in Dachau.'

Julie wiped away her tears, 'So why did they invent a story about him going to Dachau?'

'I don't know for certain – I was just the help. I heard Koppe say Heydrich's reputation was on the line. They were all SS men working across each other. Nobody knew the full picture. It was a fuck up. Koppe sorted it all out – he knew how to make your father disappear.'

They felt the carriage jolt across some points and the train slowed. Irma grabbed Julie's arm, 'Leave the train as soon as we stop, at signals, at a station, anywhere. Run and don't stop until you are away from Berlin - go south. I'll get a lot of shit from them when they realise you've escaped, so don't let me down.'

The train continued crawling for another twenty minutes until they could hear the distant wailing of sirens and see the searchlights in the sky through the cracks in the blackout. Soon they could hear the steady rumble of hundreds of flak artillery pieces and the train halted. 'We're probably here 'till morning,' Irma said, 'Go!' They opened the door and onlookers watched as Julie stepped on to the ballast of the track and took her case. A soldier shouted at them about the blackout, but Irma swore back at him with more than equal ferocity and he backed away.

Soon Julie had descended a steep embankment and was alone in a field with her luggage. The train began to pull away and presently all around her was silent, except for the distant thunder of the guns and the drone of bombers. She looked up at the moon, which occasionally broke through the clouds as they moved slowly across the night sky and felt the chill winter breeze begin to seep through her thin coat and into her fingers. In the distance she could see the outline of a farmhouse and began to make her way towards it. It was, she thought, the loneliest moment of her life and yet she seemed to be surrounded by people determined to help her survive.

She stumbled through the darkness with her heavy case, along a rough track. When, after half an hour, she came to the darkened house, knocked on the door, and was confronted with the anxious face of a Protestant pastor, she knew her faith in a benevolent God was not misplaced. He looked at her for a moment with astonishment and then stood aside, calling over his shoulder for his wife who quickly appeared, ushered Julie in, and took her coat. 'My poor child, but where have you come from?' She said with a concern that settled Julie's nerves.

Julie stood silent for a moment, her mud soaked shoes and suitcase making any pretence impossible. 'I ran away from the train.'

The Pastor shook his head, 'I thought you were the police...but never mind that. You look exhausted. You're safe here and you must stay the night.'

They sat in his warm kitchen while the Pastor's wife shared what little food they had with her. They also shared their misfortunes and were anxious to hear news from the Eastern Front, where their two sons were fighting. She tried to fill the gaps in their knowledge of events and spare them the worst, but they seemed to draw stronger inferences from her sudden arrival as a muddy bedraggled refugee than they did from what she told them.

After midnight, comforted and warmed by the broth they had given her, they showed her to their eldest son's room and left her. It was full of pictures and mementos of his childhood, certificates and sporting medals. She looked at them, at his hopeful, proud, smiling face, and prayed he might return one day to spare his parents.

She undressed and washed her feet in a bowl of water before climbing under the thick quilt. It was only then, as she lay in the darkness listening to the distant rumble of the anti-aircraft guns, that Irma's words began to haunt her and she wept and then sobbed for her father. She remained crying intermittently for many hours, clutching the pillow to her face, trying to stifle her tears, but nothing seemed able to take away the image in her mind, which replayed again and again, of him walking toward the orphanage, along the familiar pavements of Thorner Strasse, hoping to find her, and then being taken away to his murder.

The following morning after breakfast the Pastor anxiously listened to Julie's hopes of returning to Remagen-Kripp and her uncle. He exchanged glances with his wife and shook his head, 'You can't do this journey - not alone. It's too dangerous. You don't understand; the Germany you left…it doesn't exist anymore, the people are different now. It isn't safe. I'll come with you as far as Eberswalde. I have a friend there. He used to travel a lot on business. He may have some ideas – some contacts.'

Later his wife prepared a parcel of bread and some hard boiled eggs and placed them in a small sack with a pot of jam. The Pastor fetched his sons' bicycles and, after attaching her suitcase to the back of his bike, they began to cycle south.

Towards midday, as the morning haze began to clear, Julie could see a great dense column of grey smoke rising from the direction of Berlin. The Pastor looked around at her as they reached the crest of a low hill and they stopped to catch their breath and eat some lunch. They both looked towards the city in silence as they ate. 'Do you know Berlin?' he said eventually, with an air of melancholy.

'I used to live there, on the southern side of the city, in Dahlem.'

He smiled, 'Ah yes. I know Dahlem. A lovely area…still has a feel of the country about it…some fine houses too. I used to have friends near the Kaiser-Wilhelm-Gesellschaft. The manor house…the village inn…I remember them well. I think I last went there in '42.'

'Was there much damage?'

'In Dahlem? A little. But since then the bombings have got a lot worse. They've hit the Schloss, the cathedral, the arsenal and the Altes Museum. The Charité has been badly damaged…I hear

Marienfelde, Lichterfelde, Siemensstadt...they've all been levelled.' He turned to Julie hesitantly, 'My wife wanted me to ask you...in connection with our sons...the discussion last night. You said your fiancé was also in Army Group Centre.'

'Yes...he's a doctor.'

'We haven't heard from either of our sons since early May. She thought perhaps you might know a little more – that perhaps you wanted to spare her feelings last night.'

Julie nodded, 'I didn't know what to say.'

'But will you tell me...the truth?'

'My fiancé wrote to me in May, just before the Russian offensive. He said...the feeling among the soldiers was that it was better to be killed than to be captured. Unless your sons are recovering from wounds somewhere, you must hope they died quickly...without suffering.'

The Pastor nodded, 'Friedrich told us in one of his letters, that he'd been in a battalion of 120 men ordered to carry out a fighting reconnaissance, to test the Russian defences around Moscow. Seventeen of them returned. He said something quite similar to us then.' He looked away for a moment, 'I just needed to know if we should continue to hold out hope...but thank you. At least we can try to come to terms with things now.'

When they reached Eberswalde the Pastor took Julie to the house of friend Herr Pabst. After discussion they decided he would take Julie on to Neuruppin – to the north of Berlin - and avoid the city altogether. He said he had friends there who would arrange for her to be escorted further west. By these means, Julie travelled across Germany over the next month, with a series of people linked by friendship, or the church. But it was a dismal odyssey. Almost every town seemed to have been damaged by bombing, and everywhere were the homeless, the starving, the crippled and the listless. Many of them seemed only to be waiting for the end to come, sullenly watching the formations of American bombers passing overhead, passively queuing for soup and some bread with *Leberwurst*.

As Julie moved westward towards the industrial Ruhr and the city of Essen she found herself sleeping in the remains of people's houses, in basements, or in communal shelters, amid scenes of total destruction. In places, the charred naked bodies of women, children and the elderly still lay in the streets late into the afternoon, awaiting a lull in the bombing and the 'all clear', and everywhere the air seemed filled with sickening stench of burning. It was almost impossible to equate the haunted people who inhabited these ruins with the Germans she had known in 1936 when she had arrived in Hamburg. Nobody talked of the future now; they talked only about survival, how soon it would be over, and what would happen to their relatives in the East.

In early January, near Velbert, Julie caught a lift southwards towards Solingen in the back of a hay cart with 'Klaus', an elderly farmer who seemed very happy to have a passenger to talk to on his long journey. She was lying in the hay covered to her chest, trying to keep warm, when a reservist policeman halted them. Klaus and the policeman clearly knew each other and Julie could hear them speaking in lowered voices. She stood up to stretch her legs, brushing the hay away. The policeman looked up nodded. 'Stay in the cart Fräulein, keep your head down. There's some nasty business going on down the road. You won't want to look…just wait for Klaus to tell you it's alright.'

Julie sat down again, continuing to listen to their discussion. Klaus leaned down from his seat, 'Local men you say?'

'Overstayed their leave…then went into hiding. Seems they both had wives and young children. Convinced each other it would all be over soon enough. The *Feldgendamerie* caught them this morning. It won't be long now…' As he spoke there was a volley of shots nearby, and then two more, a few seconds apart. Julie shuddered and for a moment there was silence. The policeman stood back, 'Well…that's all over then…you can go on now.'

As the cart began to gain momentum, Julie felt rage rising deep within her and, hearing voices, she stood up, clinging to the side rail. A group of military policemen were smoking and drinking schnapps, while two bodies lay against a low wall. 'What about their children…?' she shouted gesturing towards the bodies. They looked up at her with surprise, but none made any reply.

The carter tapped the horse with his whip, and looked around, 'Are you mad.'

Julie lay back in the hay unsteadily and saw an officer emerge from the group of policemen, looking up the road after them, but he made no effort to pursue them.

Julie shook her head, her voice bitter, 'No, not mad...I just haven't lost my humanity yet.'

PART II

Chapter 23

Remagen-Kripp, May 28, 1945

Julie's uncle, Otto, greeted her arrival in Remagen-Kripp in mid-January 1945 with astonishment and relief. His tears had run freely and her aunt Ingrid had immediately become a mother to her. His inn, the *Rheine-Ahr*, had been in his wife's family for three generations, but the First World War had deprived them of a male heir and so Otto had become an innkeeper, against his father's wishes. In this role he had excelled, keeping a good cellar and his customers well fed with the gatherings of the forests, fields and vineyards of the Rheine meadows – the *Rhinewiesen*. It was a traditional coaching inn, being built into a row of other houses but distinguished by the large gated archway to one side through which horse drawn carriages would once have passed to the livery yard at the rear.

The only fighting they had seen was the fierce but brief struggle for the bridge at Remagen 2km away. Otherwise the sleepy village had remained largely undamaged and the ferry had continued to run over the river to Linz am Rheine - apart for a few weeks during the fighting.

But Otto's anxieties were now of another kind; with the collapse of German resistance in the east and in the west, the German forces of both fronts had been compressed into the area of middle Germany around them. And, after the German surrender on the 7th May 1945, the fear of becoming a prisoner of the Russians in the east had accelerated this process of concentration. Now the whole area of the Rheine meadows had become a series of vast improvised internment camps run by the Americans, often no more than fields in to which prisoners were forced without sanitation, water, or protection from the elements. After a few weeks in these conditions, exposed to the elements and already undernourished, even the German civilians some distance away could begin to smell the dead and dying and the ordure which flowed across these fields. They could also see starvation and medical neglect begin to kill the prisoners through the barbed concertina wire.

Otto's inn had been requisitioned exclusively for American officers of the 106th Infantry Division who administered the sixteen camps, but by some quirk of the process he had continued to be allowed to live in the self-contained domestic quarters at the rear of the premises. Later he had been asked to help the American stewards and had gradually resumed an informal role, attending to the cellar and helping restock the bar. It was from the officers he occasionally served over the counter that he began to understand the contempt in which his defeated countrymen were now held. And, since the discovery of Belsen and Auschwitz concentration camps, he had also begun to hear them talk of 'justice' and of 'punishment' and, under their breath, of beatings.

Captain Irwin Cooper was with Counter Intelligence in the 106th and a familiar face in the bar. He was the son of a disgraced Chicago city police captain who had made his 'reputation' and his money helping the mafia in the twenties and who had finally been forced to quit the police department in the thirties. However, to the army, it was not Cooper's father who mattered, but his East Prussian mother who had taught him to speak her native tongue fluently and had raised him with the same harsh discipline she had known from her mother as a child in the back streets of Königsburg. It had left him with an enduring hatred of everything Prussian - and with Prussia he now associated all of Germany.

Cooper was not an old hand in the Division. He had not been in the desperate battles of 1944 in the Ardennes, nor even been in Europe at that time and so his inner loathing for the Germans had not been tempered by respect for their toughness and courage in battle. Instead he found only beaten men which seemed to heighten his contempt. He also brought a zeal to his counter intelligence work which made others around him wary. There were even rumours among the privates that he had taken prisoners out of camp, to be found later bound and beaten down river. Tonight Otto noticed him seated at a corner table with two young lieutenants. He remained well clear as Julie took their drinks to the table, but watched nonetheless. As she set out the beers on the table Cooper caught her eye, 'Didn't I see you at the wire today?' he said casually.

Julie marked their beer mats and noticed Cooper had now had five. She looked at him but did not smile – her uncle had warned of giving the slightest encouragement to these men, who by now had established a loathsome reputation among German women for rape and violence. 'Yes.' she replied coolly.

'Were you passing food?'

'Yes.'

One of the lieutenants intervened. 'If you're seen you know the risks.'

'They're starving.' she said defensively.

'Is there someone you know in there?' Cooper asked. Julie shook her head and began to withdraw. 'I could help,' he said more encouragingly.

Julie hesitated and went back to the table, 'My fiancé was a medical officer – a doctor. I'm trying to find him.'

One of the lieutenants seemed keen to assist, 'What unit?'

'The 25th *Panzergrenadier* Division.'

Cooper shook his head, 'Well, well, didn't you guys get hit pretty bad by them at Manhay and St Vith? The two men nodded, 'So what's this doctor's name?'

'Karl Rust. He's a captain.'

'Say, we use all the doctors we can that come in. If he's there we could find him easily enough.'

Captain Cooper looked up at her, inviting her to respond but she retreated, sensing from their salacious gazes that this generosity must be at a price she did not want to pay. As she walked away and started to clear empty glasses she felt their eyes following her and moved to the other side of the bar, out of sight.

Toward the rear of the inn was a large hall which was used for weddings, parties, and meetings. The following morning, as Julie was practicing on the old upright piano which stood in the rear of the hall, she heard the sound of someone loitering at the door. She stopped and turned to see a young, rather stocky figure, in a British officer's uniform. His German was good and he seemed in a lively humour, with a bright engaging smile and intelligent eyes.

'Magnificent!' he said, 'Oh please, don't stop!'

Julie remained reserved, 'Can I help you?'

He walked towards her and held out his hand, 'Tommy Yeo, British Liaison Officer. I've been billeted upstairs. I'll be here for a few months working with the Americans. Are you a member of the family living at the back?'

247

There was something 'safe' in the manner of this *Tommy* she thought, and that allowed her at least some latitude to be polite, so she shook his hand. 'Yes, I'm Otto's niece.'

'Oh good! Then perhaps I'll hear you again sometime?'

She looked back at the piano, 'Do you play?'

'Afraid not, I'm not even really a soldier; I'm a lawyer by training. I was helping out with the War Crimes Tribunal at Lüneburg, but they found someone better and sent me down here out of the way. I'm supposed to make sure the British and Americans are joined up.' He raised an eyebrow to indicate some scepticism of his own in this endeavour. Julie smiled and hoped perhaps that this new arrival might bring some welcome colour to their lives. He didn't seem like the other officers she'd met and she warmed to him.

That evening she saw Cooper again, but now he was sober and asked to speak to her alone, outside the kitchen door under the archway. She joined him warily, making sure her back was to the open door. He stood some distance away in the gloom, his hands behind his back, contriving to look as relaxed as possible. 'I suppose you think it was just talk last night?'

Julie shrugged her shoulders, 'I don't know that I thought about it at all. People are always talking to me. It's part of my job.'

'Well, as the Lieutenant said, we may have sixteen camps and one million prisoners but doctors are something else - they now get assigned and...I found him...Dr Karl Rust.'

Julie felt a surge of hope which she struggled to contain, half disbelieving that he could be telling the truth. 'What does he look like?'

Cooper pursed his lips, 'About 5.11, dark hair, slim. He gave me this...' Cooper produced a photograph which Julie took from him cautiously. She saw that it was one she had sent Karl two years before. It was battered and creased but was unmistakeable. Cooper took it from her hand, 'He wants it back.'

He moved away from her toward the locked doors under the archway. Julie moved toward him anxious and impatient, 'Is he alright? Can't you tell me more?'

Cooper leant against the large doors and folded his arms, 'You can't be serious. Come on! They live in holes. No, your fiancé is slowly dying like the rest of them. I'd say another month on 800 calories a day and he'll be finished. He was wounded - did you know? He should be in a hospital. He needs help.'

Julie knew this detail was self-serving - that Cooper was now hoping to do a trade. The script was familiar as was the subtext – he would help Karl and in return Julie would give herself to him. She turned back toward the door, tormented and disgusted, but his voice carried after her, 'Of course, if food was denied altogether…for disciplinary reasons…as a punishment for lack of cooperation.'

Julie turned and looked at him angrily as he moved toward her. 'You'd kill a man for this?' she said gesturing at her body.

He stood looking at her and brushed her hair with his hand, 'And you would allow a man to die for your little bit of pride?'

She felt his hand touch her breast and slapped him as hard as she could, trying to turn towards the door of the kitchen. He grabbed her waist and kicked the door shut. They struggled for a moment and then, as quickly as it had begun, Cooper let her go again as the stocky figure of Major Yeo emerged from the rear entrance of the inn and began advancing toward the commotion. Julie ran blindly into him and he clutched her arms for a moment to steady her, 'Fräulein Scholl, please excuse me!' She looked startled, gestured her apology and passed quickly back into the safety of the inn.

Tommy stood looking at Cooper. 'Thought we might have a drink?'

Cooper picked up his cap, straightened his uniform and brushed past him without speaking.

Chapter 24

Captain Cooper found Karl in what passed for a medical station near the Remagen cage entrance the following morning. He was standing with the other prisoners who also had medical skills processing arrivals to determine if they carried any infectious diseases. This was not an American initiative. The prisoners had formed a cadre of doctors who could see the potential for typhus, cholera, and dysentery, to sweep through the insanitary camp. Indeed the Americans had initially seen the group as a security threat and broken them up. Now sense had prevailed and they were using them - providing delousing powder and some disinfectant.

Cooper called Karl over. He hobbled painfully toward the Captain who made him stand to attention, 'I saw Julie Scholl last night - your fiancée - as I said I would. I think you need to write to her and set things straight about your situation here.'

Karl looked nervously at Cooper; he had seen the results of his work and knew what he and his MPs were capable of, whether provoked or not.

'Yes, of course, but I have no paper, no pen.'

Cooper nodded to an MP who stepped forward with a notebook and pencil. Cooper leant forward and whispered in Karl's ear, 'I offered her a trade. She didn't take it. I want you to tell her it's ok - that your life depends on it.'

Karl paused and then put the pencil and paper down on the ground, shaking his head and maintaining the position of attention. Cooper looked at him coldly.

'You saw what I did to Oster.'

Karl nodded.

'Then keep the paper and pencil. Think about it. I'll be back tomorrow for the letter.'

Karl did indeed remember Oster, a member of the Waffen SS who'd been picked out by the guards on arrival the previous week for transfer to a special cage dedicated to the SS at Bretzenheim. He'd screamed for an hour inside the guard post awaiting his transport while the other prisoners looked on under the arc of machine guns dazed and horrified, listening to the frenzied blows and hollers of encouragement between the guards. Later Karl and two other prisoners had been ordered in to the stockade to fetch Oster on a stretcher and clean him up, but it had been a futile gesture as he was dead already, broken and disfigured beyond recognition amid a pool of blood.

That evening, as Karl contemplated his situation, more arrivals came. It was one of the first lorries to unload that caught his eye. A heavily bandaged Luftwaffe officer got off the back and fell awkwardly. The guards kicked and shouted at him and he struggled to get to his feet, but the other prisoners seemed reluctant to help him – indifferent to his injuries. Eventually two of them brought the man over to Karl where he slumped on the ground. A Wehrmacht corporal following close behind grabbed Karl's arm and pulled him to one side, 'I've been with that shit all day. He's not Luftwaffe!'

Karl looked back at the man who was bent double with pain, 'What do you mean? Who is he then?'

'I was in Poland in '39. He was in charge of the SS down in Warthegau. Our company was deployed screening an action by the *Einsatzgruppen* and German irregulars near Posen – shooting women, children, and old men. He was in charge. Don't waste good stuff on him Doctor. I hope they hang the bastard.'

'What's his name?'

'No idea. He was higher SS then and he's higher SS now.' The man spat on the floor, 'Don't waste your time. You'll know what I mean when you speak to him; he's got that way about him - they all have.' The Corporal saluted respectfully and walked back over to the group of new arrivals who were being deloused.

When Karl returned to the man he feigned ignorance of him, but as he examined his injuries he realised that the man was almost certainly Wilhelm Koppe. He tried to remember the picture he had been shown by Albert Forster in the library in Danzig. Karl looked at his dressing which covered extensive shrapnel wounds and tightened it up as best he could. As he did so he noticed the man studying him, 'You must be SS Police Higher Leader Koppe?' Karl said casually, continuing to work.

Karl felt the man tense up, 'Then you know to keep your voice down and your mouth shut.' Koppe gestured at his arm, 'The Polish resistance tried to kill me. I've still got shrapnel. They tried to operate again last month, but we were overrun.'

'You aren't *Luftwaffe*, so why the uniform?'

Koppe looked about nervously – 'Keep your voice down.'

'So you're on the run?'

'The Poles and Russians are touring the camps - looking for people. Arthur Grieser is in Austria talking wildly to save his neck - trying to make himself useful to the Americans in the hope they won't turn him over to the Soviets. I need to get out. There's something in it for you if you can help. Do you know anyone?'

Karl finished what he was doing and looked Koppe in the eyes, 'Does the name Julie Scholl mean anything to you?

Koppe looked at him askance, 'Who?'

'Julie Scholl – Danzig '39.'

Koppe thought for a moment, 'Yes, I knew a girl of that name, but that was in Posen. We tried to arrest her there.'

'No. I'm talking about after she was in Posen. I'm talking about Danzig General Hospital. You sent men there to kill her.'

Koppe sat back eyeing Karl warily, his voice contemptuous, 'Where did you get that ridiculous story from? Who are you?'

'My name is Doctor Karl Rust.'

Koppe stood with difficulty, 'So how do you claim to know about my being involved in some business up in Danzig? It wasn't even my area.'

'Because I've seen the file – and it isn't a ridiculous story. Albert Forster showed me an SD report prepared by a man called Epp. I know everything about you...what you did and why you did it.'

Koppe shifted uncomfortably, 'Why would he show *you* a police report - what's your interest in Julie Scholl?'

'I'm the doctor who treated her at the Forster's home...helped her recover. I'm her fiancé.'

Koppe's manner became uneasy. 'I had nothing to do with what happened to Julie Scholl at the hands of Grieser. He ordered her investigation. I went to arrest her at his flat, yes – when we found out about the business with Grieser, but that was on account of her father. You've got this all wrong.'

Karl shook his head, 'It was you who sent the SD men to the hospital to kill her. I was there – they were your men from Kolmar district. I saw it with my own eyes.'

Koppe looked down at his arm and winced, 'That was a rogue operation.'

'That's absurd…do you really expect me to believe that. You organised everything…'

'And you can prove that can you, Doctor?'

Karl's anger now rose inside him and his voice became harsh, 'Julie is still alive and so are you. There can still be a trial and she can still ask for justice.'

'From whom - the Americans?'

'You will answer for your crimes…one way or another.'

Koppe seemed to falter, staring at the ground for a moment with an expression of exhaustion, gathering his thoughts, 'So be it; if it's simple revenge you want I can't stop you…call the guards if that's what you really want. But think about where it gets you. It doesn't put things right for Julie Scholl. Surely there's another way – an arrangement that can smooth things over – a trade we can both be happy with. I'm told Julie took some files before she left Danzig - Kellerman told me they were stolen from Forster's safe. They're important to me. I want them back. When we're free perhaps I can buy them off you. How would that be? I can set you and that girl of yours up for life – and I'm not talking a few thousand…I can help you rebuild your lives. Isn't that what everyone wants to do now – to move on?'

Karl shook his head, 'You really think I would do a deal…for money?'

Koppe smiled, 'Not money – gold, diamonds…whatever you want.'

'You must be mad.'

Koppe shook his head, 'No Doctor, not mad. Look around you and think about it. We're all going to have to move on sooner or later…start afresh – put everything back together. Justice won't buy you bread, put a shirt on your back, build you a home, will it? Just think about that, and how you'll feel in five, ten years, when all this is behind you. You've got to think of the future now – of that fiancée of yours. She won't thank you for throwing this opportunity away will she?' Koppe squared up to Karl with a renewed sense of confidence, 'Time to face reality Dr Rust - time to move on.' He turned and began to hobble away toward the delousing queue pausing briefly to look back at Karl, 'Think about where it gets you.' And with that he merged into the mass of waiting prisoners.

The following morning Karl went to the military police post early. Cooper would arrive at some point, but he had settled on the idea that in identifying Koppe he might gain at least some protection from Cooper for Julie and himself. It was a desperate strategy but, after a sleepless night, there seemed no other option.

The MPs were reluctant to allow Karl to see a senior intelligence officer and rang around to see who might be available to take a record of Karl's sighting. Finally, they waved Karl forward to a jeep, which took him under guard to the military police headquarters in Remagen town.

Major Perkins was impatient with any interruption to his routine. He, too, was a replacement officer, a reservist, only lately arrived, and looked forward to nothing except returning home. He hated the regular army, the food, the weather, and above all, he was totally indifferent to his work. But, unable to vent these feelings on any of the responsible agencies his ire now fell on any German, for they alone he felt had engineered his discomfort and now, he reasoned, they should pay.

However, his misery was not yet entirely complete. His commanding officer had been ordered to absorb a British liaison officer and Perkins was now saddled with him, there being in his Colonel's mind some link between his role in counter intelligence and the general pursuit of harmony between the allies. He could hardly therefore refuse to pursue the matter of Karl Rust's sighting of a senior SS officer when the MPs called him that morning, especially as he was talking to Major Yeo at the time of the call.

When Captain Rust was shown into the interrogation room Major Yeo pushed his seat back from the desk to emphasise his role as an observer, while Major Perkins shuffled papers and found a pen. Karl stood with two MPs behind him struggling to maintain the position of attention. Major Yeo could see from his eyes that he was near the point of collapse. Presently he pulled over a spare chair for him and helped him sit down, to the evident annoyance of Perkins, who chose to ignore the gesture.

'You say you have identified SS Obergruppenführer Wilhelm Koppe in the Remagen cage?'

254

Karl nodded, his voice weak and rasping, 'Yes, he was head of the SS in Warthegau – based in Posen.'

Perkins turned to Yeo, 'Is he on our list?'

Yeo nodded, 'He's been named by Grieser, the former Gauleiter there, who is currently held in Austria. Koppe's accused of mass murder – shootings, deportations, kidnap, the execution of hostages - the Poles want him badly'

Perkins finished his note. 'I'll assume you can recognise the man again?' Karl nodded. 'Ok then, I'll put you in protective custody and get one of my good field men to chase this up.'

Yeo leaned forward, 'Would you mind if I also ran along behind, so to speak.'

The thought now occurred to Perkins that this could rid him of Yeo for a few days and so he agreed, though feigning reluctance. After the prisoner had been taken out by the MPs Perkins shook his head, 'If I had my way we'd just shoot the lot of them and be done with it.'

Yeo slapped him on the back, smiling pugnaciously, 'I'm sure that's exactly what they thought when they cooked up the Final Solution - easy to say when you're on top.'

Perkins thought for a moment and then looked around at Yeo with unease, 'Say, you've got that weird English sense of humour, haven't you…'

That afternoon Major Yeo talked his way past the guards to see Karl before the appointed time for his further interrogation. As he sat opposite him he slipped him some sugar and a few squares of chocolate, which Karl ate with pitiful gratitude.

When Cooper came in their eyes met and Yeo registered his irritation. Cooper chose not to salute and Major Yeo didn't take issue, but remained studiously passive and observant. Cooper had not anticipated being thwarted like this over a simple bit of blackmail and 'seduction'. Karl had been resourceful he thought to himself, he had surrounded himself with the protection only a 'big story' could provide. He sat down and looked at the prisoner critically, his voice harsh and sceptical.

'You are Captain Karl Rust lately a medical officer of the 25 *Panzergrenadier* Division. You have reported a sighting of SS Obergruppenführer Wilhelm Koppe in the Remagen cage?'

Karl nodded, 'He arrived at 20.00 last night.'

'I have a file from the British who have detained a Gauleiter named Albert Forster: *'arrested by a member of the 53rd (Welsh) Division in Hamburg, 27 May, 1945. Then interned at the British-administered Lager Fallingbostel'*. He alleges that Koppe had been injured in Cracow - tell me what injuries this man had?'

'He was partially paralysed in the right arm. He showed evidence of shrapnel wounds to the neck and face. He limped in the right leg.'

Cooper sat for a moment looking at the notes. 'How did he get these injuries?'

'He told me the Polish had tried to assassinate him.'

'How was he dressed?'

'In a Luftwaffe officer's uniform.'

'Did he give you an assumed name?'

'No.'

'Did he say anything else?'

'He said he was going to get out. He wanted my help.'

'Did he say how?'

'I assume he has a plan. But since he's only just arrived and he's wounded I imagine he'll try to buy his way out – he offered me money.'

'Buy his way out?'

'I've heard rumours.' Karl said cautiously.

'About?'

'People buying their way out.'

Cooper scoffed, 'I wouldn't believe every bit of camp gossip.' His eyes now moved down the British report and he dwelt for a moment on a paragraph of seeming significance to him but said nothing. He turned to Yeo, 'Do you have any questions Sir?' Yeo shook his head.

Cooper then turned to Karl, 'You will be held here overnight and we will go to the camp tomorrow to find Koppe together. You must understand that you will be returned to the cage subsequently.' Karl nodded.

As Major Yeo and Captain Cooper left the building, walking in step, Yeo looked over at the Captain critically, 'Is that really wise? Shouldn't he be moved to another camp after this?'

256

Cooper looked at him with irritation, 'You think he would be harmed if we returned him?'

'It's possible – as an informer. Of course, it's not for me to say – just a thought, but we lost an informant like that some weeks ago up in Hamburg.'

Cooper smiled and they walked on a little way in silence, 'I think I'll go and see the innkeeper's niece again, you know, the one that got away the other night. Do you think she's worth another try?'

'I got the distinct impression she wasn't interested.'

As their ways parted Cooper chose this moment to salute the Major, who returned it without enthusiasm. 'I don't know Major, I'm feelin' kind'a lucky!'

That evening Otto was feeling on edge. The Americans had been drinking hard and the stewards were struggling to cope, so he was helping to draw supplies from the cellars. There was talk of the camps being taken over by another Division and the 106th being sent elsewhere; and of course that might mean home, or the Pacific, but anywhere except their current guard deployment now seemed attractive.

When Major Yeo arrived back at the hotel he quickly found Otto, warning him of Captain Cooper's intention to make another attempt on his niece. Otto was a man of inflexible views and inclined to bold action where required. He had also fought in the First World War and so knew soldiers and their ways. He thanked the Major and pulled Julie from her duties and into the seclusion of their own quarters. He handed Julie the key to the door and she locked herself in with Ingrid for the evening in the parlour.

Julie found Ingrid sitting in a chair by the stove darning a sock. Julie sat opposite and sighed resentfully. Ingrid looked up. 'More trouble with the American?'

'Yes, Auntie. Uncle says he's looking for me – it seems that rather pleasant Englishman had a word with him and warned him.'

Ingrid continued to work, 'When I was a girl the Americans and the French were here you know. It's ironic really, the bridge was only built to enable the German army to attack France, it was never a commercial venture – at least I never saw any ordinary trains on it. And in both wars it's served our enemies.'

257

'What were they like in the last war – the foreign soldiers here?'

'Oh, I think they were better behaved – certainly the Americans.' She paused and looked up, 'They didn't loot so much, there's been too much of that here, and their manners were better.' Ingrid gestured at a thin English language newspaper which lay on the table. 'Of course this has been a different sort of war – I mean the concentration camps have made them very hateful towards us – as if we all approved.'

Julie picked up the paper and looked at the headline, '*The Blonde Beast, Kramer and 43 others to stand trial for Belsen Crimes.*' There was a picture of Irma Grese - the 'Blonde Beast', and Josef Kramer, the camp commandant, standing together with a guard carrying a machine gun behind them. Julie stared at the picture, unable to believe her eyes. Finally she put the paper down and turned to Ingrid, 'You can't read English can you Auntie? Who read this to you?'

Ingrid shook her head. 'Oh, Otto has a few words, but revenge…victor's justice; it's the same in any language.' Ingrid pointed to the paper, 'What about Dresden, Cologne, Hamburg, Lübeck – the women and children burned to death by the RAF? And what about the American camps here with no food and water – the prisoners starving to death?' Ingrid's voice faltered, 'I mean look at that silly girl, Irma Grese. How old is she? Julie, she could be you. I simply can't believe what they say about her.'

Julie stared at the newspaper, her face more sombre, 'Auntie, you have to understand that the Nazi's were very clever.'

'What *do* you mean? I always thought they were rather stupid.'

'I saw how they drew people in, manipulated them – even *silly girls*…and I'm afraid I was one of them…in Posen in October '39.'

Ingrid leaned forward anxiously, 'Julie, whatever are you saying?'

'I was at the orphanage at the time. One day all of us were made to line up by the side of the road. We were asked to try and identify the Polish men who had attacked us a few weeks before. Some suspects were taken from the back of a lorry and stood in front of us. A few Polish people were passing by, watching us, wondering what we were doing. As it happened some of the men were part of the mob that came to the orphanage and most of the girls made at least one or two

258

identifications. I didn't want to, but then the policeman saw me holding back and challenged me and so I had to do as I was told and join in with the others. And then after, when we had made our identifications, the policeman told us that the men would be shot. There was going to be no trial, no further questions – we were young innocent girls and they'd turned us into their accomplices, into those men's executioners, and nobody could refuse to take part in it. I don't suppose it was much different for Irma Grese.'

When Major Yeo returned to the bar after washing and changing, Otto emerged from the cellar and handed him a beer, 'Anything, my good friend, anything I can do - you tell me.' Yeo nodded, slightly embarrassed to accept the gratuity.

When Cooper arrived Major Yeo watched him from a corner table, unobserved in the crowd. Cooper was certainly keen, Yeo could see that as Cooper's eyes scanned the room for his quarry. When Julie could not be found he began to drink aggressively and waited. Yeo sensed that he should remain and that Cooper would soon become volatile. Finally he saw him accost Otto, at first with impatience at the bar and then with physical force to one side of it, pushing him further out of sight. Tommy stood and moved around the bar to get a better view. By now Cooper had seized Otto by the neck in a narrow passage which led to the stables. They were shouting at each other, but it remained inaudible amid the general din. Finally, as Cooper began to choke Otto, Yeo decided he must intervene, and although not of Cooper's size, his stocky toughness, learned over many bruising years on the rugby field, counted for something toward his confidence if it came to blows.

He stood squat in the passageway and shouted over the noise, 'Captain Cooper, people are waiting for a drink!'

Cooper looked around with an expression of cold fury and then slowly disengaged. 'You again! What's your thing with this family, eh?'

'I just wanted a drink. I was looking for Otto. I found you…having a word.'

Cooper bit his lip and straightened his tunic, while Otto moved back to the bar hastily.

They exchanged glances for a moment and then Cooper seemed to become unnaturally cordial, 'Oh, about Koppe. We can't go

259

looking for him tomorrow, there's too much going on. We'll delay 'till Thursday. We'll meet at 07.00 at MP HQ. Ok?'

Yeo nodded and Cooper left, pushing aside the gathered junior officers at the bar with renewed impatience.

It was noon the following day when Koppe found himself the particular attention of a number of other prisoners. They eyed him from a distance, exchanging glances with the guards and gesturing toward him. Soon two heavily armed MPs closed in. He made no move to evade them and awaited arrest, cursing the doctor under his breath as they handcuffed him.

'How did you find me so quickly?' Koppe asked as he slumped into a chair in the interrogation cell looking at Cooper.

'You met Doctor Rust I believe – he came to us yesterday...told us who you are. As for the search party; your comrades are starving, I gave them a few pieces of food - that's all it takes these days. Anyway it's safer for you this way. I don't want Rust to know we've met – not until we've talked.'

Koppe seemed resigned to his fate, 'So what happens now?'

'That's up to you.'

'Aren't you going to hand me over to the Poles - the Russians?'

'I read Albert Forster's debriefing about you.'

'So what! The man's under pressure, he'd say anything.'

'Look, let's not fuck about here. I read a report from the British up near Hamburg. Forster says you made yourself very rich one way and another. Forster says you were all at it: gold, diamonds, money, art. He says *you* were very active.' Koppe looked impassive but Cooper persisted, 'Look the war's over, I couldn't give a fuck what you did to get rich, but I want some. We can do a trade?'

Koppe looked sceptical. 'For what?'

'Money, diamonds, gold, whatever you have; for that I cut you free.'

Koppe remained stubbornly unmoved, so Cooper rose from his seat and grabbed his arm. Koppe grimaced with pain, but Cooper rolled up his sleeve, pulled back the bandage and exposed the SS blood group tattoo, 'That will get you every time!' He stood back. 'They've started screening the camps for that. It's only a matter of weeks before they find you.'

260

Koppe studied Cooper cautiously, 'So, what are you offering? I give you gold and you get me out?'

'Gold, gems...I don't give a shit.'

Koppe thought for a moment, 'But it's all in Switzerland.' How does that work if I can't get to it?'

'All of it?'

'I have some gold here in Germany – and some diamonds. I can pay you perhaps the equivalent of $5,000.'

Cooper looked up and shook his head, 'Your life is worth more than that!'

Koppe began to make further calculations, sensing Cooper's willingness to go further, 'And what about the evidence against me - the witnesses? What about Rust and his girl Scholl? They can name me; he knows I'm here. She has a file.'

Cooper sat, 'What about them? What are you asking for?' Koppe remained silent but Cooper quickly understood his meaning and leaned towards him, 'Ok, Rust would be easy. He's probably on his way out anyway. He wouldn't stand out – not at the moment. Scholl is more difficult - she's a civilian and a woman. She would have to disappear...that's a risk - more expensive?'

Koppe shook his head, 'But she has the evidence – the files from Danzig – possibly even a film. My freedom's no good to me without them.'

Cooper weighed up the odds and then recalled the Oster incident and the outright hostility of Major Perkins to any talk of an investigation – his willingness to let Cooper make the running.

Cooper stood, put his hand on Koppe's shoulder and leaned down, whispering in his ear, '$30,000 - for that you get your freedom and no loose ends.'

As he stood back Koppe slapped the table with his left arm, 'Robbery!'

Coopers voice was caustic, 'Not when your life depends on it - $5,000 on your release and $25,000 after.'

Cooper loomed over Koppe, 'She's here in Remagen you know, right here, I've met her; I can fix it. But, it's your choice.' He stood back and folded his arms, looking at Koppe expectantly.

Koppe pondered for a moment and then nodded, 'Alright...but no loose ends.'

261

'That's the deal and I guarantee Rust and the girl, but we need to keep you out of sight. There's a Brit around. We're going looking for you in the camp tomorrow with Doctor Rust. I threw him off so we could talk. There's a place I use, *the barn* we call it. I'll keep you there from now on. I've a couple of guys who help me with irregular stuff. The main thing is to keep you off the camp until we do the deal, and when the money is there your past will disappear...and so will they.'

Chapter 25

Julie met Major Yeo in the doorway of the inn that lunchtime after he had made a fruitless search for Captain Cooper. He knew now that he'd been given the slip, because whatever Cooper was doing he had not left any note of his whereabouts with the usual sources, nor apparently even with his MPs. Julie extended her hand, offering to take his dripping umbrella.

'Horrible weather.' he said, wiping his boots on the mat inside the entrance.

'My uncle told me what you did last night. Thank you.'

Tommy paused, 'Ah, really – well, don't let on, these Yanks are terribly sensitive you know.'

'I wondered if you would like a coffee in the parlour.'

'Is that allowed? I mean your uncle and aunt - it's their home.'

'Oh, don't worry; you are now the acceptable face of occupation. He thinks you are very honourable. He quite likes the British anyway - ever since he was in the trenches on the Western Front.'

Yeo smiled, 'Odd isn't it, that these days one's qualification to be a decent chap is to have tried to kill your uncle in the last war.'

Julie looked around, 'Yes, but he's very grateful you didn't!'

Tommy raised his eyebrows and smiled, 'Well, quite.'

When they went through to the gloomy parlour at the rear of the inn Tommy could see the cramped conditions in which they lived and it touched him that they should welcome him as a stranger. Otto was sitting sipping a bowl of watery soup and playing with a kitten with some string. When they entered he stood and they shook hands. Otto insisted the formal 'Sie' was dropped and 'du' was used and offered Tommy his seat. It was the only place Tommy could sit, but after protest he was firmly pressed into the back of the chair. 'And now that Julie is here I must go to work. My apologies and please enjoy our hospitality. I know my niece wants to talk to you.'

Tommy sat slightly disconcerted by the prospect of being alone with Julie and wondered what subject could possibly be in prospect. He had always been wary of attractive women. They had generally disturbed his equilibrium and made him unhappy and he had already decided that Julie had the looks to down a bull elephant at twenty paces with a coquettish smile. He was happy to save her blushes with Cooper, but not if this now meant his own undoing. Nevertheless he watched her for a few moments with pleasure as she prepared coffee.

Finally she sat, looking at him earnestly over the steaming cups, 'When we first met you said you had been working with the War Crimes Tribunal at Lüneburg?'

Tommy sat back 'Oh, this is a *serious* conversation! I see. Well yes, that's right.'

'Did you work there for long?'

'A few weeks. It was really a bit of a shambles. There had to be a legal process and I happened to be a trained lawyer serving with the Royal Artillery in the area. They quickly got someone better, a Major Cranfield took over after a few days and we worked together until some other chaps had been recruited. Then I got moved here.'

'Did you ever meet a woman called Irma Grese?'

His manner became more reserved, 'Yes.'

'I read in the paper that they want to hang them – the forty five from Belsen.'

He paused, 'Julie before we go further you must tell me if this conversation has a deeper significance. There are rules on fraternisation you know. Most of them are nonsense, but if you have some purpose in this you should tell me – in fairness? I can get into trouble.'

Julie nodded, 'You are quite right. I'm sorry, it's just that I met Irma Grese in November '44 and I simply don't recognise her from what I read in the papers.'

Tommy leaned forward, 'Met her - how?'

'We were on a train from Zoppot to Berlin. She'd been sent to deliver me to the SS in Berlin and then take me to Bergen Belsen. Instead she helped me escape.'

Tommy looked at his dirty shoes both surprised and intrigued. 'Tell me the story?'

Julie looked at him reproachfully, 'It isn't a story.'

Tommy sat back, 'I'm sorry – my German is not always *correct*. Please tell me what happened.'

Julie began to tell him of her past, the encounters of her life from the moment she had arrived in Posen in August 1939. As she

264

faltered occasionally during the telling, stumbling on her words, searching for less painful expressions, and sometimes pausing to catch her breath and hold back her tears, Tommy's realisation grew that he possibly held something very precious in his hands, the truth of a story Irma Grese had told them three weeks earlier and which Major Cranfield had refused to believe.

When Julie finished Tommy sat forward and clasped his hands together. He paused looking into her reddened eyes, 'Julie I can't say very much, but I can tell you that there were gaps in Irma's life - in her SS file. It had been filleted by someone with access to the highest levels of the SS and camp administration. We didn't believe her story about Posen – why should we, there was nothing to confirm it. But now you've corroborated her story that's rather changed the game.' He stood. 'But as a serving officer I'm afraid this can't remain a matter between us. If, as you say, you also have evidence of the crimes, a film, internal German security reports of the period, then they'll have to be seized. Are you prepared to give them to me now?'

Julie shook her head. 'No.'

Yeo sat again, slightly taken aback, 'Why?'

'My fiancé is being held in the Remagen camp. I know because Captain Cooper found him. That's what our argument was about the other night when you found us under the archway. He wanted me to give myself to him in exchange for Karl's life. He says Karl will be allowed to starve to death unless I agree.'

'But you will give me the papers in exchange for help in securing your fiancé's safety, his freedom - is that it?'

'Yes. But please don't think you can take the inn apart and find the material, it's very safe somewhere else.'

Tommy stood slightly offended, 'Not my style at all! And what's his name, this fiancé of yours?

'Captain Karl Rust…'

'…of the 25th *Panzergrenadier* Division?' Tommy interrupted seamlessly. I can tell you Julie, your fiancé is in custody and being fed. But he says SS *Obergruppenführer* Koppe is *here* - in this cage. Karl is safe but Cooper seems to have managed to become the investigating officer, so Karl is not quite in the clear yet.'

'Irma told me that Koppe killed my father, personally, in November '39, together with a Gestapo man, Müller.'

265

'Koppe has a lot of blood on his hands – he has a lot to fear if he's caught.'

'What will you do?'

'I'll need to get away from here for twenty four hours and speak to Major Cranfield. Until then stay here and stay out of sight – and away from that blasted Captain Cooper. I just need a little time to get things sorted out.'

That night, after Otto had closed and bolted the doors and shutters at the front of the inn, he heard the whine of jeeps pulling up outside and the rapid footfall of troops deploying. The outer doors were beaten with a rifle butt a few times and Otto impatiently undid his work. Captain Cooper stood in front of him with a warrant, which he neither understood nor recognised, while four MPs barged their way past him into the lobby and ran upstairs. Otto shrugged, 'But what do you want?' Then Otto heard Julie scream and turned towards the stairs but Cooper grabbed him around the throat, 'Your little Brit fuck is on leave, so it's down to you Otto, what's it to be, eh? Otto felt Cooper's Colt .45 at his temple and ceased resisting. As he did so Julie came to the base of the stairs supported by two MPs. She was handcuffed, bare footed and in nothing but her nightdress overlaid with a thick dressing gown.

'Watch those hands, soldier, and keep those cuffs on, she has a real mean streak.' Cooper said as they passed by. He released Otto and withdrew into the darkness.

'But where are you taking her like that?' Otto shouted, enraged and horrified.

'Protective custody.'

'But that's what the Nazis called it! The war is over! What are you doing? What has she done?' But Otto's words echoed into the empty darkness and soon the jeeps were gone.

When Ingrid found him a few minutes later he was slumped in the doorway with his head in his hands. She placed her arms round him and raised him up, 'Tomorrow you will go to the camp commandant, to the military police - they must do something about this.'

Otto shook his head, 'They are Barbarians. All of them! They've taken Julie…they've taken her, and we can do nothing.'

The following morning Julie awoke shivering in the first light of dawn in a basement cell at Military Police Headquarters in Remagen. It was small, gloomy, damp and cold. She looked at the empty bucket in the corner in which she was expected to relieve herself and decided she could wait. She sat for a moment on the edge of the bed, listening for the sound of other prisoners, or guards, but everything was silent. She looked down and noticed her filthy feet and ankles and tried to wipe them clean with the corner of a blanket. The gesture brought back memories, a vivid impression of how she had tried to wipe the blood off her shoe in the stinking foetid cell in Fort Winiary. She remembered the terror with which she had awaited interrogation then and contrasted it with her mood now. It was cold and she felt tired, dirty and apprehensive, but she understood things better - the need to maintain some kind of self-possession, a sense of detachment if she was going to get through it.

When the cell door opened an hour later Captain Cooper entered alone carrying a chair and sat down facing her as she huddled uncomfortably on the edge of her bed. He looked at her for a moment and noticed she was shivering, 'Would you like me to send for some clothes?'

Julie gathered the dressing gown around her neck. 'I'm fine.'

Cooper smiled, 'We have detained SS Obergruppenführer Koppe. Do you know that name?'

'I do.'

'Are you aware he had your father killed?'

'Yes…he murdered him in Posen.'

'And can you prove that - do you have evidence against him? If you do we need to see it – to bring a prosecution. I've been appointed the investigating officer.'

'No…I have no evidence.'

Cooper frowned, 'I was told you had files.'

Julie looked down at her bare feet, 'No, I don't. Who told you that?'

Cooper hesitated momentarily, 'According to your fiancé.'

'We haven't met for three years. How could he know whether I have evidence against Koppe?'

'Someone must have told him. Look, does it matter who?'

'I suppose not.'

'So where is the evidence against him?'

267

'I don't have any evidence – it was just something I was told.'

'Well, people say you do have evidence.'

Julie looked at him coldly, 'They can say what they like – and you can repeat the question as many times as you like. I've nothing more to say to you or anyone else. And I want to see your commanding officer. I want to complain.'

Cooper stood, smiling, looking down at her with steely eyes and then slapped her hard across the face. The blow sent her headlong into the wall and rolling off the narrow bed onto the floor. She lay still for a moment, stunned and bruised. As she got up unsteadily he rubbed his hand, 'I guess that makes us even. Sit down.'

Julie sat down warily, but did not otherwise show any emotion. He stood weighing her up for a moment; she wasn't what he'd expected - she'd adjusted quickly to the conditions he'd put her in: the cold, lack of sleep, lack of clothing, the isolation. Even the slap seemed to have miscarried - leaving her sullen rather than shaken. He resumed in a more measured tone, trying to feel his way back into the interrogation - to work out another strategy. 'Ok, let's just say you do have evidence because I know it for a fact. The SD file went missing in Danzig – the day you left. Gertrud Forster admitted giving you the file and there's no reason for you to have ditched it – am I right? The question then is what will it take to make you give it to me? You want justice surely – for your father?' And is there is a roll of film? Do you have that too?'

Julie looked at him defiantly, 'How can you claim to know all this from Karl? Who's giving you all this information? Are you working for the fugitives in the SS now – the Gestapo perhaps? Are you studying their techniques? Perhaps Koppe and you have done a deal, like the one you offered me.'

He stood, throwing the chair to one side angrily and then swung at her with his fist. Her body sprawled along the bed with the force of the impact and she collided head first with the wall but, this time, she remained crumpled on the floor, concussed by the collision and unable to move. 'I don't have....' she whispered barely audibly before lapsing into unconsciousness.

Cooper paced the cell shouting, 'I don't believe you. Now get up – get up!' He picked up the bucket in the corner of the cell and threw it at her but she didn't react to its impact, nor did she appear to register his repeated kicks. Cooper clenched his fists in frustration and

268

finally threw his chair at her. It narrowly missed, bouncing off the wall and landing at his feet again. He kicked it to one side. 'Who are you calling the Gestapo you fucking kraut bitch? Fucking whore!' Still seething with anger Cooper left the cell and slammed the door shut. When he reached the end of the corridor a young MP was standing the other side of the grille, alerted by the noise and the shouting. He unlocked the door, standing crisply to attention after doing so. His face was fresh and keen but he eyed Cooper in a way to which he took exception.

'What are you looking at, soldier?' The MP remained rigidly at attention and said nothing. Cooper inspected him carefully. 'Where are you from?'

The young man shouted his reply, 'Iowa, Sir.'

Cooper noted the starched puttees, glistening boots, and the immaculate uniform. 'Very smart.' he said eyeballing the young man. 'Name?'

'2307202 Private Jensen, Sir.'

Cooper returned Jensen's salute casually. 'As you were, farm boy.'

When Cooper had gone Private Jensen unlocked the grille door again and walked toward the cell from which Cooper had emerged. He moved the spy flap to one side and saw part of a young woman's body in a dressing gown and nightdress lying on the floor, a chair overturned to one side. He stood back for a moment struggling to take in what he had seen. His family were devout Christians and his father had more lately become a lay preacher back in his home town of Emmetsburg. After the Civil War the county had become populated with many Norwegians, Poles, Danes and Germans and it was from the last two nationalities he was descended. He asked himself what 'Pop' would do; what his Mom would say if she knew he had witnessed *this* and simply walked away. After a moment of hesitation he unlocked the cell and entered, knowing his conscience and his duty and prepared to defend both and take the consequences.

By the time he left the cell again five minutes later he had placed Julie on the crude bed and done what he could to make her comfortable. He was not certain she would be alright, how could he be, but he saw no way to complain. Cooper's harshness was a legend and Major Perkins, the man who could and should act, was a broken reed. He sat, disconsolately, listening for sounds of movement until he was relieved.

Cooper returned later that day bringing two MP's with him and placing Karl in the cell next to Julie. When he entered her cell their eyes met with mutual hostility. He stooped slightly, 'I don't have time to waste.'

She glowered at him, 'I do. You can't keep me here for ever.'

'It won't come to that.'

'So…what's next? You can't keep beating me either.'

Cooper smiled and stood back again, noticing the dark red blood trails running down her neck from the hair line and congealed into large patches on the collar of her dressing gown. He stretched nonchalantly and paced about slowly with his arms clasped behind his back, 'Do you know who's next door?' Julie looked at him warily, 'Dr Karl Rust…with two MPs. He's about to assault them and they are about to use reasonable and proportionate force to defend themselves and pacify the prisoner. For a man in his condition he seems remarkably difficult to control – even by two of my more muscular MPs.' Julie shook her head knowing that this would be his death sentence.

She met Cooper's eyes, 'Can I see him?'

Cooper shrugged, surprised by her composure, 'Sure…why not.' He grabbed her and she cried out, clutching at her ribs. She hobbled into the corridor where Cooper removed the spyhole cover on the adjacent cell and pushed her head towards it. Karl was sitting, barely conscious, on a wooden bench, leaning against the wall. He was gaunt, unshaven and dressed in what amounted to no more than dirty rags. His hands were emaciated, the yellow parchment skin stretching between the bones, the tendons accentuated by the deep hollows and wasted muscle. She stepped back, buried her head in her hands and sank to the floor. Until this moment she had remembered him as the tanned confident soldier she had parted with in 1941. She had prepared herself for the fact that he would be different - perhaps thin and weak - but the man she saw now was a ghost, aged, frail, and scarcely alive. Cooper looked down impatiently and nudged her with his shoe, 'So?'

She looked up, 'He has to be helped. If I give you the evidence, will you let me help him?'

Cooper smiled. 'No. Fuck no. He'll live – for now. That's my offer.'

Julie lowered her head again, 'I'll have to show you where the file is. I can't describe it. It's in a ruined building near the river.'

Chapter 26

It had been a mad dash to the Headquarters of the American 106th Division and whilst Major Cranfield doubted the urgency of the situation and protested, Tommy Yeo had maintained the momentum. They had cleared it with Montgomery's Staff HQ and then with Major General Stroh of the 106th, they had surmounted Colonel Dix's misgivings and now they began their final leg to the Military Police Headquarters in Remagen. But Major Yeo was also calling in favours, and as they arrived an officer from the American Judge Advocate General's Corps stepped from a car and shook Tommy's hand, 'Thanks for coming, I thought you should be here. Good to put a face to the voice.' Tommy said.

The American, Major Jimmy Torrens, whom Tommy had known only as a voice on the telephone when he had been putting together the Lüneburg legal framework, looked over their subpoena and the various consents and waivers that had been given by higher authority. Finally he nodded, 'Shall we go in?' he said in an educated Boston accent.

They had arrived at quarter to four, while Major Perkins was making ready to leave the office early, but he had failed to make good his escape and was now back at his desk, sullen and resentful, his greatcoat discarded on the floor. He looked at his adjutant who was studying the papers Tommy Yeo had served on him. He had not bothered to look at them himself, a gesture of disdain that was lost on nobody in the room, 'So what does it mean?' he said looking over his shoulder at his adjutant.

Torrens was having none of this and erupted impatiently, 'You Sir, are a United States officer. You have been served with a lawful subpoena by the Lüneburg Military Tribunal. I am here to ensure that the US Army will comply. That is *you* Sir, not your adjutant.'

Perkins turned hesitantly, 'I don't even know if we hold Captain Rust. I think he was sent back to the cage.'

The adjutant leaned forward, 'Captain Cooper left with Captain Rust and a girl about an hour ago, Sir.'

Torrens stood alert, 'A girl, and who is she?'

'A civilian Sir.' the adjutant replied, 'Julie Scholl. She was held overnight. She lives in the village.'

Major Yeo looked at Perkins incredulously, 'Julie Scholl is a German civilian; what the hell was she doing in a military prison?'

Perkins shook his head. 'I don't know, I don't know. Cooper's a good man - he knows what he's doing. He must be on to something.' Perkins looked around him at the open hostility of Cranfield, Yeo and Torrens, 'Ok, ok, have them, I don't give a shit - but they're not here.'

Torrens stood back, 'Major Perkins, those prisoners are and we must presume remain in US Army custody with Captain Cooper who is an officer under your command and you *will* find them.'

Perkins picked up the phone and spoke to a Staff Sergeant. He dwelt on the answers with increasing unease. Finally he stood with a look of apprehension, 'Give me two minutes, Sirs, and I'll be back.'

They waited for five minutes until a young keen faced MP appeared, saluted sharply, and ushered them to three Jeeps at the rear of the building. He seemed to have 'replaced' the Major who now sat two Jeeps behind them. Four MPs armed with rifles slipped into the second jeep and they sped in convoy onto the road.

Torrens leaned across from the front passenger seat as the jeep rattled over the cobbled road with increasing speed, 'What's your name MP?'

'Private Jensen, Sir.'

'Iowa?'

The private smiled, 'Yes, Sir.'

'What's going on?' he shouted in Jensen's ear above the whine of the engine.

'I don't rightly know what's goin' on Sir, I just know the Cap'ns made a lot of guys nervous - me included. He's kinda out of control – you know what I mean, there ain't no rules no more. He beat up on the girl today pretty bad in the cells – clean knocked her out – cut her head pretty bad. It ain't right, no way Sir.'

Jensen was now driving hard and fast, dodging lorries and taking to the verge occasionally to maintain momentum while the other jeeps determinedly clung to their tail. Yeo shouted in his ear from the back seat as they left the road and began to follow a narrow track along the Rheine meadows. 'So where the hell are we going.'

'The Cap'ns got this place. Shit I don't know, he brings people here, prisoners - him and a couple of the bad ass sergeants.'

273

Yeo grabbed the MPs arm, 'When we get near kill the engine and let's do the last bit by foot.' Yeo drew his Webley revolver but then re-holstered it after further reflection.

Cooper had reconnoitred the place he called 'the barn' early in his posting at Rheine meadow camps, when it had become apparent that he enjoyed unfettered power under the dysfunctional Major Perkins. He had begun to use it to negotiate with prisoners in late April when some of them had suggested that money could be arranged to ease their existence or even buy freedom. But once Cooper realised the size of sums available, in some cases, his greed had rapidly escalated to extortion and violence.

Its appearance was innocent enough - a small squat bleached grey wooden shack, like so many old agricultural buildings dotted around the fields and meadows. It seldom attracted the attention of passers-by and so was ideal for the purposes to which he put it.

When Julie and Karl arrived at the barn they were still handcuffed. Karl was conscious but half blind and barely able to walk, while Julie was tired and bruised, but now alert again after her concussion. She looked at the manila envelope at her feet in the front passenger foot-well of the jeep and despaired. As they stopped, the MP next to Karl in the back leaped out and another MP emerged from the wooden shack to greet Cooper with a thumbs-up. When Julie entered the barn she saw a tall man in a brown suit apparently waiting for Cooper. He smiled at her with surprise, 'So, finally we meet, what an unexpected pleasure.'

Cooper looked at Julie, whose expression remained blank, 'But of course, you've never met have you?' Cooper gestured an introduction, 'Fräulein Scholl may I introduce SS Obergruppenführer Wilhelm Koppe.'

Julie hesitated and then lashed out with her bare foot, narrowly missing Koppe, who stepped back deftly to avoid her. Cooper bowled her over into the hay with a look of irritation and she fell heavily, but her voice was still fierce, 'Only once, outside the orphanage…that was enough!'

While this was happening a woman in her late forties stood back a little in the shadows with a small suitcase watching events. Koppe turned and gestured to her and she stepped forward to a rough wooden table, drawing finger sized ingots of gold from it and placing them on the table. While Cooper weighed these Koppe knelt down to look Julie in the face, 'How could you be so difficult to kill when your father was so easy? It's such an enigma to me.'

Julie looked back at him but said nothing. She simply took in the face of the man who had murdered her father and tried to fix it in her mind. He stood and glanced at the opened manila envelope.

'And you won't let me take it now?'

'And trust you to come back from Switzerland!' Cooper said with incredulity.

With this Koppe picked up the suitcase, took his female companion's arm and walked out of the barn into the gathering dusk. Cooper held the gold ingots in his hand and smiled, 'Thank God for war!'

The MP at the door nodded, 'So we've got to babysit this for two weeks?' He said pointing at their captives.

'No, it's too risky, we'll do them tonight. We can't hang around. He'll be back for the papers, no sweat.' Cooper lifted Julie to her feet and reached for his Colt .45, 'Time you learned your place, young lady.' But before he could move further one of the MPs thought he saw something moving in the dusk toward the river, 'Captain, I thought I heard Jeeps and...'

Cooper looked over, 'Coming this way?'

'I don't think so - the sound's stopped, but I thought I saw somethin'.' Cooper went to the door and peered across the meadow towards the river. Then he suddenly saw silhouetted figures advancing toward them and one stocky man stood out in particular, 'Fuck! It's that Brit Yeo... and the Major!'

While the MPs took to their heels Cooper hesitated, mesmerised by the gold, the evidence which lay on the table and the prisoners, which must all now be in some way explained. He pulled the door shut, drew his pistol and took Julie by the hair, placing the gun against her temple.

Footsteps approached, the door shook and creaked on its hinges and someone fumbled with the latch. When the door had been dragged open enough an MP entered cautiously with a flashlight. The beam from his light fell immediately on Julie, the nickel plated pistol glinting at her temple, and behind her, Captain Cooper, agitated, his eyes flickering with indecision. The MPs rifle was slung and his sidearm holstered, but he registered Julie's look of panic as Copper drew back the hammer of the pistol, and so hesitated. When Major Yeo and then Major Torrens entered the hesitation between both men became more uncertain. The MP moved to his weapon. Cooper saw the motion and fired twice. The MP went down heavily, while Major Yeo and Major Torrens remained motionless. Outside the sound of footsteps increased. Weapons were cocked and made ready. In a last desperate gamble Cooper pushed Julie violently toward Major Torrens for cover and vaulted across the barn flinging himself through a flimsy side door which broke from its hinges. He picked himself up and started to run across the broad open meadow.

Yeo reached down and unslung the wounded MP's rifle and moved to the shattered doorway. He cocked the weapon, lingered on his target for a moment and then fired a single shot. He lowered the rifle slowly and, when he turned, found Major Torrens looking over his shoulder nodding appreciatively. 'Well, that certainly clipped his wings.'

Major Yeo shook his head and looked at the rifle critically, 'I was aiming for his leg.'

'He'll hang for this either way – that MPs dead.'

Shadowy figures now roamed across the area, galvanised by the shooting and Captain Cooper's screams. He was soon placed in a Jeep, bleeding profusely from a shattered elbow, surrounded by angry jostling MPs, now aware that he had killed one of their own.

Major Torrens found some keys and un-cuffed Karl and Julie, but Karl was too weak to stand and fell back to the floor where Julie tried to make him comfortable. Major Torrens looked down at her and noticed the bloody matted head wound and the stains on her dressing gown. He removed his coat and placed it over her shoulders.

Major Cranfield entered the barn cautiously and walked to the table, picking up the manila envelope. He looked down at Julie and she nodded. Tommy turned to see Major Perkins belatedly follow him, brandishing a gun. 'For God's sake!' he snapped gesturing toward the lifeless body of the MP on the floor, 'It's too late for that. He's dead, I'm afraid; there was nothing we could do. *Your* Captain Cooper shot him.'

As the MPs body was placed on a stretcher Cranfield began to finger through the contents of the file stooping to examine certain papers and calling for a flashlight. Finally, after many minutes, he straightened up, his voice relieved and reassured by what he had

276

found, 'These are quality documents. The deal's a good one Tommy – you did well.' He looked at Karl, 'Take him where you can help him - he's a free man now.'

Julie looked over to Major Yeo, 'There's a film too – undeveloped - back at *Rhein-Ahr* Inn. They didn't know for certain I had it.'

Julie knelt down again cradling Karl's head and whispering softly into his ear, desperate to reassure herself he would live, 'Now it's my turn to nurse you back to health. Stay with me – please, stay alive!' She kissed him and stroked his hair. His eyelids flickered and she thought she detected the glimmer of a smile on his lips.

The following day Tommy called on Major Cranfield at his lodgings.

'You promised me.' he said seeing that the Major was packed and ready to leave.

Cranfield looked at him, 'Very well, if you think this is really necessary.'

Yeo nodded, 'I do.'

The two officers approached the main Remagen camp along a straight cobbled perimeter road, to the side of which extended several miles of concertina wire and stakes. They drove until they reached a sandbagged command post which marked the entrance. Under the sceptical eye of the American guards they abandoned their Jeep and walked through the gates into the camp. As they left the last secure area a Sergeant offered them a machine gun and, when they declined, made it clear they could not rely on assistance if they were overpowered. Yeo looked at him with despair and removed his own side arm, thrusting it towards the Sergeant, 'Take it!'

'Sir?'

'I said take the bloody thing. I don't need a side arm.'

Cranfield did likewise and they moved forward, through the gates, into a scene of near biblical horror, their nostrils assailed with the indescribable stench of filth and decaying humanity. He had only known such a smell once before at Bergen-Belsen, before the mass graves had been limed and filled in.

They could see no path leading into the interior of the camp, so they picked their way over the bodies of the living and the dead, many bathed in their own bloody excrement as the last stages of malnutrition began to grip them. They saw the holes dug with bare hands in which the men had sought shelter from exposure. A few of them nursed dying comrades, murmuring prayers as they cradled them in their arms.

Cranfield stood red faced, looking ahead of them at an endless sea of similar degradation and suffering. 'Where is their equipment, their tents, their mess kits?'

'They were stripped of everything. There are 134,000 in this cage and there are sixteen cages in the Rheine meadows. I understand there are around 900,000 men in total. Ten thousand arrived needing urgent medical attention...they've had none.'

'Where are the latrines, the medical facilities, the stand pipes for water? What are the Americans doing?' Cranfield said with rising indignation.

'Watching them die.' Tommy replied sombrely.

Cranfield studied the emaciated faces that looked up around them, their sunken eyes and hollow cheeks testimony to the length of their ordeal. He saw, too, the bloated bellies, the empty toothless mouths and the weeping infected ulcers.

Major Yeo turned, 'Belsen had toilets, even Belsen had water! Will you say something about this?'

Major Cranfield took some chocolate from his pocket and broke it up for a few of the prisoners whose arms were raised. As he did so Tommy noticed his hands were trembling.

As they walked on a prisoner proffered some tattered paper and pressed it into Major Yeo's hand. Tommy looked at it. It was a note to the man's wife in Füssen, a farewell to her and his children. He promised to send it, but found it difficult to look the man in the eye.

As they picked their way over the prisoners, making their way back to the entrance, Tommy grasped Major Cranfield's arm with a look of despair, 'Look, there's another camp I went to, up at Heidesheim...Captain Cooper took me there before all this business with Julie Scholl. I'm not supposed to talk about it. But I can't...'

Cranfield looked at him warily, 'Can't what?'

'Can't keep it to myself...can't ignore it.'

'So, what was there?'

'When we went in, I found children there - fourteen year old boys. When I asked about them, why they were dressed in nothing but their pyjamas, he told me they had been arrested at night – taken from their beds the week before. They are living in the open, with the other prisoners. All they have is their pyjamas.'

Cranfield stared at Tommy for a moment and then began to walk on. Tommy followed him, 'What are we becoming, Major? What are we turning into?'

When they got back to the command post they were met by the Captain of the Guard who drew Tommy to one side while Major Cranfield looked on. The Captain gestured at his binoculars, 'Major, I believe one of the prisoners passed you something?' Tommy remained silent. 'Look Sir, I'm just doing my job…it's up to you how we deal with this?'

Their eyes met and Tommy reluctantly reached into his tunic pocket and held out the tattered letter he had been given.

The Captain took it, read it, and then tore it up, working the shreds of paper into the mud with his boot. 'Prisoners cannot communicate with the outside world…you should know that, Major.'

'It's a letter to his wife and children for Christ's sake. The man's dying!' Yeo said with barely repressed anger.

'They're all just fucking Nazis as far as I'm concerned.' the Captain replied coldly. He saluted, and withdrew to the command post.

As they got back to the Jeep Cranfield paused and shook his head with an air of dejection. 'I have no power over the Americans, you know that Tommy.'

'Isn't that the point of the Belsen trial - to stop *this*?' Tommy replied bitterly.

Cranfield looked at him sharply, 'Is it? I see no fear of justice being done here – do you?' He paused and collected himself and then shook Tommy's hand apologetically. 'You're right of course, I can't ignore it. I'll send a report in writing to CIGS, Monty, and everyone I can. This is…'

'A crime?' Tommy said looking back toward the camp.

Cranfield looked back too but said nothing. Finally, when he had started the engine Tommy leaned into the Jeep, 'The Red Cross have tried, you know. They sent a train load of supplies. The Yanks lied and said they weren't needed and now they've reclassified them as Disarmed Enemy Forces so the Red Cross can't get to them at all. They simply don't want them here. Just do what you can - please.'

Cranfield engaged gear and began the long journey back to Lüneburg; but he was distracted by what he'd witnessed. Up until today, he'd believed in a higher purpose to what they had done with the Americans – to prevent Europe plunging into this new 'dark age'. Now his mind reeled and he began to feel a deep sense of unease, a sense that he too, as part of the army of occupation, was complicit in what he had seen.

Chapter 27

Karl was sitting up in a chair looking out of the window when Julie entered his room after breakfast. It had been two weeks since his arrival at the *Rheine-Ahr* and since then the Americans had returned the inn to Otto at the insistence of Major Torrens. With rooms now available, Otto had insisted on looking after Karl in one of the large, bright airy rooms on the second floor, and while he had been too weak to wash or shave had performed these tasks himself. Their retired neighbour, Dr Wittig, had been able to restore Karl's eyesight and physical balance with the steady reintroduction of nutrients into his food. In Dr Wittig's day starvation had been a familiar condition in general practice, particularly at the end of the First World War and the remedies he had perfected then had proved effective in ensuring Karl's recovery. Now, after the morning's routines, it was time for Julie to spend a few uninterrupted hours with him before she started work. 'Have you seen yourself?' Julie asked as he extended his hand in greeting.

He smiled, 'Yes. Otto missed the jugular and the windpipe, but I'm a bit of a mess otherwise!'

Julie got a jug and bowl and dabbed away the evidence of Otto's attempts to shave him. They sat for a moment holding hands. 'Any news of Koppe?' He asked hesitantly.

'No. But let's not talk about *that*.'

Karl sat up, 'Yes. Sorry.'

'Do you realise we have never shared a moment of peace like this?' she said cheerfully. 'We can do anything - we're free.'

Karl leaned forward and kissed her, 'I thought I might take you to Ulm before we get married and perhaps afterwards we can live at my mother's house there - if it's still standing. It's not much but it has some land. I'm sure we could be happy there – very happy.'

'Will we get married *soon* do you think?' she said with a note of gentle impatience.

Karl smiled, 'As soon as we can.' He sat back and looked at his thin hands and bruised feet. 'But if we are to marry I will need to practice again, to study – my God I have probably forgotten it all - the general practice part at least. I shall have to become a wealthy man as well; I seem to remember you wanted a large family!'

Julie laughed, 'Oh how you taunt me with my words. At least I know your memory is still good though.' She tapped his head gently with her fingers and then ran them through his hair. 'And now we have a little mystery to solve together.'

Karl looked quizzical, 'How do you mean?'

'An envelope Gertrud Forster gave me last November.'

Julie stood, moved to the fireplace and reached inside the chimney. She pulled out a large tin and unscrewed the lid. Inside was a crumpled manila envelope. She brought it over and sat with it on her lap. Karl looked at it suspiciously. Julie probed the envelope with her fingers, 'When I left Danzig Gertrud gave me two envelopes. The first she said was the police file about Posen, but the second she was rather vague about - she said it was to rebuild my life. I never wanted to open it before. I wanted to open it with you - so now we can see what it is together.'

'She said *nothing* about its contents?'

Julie shook her head and slowly broke open the tab and removed a heavy cloth bag. She felt it and shook it. Their eyes met and she pulled at the thin string that secured the neck. She opened the bag and placed it on the table. As she did so there was a cascade of brilliant sparkling cut stones of various shapes, sizes and intricacy. They looked at them and then at each other, 'Diamonds…but there must be a fortune here!' Karl whispered with astonishment.

Julie disturbed the pile of stones with her finger, 'There are…hundreds of them.' Julie sat back and closed her eyes, 'Oh Gertrud, what has become of you. What have you done for us?' She peered into the empty bag and withdrew a slip of paper on which Gertrude had written a note;

'*My dearest Julie, I believe some of these belong to you. They came up to Danzig with your friend Herr Rath in a red leather case. I am ashamed to say Albert had the necklace and earrings broken down for the gold, so I have placed a few of my own stones in here by way of atonement. I hope they will, in some way, make up for the lost years. I wish you every happiness. Gertrud xxx.*'

Julie replaced the diamonds and re-secured the bag, withdrawn and thoughtful.

'What is it?'

Julie shook her head, 'Nothing.'

Karl took the note from her and read it. 'Was it your mother's necklace?'

'No, it belonged to someone I knew.'

'Should we accept them?'

'Yes Karl...I've already refused them once, but if Gertrud wants us to have them, and if they can make up for the lost years, if they can do good, then yes, we'll take them.' She smiled, 'So Karl, it seems there is no escape for you. Now your last hope of penury has vanished...and with it all hope of keeping your freedom. You simply have to marry me!'

'In Remagen?'

'Yes...though I suppose, when we talked about it before, in '41, we were going to honeymoon in Paris. But I'll settle for Linz.'

'Linz...Austria!'

Julie laughed, 'No, Linz across the river!'

Karl smiled, 'And I was going to order room service so we could stay in our room for days on end, without ever leaving...'

'...For three days.' Julie said with a mischievous smile on her face.

Karl looked at his still frail hands, 'This isn't quite what I had wanted for you, but it really doesn't matter does it.'

She sat next to him, 'No, nothing matters any more except being alive.' She hesitated, 'Karl, when we parted all those years ago I said I wanted to give myself to you. I said I would be here for you when you got back.'

Karl looked into her eyes, 'I remember.'

She leaned forward and kissed him tenderly whispering in his ear. 'I don't want to wait...not any longer.'

For four years Karl had dreamed of Julie, through the Russian winters and the hardships, the fighting and the horrors, and now he looked at her and realised that she was every bit as beautiful as he had remembered her then, her eyes sparkling with the life that had drawn him to her at the Posen ball, her figure still as graceful, her skin still soft and delicate. He stood and took her hand, raising her from the chair. They kissed again, but now the kiss deepened into a passion that overwhelmed them. They began to undress each other trying to contain the urgency they felt, both wanting the moment to last, to be special.

When they stood naked, Julie drew him towards the bed, still looking into his eyes. As they passed the wardrobe mirror he glanced up and noticed her reflection, the scars still visible on her back, and suddenly understood her gesture. When they lay down he looked into her eyes, 'I want you for who you are, as you are now - no other way…you do understand that don't you.' She nodded and kissed his hand. But Karl could feel the apprehension in her as they began to caress each other, her movements hesitant, her limbs tense. He lay with her for some time, gently kissing her and loving her as reassuringly as he could. Soon she relaxed and lay back, deeper into the bed. She smiled and drew him to her. She kissed him and he entered her gently, looking into her eyes as he did so, her anxieties gradually leaving her, her arms drawing him on. He smiled and slowly began to roll over. He drew her around with him, still locked together, until she lay on top of him. She smiled, kissing his chest as they rocked slowly together. Soon Karl's breathing became heavier and his expression more intense. He reached up for her, drawing her to him, kissing her passionately. She felt him shudder and he smiled. She lay her head on his chest, her arms holding him tightly, as she felt him shrink within her.

When, finally, they lay next to each other, Julie placed Karl's hand on her abdomen and crossed her legs slightly, as if trying to secure within her the precious hope of life he had so tenderly planted there.

He ran his hand down the side body and gestured towards the bruises on her ribs and hips. 'Who did this to you?' he whispered.

Julie shook her head, 'Cooper.'

Karl kissed the bruises and then, moving over her, he kissed the scars on her back. 'Nobody will ever hurt you again – I promise, and I never want to be parted from you. We can start again…just the two of us.' He kissed her.

'I want that Karl…I've dreamed of that.'

'And you really want children?'

'Yes.' she said, pulling back from him and fixing him with a glint in her eye, 'I want children…our children. I want a family Karl…I want a future for us.' She smiled, 'Do you realise, I have no inhibitions any more – can you imagine that – no fear. Not now…not after this. I only feel excited – about everything, about tomorrow…when we shall be alone again!' She kissed him on the lips, and then on the chest, and then on each frail hand.

Karl slumped laughing gently to himself, 'Remember, I'm still in a weakened state.'

Julie sat up and loomed over him energetically, 'Oh don't worry, and I'll feed you up. I'm sure there's a diet for this too.'

Karl groaned and put a pillow over his face.

It was a few days later that Dr Wittig stood with Otto, Ingrid and Julie in the hallway of the inn. He was a delightful old character who seemed to have been revived by his sudden return to general practice after years of inconsequential retirement. He removed his *pince-nez* and put down his leather medical bag stiffly. 'He does seem to have weakened slightly in the last few days.' he said with an air of bafflement. 'I *am* concerned about his stamina - he seems very tired suddenly, but I think in general his progress is good. The main thing is that his spirits be kept up. That's important for recovery.'

Ingrid clasped Julie's hand, 'I'm sure this is only temporary.'

Dr Wittig leaned forward, 'Perhaps you should try to cheer him along a little more. He seems to like it when you read to him – he tells me you read very well.'

Ingrid seemed to agree, 'Perhaps you should go to him now and give him another few chapters – take his mind off things.'

Julie tried to remain composed, 'He had three chapters this morning, Auntie, there's only so much I can do.'

As the doctor left, Tommy Yeo arrived and greeted them all with great enthusiasm, 'Good news!' he said fixing Otto with a bright smile, 'Toilets, food, tents, water bowsers, the lot - the Americans seem to have woken up at last.'

Otto nodded, 'Thank you.'

'No Otto, not me, Major Cranfield…I think. He went back and shamed the top brass I hope.' Tommy gestured to Julie and they walked into the rear of the inn and sat alone. 'It seems I'm going back to work with Major Cranfield up in Lüneburg. I've been asked to return, but I'm afraid I need you to come with me. You're being called as a witness for Irma Grese.'

Julie's eyes wandered anxiously, 'But Karl needs me here. Must it be so soon?'

Tommy looked at her with understanding, 'I am sorry, but your evidence…it may change things slightly. I'll take you myself and I will bring you back. It will be door to door and I will be your escort - how's that?'

'But will it save Irma do you think? What can I say that would do that?'

'I'm afraid I can't answer that. That would be coaching a witness. No, you will need to answer questions and tell the truth. We will decide what to do with the answers.'

'When do we leave?'

Tommy smiled apologetically. 'Tomorrow morning at seven.'

Julie wilted slightly and then remembered something else, 'I meant to ask about the film – the pictures. What was on the film Irma gave me?'

Tommy shifted uncomfortably, 'Oh, we'll deal with that tomorrow, too.'

When Julie found Karl later he was reading a medical textbook which Dr Wittig had left him. He put it down, 'It's hardly current – 1911 – but it's a start!'

Julie sat on the chair next to him, 'Major Yeo says they have brought food, tents, toilets, and medical facilities to the camps; that the Americans have started to improve things.'

'Are people still throwing food over the fence?'

'Yes, and the Americans have stopped shooting at them.' She looked around the room despondently, 'Look, Karl, I have to go away with Major Yeo. They want me to go to Lüneburg to give evidence about Irma Grese - about Posen and my father as well I suppose.'

'When?

'Tomorrow.'

'You should be careful.' he said reaching for her hand.

'Why?'

Karl pointed to a pile of newspapers on the floor, 'Look at the English and American press. Think about it, Julie; they've been more or less condemned already.'

'But Karl, she saved my life!'

'And you think you alone can save hers - against a tide of outrage like that?'

Julie stood up and began tidying the room, 'Major Yeo says I need only tell the truth. And it's not just about Irma, it's about my father too, it's about what is in those photographs, the pictures that cost Dr Hertz and Rath their lives.'

'Did he say anything about the photographs?'

'No…he just talked about Irma.'

The Rathaus (town hall) Lüneburg, 4 July, 1945

Major Cranfield stood up as Julie entered the small interview room in the town hall at Lüneburg and shook her hand courteously. He nodded at Tommy and they all sat around a small table.

'How is Herr Rust?'

'He's much better. He asked me to thank you for his freedom and for the help you have given at the Rheine-meadow camps. A lot of men owe their lives to you.'

The Major shook his head, 'And what a lot of trouble I have caused there! Never mind though.

'You may call me Major Cranfield, or just Sir. Is that alright?' Julie nodded. Cranfield paused and looked at Major Yeo darkly before resuming. 'As you may know you passed us a file compiled by SS Obergruppenführer Hildebrandt. This was, it seems, the result of your arrival in Danzig in November 1939, when he became aware of unauthorised operations by SD men from Kolmar District under the control of SS Obergruppenführer Wilhelm Koppe. It appears they had intended to kill you. He later employed an agent, Epp, to follow things up and verify some of the facts you had provided regarding your imprisonment and assault by a Gauleiter by the name of Grieser. He established that a Captain Gerhard had gone to Posen to look for you in connection with enquiries into your father, that Koppe wished to deflect his search for you, that subsequently your father was sent for trial in Berlin...'

Julie held up her hand, 'I'm sorry Major Cranfield, but my father was murdered by SS Obergruppenführer Koppe in Posen in November '39, when he went to find me at Thorner Strasse orphanage. Epp's report was wrong.'

Cranfield shook his head. 'Yes, but you got that from Irma Grese verbally and Epp's report tallies with the records at Dachau - we checked.'

Julie shrugged. 'Why should she lie?'

287

Cranfield paused, 'There can be many reasons for an accused person to lie; to appear more creditable, or helpful? Perhaps even to offer evidence against a higher ranking official in the hope of a lesser sentence. Indeed, she now has the most basic reason - to save her own life.'

Julie leaned forward. 'But Sir, Irma told me this in December '44, on a train from Zoppot to Berlin and she had no reason to lie then. And Major Yeo has already told me that Irma's SS file had been tampered with so surely the Dachau records could also have been altered just as easily.'

Cranfield paused and made an entry in his pocket book, 'Noted.' He sat back. 'Epp's report then refers to the death of a Gestapo man, Müller. There's an implication that he was to be questioned by Captain Gerhard about your disappearance from Fort Winiary. It seems that the SD file which Koppe had did not explain what had happened to you – where you were held, why you were taken from your interrogation - this was an effort to silence him.'

'Sir, I'm sorry but again that isn't what I've been told. Irma told me that Müller had been ordered to murder my father and had refused. Koppe shot my father and then shot Müller – she said there were to be no witnesses.'

'And apart from Irma's third party account, her hearsay evidence, what do you rely on in believing her story above the official records? I have to have hard evidence Fräulein Scholl. You must understand that what Irma might say will only carry weight if it is supported by witnesses - evidence.'

'But she told me there were others involved, an SS Dr Fischer, SS Captain Kellerman. Can't they be found? And the girls, they were being sent to Gnesen. Irma said my father caught them loading the girls onto lorries in the middle of the night. Someone would have seen something.'

Cranfield seemed suddenly surprised, 'So you knew?'

'Sorry?' Julie said confused.

'You said your father found them loading the girls on to the lorries.'

Julie frowned, 'Yes – they were to be taken to Gnesen.'

'In boxes. They were loaded onto the lorry in boxes - they were all dead. They were being taken to Gnesen for burial.'

288

As Julie broke down, her head falling forward into her now trembling hands, Cranfield realised he had misunderstood her German - that she had not known. And now she sat, clinging to her composure, weeping and rocking gently. Her voice was now quiet, no more than a whisper between her sobs, 'Helene, Birgit...little Viktoria...' And at that moment she remembered them as they had been when she first arrived at the orphanage, excited, inquisitive, and generous. She also remembered Helene holding out her hand with a smile as she sat on the edge of the bed that first morning in August 1939, offering her friendship when she had felt lost and frightened. But she was determined not to allow herself to break down completely, and so she sat up again wiping her eyes.

Cranfield looked at her apologetically and then rose from his chair and moved to a narrow bench at the side of the room. He opened a heavy envelope and set out some photographs. He looked round at Major Yeo, 'Tommy, there's no way around this. I'm sorry Fraülein Scholl. Please can you come and identify these photographs; the location you think they were taken, the date and any of the people in them. This is from the film Irma gave you. I'm afraid it's rather harrowing.'

They stood and Julie began to move apprehensively toward the pictures on the bench. Cranfield held a file over the adjoining photograph to prevent Julie from being distracted and began to work along them, left to right.

She looked down at the first picture, 'That is the dormitory where we slept. I was there for over two months. All sixteen of us slept there. It was in Thorner Strasse, in Posen. I arrived 28 August '39.'

Cranfield moved the file to uncover the next picture. 'This is the school room where I practised. These are the stained glass windows.'

Cranfield repeated the process, 'Oh and Karl took this of the girls together – I must have been waiting for him in the office. It was the day we went sightseeing. Yes, it's all fifteen of them.'

'Can you name them?'

'That's Agnes, Erika, Gabriele, Dorle, Edda, Jutta, Klara, Ottilie, Birgit, Claudia, Therese, Ursula, She is Viktoria and that is Waltraud. And there is Helene, the Head Girl – she was my closest friend there.'

Cranfield looked at her 'No surnames?'

289

'I can't remember. No.'

'Date?'

'October, the twenty *something* of October '39.'

Cranfield hesitated and looked at Tommy, who nodded and drew closer. He moved the file obscuring the next picture. Julie peered at it uncertainly. It was grainy and dark but as Julie began to recognise the outline of familiar shapes, the handrail by the mirror, the bedframes, the windows, she suddenly cried out; it came from deep within, an indescribable sound, as though their horror spoke through her. Then, for a moment she was silent, bent over, her hands covering her face. After a few minutes she turned to Cranfield, still speechless, tears rolling down her cheeks.

He too seemed to struggle. 'They hanged themselves...all of them. It was...a desperate act...'Cranfield paused. 'It seems they stood at the ends of their beds and jumped into the void. They used bed sheets attached to some old pipes in the ceiling. Irma says they had become hysterical that night, but later they seemed to settle. When she went back at midnight they were dead - all of them.'

Julie's voice was distraught, 'But why?'

'Irma says the SS were going to *use* the girls. She says it seemed that the SS simply saw it as an opportunity - somewhere for their men to go. They were orphans after all - there was nobody to answer to. And in the longer term it seems they hoped the girls would produce children. Irma believes there was also an element of punishment – after some incident.'

Julie wiped her eyes with her hands, 'Thank you, I will go on,' she said with a fierce determination.

Cranfield uncovered the next photograph which more clearly defined the image, 'That's Helene and Edda,' she paused 'Waltraud had been raped before.' She covered her face, 'Little Viktoria - how could they...' Through her tears she tried to finish her sentence but now broke down completely. 'I could recognise some more of them if you needed me to but...not now, please. I can't look any more.'

Cranfield persisted and produced a pencil pointing to the mirror which ran the length of the dormitory and which caught the reflection of the photographer between the limp lifeless bodies of the girls, 'Nobody noticed the reflection at first – it was one of our analysts who pointed it out - it's the photographer.' Cranfield said quietly.

290

Julie wiped her eyes again suddenly perplexed, 'Irma took them! But why?'

'Do you know her background?'

'A little?' Julie said moving back to the desk.

He sat and opened a file, 'Irma was fourteen when her mother hanged herself after she discovered her husband was having an affair with the daughter of a local innkeeper. Irma found her mother's body in a barn. Her sister Helene says she had stayed in the barn for an hour before they found them both - Irma just sitting with her mother, staring up at her. Her father was an agricultural worker – a fairly brutal man by all accounts. He remarried quickly, leaving Irma as one of four children without their mother. It seems what happened at the orphanage carried too many resonances – it became her obsession.'

Julie nodded, 'She said I would understand when I saw the pictures. She sent me my mother's letters too – I didn't understand that at the time. It seemed such a strange thing to do.'

Major Yeo stopped examining the pictures and looked over. 'And then of course, after the incident at the orphanage in Posen, she re-joined the camp system and all the brutality that went with it. She was certainly promoted with a dazzling regularity. Did she mention Wolfgang Hatzinger to you at all?

'No.' Julie said.

'He was head of construction at Belsen – died there of typhus. She asked to stay there so she could be with him while he was dying – they were lovers. They'd worked together at Auschwitz too.'

Julie looked at him 'But why are you telling me this?'

Major Yeo bit his lip, 'Probably because I'm still trying to work out who she is; and because at the moment I'm having problems with explaining it all myself. She did some appalling things and yet…at the orphanage…in a different context. She speaks very fondly of them you know.'

Cranfield stood, 'For now that's all. Major Yeo will take all the necessary statements this evening and arrange your transport back to Remagen.'

Julie looked at Tommy, 'Is that all you need me for - what about my father?'

'For the time being.' Cranfield interjected. 'Stay here tonight with Major Yeo as your escort and we will send you back tomorrow.'

Julie turned to Tommy, 'I thought you would return with me.'

'I'm afraid since we spoke the Americans have marked my card - they've accused me of breaching the rules on fraternisation while I was with them - which of course I did.'

Julie shrugged her shoulders, 'I don't understand?'

'It seems they don't want me back in Remagen – even as a visitor.'

Julie embraced Major Yeo to his evident surprise and in doing so solicited a crooked smile from Major Cranfield. By the time she let go she had regained some of her composure. 'Karl and I will get married soon. You saved his life. If we can ever repay your kindness please let us know. And when the Americans are gone come and see us.'

'And now we must go and see the Colonel for a little chat!' Major Cranfield said looking at Tommy lugubriously.

Chapter 28

When Majors Yeo and Cranfield presented themselves to Colonel Watson in the imposing library of the town hall they found him seated with two others. A man in his fifties with a grey moustache, silver hair, and a suit better fitted to Whitehall than Lüneburg stood up and shook their hands, introducing himself as Charles Addes from the Foreign Office. The other, a Major, simply introduced himself as holding a 'watching brief' for the Chief of the Imperial General Staff, Alan Brooke, 'Just call me Major John.'

When they were seated Colonel Watson began. 'This memo you sent…about the Rheine-meadows camps. I've had it withdrawn. I've had the copies returned. It's caused a bit of a rift with the Americans.'

Major Cranfield made no comment and remained expressionless.

'Very well, I take that as an acceptance of the position – sorry, but that's the way it is.'

Addes spoke, with the emollient authority of his office, 'I understand that things are being done to improve the situation in the camps, but we don't want a fuss about it, not now, not with so many issues coming up.'

The Colonel pondered for a moment, 'Yes…and there is this other business - the Belsen trial. I'm told that you have some fresh line of attack, some new evidence for the defence. Does it really change anything?'

Cranfield looked at Tommy uneasily. 'I'm not sure in what sense you mean *change*. I couldn't possibly discuss it at this stage. We are preparing Irma Grese's defence. She is my client.'

Major John leaned forward, 'She's not your client and you are a serving officer appointed under the Army Act, King's Regulations and the King's Warrant to conduct a defence. Now, do you intend to deny the charges or to plead in some other way - mitigation or such-like?'

Cranfield drew breath, 'We have new evidence - it's true. It seems that in 1939 Irma Grese was sent to serve in an orphanage run

293

by the SS in Posen. While there she witnessed certain criminal acts. She gathered evidence about them and kept it. She even saved the life of one of the witnesses, a girl called Julie Scholl. If the death penalty is asked for we'll demonstrate that Irma Grese may also be a key witness in other trials which her immediate execution would prejudice - trials of more senior and significant criminals in the SS. We're hoping to use her conduct in the orphanage, and later, as evidence that she was not naturally brutal, but was brutalised by the camp system and the Nazi regime.'

This answer produced unease in the room. Major John looked expectantly at Addes who seemed deep in thought for a moment. Finally he spoke, 'I respect and understand your best intentions gentlemen but how is the public supposed to interpret such a defence?'

Cranfield looked surprised, 'The court is concerned with law and fact, the court is not concerned with public opinion.'

'But this is a very public crime and it's being tried by a British Military Tribunal. Our allies – the world – will be watching. We need to make a show of things, not a spectacle of ourselves trying to defend the indefensible.'

Cranfield sat back, 'But Major John has just articulated our role in this trial Mr Addes. We're appointed to defend the accused by the army and we have a duty to obey. We have to mount a defence - that's what we've been ordered to do. I just don't see how the introduction of mitigating evidence threatens to make a spectacle of things?'

Addes raised an eyebrow, 'We need to draw a line Major. We need to be quick and decisive and move on. We can't parade Irma Grese to the world as one of Hitler's victims - it'll make us a laughing stock. Churchill won't stand for it and neither will Monty, or CIGS.'

Major Cranfield looked at Major Yeo, who shifted uneasily on his seat, and then stood, assuming the position of attention, 'Sir, I really must protest, and I reserve the right to refer this discussion to the Judge Advocate General – with respect Sir, this is nothing short of interference with the conduct of the defence.'

Addes looked at Major Cranfield sharply, 'Don't you understand man, it's essential to ensure there is no chance, not the remotest possibility, of the return of National Socialism? If that means culling the military instincts of the German people then so be it...'

Major John leaned forward, '…and public opinion will be more easily reconciled to a new Germany, if the old one has been very publicly consigned to the gallows.'

Addes gestured that Major Cranfield should sit again. 'Because there is the bigger concern, and that is about our ability to maintain the post-war consensus. The Soviet Union is a potent force in Europe now. We need to balance this with a strong but de-Nazified Germany. That means getting the show back on the road – getting Germany back to her place in the community of European nations.'

Major Cranfield's expression hardened, 'Forgive me Sir, gentlemen, but am I therefore to understand that this trial is a purely technical exercise, that the outcome is already known?'

Colonel Watson leaned forward, 'Don't play the maid Major; we're all simply concerned that the trial is managed sensibly. Not simply that justice is done, but that it is also seen to be done. We won't stand by and watch the defence making a mockery of things – going off on whimsical flights of fancy. It should be perfectly clear to you already what sort of person Grese is - and the rest of them for that matter.'

Major John looked at some notes on his lap, 'Didn't she make the selections for the gas chambers at Auschwitz as the overseer, and isn't that damning enough.'

Cranfield nodded, 'Yes, she made the selections, but someone selected her and she was eighteen when they got their hooks into her - poorly educated, and by all accounts did everything she could to get into nursing. My point is simply that without the Nazi regime Irma Grese would probably have been a very ordinary member of society.'

Colonel Watson looked at Addes who shook his head with an air of exasperation to indicate he had no further questions, 'But all this discussion about Grese is not really why you're here, helpful though it is to understand your approach. No, we're here really about other developments in your work on the defence.'

'Other developments, Sir?'

Major John sat forward clasping a telegram he had removed from a file on his lap. 'Your trip to Remagen. The Americans are anxious you may intend to make a link between Bergen-Belsen and what you saw in the Rheine-meadows camps. They wonder if you intend to make a connection in your defence of Irma Grese - of your other *clients*. We want to know - for the sake of harmony with our American allies?'

Cranfield shifted on his seat uneasily, 'It is not currently my intention...'

'Currently!' Major John snorted, '*Currently* isn't quite good enough I'm afraid. Not now they've been visited – not now that you might be tempted to draw parallels. You see there's another American cage for the *Waffen* SS near Bretzenheim, it's a lot worse than the one you saw and the Yanks are rattled. It's now been taken up in Washington and that's why we're here. The world's press will be at the Belsen trial. They don't want the world's press at Bretzenheim. I just have to make it clear now that should you make a link it would constitute a major embarrassment to HM Government. You need to understand that you simply can't make such a link - it *won't* be permitted.'

Major John leaned forward, 'So that's it gentlemen. Message delivered. You may go.'

The room fell uncomfortably silent while Major Cranfield and Major Yeo stood, saluted stiffly, and left. After the door had closed behind them Colonel Watson turned to Major John with an air of disquiet, 'This place Bretzenheim, what is it then?'

Major John turned, 'The Americans say around 18,500 SS men have died there since April. They are looking at about 50,000 deaths for the Rheine-meadows camps in total. It's not official policy as such, but there's a view the SS are a special problem for post-war Germany - that they won't be re-socialised, that they need their own *special* solution.'

Stillness fell over the room and the ticking of the grandfather clock now filled the void. This silence grew in intensity until Colonel Watson stood abruptly, his face flushed, and walked out, slamming the door behind him.

Addes looked over at Major John, 'I had hoped this little chat might settle things, but I'm not so sure. If this ends in a *buggers muddle* you do realise heads will roll?'

Major John began to gather his things, 'It does rather seem that they've decided to rise to the occasion. But you're right of course; this'll have to be dealt with - it'll be our heads on the block as well as theirs. Look - there's a man in the Intelligence Corps, a Yorkshireman by the name of Ching – bloody strange name for a Yorkshireman but there you are - he's good at dealing with this sort of thing. Leave it with me.'

Chapter 29

When Julie returned to Remagen-Kripp the following evening Karl was sitting in the parlour with Ingrid. He stood and embraced Julie with passion and relief while Ingrid put down her knitting and made some excuse to leave, kissing Julie on both cheeks with a twinkle in her eye. After she had gone they sat together.

'She is such an interesting lady, your Aunt; such a mine of information. She was just reminiscing about life before the last war.'

Julie raised an eyebrow, 'Don't be fooled, she will have got more out of you than you are ever aware of, just by telling you a few stories.'

'And how was the trip?'

Julie looked deflated and Karl put his arm around her shoulder, 'Was it that bad?'

'I'm afraid I had too many expectations. At first it was very business-like, very formal. They asked me lots of questions. They showed me the photographs...' she halted and Karl could see her struggling for a moment. 'I had no idea, I was completely unprepared – don't ask me about them please.'

He reached out and held her, 'And then?'

'Then it seemed to be left in mid-air. They had gone to a meeting with a senior officer and when they got back they just seemed to have changed their outlook on the whole case. They were *terribly polite* – typical English manners, but no, their minds were changed.'

'And your father?'

'Major Yeo said it wasn't within their legal powers to pursue the matter. He didn't elaborate.'

'And the orphans? Do we know what happened to them – did they make it back to Germany?'

Julie became glacial and there was a long pause, 'They're all dead...they killed themselves in '39 – just before I left Posen.' she said quietly.

Karl sat for a moment unable to take in what she had told him. Then he got up and kissed her on the head and held her tightly, 'I'm so sorry...those lovely girls...how could such a thing happen?'

Julie looked up at him with tears in her eyes 'I can't...I can't talk about them - it's impossible...Karl, it has to end here. We have to start again and leave this behind...we can't live with this for the rest of our lives.' Karl sat and they held hands for a moment in silence, but her gaze was distant, and her mind consumed by the need to escape the past, the memories and horrors to be locked away and never revisited.

It was two days after their encounter with Major John and Mr Addes that Tommy and Major Cranfield were able to share lunch together in the officers mess and digest the encounter. After talking it over for some time Cranfield sat back and shook his head, 'You know it's no use, Tommy, we're completely cornered and we both know it. We can't take on the army let alone the establishment back home. We've simply got to go along with it – accept the limitations...do what we can.' He paused with a look of dejection, 'But it does bring me back to something I was mulling over on my way back from Remagen - after seeing the camps; if we as British officers can't do anything to stop this, if we're really part of the same machine, then what the hell did we expect an ill-educated eighteen year old peasant girl like Irma Grese to do under the Nazis? How was she supposed to decide things for herself? It's absurd.' He got up from the table and grasped his cap, patting it into shape, 'War is a great leveller isn't it Tommy! It doesn't matter where you start from, how moral the cause in the beginning, we're all just basically butchers by the end of it.'

It was nearly two thirty by the time they finally got back to the small office they shared in a requisitioned building near the town hall to resume their work on the defence. As Canfield turned the key in the door, a Lieutenant Colonel accompanied by two members of field security hailed them from the end of the corridor. The Colonel, a wiry diminutive man approached them briskly and returned their salute before extending a document. Major Cranfield took it, glancing at the field security men uneasily, and read it thoroughly before passing it to Major Yeo.

It was an hour before Lt Colonel Ching, a rather grizzled Yorkshireman, finally finished examining the Gestapo and SD files, documents and photographs, which Julie had provided. 'Has this material been included in your list of documents?' he said brusquely.

'We haven't exchanged lists with the prosecution yet.' Major Yeo said.

'Well you can't use it – not until it's been cleared – sorry, but that's it. We have to examine it first, and we have to show it to the Poles.'

Cranfield leaned forward, 'May I ask your authority, Sir.'

'CIGS.' Ching snapped.

'General Alan Brooke – Chief of the Imperial General Staff?' Major Yeo said incredulously.

Ching sat back. 'He's the PM's advisor too. I would have thought your encounter with Mr Addes of the FO and Major John, would have sobered you up. We're not buggering about here. You have your brief – stick to it.' Ching stood and tapped the folder, 'You're both lawyers - what do you think it is you have here - eh?'

Cranfield stood up exasperated, 'Mitigation.'

Colonel Ching shook his head, 'A bloody mess, that's what you've got here. Sit down.' Cranfield and Ching both sat again eyeing each other with hostility. 'If the Germans killed their own people it's no matter for a military tribunal. The tribunal is interested in crimes of war – Germans killing other nationalities contrary to the laws and usages of war.'

Major Yeo leaned forward, 'But Irma Grese *wasn't* a combatant - she was a prison wardress sent to Ravensbrück by the labour exchange.'

Ching frowned, 'An argument on a point of international law which I'm sure you will test in court.'

Cranfield shook his head, 'With the resources we have! Are you aware that none of us are experts on international law - that we have no texts; that we are both ordinary solicitors plucked from the ranks of the Royal Artillery? We asked for an English authority on international law; we've been told we can have one - if the defendants pay their expenses. And, if we want to go to London to do research we must pay the costs ourselves. In practical terms *no*. It's simply impossible for us to act effectively.'

Major Yeo interjected, 'This is a trial of a capital offence Sir. We must be allowed to use what materials are available. If you take away these papers there's almost nothing left to us. We need materials to work with.'

Major Ching got up, 'But not *these* materials and this is not relevant evidence. From a cursory glance it can only muddy the waters. I'll need to pass this around a while - let the Poles have a look - that could take months.' He walked toward the door, grasped the handle and then turned. 'And may I remind you both that you are still serving British officers and subject to military discipline. I suggest you bear that in mind in future when you are dealing with your German witnesses. Perhaps Major Yeo you need to be a little more discreet when you fraternise.'

'Fraternise Sir?'

'I want no further informal communication with Julie Scholl, or anyone else outside the chain of command. Do you understand? No more fireside chats. And don't assume it's all *Marquis of Queensbury* in the army. If you cross me, or pull any *rabbits out of the hat* at the trial, your feet won't touch the ground; you'll disappear and we'll throw away the key - understood?'

It was November 1945 before Karl finally encountered a source through which he could trade a few of their diamonds for dollars. The Americans were importing financiers, economists, and industrialists, to assess the state of post-war Germany, and a few were passing through Bonn. Soon, loitering around the hotels and cafés, Karl overheard the ambitions of an ageing American mining magnate to take a stake in the Saar coal fields, but cursing the French for blocking him. He talked angrily to his business associates of taking his fortune home with him and the stupidity of the Allied Control Commission. They seemed equally at a loss to know how to exploit the post-war landscape, or deal with the labyrinthine administration put in place by the occupying powers. Soon Karl had introduced himself and, after some cautious probing and a large amount of American bourbon consumed in the privacy of a hotel room, a deal was reached under which Karl would receive not only dollars, but critical medical supplies, in return for diamonds. With these dollars Karl and Julie paid the rental for a large house in Linz am Rhein, leased with the help of Dr Wittig who knew the elderly owner. Their new house stood high above the small town and held panoramic views of the river valley and beyond. It soon acquired a good Steinway piano, some excellent second-hand furniture, a consulting room, a library and a nursery, which was being prepared for the arrival in April of their first child. It also had an annex which, in a more prosperous age, might once have housed domestic servants and from which Julie could see her uncle's inn.

Otto and Ingrid might once have been scandalised by the circumstances of Julie's marriage, but now looked forward happily to the arrival of 'their' first grandchild – as Otto insisted on calling it. They married at the Protestant church a short distance from the *Rhein-Ahr* in early December. Otto gave his late brother's daughter away with unbounded pride and was unstinting in his hospitality. A small band was found to accompany the celebrations and the event seemed momentarily to raise everyone's spirits. But the autumn had been difficult, and early winter had been harsh - starvation and disease becoming commonplace in the towns and cities. Food was scarce, even in the villages with ready access to the countryside, and Karl's anxieties about the future began to mount. Then, in late November, the occupying forces announced rations were being cut still further, to 1,000 calories a day. It seemed that all Europe was on the move, begging, stealing, and scavenging for anything that might be eaten or provide fuel. Likewise, Karl and Julie picked berries, mushrooms, nettles and leaves, to supplement their rations and keep them and their unborn baby adequately fed, while Karl collected firewood in an old pram, hunted rabbits, hares, and wildfowl, in league with their neighbours. Barter was the new currency in preference to the new and worthless Occupation Marks issued by the allies, and Karl became a familiar figure in Remagen, Unkel, Linz and Sinzig, pedalling his bike and trading whatever he had for a small bag of flour, a pot of lard, milk, tea, or a few kilos of beef.

It was December 16th, 1945 when Julie got back into bed one morning, shivering, with a letter from Helene Grese. It seemed strange that she should have written to her, since Julie's only act had been to write a letter for Irma on the train from Zoppot and to post it - and that had been a year earlier. She could only imagine Irma had asked her to write and so settled into Karl's arms and started to read, while his hand gently caressed their unborn child.

'*Dear Fräulein Scholl, You may know by now that General Montgomery has refused my sister clemency. In this event she wanted me to write to you and ask you for your help – even now, when all hope for her has passed.*

302

Irma says that you gave a statement in Lüneburg to Major Cranfield. It was about Irma, but it was also about Wilhelm Koppe and the orphans in Posen.

Irma wanted you to know that the papers and photographs you gave the Major in Remagen were taken from him and were not returned before her trial. He was given several legal reasons Irma could not explain or remember. It seems that they needed Irma to be a 'Beast' right to the end and I'm afraid Cranfield seemed much less willing to argue Irma's defence than she had expected. I'm afraid she lost her temper with the prosecution in the end which did her no good.

Major Yeo has not written or been to see us as he promised. Did he contact you at all? Has he explained anything? If so, please let me know.

So, now my sister will probably die. When you read this she may even already be dead. She is to be hanged on 13th December.'

Irma just wanted you to know that nothing now seems to be happening about the orphans. She hopes you will ask questions when and if you can to keep the hope of justice for them alive.

She thanks you for your help and says you should not feel anything for her. She accepts her guilt and hopes now to be at rest finally with our mother. She wishes you a very happy life.

I wish this for you also…
Yours
Helene Grese"

Karl also read the letter, paused, and then put it on the bedside table. He kissed Julie looking for reassurance, 'Will you do anything?'

Julie seemed unsettled but shook her head. 'I can't. It wouldn't bring anything back would it? No, I'll write back. I'll thank her and say a few things about Irma, but I can't help - we have to move on...' she put her hand over Karl's which lay on her belly and their fingers meshed, '…for the children.'

Karl kissed her and smiled. 'The baby - have you thought of any names?'

'Oh, I'm not sure. I'd like to get away from some of the traditional names.'

'Won't that be a little difficult?

'Why?'

'Well, isn't there supposed to be some reference to our family, grandparents, great-grandparents, aunts, uncles, sisters, brothers, cousins, second cousins, mothers, fathers…what's left? We have to have a family name.'

'Well, there must be someone among them who has an unusual name, someone a bit different.'

'I had a second cousin called Clytemnestra.'

Julie giggled, 'You should worry then – didn't she drown her father!' She began to beat Karl with a pillow until he begged for mercy.

As she lay poised to strike again he spoke, 'So they won't be names dredged from the past then?'

Julie narrowed her eyes, 'All right, all right; what about Eric after my father, or…'

'Sophie after my mother…?' he said edging out of bed.

Julie unleashed a flurry of pillows as Karl retreated to the bathroom. 'And don't forget, I'm going to Bonn today…' she shouted after him, '…and I'm beginning to be attracted by the name Clytemnestra!'

Julie arrived in Bonn at noon by train. She felt well and contented and imagined the baby was lying comfortably inside her, warmed against the chill winter breeze. She felt happy to be pregnant, happy to be able to walk freely along the sleepy streets, happy that, however difficult their life was now with the shortages and rationing, her baby would grow up in peace and with more advantages than she had known. She also enjoyed the lingering pleasure of knowing that Karl was at home, safe in his consulting room, dispensing his services and often his medicines, without recompense and with a quiet admonishment that he would carry the cost. It was in this way that he now used their wealth discreetly, to lighten the burdens of their poorer neighbours and help the village to live with its privations.

At five to two she began to return to the station having combed the busy market and the almost empty shops for a few items for Karl and some toys for the nursery.

As she walked to the junction of Johannesstrasse and Limpenrichter Strasse she saw a small crowd gathered around a young woman who was lying in front of a car. She went forward and found that an argument had broken out between the driver and two of the women who were helping the injured woman to her feet. It seemed that the woman had collapsed, partly through hunger and partly through cold. She wore a thin coat and a summer dress. Her shoes had holes in them which had been stuffed with cardboard and her hair was partly matted. She was also heavily pregnant, so Julie crossed the street to speak with her. But as she did so her attention was drawn by the driver of the car, who was still haranguing the young woman, 'You could have caused an accident, you idiot, you stupid bloody Polak – now get off the road. Out of my way!' He waved her aside in a final parting gesture. She looked at him with disgust but by now he was getting back into the car so she leaned down to catch his eye and register her anger and contempt. But as she caught sight of him, mouthing to himself as he engaged gear, she suddenly saw what resembled the pockmarked profile of Wilhelm Koppe. She stood for a moment, startled, trying to see clearly though the reflection of the passenger window, but by then he was pulling away and soon he was gone, and the moment had passed so quickly she thought it must have been an illusion - a trick of the mind. Nevertheless it remained there, like a frame of film, frozen, and unsettling.

By now the two women had steadied the girl on her feet and she was begging to be left alone, but Julie caught her arm and their eyes met. Julie looked at the woman's abdomen and pointed to her own, 'My husband is a doctor and you look ill.'

The woman glanced at her nervously, 'I have no money. I have nothing.' she said in Polish accented German.

Julie smiled, 'If you come with me I can give you food, a bed, and my husband can see if you're all right.'

The woman seemed exhausted and willing to be led, so Julie took her by the arm and walked her to the station. As they sat on the train the other passengers looked over, repelled by the sight and smell of Julie's companion and began to pass comments. Julie's anger mounted as the sense of shame and discomfort in the young woman grew, and when she reached for the handle of the carriage door it was as much as Julie could do to stop her from leaving. 'The man said you were Polish?' Julie said trying to engage her and distract her attention from the hostility around them.

She looked down at the floor, 'No, I'm from Bromberg. I am ethnic-German.' The woman looked at her belly with detestation, 'And this is not mine. This is what the Russians did.'

305

Julie reached forward and took her hand, 'What's your name?'
'Dorothea.'

'Dorothea, God has smiled on you today. You will come and live with us until you are better. How much longer do you have?'

'January – I think.' she said unhappily.

'You're safe now - we can take care of everything.'

When they entered the house wearily an hour later Karl greeted Dorothea as Julie had hoped he would, as simply a welcome house guest, and she was immediately made to feel at ease in their home. Julie helped her wash and dressed her in some ill-fitting clothes. Later Karl examined her. She was weak, malnourished, and anaemic; these could be treated he said. But Dorothea could not be drawn on her feelings for the baby and this concerned him.

When she was shown her rooms in the old servant's quarters Dorothea's spirits seemed to revive. And, after further attention to her hair and hands, she emerged from her ragged former self as a younger and prettier woman than Julie had thought possible. Her hair was now revealed to be a rich chestnut colour, her delicate features and fine pale complexion lending her brown eyes a soulful depth and beauty. Julie thought how many women might envy such looks, but how they must have damned Dorothea to torments beyond imagination as she fled through the Russian lines.

At dinner Karl talked a little about Bromberg and so was able to at least share some familiar places and recollections with her, but Dorothea remained reserved and confined herself to short answers and nervous but appreciative smiles. As she ate Julie noticed that her hands trembled and that she had scars on her wrists, only recently healed.

When Julie and Karl lay in bed that night Julie's mind ranged over that day's events, of the car and its foul mouthed belligerent driver, of that moment of fleeting recognition now consigned to her imagination. But it was Dorothea who made them both feel unsettled and inwardly preoccupied. Finally Julie took Karl's hand, 'How old is she?'

'She says she's eighteen.'

Julie fidgeted with the buttons of her nightdress, 'Do you think she'll harm herself – the baby?'

Karl looked at her bleakly, 'I'm afraid I think she *could* - in her present state. Did you notice the scars on her wrists?'

306

Julie nodded, 'Should I go and see her?'

'Julie, if she wants to take her life it will be at a moment of her choosing. All we can do is provide some hope - some alternative future to whatever hell she imagines for herself with that child.'

Julie rose from the bed quickly and put on her dressing gown, 'Thank you. I'll be back soon. I'm going to talk to her.' Karl tried to protest, but realised Julie's mind was made up.

She descended the stairs to the servant's quarters and knocked on the bedroom door gently a number of times, but there was no answer. She could see the light was on and so entered cautiously, quietly calling Dorothea's name.

When her eyes fell on her she was sitting upright in bed, staring ahead of her into the distance, her hands gripping the bed sheets fiercely. 'Couldn't you sleep?'

Dorothea shook her head, her voice strangled by fear and apprehension. 'They used to hunt us at night...the Russians...I can't sleep. I can still hear the girls screaming...screaming for help.'

Julie pulled up a chair, 'Dorothea...I know what you are suffering...I was like you once.' Dorothea looked at her with wild terrified eyes and then resumed her distant gaze, 'I want you to know we will keep the child if you can't look after it, if you can't live with it. We will support you if you do want to keep it.'

Dorothea began to rock backwards and forwards, 'They made me bury my parents. They murdered them in front of me - there's no one left.'

Julie sat forward, her face stern, 'I'll remain with you day and night. You will not harm yourself.'

'You care? Why?' Dorothea snapped with tears in her eyes.

Julie's voice was now steely, 'Because I could have been *you*! Because a part of me still is *you*! And now I want to live and one day so will you.'

Dorothea stopped for a moment and looked around, her face tormented and her voice pleading. 'Can your husband help me then? I can't sleep, not with the nightmares. They won't go away...the screams.' She reached out and clung to Julie with such desperate determination that Julie comforted Dorothea to a point of near mutual exhaustion before finally being able free herself and call for Karl.

When he left Dorothea an hour later she was unconscious. As Julie and he lay together in the small hours with the light still on she recalled how Sister Schmidt had drilled the orphans in their dance steps to fend off their fears and began to make notes of the things Dorothea might do about the house. Soon she and Karl had added a few ideas together and in the morning they slowly but purposefully began to occupy Dorothea's time. It seemed to steady her nerves and within a few days Karl had also appointed her as his medical record keeper. As her work increased over the following weeks, so her darkness seemed to recede, though she remained withdrawn and rarely spoke more than a few words.

When Dorothea gave birth in late January 1946 it was to a girl. Julie was herself only three months away from the end of her term and so occupied herself with the new arrival as if it were her own, while Dorothea hesitantly nursed the child through a series of inner crises only seldom glimpsed by Julie. Over the weeks that followed both Karl and Julie could see that Dorothea was struggling to behave towards her baby with any genuine affection or concern – though she tried to maintain the appearance of it in their company. It was in her glances and in her manner with the child, the careless touch and the chilly absence of feeling that they understood, with a growing sense of helplessness, the lack of any maternal bond.

Then in early May, a few weeks after Julie had given birth to their own daughter, Sophie, they found the baby alone one morning and Dorothea gone. There was a note, an apology of a kind, but also a reassurance that she would not harm herself. She had waited as long as she could and must now begin again she said. It was a sentiment that found sympathy with Julie and so she now put both the girls to her breast as her own, knowing that only she could love Dorothea's child as she deserved. And, as Dorothea had not named the child, despite many attempts to encourage her, Julie decided to call her little 'orphan' Helene.

The months now passed in a frenzy of activity as Julie balanced the needs of her 'twins' with the struggle to maintain a household in the face of the shortages. Then, one morning in late July 1946, while Julie was sitting in the kitchen feeding Helene, and Sophie lay next to her in a cot, Karl entered, kissed her tenderly, and went to the stove for some coffee. Julie noticed he had folded that day's copy of *Die Welt* tightly under his arm, something he was loath to do normally, and beckoned him over, looking into his eyes, sensing there was something he was holding back. He smiled weakly, unfurled the newspaper and spread it out in front of her. She looked at it for a moment and then her eyes alighted on a small column heading near the bottom of the front page, "ARTHUR GRIESER PUBLICALLY HANGED IN POLAND, on the slopes of Fort Winiary....". Julie closed her eyes, pushed the paper back towards Karl and kissed the baby on the head. She said nothing then, or later, and his name was never spoken by her again.

PART III

Chapter 30

By 1948 Dr Rust and his wife had assumed a respected place among the citizens of Linz am Rhein. Their philanthropy and charity were admired and Julie began to emerge as the pianist she had once promised to be, often performing for charity or in aid of civic reconstruction.

By 1949 Bonn had become the seat of government in the new West Germany and Julie's access to the recital halls and platforms it provided, and the admiration of respected luminaries and critics, soon propelled her toward wider audiences in Germany. Family ties also strengthened with the arrival of Peter and Dorothea in 1950, and 1952. These made acceptance of the many invitations to perform abroad impractical and so Julie contented herself with domestic German audiences and a distinguished but limited reputation as a solo pianist.

And then, in January 1960, she received a letter from the past - from an old acquaintance; Edie Krebs had written on the notepaper of the Schubert Society in Vienna, to which she appended her signature as Secretary and invited her to play at their festival in early May.

The letter was greeted by Julie with mixed emotions and she talked through her feelings about seeing Edie again with Karl at some length. Finally she decided to go - but alone and only for four days. She would see Klemperer at the Philharmonie conducting Bruckner and play one recital, but she would not stay too long with Edie. She found she still needed a margin of safety from the past they shared and the emotions and memories which Edie might evoke.

When they finally met that fine Mayday morning, as she emerged from Wien Westbahnhof Station, Julie's anxieties were immediately dispelled by Edie's appearance. The sharpness of some of her features had been softened by age, contentment, and prosperity. By her side stood a pleasant if rather plain older man, with plump ruddy cheeks and a balding head, who was clearly devoted to her. He bowed slightly, holding Julie's hand delicately, 'Josef Keller', he said in a diffident tone, and took her cases. Edie hugged and kissed her as if they were sisters rather than brief acquaintances in adversity for those few weeks of 1940. She took Julie's arm, bubbling with enthusiasm and showed her to the car. They soon sped out of the city, across the Danube towards Breitenlee, sitting on the back seat chatting animatedly while Joseph whistled to himself in the front.

'I can't tell you how happy I am...' Edie continued breathlessly, '...to be able to make your dream come true. And finally you are in Vienna!'

Julie pointed surreptitiously to Herr Keller and Edie leaned closer, 'Oh, you will recall the others I might once have married? Well this is one of them - such a good man. He's changed my life.'

'And Hermann...?'

'Dead.' Edie said quickly and in a tone calculated to discourage further enquiry.

That night they all re-entered the glittering environs of Vienna, walked arm in arm, three abreast down the Bosendorferstrasse, and approached the steps of the Philharmonie. Julie had relished this rare opportunity to step out in her evening dress and wear her jewellery in the company of elegantly dressed concertgoers and felt excited and elated. Inside the building Julie's eyes were drawn by the glittering crystal of the chandeliers and the sumptuous colours of the interior. She could already feel the anticipation in those around her and suddenly recalled how vividly she had imagined this moment during those lonely wartime years when she had needed to escape from reality - and yes, it had been just like this she thought.

While they stood for a few minutes glancing at the programme in the entrance hall, Edie suddenly turned and tugged Julie's sleeve. 'There's a man over there looking at us. Do you know him?'

Julie turned and met the man's eyes, 'My Lord, I think it's Tommy Yeo – someone I met in Germany at the end of the war - how marvellous!'

Tommy walked over smiling broadly, his dinner jacket and black tie lending him a dignified but more portly appearance than Julie had remembered. He acknowledged Josef and Edie with great courtesy and then kissed Julie's hand, 'I had not dared to believe it was you.' Tommy said, in faultless German.

'And you are out of uniform at last.'

'Only for tonight; I'm now the Military Attaché here.'

311

'I thought you would go back to law.'

'I did too, but then I was recalled for the Korean War and decided to stay on – well, by then I'd spent so long in the army that it hardly mattered – my career in law was over.' He seemed suddenly distracted by others who were hailing him from a distance, 'Oh dear, I am so sorry – look I have to go, I'm on duty.'

Julie took his arm, 'But you always said you wanted to hear me play?'

He smiled mischievously, 'I already have a ticket – you and the *Wanderer Fantasy* - how apt! Until tomorrow then?' As an afterthought, Tommy drew a business card from his wallet and pressed it into Julie's hand, 'Unless you'd like to meet for coffee?'

Julie smiled, 'That would be lovely.'

Later that night, after the concert, drinks, and hot chocolate, Julie and Edie sat alone in her lounge, the fire casting long shadows in the dimly lit room.

'So you have four children now?'

'Yes. I had Helene first, then Sophie, then Peter and Dorothea.'

'And how old are they?'

'It's complicated! I had the first two within three months of each other.'

'How?' Edie said incredulously.'

'I suppose it does sound strange, but I found this girl of eighteen, Dorothea, in Bonn, just after the War. She was eight months pregnant. Her parents had been murdered by the Poles and then she'd been raped terribly by the Russians trying to flee to Germany from Bromberg. I took her into my home with Karl – she was starving. We looked after her but she was in a dreadful mental state - shattered by her experiences. When the baby was born she left…she couldn't cope and couldn't bear to keep the baby.'

'So you took the baby in as an orphan?'

'No - as my own - she was never going to be an orphan. But I did name her after a lovely friend I had at an orphanage in Posen. I felt it was a wonderful thing to be able to do in all the circumstances. It's changed all our lives and she is *so* bubbly and happy.'

Edie became hesitant and fidgeted for a moment with her cup, 'Yes, Hermann told me you'd been in Posen. He told me after that first evening at the Forster's. He said you'd had a bad time - that you were *marked.* It made me feel very guilty about the way I'd behaved towards you.'

Julie looked at Edie and felt a chill suddenly come over her as their eyes met. 'Ah?' she said apprehensively.

Edie shook her head, 'And when Hermann found out I'd gone back to see you and we'd played so happily together that day, he warned me off completely. That's when I realised I'd had enough – but I couldn't say anything to you of course. Do you know that Hermann shot himself?'

Julie rose from her chair putting down her cup clumsily, 'I'm sorry Edie, but this is all in the past. I was worried this would happen. Honestly, I have to move on and so do you. We can be friends - I want to be friends - but not if we have to relive the past...they're all dead now.'

'Not Wilhelm Koppe...' Edie said turning to look at Julie with tightened lips '...and I do know what he did to you. He's still alive and doing very well.'

Julie sat down, stunned, 'But how do you know he's alive?'

'Because he's the sales director of a chocolate factory in Bonn and calls himself Lohmann – his wife's surname.'

Julie reached out and held Edie's arm, 'But that's impossible - in Bonn.'

'He's hardly hiding is he, right under the noses of the Government there. But yes, I know he's there, living with his wife. He brings his chocolate to Vienna - he's their representative here. We met – he knew me through Hermann of course – but he wasn't concerned, not even the slightest bit anxious when I saw him. *'Nobody's interested'* he said.' Edie rose from her chair and went to the cupboard, 'Look here, he even gave me some truffles and suggested we might go to dinner together – he seemed to think I might like to get to *know* him better!'

Julie studied the chocolate box and then put it down, 'You know he murdered my father?'

Edie shook her head, 'No, I didn't. I had no idea. I'm sorry.'

Julie gripped her hand, 'It's alright. You've only confirmed what I saw with my own eyes in '45 and I chose not to believe - that he's there, in Bonn. And if that meant a life for Dorothea and her daughter that day then I'm happy - but now...'

Edie looked into her eyes, 'Now...?'

313

'I must act I suppose. Now I know he's there I'll have to confront him.' Julie stood. 'But after tomorrow - everything must wait until after the recital.'

The *Burgtheater* on the Ringstrasse had only re-opened five years earlier but had been restored to its former Habsburg glory as one the finest and largest theatre stages in Europe and one of the iconic architectural achievements of the city.

When Julie saw the stage the day before her recital she looked at Edie with disbelief, 'Isn't this rather large, Edie? How many tickets have you sold exactly?'

'Edie rolled her eyes; three hundred and fifty... but on the night...'

'And how many does the auditorium hold?'

'Well...one thousand four hundred.'

Julie wilted but then seemed to be captivated by a thought, 'Good... then I want you to throw open the doors to the city orphanages and schools.'

'I'm sorry?'

'I am happy to fill the seats with children.'

'But this is Vienna – Schubert!'

'Did he hate children?' Julie asked with mild astonishment.

Edie thought for a moment, 'Well, they always seem to be either dying or dead in his songs. But I suppose he's not as dreadfully morbid about them as Mahler!'

'I am meeting Colonel Yeo for coffee at 10.00am and will then practise for the rest of the day at the Academy.'

Edie held up her hands in surrender, 'I know that look, Julie; very well. I will do what I can but could we confine them to the first circle?'

They kissed goodbye, and as they did so Julie saw Tommy walking down the auditorium steps toward them.

Later they sat together in the nearly empty coffee lounge. He looked over at her affectionately, 'You've changed remarkably little.' Julie fixed him purposefully and he sat back with an air of resignation. 'Ah, you're about to have a serious discussion with me aren't you? I can see it in your eyes. You really don't want to talk to me about Schubert do you?'

'I was in correspondence with Helene Grese after the war.'

Tommy frowned and his voice lost its ebullience, 'So, this is about the trial is it - about Irma?' he shook his head, 'I'd really rather not revisit this...not now...it's fifteen years ago Julie.'

'I just think we were all surprised that nothing was made of the evidence I gave you, about what she did for me and the orphans – the evidence she gave about Koppe. I want to know why you never came back to me?'

Tommy looked around him at the empty chairs and then leaned forward, 'They drew a line Julie, that's what happened. We were army officers and it came from the very top. Cranfield had been in the army longer than I had. He'd never known anything like it – none of us on the defence team had. We were stripped of everything. The pressure was incredible. We had no idea how far they were prepared to go. It was largely a piece of theatre I'm afraid...even if most of the verdicts were justified.'

'But what about the evidence I gave you?'

'It was seized by a Lieutenant Colonel in the Intelligence Corps. In the end we had to proceed without it. They wouldn't let us use it. I expect it's been given to the German Government now. If they find Koppe they will no doubt use it.'

'But Irma was a key witness, wasn't she? She was there at the orphanage when it all happened. When they executed her they also killed the case, didn't they? Those photographs mean nothing without her.'

Tommy looked at her nodding his head slightly. 'In the absence of other evidence...of course. But what could we do - we were under orders.'

Julie produced the cardboard wrapper from the box of chocolates given to Edie and laid it in front of Tommy.

'There you are!'

He looked at her quizzically. 'What's this?'

'Koppe is living in Bonn. He's the director of a chocolate factory. Even if your people destroyed the chance of justice for the orphans and my father, there are still the Jews and Poles to be answered for.' Tommy picked up the wrapper and looked at it with obvious discomfort, but Julie continued, 'Ironic isn't it; if Irma had just managed to hide away for a few years packing chocolates under the noses of the German Government she would have lived. She'd probably get twenty years now and be out in ten.'

Tommy pushed the chocolate box back towards her. 'Julie, you have to understand, for the same reasons it was so necessary to hang Irma and her kind then, it's absolutely not going to be welcome if Koppe goes on trial now. It's 1960; Germany is in the front line and the Russians are pushing at the gates – you've seen the papers, they've shot down an American spy plane. Nobody wants to go back and re-examine the war - the Russians are the threat now.'

'Are you saying you won't help me?'

'I'm saying it's too late.'

Julie stood stony faced, 'I had to ask, Major Yeo: for my father, for the orphans, for the others he killed. You do understand?' Tommy registered the new tone of formality in her voice and felt uncomfortable. She leaned down, 'You saved my husband from the Americans, and you saved me from that monster Cooper - you believed in law. You were a friend to Germans when Germany was friendless, and I would prefer to remember you that way.' She extended her hand abruptly and they shook briefly before she left.

Tommy remained in his seat and toyed with the chocolate box for a moment, deep in thought, watching her walk into the distance and then disappear through the café doors.

When Julie took to the stage of the Burgtheater the following night she was largely blinded to the audience by the stage lights. She sat at the piano in the dark void of the stage, entirely focussed on the music. Perhaps it was this ability to exclude all other thoughts and feelings - the fears and terrors - that had saved her so many times when otherwise she might have lost her sanity. But as she began to play she did feel something new within her, a confidence, a new sense of purpose which did not stem only from the music, but from an inner belief - that she could now take a step of her own, that for the first time *she* could bring justice for her father and the orphans; that she might in some way claim back her past and her future. She felt suddenly liberated and it seemed to lift her playing to a new level of intensity.

In the interval Edie came to the dressing room and proudly flourished a piece of paper, 'Five hundred, Julie, one hundred of them children - it's incredible for a recital and the critics are here. You have them in the palm of your hand. And the playing! Well, you have

316

changed so much – it's electrifying. What's going on in that head of yours?'

But Edie could see that Julie's thoughts were elsewhere and she seemed unmoved by Edie's enthusiasm.

'Edie I am going back to Linz early tomorrow. I need your help to sort everything out with Wilhelm Koppe once and for all. Will you help me?'

Edie nodded warily. 'Will you tell me what you intend to do?'

'No - not now. I will telephone in a few days, but I would never do anything that would break our friendship. It's just a favour that nobody else can do.'

In the second half the *'Wanderer Fantasy'* flowed flawlessly from beneath her fingers and after tumultuous applause it remained only to conclude the recital with an encore. But suddenly Julie felt a strange yearning to play something for her mother, for the children and orphans, rather than the Schubert she had prepared. And so she began, almost inaudibly in the cavernous hall, Rubinstein's *E flat Serenade*. It was the music Edie had last heard in Danzig in the dark days of 1940, that Julie's mother had first played to her as a child and then taught her as a young girl. It was the music which Gieseking had forbidden her. It had none of the drama or display of the Schubert, but when she had finished the hall erupted again. And then, for the first, time she could hear the children, calling for more, their small hands held high with excited applause, their small feet stamping with enjoyment.

She sat again smiling as the clamour died, having already been warned that encores were the downfall of many a Viennese debutante and began to play Schumann's *'Toccata'*. Now careless of all dangers and inured to all technical difficulties, her hands fluttered and struck the keys with a bravura that halted even those poised to leave quickly for the bars and cafés. Her whole person seemed at one with the pulse of the music and the audience looked on, mesmerised by this explosive display of passion and verve.

When, at last, she brushed over the keys to render the last throw-away chords, all was pandemonium again. As the lights came up she could see the critics in the front row either eyeing her with stunned incomprehension, or scribbling furiously to catch the early editions.

Later, after the reception and much enthusiasm from invited guests, she went back to her dressing room. As she put on her coat there was a gentle knock on the door and when she answered Tommy Yeo entered bearing a bouquet. He stood, awkward and silent, 'Have you something to say to me, Colonel Yeo?' she said, taking the flowers from him and smiling appreciatively.

'Apart from congratulations...' he said cheerily, but then pushed the door firmly shut, becoming instantly serious, 'Yes, I have. I came to tell you I've cabled Bonn. I have set the wheels in motion. But I also came to advise you that you must be prepared for some resistance - even some sort of backlash.'

'To advise, or to warn?'

'That depends on the Federal Intelligence Service - on Gehlen.'

'Why should that be a problem? Who is Gehlen?'

'He's an ex-Wehrmacht Major General, he's Head of West German Intelligence.'

'In Germany everybody has a past!'

Tommy seemed momentarily exasperated, 'You have to understand the new Germany Julie – please! Nothing is new, it's all been sanitised and re-packaged. Gehlen took over intelligence operations in Germany after the war, but he was the CIA's man until '56; he recruited the first agents, his old contacts, the people who worked against the Russians during the war - the Gestapo and SS. They had the knowledge the CIA needed...He's got dubious friends - that's really what you need to understand and the Government won't thank you for exposing those sorts of links with Nazi regime. I think they'll try to dump this. The Russians are the enemy now – at least that's the way Gehlen wants us to see it.'

'And so?'

'Be careful. You have a family and a life to live. Do what you can, but don't feel you have to push this all the way. Don't try to push them further than they're prepared to go.'

Julie smiled weakly, 'Thank you.' and then she brushed his arm with her hand affectionately, 'You know, Tommy, you haven't aged well - you've lost something of your idealism. But thank you for what you were to us then.'

Julie turned to pick up the flowers and leave, but Tommy barred the door.

'Wait…please wait.' He seemed to brace himself for what he was about to tell her and then began to speak more quietly. 'When we were taking evidence from Irma Grese in June 1945 about Posen, she told us about a doctor - Hertz was his name…'

Julie nodded, 'Yes, I knew Hertz, he saved my life.'

'He and Irma agreed after the suicides that they would keep evidence about the crime – in the hope one day that justice would be done. There were two things they had: the pictures which Irma kept, and a policy paper issued by SS Dr Fischer of the Race and Resettlement Department and signed off by Wilhelm Koppe, which was sent to Switzerland – to Berne. Irma said there was a footnote in the document which proved that the girls in the orphanage were to be confined under SS guard, and hand annotations by Koppe regarding the purposes of SS access to them. Our notes were confiscated by the Intelligence Corps. The allegation about the document was never followed up. She also claimed Hertz kept other notes about Koppe. They were all in a safety deposit box. If it's true it means Koppe could still be prosecuted for what happened at the orphanage - even without Irma.'

Julie stood for a moment. 'How could we find it – the deposit box?'

He shrugged his shoulders, 'I don't know.' Tommy stood aside and placed his hand on the door handle. 'I'm sorry. That's how it was then - I was under military discipline, I obeyed orders; and this is me now - trying to do the right thing and pick up the pieces.'

Julie smiled and looked at the flowers, 'Sorry Tommy. I'm sorry I said what I did. You are still a good man.'

Chapter 31

By the time Julie departed Vienna the next day Edie had already gathered what reviews she could of the previous evening's concert and Julie sat reading them in the railway compartment. After she had digested these her eyes wandered further and she also noticed a new face emerging from the columns of political coverage about Germany - that of the Mayor of Berlin, Willy Brandt. She thought how he contrasted with the ancient Adenauer who had been Chancellor since September 1947 and whose tenure seemed a symbol of the older generation holding back the new, regardless of his achievements. Brandt was in his late forties, Adenauer in his eighties. She suddenly felt irritated by German politics, its conservatism, and its continued tolerance of the past – the reliance on people like Gehlen and his Gestapo and SS friends.

When Julie got back to Linz, Helene, Sophie and Peter greeted her with enthusiastic hugs and Dorothea with a posy of meadow flowers. Karl embraced her as he always did after any time apart, holding her long and tight to him and kissing her with a tenderness that spoke of his continuing insecurity at separation from her.

As they walked up the hill through the cobbled streets of the town their neighbours and friends acknowledged them affectionately and Julie felt suddenly contented with the world and glad to be away from Vienna. As they went on Dorothea and Peter broke off to play with other children, while Helene and Sophie met up with some school friends, leaving Karl and Julie to finish the short distance to the house alone.

After talking about the concert for a little time Karl became preoccupied and Julie sensed that something was disturbing him, 'What is it Karl?'

At first he shook his head, 'Oh it's nothing…local gossip.' Then he stopped, unable to contain his anxieties, 'Did something happen in Vienna - something else?'

Julie searched his eyes for meaning, 'Why?'

He shrugged. 'I'm not sure. It's just that people in the town started telling me things as I came to meet you with the children.

People - strangers - have started asking questions about you...about us?'

Julie clasped his arm and they continued walking. 'Who?'

'I don't know; at the butchers and in the coffee shop, it was *people* probing about the children and me. Frau Rose said they seemed odd - official.'

Julie pondered for a moment, 'Karl, they were probably journalists, you know, looking for a story after the concert.'

The following weeks were spent responding to the aftershocks from the Vienna recital. Suddenly Julie found herself with an agent in Berlin and an international profile which she seemed reluctant to acknowledge or pursue. Instead she consumed herself with the preparations for the one hundred and fiftieth anniversary of Schumann's birth on 8 June 1960 and the concert she was to give in the Schumann–Haus in Bonn on 11 June to mark the event. To Karl her attentions also seemed concerned with the actual organization of the event to an extent to which he was not accustomed. It was not only her new agent but Edie who was also involved telephoning and discussing the choreography of the concert in seemingly minute detail.

And then, at noon on Sunday 5th June, as the family prepared for lunch, four cars ascended the road from the village to the house and halted noisily outside, while a police car pulled up and maintained station at the end of the drive.

When Karl went to the door to answer the insistent knocking, plain clothed men showed their identification with casual indifference to his protests and brushed past. The senior officer, identifiable only by the authority of his commands, proceeded to order a search and made his way towards the back of the house.

The children were sitting with Julie in the living room when the door was opened abruptly. They nervously gathered around their mother as the officer identified himself. 'I am Captain Ritter of the Federal Intelligence Service. I have a warrant to search these premises and for your arrest.'

Julie stood with studied composure and kissed each of her children. Dorothea began to cry and Helene bent down to comfort her while Peter clung to Julie's arm. When Karl entered the room Julie gestured to him and he took Peter and Dorothea from her, 'You're

321

upsetting our children Captain, so I suppose we should leave as quickly as possible. May I get my coat?' she said as calmly as she could, aware that the children were still watching her. Ritter nodded and she returned a few moments later with her bag and coat.

She smiled at Karl apologetically, but he seemed inconsolable, 'What have you done darling? What's this all about?'

Her voice was composed, 'I complained Karl, that's all. I've found him...he's here...in Bonn.'

Ritter advanced and took her arm, 'That's enough. I want no more talking.'

They arrived at the Federal Intelligence Service building in Bonn at one thirty. Julie was immediately taken to a bright sterile featureless interview room on the first floor where she sat with a female officer until Ritter re-joined them a few minutes later.

He sat and put a thin file down on the desk, which he opened impatiently, spreading out the papers. His tone was businesslike. 'In '39 you were arrested and held at Fort Winiary in Posen on suspicion of espionage and working for the Polish Intelligence Services. You were held overnight and then put under house arrest. After one week you escaped from house arrest. Is that correct?' Julie stared ahead without expression. 'In May '45 you disclosed to Major Cranfield and Major Yeo of the British Army the existence of criminal files and other documents which you had obtained from sources close to the German Government then in Danzig, West Prussia. How did you obtain those papers?' Julie said nothing. 'You were in contact with Major Yeo, British Military Attaché in Vienna again on May 2nd, 1960. What did you talk about?' Julie shook her head. Ritter thrummed his fingers on the desk eyeing her impatiently. 'Have you met Major Yeo regularly since the war?'

Julie looked at her hands while he attempted to engage with her. He resumed with irritation, 'You claim that a former SS Obergruppenführer Wilhelm Koppe is now living and working in Bonn under the alias Lohmann. Is that correct?'

'Yes.' she said looking up again.

Ritter passed over a photograph of Koppe that seemed to be taken from a catalogue or magazine, 'Is that him?'

'Yes.'

322

There was a knock on the door and a slim older man entered the interview room. He was wearing an expensive suit, wore rimless glasses and had a fine mane of grey hair. He gestured with the slightest of eye movement at Ritter and the female warder who left the room without speaking. The man sat where Ritter had been and smiled benignly, extending his hand, 'Troost…Ludwig Troost.'

Julie remained motionless for a moment and then reluctantly extended her hand. 'Good!' he said nodding appreciatively, 'I am concerned about what is happening here. You should not be mixed up with the likes of us. We're supposed to be a foreign intelligence service, not getting muddled up in police work.' He took out some cigarettes and offered one to Julie. 'I know of your reputation of course, as a pianist – Vienna was a triumph by all accounts. But you are also a good mother – four children? Your husband is highly regarded and does much for the poor and disadvantaged. I think you even took in an orphan – Helene?' Julie looked at him warily, 'What I want to know is why you are pursuing this matter of Koppe through the British?'

'It was pure chance.' Julie murmured.

'Is this political?'

'How do you mean?'

'You went to the British. Why didn't you come to us?'

'The file on Koppe's crimes was given to Major Yeo in '45 - it disappeared. I wanted to find out why. When I met him in Vienna I asked him. It was a chance meeting.'

'You went further than that though, you asked him to pursue it, which means the German Government now has a formal request on file from a foreign government.'

'He murdered my father.' Julie said meeting his eye.

Troost seemed to shrug, 'Germany is full of people who did terrible things, and now they are businessmen, bankers and industrialists. Would you have them all brought to trial?'

Julie fixed Troost in her gaze for a moment, 'How do you know about my wartime police record - my detention in Fort Winiary. Why are you using my old wartime file?'

'Is there something in there that makes you anxious?'

'But that's a Gestapo file you're using - the one from Posen.'

'We have all the old files. The archives were preserved. We needed to know about you - your whole history.'

'And is that your only source?'

Troost looked at her sharply, 'Meaning...?

'Is it true there are still ex-SS and Gestapo working here in this office - for the German state? Is that why Koppe feels invulnerable? Is that why I'm here and he isn't?'

He smiled, 'Who told you that, Major Yeo?'

Julie leaned forward, 'How did you know I was put under house arrest in '39 - after my interrogation at Fort Winiary prison?'

'From your old wartime files – as I just told you.'

Julie shook her head, 'But my old Gestapo file never explained why I'd been taken from Fort Winiary – it never mentioned my house arrest. The file didn't explain why my interrogation had been stopped. Only Müller, Koppe and Grieser knew that, and the only person who's still alive is Koppe.' Julie became silent, but her eyes remained firmly fixed on Troost, 'You've spoken to him - haven't you?'

Troost thought for a moment and then nodded gently with a wry smile, 'Ok, I won't deny it. We all live with contradictions, but Frau Rust, we are not all politicians, they don't like contradictions - not public ones anyway. We have federal elections next year; the SPD is talking about putting up a young socialist, Willy Brandt, as their chancellor candidate – bypassing the party chairman. Adenauer is afraid he'll lose his majority. The Government's jumpy.'

Julie shrugged her shoulders and sat back, 'You've lost me, Herr Troost.'

'The Federal Intelligence Service is Adenauer's child, it's the product of his long chancellorship and he personally oversees it. If Koppe is put on trial his links will be exposed and the Government will be called to account for the fact it employs former members of the SS and Gestapo in its intelligence community – a necessary but politically sensitive measure in these difficult times.'

Julie looked at him sensing for the first time the malevolence in his candour, 'And why tell me this? What do you expect me to do now – abandon my allegations to save Adenauer?'

He drew on his cigarette and smiled, 'My job is to protect the Government from external shocks and alert it to internal threats. I do this best by finding common ground, in reaching an understanding, in heading them off. We are all vulnerable to shocks - governments and individuals.'

'You and your family for example live a good clean German life, but dig a little deeper and what do you find. That the state cannot account for all of your wealth, that your child Helene was not properly adopted, that your surgery is not licensed correctly, that your handling of state property during the War may be, however absurdly, indictable, that you have contacts with the British and, in the past, Polish intelligence. And now I'm like you; I have this information, so what do I do with it? Do I pass it on to the appropriate agencies of the state, or do I consider all the implications of simply throwing it into the wind and reflect on it for a while? You see, Julie, I believe that you should know why I am doing this, because if you know how serious the implications are you will believe in my willingness to act against you with all the forces at my disposal. If I say nothing about my motives and simply say *don't do it or else* then you might still be under the illusion there is a future for you and your family if you betray my trust.'

He fixed her determinedly, his voice more abrasive, 'And then there are the other issues; about old friends meeting other old friends, of Gertrud Forster suddenly arriving in Austria, of meetings with Edie Krebs and telephone calls to Linz. What are you doing Frau Rust?'

'Nothing.'

He smiled, 'What are *they* doing Frau Rust?'

Julie shook her head, 'I have no intention of allowing my family to be torn apart Herr Troost.'

'So this is simply a chain of unconnected events?'

'Yes.'

He sat back, 'My job is not to trust, but to assume the worst of you. Suffice it to say that my understanding with you here today is that the status quo is maintained. You go about your life and let Herr Koppe go about his. If you persist, however, your life will fall apart, your husband's surgery will be closed, your daughter will be put into care, and your financial affairs will be investigated. Your career will be blighted by intrigue and you will face charges in relation to the past handling of state papers and the other matters.' Troost stood abruptly. 'You will now be released and placed under surveillance for twelve months until after the elections. You will refrain from any political activity and after that we shall see whether you and Herr Koppe can coexist in peace.'

325

Julie stood, suddenly realising the depth of her naivety. She had thought it would be easier, but she had been deceiving herself. These were not the thugs she had met in '39, who defended a ruthless ideology - she could have fought against that; these were the defenders of the conservative political caste, and the economic miracle that was Germany. Suddenly it became difficult to feel any nobility in risking everything, the children, her family, the life they had built, to challenge them. Yet she felt repelled by the idea of bowing to them and their 'benevolent' amorality.

Chapter 32

Julie arrived home at twenty past five to a tense, confused, and chaotic house. The children eventually settled after much awkward reassurance and following a late dinner went to bed. When they had gone, Julie and Karl put the last few items back in place following the search carried out by Ritter's men. Karl had seemed relieved to see Julie, but angry at his ignorance of events, and now they were alone his mood became bitter again. 'Edie called today.' Julie looked away hesitantly. 'I told her what had happened. We had a long talk.'

Julie put her hands over her face, 'They are watching us, Karl. They are listening to our telephone calls. What did you say?'

'You can't do this to yourself - to us! This is now affecting us all - Peter and Dorothea especially. And Helene and Sophie aren't children anymore.' he said with a flash of anger that frightened her, 'They want answers and so do I.' She had never felt this rage in him before and now it crushed her. 'Do you remember Pastor Niemoller?' he said more calmly. Julie nodded her head. 'I was thinking of him today as the men took you away. *First they came for the Jew and I did not speak out because I was not a Jew; then they came for the communists and I did not speak out because I was not a communist; then they came for the unionists and I did not speak out because I was not a union man. Then they came for me – and there was no one left to speak out for me.'*

'I was reciting it again and again while I was waiting for you. Is this about your father? What did Edie tell you that's turned our world upside down, that means our children see their mother taken away like that? Have we so easily turned the clock back twenty years in Germany - just by asking a few questions? Is Adenauer really a fraud?'

Julie buried her head in her hands with tearful exasperation, 'I thought when I came back from Vienna I could make a stand for my father, for the orphans. I found out that Koppe is living in Bonn. I wanted the authorities to act. Now I realise that it's impossible; they will destroy us first and I can't allow it.'

Karl's anger suddenly left him and he embraced her, gently whispering words of reassurance, 'Tell me everything.' he said,

327

kissing her tears. Julie sat with him weeping for a few minutes but then began to go through a full account of Vienna; Edie, Tommy, and all that Ritter and Troost had said. When she finished it was nearly midnight. Karl rose from his seat and took Julie by the hand. He led her to the bedroom where he undressed her, kissing her shoulders, neck and arms tenderly as he did so. Then, when she was calmer, they lay naked in bed holding each other in silence, their feelings and thoughts running together. Karl kissed her and she felt suddenly safe and clasped him more tightly, 'You must forget everything except the concert. I will resolve everything - trust me. In the morning I'll leave. I will be at the Schumann-Haus on Saturday. I will arrange everything and nobody will hurt the children or you. We have to end this now, but we have to end it on our terms, not theirs.'

Julie did not demur, nor even question his intentions, or the risks he might run. She could no longer go on, and the threat to her children - and to Helene in particular, weighed on her heavily. Later, when Karl was asleep, she went to the children's rooms, checking on them to make sure they were safe, and kissing each one in turn.

Berne – Switzerland Monday 6 June, 1960

The Coue Institute in Berne had been advised of Dr Rust's imminent arrival. He felt it was less likely to arouse curiosity if the Swiss Central Medical Registry made the initial contact than if he purported to be in the area by chance looking for Frau Hertz.

He was greeted with great professional courtesy by Dr Nivelle who walked with him along the polished corridors of the old institute, toward the minimum security facility.

'I cannot tell you, Herr Rust...' the doctor said, '...how long we have hoped for some kind of interest from the Bonn government, indeed for any news of what will happen to these patients. Frau Hertz was not the only refugee with mental health problems. They are still littered across Switzerland.'

Karl smiled, knowing he was incapable of supplying any official information and hoping the doctor would not press him to do so. 'And how is Frau Hertz, what is her prognosis?'

'She is better at the moment, but the schizophrenia is always latent within her. Often she can be in a very dark place. But at other

328

times she can be productive - a model patient. That's how we have coped.'

'May I ask how this has been financed?'

The doctor shrugged his shoulders, 'As I say, when the doctor passed on we had no choice. Either we would return her to Germany, or keep her here. But in his letter, shortly before he died, he made it clear what would happen in Germany, so we did what we could to harness her skills to help here – to pay her own way. But you now say Germany may take her back - to your clinic in Linz am Rhein. That will be good for her. The area is a good one. I went there many years ago.'

When Karl met Clara Hertz he was relieved by her apparent normality. She was wearing a floral dress, low heeled black shoes and her hair was tidy and well kept. It occurred to him that she must have been considerably younger than Dr Hertz when they married before the war and that at one time she would have been something of a beauty.

Dr Nivelle left them for Karl's initial consultation and she invited him to sit while she made them a cup of iced tea in the small kitchen. When they walked together into the communal area they were alone, the sun having drawn the other patients into the warm fresh air, 'You knew Rudi, my husband?' she said with a pleasant smile.

'Yes, we met in '39 in Posen.'

She studied him carefully, 'You're not a friend of Grieser and the others are you?'

'No, I'm a doctor - I knew your husband professionally.'

She visibly relaxed and started to nod, 'That's all right then. It's just that, that...' She sighed, 'So you are a doctor?'

Karl now needed to get to the purpose of his visit quickly, knowing his Vienna train left at six o'clock. 'Your husband used to call you regularly, didn't he? You must miss that?'

Clara nodded, 'Yes, he had a lovely phone voice you know. He used to complain that I never spoke, but I loved to listen. He so missed me you know. He wrote too, especially towards the end of his life - when the war began telephones became a problem you see.'

'Did you keep his letters?'

'A few...I was a bit concerned about him to be honest – towards the end. I think...well, I think he turned a bit mad. It was very fanciful. I told the doctors here, but they just shrugged.'

329

'What sort of things did he say?'

She rolled her eyes, 'He saw conspiracies everywhere. Poor man…I do miss him… my Rudi.'

Karl tried to keep her mind focused and leaned forward, 'I study this sort of thing – people's anxieties. I would be very interested to see the letters, to understand his condition?'

Clara got up and smiled, 'Oh, you can have them. I have all sorts of other things to do these days. I don't have time to read them now. I have my own patients to care for.'

She left the room and returned after a few minutes with a shoebox of papers and thrust it into his lap. He rifled through the contents casually and then felt a small envelope at the bottom which seemed to be thicker and weightier than the others; he could feel that it contained a key. When he pulled the envelope out he saw that it carried the monogram of the Bank of Commerce and Investment in Bern. He showed it to her. 'Ah yes, he had a box at the bank. The lawyer in Berne brought that to me after he died. I didn't know what to do with it.' She made no motion to retrieve it, but stood. 'Well, if you will excuse me I must make my rounds.' With this she turned and began to wander away.

Karl arrived in Vienna late that evening having spent the afternoon in the vaults of the Bank of Commerce in Berne. It had been a strange experience to disturb the contents of the box and to expose documents that had lain there for twenty years.

Edie met him alone in a taxi rank near the station entrance and they drove quickly back to her home without speaking. When he arrived Gertrud Forster was there and they embraced and talked at length. After news of family and talk of Julie's brief arrest, Karl produced the letters which he had read on the train and the contents of Dr Hertz's deposit box. He noticed the atmosphere in the room change as they hesitantly started reading the old papers and found themselves transported back to a world they had hoped to leave behind.

Karl picked up a bundle of mixed papers held together with frayed string and untied the loose knot holding them together. The whole past of Grieser and his crimes against Anna Abetz were suddenly brought into stark relief on the table in front of him, written with clinical detachment and in the clear neat green copperplate handwriting which had been Hertz's style. He unfolded the death

330

certificate for Anna Abetz and the post mortem report of the time which brought home the cold reality of her short brutal life. But Hertz's notes also described how Grieser had progressively taken over emotional and physical control of the little girl and how he had exploited her mother's circumstances - the crippled husband, the alcoholism, and poverty. They had all made it easy for Grieser, as had the trust and affection he had cultivated as a benevolent figurehead in the place of Anna's bedridden father. But it was the physical injuries that appalled Karl, injuries even her drunken mother must have known of but ignored, injuries omitted from Anna's death certificate but privately recorded by Hertz - similar injuries to those he had found on Julie when he had first examined her. He found the parallels harrowing, knowing what Julie had endured and that Anna had been no more than a child. And then he thought of Koppe, the man who had fed Julie to Grieser, who had delivered her to Grieser's flat knowing, or at least hoping what he might do, and must have watched and listened to her subsequent agonised debauchment, calculating from day to day what value might be attached to her suffering. Karl closed his eyes, unable to read more, and then folded up the Anna Abetz papers, passing them to Gertrud with an expression of foreboding.

The other papers showed that Hertz had maintained his vigilance over the following years, with copious notes about the orders and 'position papers' prepared for Koppe and the SS by Dr Fischer regarding the orphanages. There was even a list of the girls names, ages, and academic achievements, completed in Sister Schmidt's handwriting. Later he had noted Koppe's discussions with him in every detail – of the blackmail of Grieser and his plans for the orphans. And then Karl came to the final paper on which Koppe had annotated that the orphans in Thorner Strasse should be confined under supervision and made available to the junior officers of the SS. Hertz had added a note of his own below it. '*I was ordered with Dr Fischer (absent) to make the girls aware of what was expected of them. That evening SS Dr Fischer visited the orphanage alone and did so. As the result, and despite the efforts of Overseer Grese to calm the girls, by midnight all fifteen of them had taken their own lives by means of hanging and slow strangulation.*' And there Dr Hertz's record stopped.

After they had read the papers they sat for a few minutes in silence and then Edie began to collect everything together with an air

331

of agitation. 'The Federal Intelligence Service will want this. We can't let them bury this again.'

Karl nodded, 'Troost was very specific - we are all being monitored, watched, listened to. We can hardly move can we?'

Gertrud held out her hands in a gesture of frustration, 'So how do we get this to Bonn, to the people who need to see it? The moment we cross the border we'll be stopped. So…who has an idea?'

There was a long silence. Then Karl leaned forward, 'There's one person I can think of, a complete outsider who would help, I'm sure of it. If we can stay put here until Saturday and only move at the last minute…not give them time to react, then I'm sure we can do it. I'll make some calls tomorrow.'

Edie leaned forward and grasped his arm, 'But not from here!'

Chapter 33

On Saturday the 11th June 1960, Gertrud, Edie and Karl set out for Bonn together from Vienna, while Julie and her daughters, Helene and Sophie, went to the Schumann-Haus for her final recital preparations. Across the city of Bonn others also stirred. When Ritter entered Troost's office late that morning and presented a summary of the latest intelligence on Julie Rust, Karl's activities in Berne began to alarm him and his visit to Vienna confirmed those suspicions. He ordered them all to be kept under surveillance and the train they were on to be met in Bonn. Then he decided to go home. It was a Saturday and otherwise all seemed quiet.

As he put on his coat his operational officer entered the room, 'I was just going, anything important?' Troost said casually.

Weber shook his head, 'Just to let you know Willy Brandt is on his way from Berlin with a few other SPD hacks, they've said we don't need to lay on any security this end. He'll stay with his own men when he gets here.'

Ritter nodded, 'A social trip then?'

'Yes, he's decided to go and see a show.'

Troost smiled, 'A good show, here, in Bonn! He'll be bloody lucky…should have stayed in Berlin.'

At the Schumann-Haus early that afternoon Helene had become perplexed by an 'A' board in the foyer with a large poster advertising the concert, 'But why only *Celebrity Recital*?' she asked, and why not use your name. Surely after Vienna people will want to see *you*. And I promised Peter I would take him a poster back.'

'Oh, don't worry Helene, anyone who is anybody will be here tonight – we sent out a lot of leaflets and invitations. There will be plenty of people in the audience.'

'Except us!' Sophie said reproachfully, and why no picture – you're so pretty - it's a shame.' Helene took Julie's hand, 'Can't we stay for the concert?'

Julie shook her head and looked into Helene's deep brown eyes, 'It's only for tonight. Lots of people will be here; I shall have no time for you and I don't want you to be left alone all evening.'

The administrator came into the empty hall and beckoned, 'I understand you want some reserved seats?'

Julie smiled, 'Yes, assume twenty VIPs.'

The woman looked unhappy, 'But that's nearly the whole front row.'

Julie nodded, 'And three seats on row five in the very middle.' The woman frowned and left them alone.

Helene and Sophie suddenly linked arms and looked at their mother earnestly, 'Father promised you would talk to us...about the other day?'

Julie wilted slightly and they sat on a few scattered chairs, 'Yes, I'm sorry about that. It was about your grandfather.'

Helene shook her head, 'Mother, *you* didn't kill him, so why were *you* being arrested. And why will you never tell us anything more about him, or about anything to do with what happened then – during the war. Why are you so secretive?'

'I'm not secretive...surely you understand how difficult it was for people then – the things that happened.'

Sophie shook her head, 'Yes, we know the history from school, but this is about you and father and our family. And you say you're not secretive but nobody else at school seems to have a mother like you. Even dad is happy to tell us things until we ask where you were at the time - what you were doing - then he just shrugs and tells us to '*ask your mother*'.'

Helene leaned forward, 'So why were you arrested on Sunday? Is that something to do with what happened in the war to grandfather - is that why you won't explain anything?' Julie suddenly found herself avoiding her daughters' gaze and began to knit her hands together tightly, unable to answer them, unsure what to say - how to react. Finally Helene seemed to become frustrated, 'Can't you at least tell us how you got those scars?'

Sophie turned to Helene with disbelief, 'Helene, how could you!'

Julie closed her eyes and her face became suddenly wracked with emotion. Sophie stood and quickly moved to put her arm around her mother. She looked back at her sister with exasperation but also for reassurance, however Helene now also looked desperately upset, 'I'm sorry Mother. I didn't mean...it just came out. We are concerned for

334

you. Tell us that everything is alright. We just want to understand what's happening.'

Julie's eyes opened and she tried to smile but they glistened with suppressed tears, 'Helene, you have the right to ask, you know that, you all do. It was a difficult time for everyone, but I can't answer. I'm sorry. So much happened to me then – too much for one lifetime. It's all buried...locked away. One day perhaps I will be able to talk about it, but for now it's too difficult - too frightening; even now after twenty years. I'm afraid if I open the door I won't be able to close it again. Please...please understand.'

Sophie kissed her mother on the head and sat down again, 'But they're not going to arrest you again are they?'

Julie dabbed her eyes with a handkerchief, 'No, we've gone past that sort of thing.'

'And you're not in trouble?'

'No!'

Helene leaned forward, 'So why can't we stay for the concert - we're fourteen now?'

Julie sat up, 'Because I have plans for this evening. Your father is coming from Vienna with friends of mine. We're going to make a night of it.'

Later, as Helene and Sophie were about to return home, Helene took Julie's hand, 'Will you still keep your promise - to help me find out about Dorothea when I am old enough?'

Julie smiled and kissed them both, 'Of course, that's a promise and do you know, you look *so much* like her. I wish she could see you now. You'd make her very happy.'

It was six fifteen when Troost found his evening thrown into confusion. His wife came into the garden where friends had gathered around an outdoor grill. He removed his apron swiftly, even before his wife had finished relaying the message and began hurrying toward the open patio doors. At the front gate he found Ritter, breathless, a car door left open in the street. 'It's Karl Rust...it's serious...you'll need to come back to the office.'

Troost looked at him impatiently, 'Exactly how serious?'

'We just got the notes of a telephone call from Vienna to Linz made last night. It seems Karl Rust is bringing a lot of papers about

335

Koppe with him back from Austria - some papers from a safety deposit box in Berne.'

'But you have them under surveillance – they're being met.'

'I've got no orders to stop them, just to meet them…keep them under surveillance.'

'And these papers, do we know where they are taking them?'

'To the Schumann-Haus…there's a show on there tonight.'

Troost's eyes suddenly glared furiously, 'A *show*…Brandt! They're going to show them to Willy Brandt - Jesus!'

It was six thirty when Julie met Willy Brandt in the administration office of the Schumann-Haus. He arrived with three of his trusted political advisors and six security men who sealed access to the room. He greeted Julie with great charm and she felt a frisson of charisma in his warm weathered smile as he introduced his colleagues.

Finally they sat and he looked at her expectantly. 'You have something of constitutional significance to discuss with me I believe? I don't usually attend concerts and I don't usually come to Bonn, but I'm told by an intermediary who went to Vienna that this is a very serious matter, and your agent in Berlin was most insistent you were *unable* to come to me…for reasons which I assume will become apparent?'

Julie looked apprehensive but smiled. 'I'm still awaiting the papers I need to show you but yes, this concerns you directly – that is as the candidate to challenge Adenauer as Chancellor next September.'

Brandt looked momentarily stunned, 'Where did you get that from - nobody knows about that?'

Julie met his eyes, 'It came from the Federal Intelligence Service, a man called Troost. They know the SPD is looking to bypass the chairman of the Party. You're being monitored…and so am I – that's why I couldn't come to you.'

Brandt looked around warily at his colleagues, 'But that's out of the question - we don't do that sort of thing in Germany – not any more. Has anyone heard of this man?'

One of the security detail stood forward, 'Herr Brandt, Colonel Troost is number two at the Federal Intelligence Service here in Bonn, he's the Assistant Reporter to Adenauer.'

Brandt sat back anxiously, 'And you can explain everything tonight?'

336

'Yes.'

He broached a craggy smile, 'Very well, then we shall wait a little while for the papers. And, while we wait, tell me a little about yourself?'

When Karl, Gertrud and Edie arrived in Bonn at six forty five they had expected to be stopped, but instead they outpaced their 'shadows' and got to the taxi rank with enough leeway to leap into a Mercedes and pull away unhindered. Karl could see men bundle themselves into a waiting Citroen and begin to follow them. Edie saw them too and smiled at Gertrud, 'Take us to the Schumann-Haus, Sebastianstrasse...' Karl asked the Turkish taxi driver nervously, '...and don't lose the Citroen behind us, it's the police, they're trying to follow us.' The driver looked in the mirror and smiled uneasily, unsure how to react to these apparently respectable middle aged fugitives.

When they were a short distance from the driveway leading to the Schumann-Haus they abandoned their taxi and began to separate and merge into the concertgoers. As they did so each saw their shadows pursuing them and paced their advance accordingly. Troost stood high on the steps of the concert hall, watching and waiting for his men to strike and, in turn, Edie, Karl, and Gertrud were first corralled and then jostled to the side of the driveway where they were cursorily searched. From each of them an envelope was recovered and then held aloft.

Troost gestured to his men in acknowledgement and stepped down from his vantage point walking through the melee toward the group smiling. He stood, looking at his three detainees for a moment, with quiet satisfaction. Karl stepped forward, 'You are?'

Troost shook his head, 'It is irrelevant now who I am, Herr Rust. Your wife promised me - she gave me her word. She's broken our agreement.'

'Herr Troost then is it? She did give me your name.'

Troost nodded, 'You will regret this adventure, Herr Rust. I could not have made the consequences clearer for your family.'

Karl shook his head, 'It's over, Troost. You can't control things like this anymore – *Sippenhaft* died with the Nazis surely, you can't condemn whole families.'

337

'Even the democratic state must be protected.' Troost said laconically as he took the envelopes from Ritter and held them. But then his manner became uneasy and his eyes began to nervously dart between Karl, Gertrud, and Edie, sensing their lack of indignation at his apparent success. 'Three envelopes!' he exclaimed and knelt down, rapidly undoing them, tearing clumsily at the flaps. He drew out a copy of the day's *Wiener Zeitung* newspaper from each and then stood looking at Ritter, 'Is Brandt here yet?'

Ritter looked at one of the other officers who stiffened, 'Sir, he arrived early, about six thirty, and went to the administration offices.'

'And Scholl?'

'She's been here all day.'

Troost looked back at the hall and shook his head. 'Well, it's probably too late then.'

It was at this moment that one of Brandt's security men admitted a plainly dressed but attractive middle aged woman into the administrator's office. She nervously asked for Frau Julie Rust and drew a large file out of a case which Julie hurriedly opened and placed before Brandt. Julie hugged her, 'Please see me after the concert?' The woman nodded, but did not withdraw. 'I have something else...something from my brother.'

Julie shook her head. 'I don't understand.'

Without speaking Helene Grese took out an envelope from beneath her jacket and gave it to Julie, 'My brother Alfred was an amateur photographer; he ran off some prints for Irma when he was on leave from the Russian Front in '43. She wanted to know if the negatives were good.'

Julie looked at the envelope with misgiving. 'I hoped I would never have to see these again, but thank you, they are important.' Helene kissed Julie on the cheeks and left the room.

'Who was that?' Brandt asked, as Julie sat next to him.

'That was Helene Grese - Irma Grese's sister, but we will get to that later.'

Brandt looked sideways at Julie with an air of disquiet, but soon focussed on the papers in front of him as Julie laid out the evidence on which her indictment of Wilhelm Koppe rested, of the efforts of the security services to silence her, and their motives for doing so. As she worked through the papers Brandt began to murmur

338

to his colleagues and they, too, began to look intently at the documents, passing them to one another.

It was when they saw the photographs from the orphanage that Julie's narrative broke down and a chill spread throughout the room. Brandt shook his head, remaining tight lipped as he looked at the grainy photographs of the young girls' lifeless bodies hanging in the orphanage, each in her nightgown, each hanging in the void at the end of their bed into which they had leapt to escape the terror which Koppe had brought to them, their innocent faces staring back from the pictures pitifully. 'And they would protect a man who could do this, to save the reputation of Adanauer!' Brandt exclaimed, quietly repressing his anger.

It was at this moment that Troost and Ritter tried to force their entry into the room, but Brandt's security were unmoved by claims of higher authority. Brandt had known the fear of arrest by the Gestapo as an anti-fascist in pre-war Germany and was in no mood to defer to men he now saw as little more than their heirs and successors. His men barred the door and made it clear that force would be used if necessary, drawing their handguns and cocking them.

When, after a few more minutes, Julie finished her narrative, Brandt closed the files and looked around him at his colleagues. 'So, what can we do? Julie Rust speaks for the post-war generation now. She's come to us to seek both protection and justice from the German state. If the security apparatus silences her, then it can silence all of us. And from what we now know of Troost, the SPD - my candidacy - is as much a part of their thinking as anything else, which is a constitutional issue for the future of a democratic Germany.'

Brandt stood and looked at his watch. 'Julie, I need to talk with my colleagues about how we deal with this. It's nearly quarter to eight and you must play in fifteen minutes, but I give you my word that you will not be harmed, nor your children, or husband – not in the name of Germany. I will be placing the activities of the Intelligence Services before the Constitutional Court - there's no other way.'

Julie stood and there was a ripple of encouragement as she left the room. Outside she brushed past the waiting Troost and Ritter and met their looks with cold indifference but they made no move to stop her.

When Julie took to the platform that night she noticed Edie and Gertrud sitting either side of a tall older man in a blue suit, white shirt, and red tie. Her eyes also met those of Willy Brandt, who nodded reassuringly at her as he sat, amid murmurs of recognition from the audience. She also noticed Troost standing at the back of the hall, sullen and malign, his men scattered around the edge of the hall.

She began the recital with Schumann's *Davidsbündlertänze*. She was mentally unprepared, but the shortness of each of the pieces allowed her to progressively settle and compose herself. She had deliberately chosen the *Arabesque* to finish the first half of the performance. It allowed her the scope to be distracted without risking catastrophe, for she had known and planned this scene with Edie and Gertrud a hundred times.

During the interval she hovered in the margins of the hall, watching Gertrud and her companion from a distance, praying that nothing would come between her and the moment she had chosen to deliver the final act of the evening.

When the audience had reassembled for the second half she played Schumann's First Sonata. She found herself suddenly nervous and clumsy and fought back against her wandering thoughts and wayward fingers with unusual difficulty. When at last she stood at the piano to receive applause she looked out into the audience unyielding; awaiting silence.

When all was still, she caught Troost anxiously looking around the hall, sensing something was about to happen. But her voice was firm and clearly audible, 'Distinguished guests, Ladies and Gentlemen. It has been a great pleasure to play for you this evening to celebrate the 150th anniversary of the birth of Robert Schumann. He was a man of vision and intelligence, of artistic principle and great industry, qualities very much in evidence today as we also celebrate the miracle which is the maturing of a new Germany. In this audience tonight are many of the people who have made this possible, Herr Willy Brandt for example, the Mayor of West Berlin, who has rebuilt that great city and made it a showcase for the world. He has come here tonight specially to join us and I thank him.' There was a murmur in the audience and a small ripple of applause.

'But it is not simply about great men; the story of the new Germany is also about individuals, very many of them unnoticed, modest and self-effacing, like Herr Lohmann who I see sitting in this audience tonight, a humble man who has been invited especially.' Julie gestured at Edie and Gertrud who made Herr Lohmann stand uncomfortably in the middle of the audience. 'Herr Lohmann is a man who, like the rest of us, has embraced the new Germany, a man who has turned his back on the past. But, of course, not all of us are entitled to do this, not if, like Herr Lohmann, you arranged for the rape of young German girls at an orphanage in Posen in 1939, the murder of mental patients, Poles, Jews, and Germans, and ordered my own murder at the hands of the Gestapo in 1939 when I was fifteen. Well SS Obergruppenführer Wilhelm Koppe, what is your answer? What do you have to say?'

Koppe began to gesture violently at Gertrud to make way for him, but they were seated midway in a long row of tightly regimented chairs. He pushed her and forced his way past as members of the audience began to break into animated conversation, a few standing and demanding an answer from the man in the blue suit who beat his way along the line of chairs. When, toward the end of the row of seats, a man stood and barred his way, Koppe lashed out. The man fell to one side and Koppe made for the rear of the hall where Troost remained frozen by indecision. Willy Brandt stood with his security men eyeing him. Finally Troost buckled under this recriminatory gaze and angrily directed his men to apprehend Koppe, himself moving to check his exit from the hall.

While all this was happening Julie stood watching from the platform and when Koppe finally stood handcuffed between Ritter and Troost she made her way to him. She looked into his pockmarked face which was now purple and ran with rivulets of perspiration, while members of the audience began to gather around them, 'Where did you bury my father?' Julie said angrily staring into his agitated eyes. 'At least tell me where you took the German orphans you terrorised to death.'

Koppe shook his head, trying to catch his breath, and looked at Ritter, 'Will you allow this spectacle? Well? Get her away from me. This is madness. I was a soldier. I was never in the SS...'

'Then why use a false name? Why pretend to be someone else, Herr Koppe?'

Troost pushed Koppe away, anxious to end the public spectacle and moved him toward the exit. Julie remained where she stood and then, when Koppe was out of sight, turned and hugged Gertrud for the first time in sixteen years. They remained for a long time in this embrace as members of the audience began to file past and out of the hall in animated conversation.

As Brandt left, tightly clutching the papers and closely guarded by his security team, he nimbly approached them and kissed Julie's hand, 'I don't go to many concerts, but I might be persuaded by this experience – quite an encore. And don't lose any sleep...' he tapped the file.

When, finally, the last of the audience had left they rearranged some of the chairs and sat in the hall. Gertrud smiled, 'Karl tells me that you have a family now.'

Julie reached over to her, 'Yes – four children, but what of Inga and Peter? What of them?'

'Oh, they've finished university now. But Albert? He was sent to Poland by the British. You know they hanged Grieser in public, and Hildebrandt and Kellerman too, but I heard nothing about Albert. The Poles remained silent for years. It was '54 before they told the Foreign Office that he'd been hanged in the courtyard of Mokotow Prison in '52, after the Polish President had declined clemency. So that was it - no farewell.' She sighed, 'But you have prospered?'

'Yes - thanks to you!'

Gertrud shook her head, 'I hope you didn't think they were tainted in any way...that's why I wrote you the note.'

Julie looked at Karl. 'We used them to help people...and yes, we also rebuilt our lives.'

Gertrud shook her head 'I'm just sorry Albert had it broken down for the stones and gold, was it your mothers?'

Julie shook her head 'No – it belonged to someone I knew. But are you alright - are you coping without Albert?'

Gertrud smiled, 'I'm very well – but of course, I miss him.'

Karl stood up noticing that the caretaker was hovering and wanting to lock up, 'Do you think Willy Brandt can help?'

'Yes...' Julie said decisively, '...he's got a look about him. It's not his real name you know. It was his assumed identity before the war and then afterwards he just kept it.'

'We all had assumed identities during the war,' Edie said quietly.

As they left the Schumann-Haus Edie and Karl talked, while Gertrud and Julie walked ahead slightly, arm in arm, as they had last done in Danzig in 1944. 'Have you met Edie's new husband? She seems a different woman, doesn't she?' Julie said.

Gertrud nodded, 'Yes…when she called me about your situation I was so surprised - you can't imagine. I was so pleased to think of seeing you again after all these years.'

'I notice you didn't mention Hermann. Edie told me about him though - about his committing suicide.'

'But did she say when?' Julie shook her head. 'It was after that dinner, when he asked you to help him. I thought you would be too upset at the time; but what a thing to do?'

'I couldn't have saved him.'

'But I think Edie felt slightly responsible. You see when he left that evening he telephoned her – normally she had Josef field her calls but he was away. He'd been drinking – with us and then alone later. He wanted Edie to help him, but she put the phone down. I suppose, however you feel about him, she must have felt she could at least have listened.'

Julie shook her head, 'No, Gertrud, she couldn't. He had turned her inside out in his time. She didn't trust herself with him. She said he was a manipulator – I sensed it myself but by then drink had taken over. She knew he could control her if she listened to him for long enough, and when the spell was broken she must have wanted to run away, be ordinary again, and never look back.'

Gertrude nodded thoughtfully, 'Yes, I suppose we've all felt like that…at one time or another.'

That night when they were alone in the bedroom Julie turned and looked at Karl, 'You know I feel almost the way I did then, at the end of the war I mean, when we first made love. I suddenly feel such a huge relief. I feel free and as if everything around us is changing for the better.'

Karl took her in his arms, 'And you have a glint in your eye, what is it?'

She smiled coquettishly, 'It's the glint I had at the end of the war…' she said advancing toward the bed and beginning to slip off her dress.

Karl shook his head looking at her in her semi-nakedness, 'Our children will soon begin to look at us with disapproval you know!'

Julie smiled, 'Because we're still young and in love.'

'Or is it because we still behave like shameless newlyweds?' he replied with playful sternness.

Julie got into bed and pulled up the covers, 'I am still enjoying myself. I don't want to be respectable just yet...this is still our generation and we've just won it back. We do have a little more to give before we pass on the torch to the children...surely?' She held out her hands toward him.

'So the long struggle is over?' Karl said beginning to undress.

Julie patted the duvet, 'No, the long struggle is just beginning. Do you remember when I used to come to your room and read to you - when you were sick? Do you remember how I used to put a chair against the door?'

'How could I forget those mornings!'

'Well, tonight I want two long thrilling chapters from you with a good plot, lots of twists and turns, and plenty of ups and downs.'

Karl began to smile, 'Two chapters!'

'Karl, I want one last child. I dreamed about her last night. She was so beautiful, so playful and mischievous. She reached out to me and I wanted to bring her back with me from the dream.'

Karl got into bed next to her and looked into her eyes. 'Sometimes you know, I think you see beyond this world.'

'I am sure I do. My mother never left me - and they are still there you know, the orphans and my father. I still see them sometimes when I close my eyes at night. We often talk together.' Julie shook her head slightly, 'I just hope that one day someone will find them and we can lay them to rest properly. I'm sure that's what they are waiting for.' Karl kissed her gently and she smiled with a tenderness and beauty that recalled earlier times, and soon they were making love with a passion which seemed to bring together all their hopes and desires, their tenderness and longing.

344

It was a sultry July day, but from Julie's vantage point high above the village of Linz it felt as though Germany had been quietly abandoned. There was nobody on the streets, nor cars on the roads for as far as the eye could see and an eerie silence had descended over the whole country. Only the occasional roar of long freight trains and the barges slowly chugging their way along the Rheine seemed to offer any sign of continuing normality. But, as Julie meandered through the garden towards the house, she could soon hear Peter and Karl through the open veranda doors shouting for Germany over the voice of the commentator, the commentator shouting over the roar of the crowd, as the World Cup Final grew to its first climax – and then it was bedlam.

Julie smiled to herself, put down her basket and gardening gloves, and sat on a swing chair watching Viktoria who was happily continuing to colour in the flagstones on the path with bright chalk pictures of the cows and sheep she could see grazing in the fields beyond the garden fence. Viktoria was now five and the last of Julie's children; a bright, smiling, inquisitive child who seemed to have so much in common with the young girl whose name she shared and happy memory she embodied, that Julie often found herself thinking that a little bit of Viktoria had somehow found its way into her - that she lived on behind her daughter's mischievous smile and playful excitable eyes.

As she began rocking gently backwards and forwards, her dress coolly flapping about her legs, she looked down over the broad river, across the meadows toward Remagen and the piers of the old bridge, and beyond that to Unkel, and her mind began to wander. At first she simply wondered about Dorothea and what might have become of her, what she would feel if she could see her beautiful daughter Helene - now twenty. Then she thought more distantly of the Helene she had known in 1939, the girl who had taken her hand that first morning in the orphanage, when she felt lost and frightened; how Birgit had crept into her bed when gunfire had first echoed across Posen and they had huddled together telling stories to keep their fears at bay. She thought of Viktoria and Erika, giggling to each other in the school room, as they talked of travelling the world together and the rich American husbands they would marry. She felt a wave of sadness as she thought of their short lives and the hopes she had briefly shared with them and opened her eyes to stem the tide. She sat for a moment, the swing now motionless, blinking in the sunlight, unsettled by her memories. Then her eyes fell on Viktoria, watching her intently as she coloured in the pictures she had drawn, studying her with a quiet sense of reassurance. After a few minutes Viktoria noticed her mother's gaze and after a playful tussle drew her over to the pictures to sit and colour them in together.

This surge of memory had been partly caused by that morning's post in which there had been a letter from the State Prosecutors Office - very dignified and very understanding, but telling her that in view of the deterioration in the health of Wilhelm Koppe and the likelihood that he would remain unfit to stand trial, no further attempt would be made to prosecute him for the murders and other crimes for which he had been indicted.

Karl had not understood her silence then, as she laid the letter down on the kitchen table and cleared away the breakfast plates, but later, when he was alone, he had quietly read it and put it away at the back of a drawer. It seemed, for the moment, the only thing he could do – a gesture where words seemed futile. Later, when Julie came back from the garden, she did not ask where the letter had gone. Instead she busied herself arranging some freshly cut red roses in a vase before going to the music room to practice at the piano.

It was when she returned an hour later and they sat drinking coffee in the kitchen that Karl leaned over the table and took her hand, 'I read the letter...I'm sorry.'

She looked at him and smiled gently, reluctant at first to say anything, but then she spoke, her voice quiet and subdued. 'I was fifteen when he murdered my father. I didn't know it then but that made me an orphan too. And now I'm the last of them still alive. That's why they hunted me all those years wasn't it, so that there would be no one left behind who would remember them - but I'm determined to, Karl, and I can't grieve for them, nor for my father...not until we find them and give them a proper resting place.'

Karl shook his head, 'But Julie they're in Poland - in the communist East; it's impossible now.'

Julie nodded, 'Perhaps now, but almost the last thing my professor said to me as I left Warsaw in '39, was not to give up hope...that all this would pass...that I must believe in a future. Well

346

Karl, I do, and I always will. So we will find them eventually – perhaps not next year, or for many years, but things will change, and then we'll go there and look for them - it's a promise I've made.'

Karl leaned forward, 'To them?'

He felt her grip on his hand tighten, 'No Karl…to myself.'

Postscript

SS Obergruppenführer Wilhelm Koppe - After his arrest in 1960 Wilhelm Koppe was imprisoned for two years awaiting trial but was finally released on bail on 19 April 1962. His trial opened in Bonn in 1964. He was accused of being an accessory to the murder of 145,000 people. The trial was adjourned due to Koppe's ill health and in 1966 the Bonn court decided not to pursue the prosecution for those reasons. The German Government refused a Polish request for his extradition. Wilhelm Koppe died in 1975 in Bonn.

David Lane, 1 November 2012

If you wish to contact the author in connection with this work or comment on any aspect of it please email: orphansposen@yahoo.co.uk

AUTHOR'S NOTES

Polish expansion 1919-39

The Poland born as the result of the First World War, from elements of the Russian, German, and Austro-Hungarian empires, was anything but united. Of a total population of 34,900,000, it contained 7 million Ukrainians, 2 million White Russians, 3,200,000 Jews, 200,000 Lithuanians and 1,400,000 Germans. Its eastern borders were ill-defined. By 1921 Poland had already fought a seven day war with Czechoslovakia, occupied part of Lithuania, fought a war against Russia/Ukraine, and savagely suppressed the separatist Ukrainian minority in eastern Poland.

On March 21st 1921, after a plebiscite to determine whether Upper Silesia should remain part of Germany or be incorporated into the new Polish state, 707,393 votes were cast for the status quo, while 479,365 were cast for incorporation of the area into Poland. On May 2nd 1921, patriotic Poles stormed Beuthen, Pless, Rybnik, Gross-Strelitz, Gliwitz and Kattowitz, under Poland's Commissar for the Plebiscite, Woiczech Krofantny. The Germans protested and Krofantny was replaced. Sixty Germans were murdered, but French peacekeepers refused to intervene to stop the Polish occupation. When Italian troops did intervene, 30 were killed and 50 wounded, and when Germans in Kattowitz expelled the Poles, a short siege ensued. The reprisals and persecution that followed were internationally condemned, but over 70% of Germans in Upper Silesia, which was ceded *de facto* to Poland on 20 June 1922, had left by 1931 – a total of 156,000 Germans.

Poland had also been in conflict with Czechoslovakia since 1919 over their respective claims to part of the former Duchy of Teschen, awarded to Czechoslovakia after the First World War. The area comprised 1,683 square kilometres (650 sq miles) and 228,000 inhabitants, of whom 133,000 were Czechs and the remainder Poles. In the summer of 1938 the Germans learned that in return for allowing the Poles to seize Teschen from the Czechs, the Polish Government would refuse to allow Soviet forces to cross Poland to assist Czechoslovakia if attacked by Germany. Hungary reached a similar agreement. As William Shirer states of this inglorious chapter in

Polish/Hungarian history, "The Poles and Hungarians, after threatening military action against the helpless nation, now [November 1938] swept down, like vultures, to get their slice of Czechoslovak territory." At the same time the Germans took over the ethnically German areas of Czechoslovakia (the Sudetenland) following the Munich Agreement, but in March 1939, in breach of the terms of the treaty, seized the remainder of the country.

Following the Second World War Teschen was reluctantly returned to Czechoslovakia by Poland, but only after Stalin's intervention.

The German Minority in Poland

The persecution of Germans in Poland between 1919 and 1939 is now largely forgotten. From a population of 1,400,000 ethnic Germans in 1919, there remained less than 491,000 by 1939.

Aside from the special circumstances of Silesia (above), a significant element of the Polish policy for removing the German ethnic minority from Poland was represented simply as land reform. Large estates were broken up, nominally to provide homes for the landless and greater social equality. In Posen and the Polish Corridor where high concentrations of Germans remained, 63% of the land seized in this way was from ethnic Germans, and exclusively redistributed to Poles. Polish citizenship also became a condition of land ownership, forcing many to abandon Poland and return to Germany. Equally the failure to hold documents of title could invalidate possession, and 3,964 ethnic Germans were deprived of their land in this way without compensation.

At an economic level German businesses were boycotted, taxed selectively, or denied state contracts. German directors, managers and employees were sacked from Polish businesses, and ethnic Germans were excluded from the professions and civil service. The Protestant Church was also persecuted and its property seized, and in 1923 the main cultural organisation representing the interests of the German minority (the *Deutchtumsbund*) was banned, its offices closed, and its leadership arrested for treason[3]. German language newspapers

---

[3] By 1924 there were over 3,000 political prisoners in Polish jails. Two years later the 'democratic' government was overthrown in a military coup by General Pilsudski.

were routinely seized and German schools and kindergartens closed to suppress the teaching of German language and culture.

At its most basic level there remained among many Poles a sense of racial, religious and cultural hostility, and a belief that their German neighbours had prospered unfairly under Prussian and German rule and continued to enjoy the spoils, while many Poles lived in poverty.

There can be little doubt that this toxic mixture of state sponsored persecution and historic hatred toward the German minority fuelled the massacres of ethnic German civilians between late August 1939 and the 17th September - by which date Poland had been largely overrun. The largest massacre took place in Bydgoszcz (Bromberg) on the 3rd September when over 1,000 men, women and children were murdered by their Polish neighbours in an orgy of violence and looting.

The total number of ethnic Germans estimated to have been murdered during this period by the Polish State (elements of the army, police and militia), or by mobs, varies from between 5,000 and 12,500. The figure quoted by the official German Foreign office report (second edition), published in 1940, was 58,000; but the figure has been discredited.

The Orphans of Posen

The events described in this book did take place at an orphanage in Thorner Strasse, though in Bromberg, not Posen. However I have followed the chronology and the conduct of the searches made by Polish soldiers and 'militia' exactly, based on witness statements taken at the time. Sisters Schmidt and Olga did exist, though the characters of the orphans have been fictionalised.

I have added to these events a separate incident which occurred at a convent for girls in 1941 in the Ukraine, which forms the basis of my account of what happens to the orphans of Posen.

Posen - Poznan

There is now little left of the old Imperial German city of Posen, though the places visited by Julie Scholl with Karl Rust in this book all survived the war. Hitler declared it a fortress city in early 1945 and the Russians bombarded it. The Poles have rebuilt part of the old town, and of course, it is now the thriving Polish city of Poznan, but evidence of German habitation (monuments, place names, churches, and cemeteries) has now been largely eradicated as a part of the post-war policy of 'cultural cleansing'.

The Gauleiters and the SS

Arthur Grieser, Albert Forster, SS Obergruppenführer Wilhelm Koppe, and SS Obergruppenführer Richard Hildebrandt imposed their authority on the world around them much in the way I have described. Arthur Grieser was hanged on the slopes of Fort Winiary in July 1946 and holds the dubious distinction of being the last man to be hanged in public in Poland. Albert Forster was handed to the Poles by the British and hanged in 1952. Richard Hildebrandt was first tried at Nuremburg and sentenced to 25 years then handed to the Polish Government for trial and hanged. Wilhelm Koppe evaded justice, dying in Bonn in 1975.

Heim ins Reich – the resettlement of Germans from the Baltic and Russian occupied Poland

The chaotic resettlement of Germans from the east and the Baltic States and the drive to repopulate Warthegau and Danzig-West-Prussia all took place amid the in-fighting and disagreements described in this book.

Albert Forster and Arthur Grieser clashed on resettlement policy and on how to 'Germanize' their populations, Forster taking a more 'liberal' approach than Grieser, who was far closer to the SS. A deep loathing for each other had its origins in their rivalry as members of the Danzig Senate, but also owed something to their different origins. Grieser was a veteran of the First World War and an 'old fighter' for the Nazi cause. Forster represented the more 'professional' image of the Party; a bank employee but at the same time a charismatic socialite, he had charmed and impressed Hitler, Hess, and Bormann.

Hitler's plan for a Polish State

On the grounds that it might later be used by the Germans against him, Stalin vetoed Hitler's plans to make a rump state of Poland in 1939. Hitler accepted the veto, knowing that he dared not risk conflict with

Russia while France and Britain were poised to attack Germany from the west. He appointed Hans Frank Governor General of Poland. A chess player, a pianist, and a lawyer, Frank's name was to become synonymous with the cruelty of the Nazi regime towards the Polish people, and with the Holocaust. He was hanged in October 1946.

The economics of war and the 'Zossen putsch'

By the end of the Polish campaign Germany had almost no reserves of ammunition left. Hitler had been planning for war in 1943, not 1939. The High Command of the German Army in Zossen did briefly consider overthrowing his regime after the Polish campaign. Before doing so they tried to present Hitler with economic evidence to support their view that a war could not successfully be waged in the west. Their efforts failed and so, too, did their nerve, allowing Hitler to resume his campaign in June 1940, after which success in the west he was unassailable.

Gertrud Forster and women

Gertrud Forster was featured in *Life Magazine* in August-September 1939 at tea with Hitler. However the role of women in the Third Reich was highly circumscribed. Women were specifically excluded from politics, the army, and the administration of justice. When the Nazi Party gained power in 1933, they aimed to remove 800,000 women from employment over four years. Motherhood was celebrated; couples were offered loans to set up homes and start families, with grants for larger families and heavier taxation for single men. Mothers producing four or more children received the *Ehrenkreuz der Deutschen Mutter* - Cross of Honour of the German Mother. Ultimately the Nazi ideal of women as mothers and homemakers ('faithfulness and beauty') collided with reality. In 1938 there were only 25,000 women in employment. By 1945 there were 7.5 million serving in auxiliary military units, signals, anti-aircraft, or base office work.

The execution of German soldiers for military offences

Between 1914 and 1918, 150 death sentences were passed on German soldiers of the Kaiser's army, of which only 48 were carried out.

Between 1939 and 1945, 15,000 official military executions were carried out. In the final days of the war it is likely that many executions for desertion and other offences went unrecorded and were carried out without due process. The figure for German soldiers executed by their own side is therefore likely to be much higher.

The Rhinewiesenlager - the Rheine meadows camps

The Rheine meadows camps were as I have described them – open fields, surrounded by barbed wire, with no protection from the elements. It has been suggested by James Bacque in his book, *Other Losses*, that 800,000 Germans died in the sixteen camps. A 1962 German parliamentary enquiry chaired by Eric Maschke produced a figure, on incomplete evidence, of 4,537. Historians generally accept that the total did not exceed 50-60,000, but from the chaos of post-war Germany precise numbers are impossible to obtain. However, taking into account the conditions described by witnesses and contemporary accounts of the care and levels of nutrition and water given to the men, it is certain that the casualties far exceeded the level accepted by the Maschke Commission - particularly given the prisoners generally poor condition on arrival in the camps. For example, at Bad Hersfeld the prisoners survived on 800 calories a day until a fifth of them became skeletons, while at Bad Kreuznach, prisoners were given no bread for six weeks, merely a few spoonsful of vegetables and fish each day. In Heidesheim there were examples of fourteen year old children who had nothing to wear but their pyjamas, because that was what they had been wearing when they were arrested.

Sanitation was almost wholly lacking. At Rheineberg, the camp became a giant sewer, men defecating where they stood for lack of anywhere to go, amid chronic overcrowding. Böhl, a camp designed for 10,000, held over 30,000. Remagen had 134,000 against a capacity of 100,000. At Bad Kreuznach the camp became 'a sea of urine'. Dysentery quickly became endemic in all the camps.

Despite the proximity of the Rheine, water was also inadequate, prisoners drinking their own urine to stay alive. At Bad Kreuznach there was one tap for 56,000 men and at Büderich five taps for 75,000 men. When the commandant of that camp was asked why the prisoners were being kept in such inhumane conditions he allegedly replied, 'So they will lose their joy of soldiering once and for all.'

The initial involvement of the Red Cross, the re-designation of the prisoners as Disarmed Enemy Forces by the Eisenhower administration to place them outside Red Cross jurisdiction, and the refusal to allow prisoners to communicate with the outside world, are fact.

Irma Grese

The history of Irma Grese and her family circumstances are largely as related in the story, though her mother died from drinking acid rather than by hanging. I have also altered the dates slightly to allow Irma Grese to be a part of this narrative. She did not in fact join the camp system until 1942.

The bombing of Germany

Over 200,000 German civilians died in bombing by the British and American air forces. Cultural heritage and treasures accumulated over centuries were lost. Specific targets (ancient cities with wooden houses set close together), were identified as suitable for fire-bombing with incendiaries, the intention being to generate firestorms which would lay waste whole areas and be impossible to extinguish. In July 1943 such a firestorm in Hamburg killed 40,000 people and destroyed 250,000 dwellings. (The total number of British citizens killed by bombing of all kinds in the war was 60,595). As early as 1941, the British Government was warned that indiscriminate bombing was ineffective and did not significantly inhibit the German war effort. In fact German munitions production peaked in September 1944 despite the devastation.[4]

After the war many Germans questioned the targeting of civilians by allied bombing, considering themselves victims twice over: first of the Nazi regime and then of the Allies. Others, reputable historians amongst them, argue that it was necessary for German

---

[4] The Thirty Years' War (1618-1648) and the slaughter at Magdeburg represented a proportionately higher loss of German lives, but the physical destruction of Germany in World War II remains unparalleled in history.

civilians to die indiscriminately as the result of area bombing in order for a greater evil to be defeated. It is a view which relies on a comparative morality that I find deeply troubling.

The Belsen Trial

Bergen-Belsen concentration camp was liberated by the British 11th Armoured Division on 15 April 1945. When they entered the camp under a truce, following an outbreak of typhus, they found 13,000 unburied corpses and 53,000 prisoners, many close to death. After liberation a further 13,994 died as the result of typhus or advanced malnutrition. Initially only the commandant of the camp, Josef Kramer, was arrested, to be followed only later by the rest of the guards that remained at the camp.

It is believed that 20,000 Russian prisoners of war and 50,000 others perished in the camp between 1941 and 1945. Up to 35,000 perished in the first few months of 1945 due to the outbreak of typhus.

The circumstances of the Belsen Trial are as related. The lawyers were not by modern standards qualified for their role. They were simply serving officers who had been solicitors or barristers before the war. Lacking resources and denied expert advice on international law, they were also refused funds to carry out legal research in London.

Irma Grese was typically described in the London press as 'The Blonde Beastess'. She was specifically charged at the Belsen trial with: shooting three female prisoners, ill-treating prisoners by beating and kicking, and making selections for the gas chambers at Auschwitz.

The Belsen trial, which lasted from 17 September to 17 November 1945, was criticised for being over-long. Officers defending the accused found themselves receiving abusive mail. A number complained that their demobilisation was being delayed because of their role in the trial. Of the forty-five accused, eleven were sentenced to death. They were executed by hanging on 13 December 1945. Among them was Irma Grese, at 22, the youngest person under British jurisdiction to be hanged in the twentieth century. (Her executioner was Albert Pierrepoint.)

The ethnic cleansing of Eastern Europe

At the end of the war the Polish border with Russia moved westwards, while 112,000 km² of pre-war German territory was given to Poland[5]. Seven million Germans now found themselves within the new border. Between 1945 and 1949, together with 3 million Germans from Czechoslovakia and 1.8 million from other lands (11,730,000 in total), these seven million were forcibly returned to Germany.

These are figures that convey nothing of the true magnitude and horror which befell the Germans in these areas, mainly women and children and the elderly. Murder, rape, beatings and torture, in the many Polish concentration camps became commonplace - camps such as Zgoda, Trzebica, Kłodzko, Potulice, and Łambinowice. The death toll was estimated by the German Parliament in 1974 to have been 100,000. The Polish Ministry for Public Security put the figure at 6,140.[6] There were, besides, spontaneous expulsions and forced marches, as well as private acts of revenge.

Those ethnic Germans who attempted to flee back to Germany before the arrival of the Red Army often delayed too long, swayed by optimistic reports of German counter attacks, only to encounter Polish or Russian soldiers, or militias, bent on robbery, murder and rape.[7]

---

[5] Including Pomerania, Lower Silesia, Mecklenburg, Saxony (part), Brandenburg (part) and Border Mark as well as East and West Prussia.

[6] The Poles were not the only nation to take over former German concentration camps. For example the Russians continued to use Sachsenhausen and Buchenwald until the mid-1950s. It is estimated that 14,000 Germans were murdered or died of neglect in Sachsenhausen alone before it was turned into a museum - to commemorate victims of the Nazi regime. It is estimated that up to 40,000 Germans and 10,000 Russians died of illness, starvation and neglect, in the ten camps run by the Russian NKVD in East Germany between 1945-53.

[7] The magnitude of crimes against women at the end of the war defies comprehension. In Berlin it is estimated that 110,000 women were raped by the Red Army, in Vienna 87,000. The U.S Army stands accused of 17,000 rapes in North Africa and Western Europe between 1942 and 1945 (figures for other nations are not recorded). In Germany as a whole, 2 million women are believed to have been raped by occupying forces in the aftermath of the war. As the result of sexual violence and exploitation it is estimated that 2 million illegal abortions were carried out each year in the immediate aftermath of the war and between 150,000 and 200,000 'foreign babies' were born, some of which were the result of rape. The effect of these sustained attacks (1945-48) on women and, often, young girls, is incalculable. It certainly discredits any notion that these were spontaneous acts of reprisal.

It is estimated that between 1945 and 1949, 500,000 ethnic Germans died, or were murdered, during 'cleansing' operations in Eastern Europe.[8]

Reinhard Gehlen

Head of West German Intelligence from 1956 to 1968 and a former Wehrmacht Major General, Gehlen was initially recruited by the Americans to spy on the Russians, taking up his post in Germany in 1946. He employed ex-SS and Gestapo men, principally because of their wartime experience. In 1968 he resigned when his relations with German Chancellor Adenauer became strained.

Willy Brandt

Willy Brandt, real name Herbert Frahm, was Mayor of Berlin from 1957 to 1966. He had been an anti-fascist before WWII and was obliged to change his name to avoid arrest by the Gestapo. German Chancellor from 1969 to 1974, his most important legacy was *Ostpolitik*. A policy that proved controversial in West Germany, it was aimed at improving relations with East Germany (the then GDR, or German Democratic Republic), Poland, and the Soviet Union.

---

[8] It was not simply Germans who suffered at the hands of the new Polish State. Between 500 and 1,500 Jews were also murdered in Poland between the German surrender and June 1946. Many were returning from German concentration camps to try and trace their relatives and reclaim their property. After a pogrom in the Polish town of Kielce, on 4 July 1946, in which 42 Jews were murdered, approximately 95,000 Jews fled Poland – many back to the relative safety of Germany and then Palestine/Israel. The Ukrainian minority in Poland was also cleansed. 'Operation Vistula', begun in April 1947, was intended, in the words of the Polish military, as a 'final solution' to the Ukrainian question. It involved the forcible relocation of ethnic Ukrainians to western Poland (much of it former German land), the eradication of their language, culture and communities. Many died in transit, were imprisoned, or, in some cases, were murdered. These acts against Germans, Jews and Ukrainians were not, as some historians have argued, a 'reaction' to the Second World War and its aftermath. They were, in fact, no more than the continuation of pre-war policies which could now be pursued without moral restraint, or the fear of intervention.

The Rhein-Ahr Inn

Finally, the *Rhein-Ahr Inn* in Remagen Kripp does exist, though it, nor anyone associated with it, played any part in the events as described in this book. It is a delightful family establishment from which to explore the Rheine meadows and, across the river, the beautiful old town of Linz am Rhein.

List of principal or historical characters, place names and expressions

Addes, Charles - British Foreign Office representative.
Anschluss – the union between Germany and Austria affected by Hitler in 1938.
Beck, Sophie, Albert, Maria - Guardians to Julie Scholl in Warsaw.
Brandt, Willy* – German Social Democrat politician and Mayor of Berlin 1957-66.
Blitzkrieg – the term given to the German strategy of attacking with lightning speed and quickly outmanoeuvring and overwhelming the enemy.
Bromberg (German) Bydgoszcz (Polish) city now in western Poland.
Brooke, Alan* – British Army, Chief of the Imperial General Staff.
Ching, Lieutenant Colonel – British Army Intelligence Corps.
CIGS – Chief of the Imperial General Staff (the most senior British General.)
Cooper, Captain – Intelligence officer US 106 Infantry Division.
Cranfield, Major* – British Army attached to the War Crimes Tribunal Lüneburg.
Danzig (German) – Gdansk (Polish) northern Baltic port in West-Prussia (Poland).
Drzewiecki, Zbigniew* – Polish pianist and teacher.
Einsatzgruppen – SS killing squads who operated in the eastern conquered territories.
Epp – SD officer attached to Danzig SS HQ.
Ethnic German – a person of German descent living in Poland.
Fischer, Dr Captain* – SS Race and Settlement Division attached to Posen SS HQ.
Forster, Albert* – Gauleiter – Civil Governor of Danzig West Prussia.
Forster, Gertrud* – Wife of Albert and mother of Inga and Peter.
Funk, Walther* - German Minister for Economics 1937-45.
Gehlen* – ex-Wehrmacht Major General Head of West German Intelligence.
Gerhard, Captain - Working for Colonel Hopp Berlin SD in Posen.
Gieseking, Walther* - German pianist and teacher.
Grese, Irma* – SS Auxiliary.
Grese, Helene* – sister of Irma.
Grieser, Arthur* – Gauleiter – Civil Governor of Posen.
Heider, Max, Medical assistant to Dr Hertz in Posen.
Hertz, Rudi Dr – Head of Medical Services for the Resettlement programme in Posen.
Hildebrandt, Richard* – SS and Higher Police Leader Danzig West Prussia.
Himmler* – Head of the SS *Reichsführer.*
Hopp, Colonel – Security Police 'SD' Berlin.
Jensen – Private, US Army Military Police.
Jungvolk – Nazi youth organisation for boys between 10 and 14 years.
Jungmädel – Young Maidens, Nazi youth organisation for girls of 10 to 14 years.
Kellerman* – Captain SS Adjutant to Wilhelm Koppe.
Koppe, Wilhelm* - SS and Higher Police Leader Posen.
Krebs – Hermann Captain SS and Edie, his wife, residing in Zoppot..

360

Krill – Sergeant, Gestapo, Posen.

Mensch, Peter - Administrative Head of Resettlement under Dr Hertz in Posen.

Magdeburgisieren – German expression signifying total destruction originating from the razing of Magdeburg and slaughter of its entire population during the Thirty Year's War 1618-48.

March Violets – the name given to Germans who joined the Nazi Party after it came to power in 1933 and who were generally seen by more long serving members of the party as opportunists and careerists.

Müller, Captain Gestapo liaison officer between Gauleiter Grieser and the SS in Posen.

Olga, Sister* - Nun at the orphanage on Thorner Strasse.

Paderewski* – Polish pianist credited with beginning the Greater Polish Uprising after a speech in Posen in 1918 and first Prime Minister of the Second Republic in 1919

Pilsudski* – President, First Marshall and Head of State in Poland (died 1935)

Posen (German) – Poznan (Polish) former city/administrative province of Prussia/Germany 1815-1918 now in western Poland

Poznan (Polish) – Posen (German) see above

Rath, Gunther – German businessman operating in Posen

Reichsgau Wartheland - (1939-45) Nazi administrative province of Posen

Ritter – German Federal Intelligence Service Bonn

Röhm, Ernst* – notorious homosexual and leader of the SA – the Nazi Stormtroopers

Rubinstein, Anton* - Russian Jewish composer and pianist (1829 -1894)

Rust Karl Dr - attached to the German Foreign Office investigation into Polish atrocities

SA – a Nazi party organisation also known as Stormtroopers.

Selbstschutz – literally 'self-protection'. Ethnic German militia.

Schmidt Sister* – Catholic Nun overseeing the orphanage in Thorner Strasse Posen.

Scholl Julie – German music student daughter of Eric.

Scholl, Ingrid – Aunt of Julie Scholl.

Scholl Eric – Father of Julie Scholl and an economist working for Walther Funk.

Scholl, Otto – Eric Scholl's older brother.

Sikorski Kazimierz* – teacher of Composition at the Warsaw Conservatoire.

Sippenhaft – the practice of arrest because of kinship with an accused person - operated during the Nazi period 1933-45.

Sonderkommando Lange - In Posen in the beginning of 1940 Herbert Lange assumed command of a group tasked with extermination of mentally ill in Warthegau area. The unit, equipped with gas vans shuttled between hospitals, picking up patients and killing them with carbon monoxide.

Straż Obywatelska – Polish militia, translated as 'Citizens Guards'.

Torrens,- Jimmy US Judge Advocate General's Corps.

Troost Ludwig – Deputy Head German Federal Intelligence Service Bonn.

Völkischer Beobachter – Nazi Party Newspaper.

Vogler, Gottfried - Head of the Civil Service for Gauleiter Grieser in Posen.

Wolff, Karl*- Chief of Staff to Himmler.

Yeo– 'Tommy' - Major British Army attached to the War Crimes Tribunal Lüneburg.
Zoppot (German) – Sopot (Polish) Spa town on the Baltic coast near Danzig.
Zossen – Army command headquarters near Berlin.

*Based on historical characters.

Bibliography:

Rauschning, Hermann, 'Hitler Speaks', Thornton Butterworth 1940.

Shirer, William, 'Berlin Diary', Alfred A Knopf 1941.

Shirer, William, 'The Rise and Fall of the Third Reich', Secker and Warburg 1970.

Wheeler-Bennett, 'The Nemesis of Power, The German Army in Politics 1918-45', Macmillan 1967.

Kershaw, Ian 'Hitler', Allen Lane 2008

Hastings, Max, 'All Hell Let Loose', Harper Press 2011.

Bullock, Alan, 'Hitler a Study in Tyranny', Odhams Press 1954.

Transcript of the Official Shorthand Notes of 'The Trial of Josef Kramer and Forty Four Others. http://www bergenbelsen.co.uk/pages/Transcripttrial

de Colonna, Bertram, 'Poland from the Inside', Heath Cranton 1939.

German Foreign Ministry: Atrocities against the German Minority in Poland – 2nd edition Volk und Reich Verlag 1940.

Knoke Heinz, 'I Flew for the Führer' Evans Brothers Ltd 1953

Egremont, Max, 'Forgotten Land - Journeys among the Ghosts of East Prussia' Picador 2011

Blanke, Richard, 'The Orphans of Versailles' – The University Press of Kentucky 1993

Lorant, Stefan, 'I was Hitler's prisoner' – Penguin Books Ltd 1939

Davies, Norman, 'White Eagle, Red Star –The Polish Soviet War 1919-20' – Macdonald 1972

Lowe, Keith, 'Savage Continent – Europe in the aftermath of World War II', Penguin Viking 2012

Dowling, Alick, 'Janek – a story of survival', Ringpress Books 1989

Wolf, Abraham 'Ze'ev' - (Unpublished – recollections of the life of a Polish Jew.)

MacDonogh, Giles, 'Berlin' - St Martin's Griffin 1998

Acknowledgements

I would like to thank my readers: my wife Penelope and step-daughter Leonie Boyle, Susan Bryant, my parents Arthur and Margret Lane, and Robert Lloyd, for their help and suggestions when preparing this work for publication, and my good friends, Ute Emmerich and my German reader Elke Jury, for their advice and guidance on all matters German.

My thanks also to Linda Fowler of Glint Print, for her help, patience, generosity, and creative flair in designing the cover for this book, and Esther and James at DPS Print in Kidderminster for their help and support in preparing the many drafts of this novel.

I would especially like to thank those people whose friendships made in Greece and Germany have made writing this book possible: Britta Werner, Juliana Leiacher, Birte Strohmayer, Ingrid Pintgen, Klaus and Inge Klabunde, and of course Noula Gemetzi and Ute Emmerich.

I would also like to thank the German Institute in London for guiding me to additional sources of information on Posen and the history of the German ethnic minority in Poland, and David Pearson of Worcestershire County Council (Libraries) for sourcing other research materials.

Finally I would like to thank again my editor Stephen Chappell who transformed this book into something more readable!